KILL TEAM

Iyle raises a hand and I give him the nod to speak. 'Who the hell are you, sir?' he asks, hands on hips.

'I am the man the Colonel visited a dozen kinds of hell upon and survived,' I reply slowly, gesturing for the others to gather in front of me. 'I am the man who helped the Colonel kill three million people. I am the only man to survive when four thousand others died on the battlefield. I have killed men in their sleep. I have shot them. I have stabbed them. I have strangled them. I've even beaten them to death with my hands and fists. I've fought tyranids and orks, I've marched across searing deserts and frozen wastelands. I've nearly died six times. My own men have tried to kill me on more than one occasion. I've fought things you don't even know exist. And I killed them.'

Every word of it is true as well, and they can tell it by the look in my eye.

More Warhammer 40,000 from the Black Library

• LAST CHANCERS •

13TH LEGION by Gav Thorpe

• GAUNT'S GHOSTS •

FIRST & ONLY by Dan Abnett

GHOSTMAKER by Dan Abnett

NECROPOLIS by Dan Abnett

HONOUR GUARD by Dan Abnett

• EISENHORN •

XENOS by Dan Abnett

• SPACE WOLF •

SPACE WOLF by William King

RAGNAR'S CLAW by William King

• OTHER WARHAMMER 40,000 TITLES •

EXECUTION HOUR by Gordon Rennie

PAWNS OF CHAOS by Brian Craig

EYE OF TERROR by Barrington J. Bayley

INTO THE MAELSTROM
eds. Marc Gascoigne & Andy Jones

STATUS: DEADZONE
eds. Marc Gascoigne & Andy Jones

DARK IMPERIUM
eds. Marc Gascoigne & Andy Jones

A WARHAMMER 40,000 NOVEL

The Last Chancers

KILL TEAM

Gav Thorpe

For the staff of Bugman's and their liquid inspiration (cups of tea, obviously)

A BLACK LIBRARY PUBLICATION

First published in Great Britain in 2001 by
Games Workshop Publishing
Willow Road, Lenton,
Nottingham, NG7 2WS, UK

10 9 8 7 6 5 4 3 2 1

Cover illustration by Kenson Low

A CIP record for this book
is available from the British Library

ISBN 1 84154 155 9

Set in ITC Giovanni

Printed and bound in Great Britain by
Omnia Books Ltd., Glasgow, UK

See the Black Library on the Internet at
www.blacklibrary.co.uk

Find out more about Games Workshop
and the world of Warhammer 40,000 at
www.games-workshop.com

KILL TEAM

ONE
PROLOGUE

THE AIR WAS filled with swirling grey dust, whipped up into a storm by a wind that shrieked across the hard, black granite of the tower. The bleak edifice soared into the turbulent skies, windowless but studded with hundreds of blazing lights whose yellow beams were swallowed quickly by the dust storm. For three hundred metres the tower climbed into the raging skies of Ghovul's third moon, an almost perfect cylinder of unbroken and unforgiving rock, hewn from the infertile mesa on which the gulag stood.

A narrow-beamed red laser sprang into life from its summit, penetrating the gloom of the cloud-shrouded night. A moment later it was answered by a triangle of white glares as a shuttle descended towards the landing pad. In the bathing glow of the landing lights, technicians scurried back and forth across the pad, protected against the violent climate with bulky work suits made from a fine metal mesh, their hands covered with heavy gloves, thick-soled boots upon their feet.

With a whine of engines cutting back, the shuttle's three feet touched down with a loud clang on the metal decking of the landing area. A moment later a portal in the side swung open and a docking ramp jerkily extended itself on hissing

7

hydraulics to meet with the hatchway. A tall figure ducked through the low opening and stepped out on to the walkway. He stood there for a moment, his heavy dress coat whipping around him, a gloved hand clamping the officer's cap to his head. With his back as straight as a rod despite the horrendous conditions, the new arrival strode across the docking gantry with a purposeful gait, never once breaking his gaze from directly ahead of him.

Inside, a black-clad guard saluted the man and without a word gestured for him to proceed into the open work iron elevator just inside the landing pad building. With a creak of rusty hinges the warden swung the doors shut and jerked a lever to start the conveyance descending with a rattling of chains and grinding of gears.

'Which level is the prisoner on?' the officer asked, speaking for the first time since his arrival. His voice was deep and quiet, the authoritative tone of a man used to being obeyed without question.

'Level sixteen, sir,' the guard replied, not meeting the piercing blue gaze of the officer. 'One of the isolation floors,' he added hesitantly. The visitor did not reply but merely nodded.

The lift rattled on for a couple of minutes, passing slowly down through floor after floor, an illuminated dial marking their descent. When it reached seventeen the guard hauled back on the lever and a moment later the shaft echoed with a screech of badly oiled brakes. The elevator shuddered to a halt a few seconds later.

The officer glanced up at the floor indicator, which now was shining through number sixteen.

'The tech-priests promised to look at it, sir, but say they are too busy,' the warden answered apologetically at the officer's questioning glance. The prison guard was old and haggard, with thinning tobacco-stained white hair and an ill-fitting uniform. Coughing self-consciously the guard flung open the doors with more screeching and stepped out of the way.

The level onto which the tall man stepped was as round as the tower itself, heavy armoured doors spaced evenly around its wall. Everything was the colour of ageing whitewash, a pale grey stained in places with patches of reddish-brown.

'It's this one, sir,' the guard said, walking around to the right of the elevator door when he realised the officer was waiting for directions. Another guard, younger and sturdier than the one who had been waiting at the landing pad, was standing by one of the doors, dressed in the same plain black uniform, a heavy cudgel hanging from his belt. The first guard led the officer over to the door and flipped down a small viewing window. The smell of stale sweat swept out of the small grille, but the officer's face remained impassive as he gazed through the narrow slit. Inside, the cell was as bare as the hall outside, painted in the same drab colour. Only a few metres square, the room was illuminated by a single glow globe set into the ceiling behind a wire mesh. Its lacklustre yellow light cast a jaundiced tinge across the room's occupant.

He was stretched out on the far wall, wrists manacled to the corners of the ceiling with heavy-linked chains. His feet were similarly restrained to the floor. His head hung down against his chest, his features hidden by a long, bedraggled mane of unkempt hair. He was clad in nothing but a rag about his waist, the dim light showing up his taut, sinewy muscles. His chest was criss-crossed with scars, some new, others years old. His arms were similarly disfigured, a particularly prominent slash across his upper right arm obscuring what was left of a tattoo. His left thigh was marked on both sides by large puncture scars from a wound that had obviously passed completely through his leg.

'Why was he moved here?' the officer asked quietly, his voice causing the prisoner to stir slightly.

'In the first month he was here, he killed seven wardens and five other prisoners and almost escaped, sir,' the older guard explained, casting a nervous glance through the slit and exchanging a look with the other guard. 'The commandant has had him confined to isolation for the last five months for the safety of the other inmates and the guards, sir.'

The officer nodded and for a fleeting second the warden thought he saw what looked like a satisfied smile pass across his lips.

'And his mental condition?' the man asked, moving his gaze from the warden back into the cell.

'The chirurgeon has examined him twice and has declared him psychopathic, sir,' the guard replied after a moment. 'He seems to hate everyone. He refuses to eat anything except protein gruel. The only time he allows us near him is when we take him down to the exercise hall. We can't allow him in there with other prisoners though, and no one is allowed to carry anything that might be turned into a weapon in his presence. We learnt that when he tried to escape.'

The officer turned back, an eyebrow raised in query.

'Nobody thought to count the spoons in the mess hall,' the warden replied, ashen-faced.

The man turned his attention back to the cell once more.

'Perfect,' he whispered to himself. 'Open the door,' he ordered the younger of the two guards, before stepping back and to one side.

As the sullen, dark-haired warden did as he was told, the door screeching open, the prisoner looked up for the first time. Like the rest of his body, his face was a mass of scars. A long beard hung down over his chest. The warden's look was returned by a venomous stare, hatred burning in the dark eyes of the inmate, a feral intensity shining in them. The second guard took up position on the other side of the prisoner, dragging his heavy club free and holding it easily in his right hand.

'Now the manacles,' the officer prompted.

'I don't think that's a good idea, sir,' the ageing guard replied with a startled look. The prisoner's eyes hadn't moved, continuing to burn straight through the warden.

'S-s-sir?' the younger prison official replied with a horrified stare. 'Did you hear what he told you about this animal?'

'He is not an animal,' the officer snapped back. 'The manacles.'

Visibly shaking, the white-haired warden crept forward and fumbled with his ring of keys. The other guard followed him, dragging his cudgel free from his belt. Hesitantly the crouching guard unlocked the left leg first, flinching nervously, expecting the foot to lash out at him. A bit more confident, he unlocked the other leg. He glanced up at the prisoner's face, but the inmate's gaze had not left the face of the other security man. Quickly he undid the wristlocks and took a few hurried steps back, ready to bolt.

The prisoner took a step forward, rubbing his arms to revive the circulation. Then, without a word, the inmate stepped to his left, his right hand lashing out, sending the maul spinning from the younger warden's grasp, who yelped and clutched his broken wrist. The other guard stepped forward, but the prisoner was quicker, twisting on his heel to deliver a spinning kick to his midriff, hurling him back against the wall with a thud and a hoarse cry of pain. The guard with the mangled wrist had recovered now, but the prisoner turned his attention back to him, smashing rigid fingers into his throat then wrapping his arm around the guard's neck in a headlock. There was an audible crack as the guard's neck snapped, and the prisoner gave a satisfied grunt as he let the body slump to the ground. He took a step towards the surviving warden and was about to repeat the move when the officer stepped into the room.

'That is enough, I think,' the visitor said quietly, and the prisoner looked round, a wolfish grin of savage joy splitting his scarred face.

'I'm fraggin' happy to see you, Colonel,' the prisoner said, laughing hoarsely. 'Do you need me again?'

'Yes, I need you again, Kage,' the Colonel replied.

TWO
VINCULARUM

+++*The playing pieces are being assembled, the strategy is in motion*+++

+++*Time to prepare for the opening moves*+++

It is with a mixture of relief and dread that I look at the Colonel. On the one hand, the fact that he's here means an end to six months of misery and boredom. On the other, his presence means I could be dead any time soon. I've been hoping for and dreading this moment for half a year, torn between expectation and apprehension. All in all, I'm pleased to see him though, because I'd rather take my chances with the Colonel than rot in this damn cell for the rest of my life. He just stands there, looking exactly the same as he did the last time I saw him, as if he'd just come back in after a moment, rather than having abandoned me for nearly two hundred days to stare at four bare walls.

'Get him cleaned up then bring him to the audience chamber,' Schaeffer tells the guard curtly, giving me a final glance before turning and striding back out of the door.

'You heard the officer,' the warden prods me into life as I stand there staring at the Colonel's retreating back. He casts a nervous glance at the corpse in the corner of the cell and takes a step away from me, his eyes wary, hand hovering close to the pistol at his belt.

I follow him to the lift, and wait there in silence for a few minutes while the elevator takes the Colonel back to the top of the tower. My mind is racing. What does the Colonel have in store for me? What's the mission this time? Commander of the 13th Penal Legion, known commonly as the Last Chancers, Colonel Schaeffer led me and nearly four thousand others in bloody suicide missions across a dozen worlds last time around, and all to whittle us down to a few survivors. Would it be the same again? Was I going to spend the next two years being shipped from battlezone to battlezone, wondering every time if this was the fight that would be my last? To be honest,

I don't care one bit. If my time in this stinking prison has taught me anything, it's that life on the battlefield, fighting for your life, is far more desirable to sitting on your arse for nine-tenths of the day.

I knew he would come back for me, though. He didn't say anything when he left, but I remember his words when we first met, just over three years ago. 'Just my kind of scum,' he had called me. Shortly before knocking me out, I might add, but these days I wouldn't hold that against him. He's done a lot worse, to me and others.

With a shuddering clank the conveyor arrives and the warden ushers me inside. We rattle up a couple of floors to the wardens' level where the washrooms are. I've never come this way before, for the last five months my washing routine has consisted of being hosed down with cold water every other day. I follow the guard without much thought, my mind still occupied with the Colonel's arrival. It guarantees nothing but bloodshed and battle, but then that's all the Colonel has ever represented. That and an unbending, uncompromising faith in the Emperor and unswerving loyalty to the Imperium.

I've always had plenty of faith, but it wasn't until the Last Chancers that I realised my part in the grand scheme of things. I'm a murdering, cold-hearted bastard, I don't mind admitting. But now, I'm one of the Emperor's murdering, cold-hearted bastards and He has a use for me again. It gives me some small measure of satisfaction that although all I know how to do now is to cripple and kill and maim, I have a sense of purpose I never had before. It's a cruel, hard galaxy out there, and if you're going to survive you have to learn some cruel, hard lessons. I learnt them while four thousand other Last Chancers didn't, and I'm still here. I figured all the time I was in that cell, remembering every battle, every gunshot and stab, that the Emperor and the Colonel weren't finished with me just yet. I reckon neither will ever be finished with me, not even after I'm dead, I'm sure.

I pull off the rag and step into the showering cubicle. The guard turns the water on from outside and a scathing jet of hot water cascades down on to me from the grille in the ceiling. He tosses in a gritty bar of soap and I start scrubbing and scraping.

'I need to shave,' I call out over the splashing of water. The guard mumbles something back that I don't hear over the water drumming off my head. 'I said get me a blade, I need to get rid of this fraggin' hair and beard!'

'You're not allowed sharp implements, Kage,' the guard calls back. 'I'm under orders.'

'For Emperor's sake, you sack of crap, I can't go in front of the Colonel looking like a sodding beggar,' I argue with him, stepping out of the cubicle. He retreats quickly. I point to the pistol and then the knife in his belt.

'If I wanted to kill you, you'd already be a cooling body,' I tell him with a smile. 'Give me your damn knife before I come and take it off you.'

He unbuckles the sheath and tosses it over to me, looking ready to bolt at any point. The look of fear in his eyes sends a shiver of pleasure through me. What I would have done to have had a reputation like this a few years ago back on Olympas. It would have made things a lot easier for me growing up, that kind of terror.

I step back under the stream of water and lather the soap across my face and head, then pull the knife out and throw the sheath back out on to the tiled floor. I start with hacking off the hair as close to my skin as I can get it, dropping the ends in tufted lumps to swirl down and block the plughole in the floor. I then shave the beard off, scraping the knife across my cheeks and chin, removing a layer of skin at the same time. It stings more than a las-bolt wound, but I don't mind. I rub my hand across the smooth skin, enjoying the sensation of cleanliness for the first time in ages.

My hair is a bit more difficult, but I eventually manage to cut all that off as well, leaving a few nicks and cuts across the back of my scalp where the angle was awkward. Hey, my face was ripped apart and put back together again years ago, so I'm never going to win any medals for looks anyway.

Satisfied that I'm as presentable as I'm going to get, I dry myself down with the coarse, scratchy towel proffered by the guard while he goes to fetch me something suitable to wear. He returns a short while later with standard prison fatigues – badly made grey, baggy trousers and shirt woven from raw linen, and a pair of ill-fitting laceless boots. I feel like a right idiot wearing these clothes, like a small kid who's dressed up in his older brother's gear. I follow the guard back up in the elevator for my talk.

The guard knocks at the door and the Colonel calls me in. Unlike the rest of the prison tower, the circular hall is decorated with a bright mural that runs continuously around its walls, depicting some Ecclesiarchy scene as far as I can tell. Some saint's martyrdom judging by the final images which portray a man with a glowing halo being torn apart by greenskinned monsters which I take to be fanciful interpretations of orks. I've fought real orks, and in the flesh they're even scarier than the grotesque parodies painted around the hall.

The Colonel is sat to one side behind a plain desk of dark, almost black, wood. A simple matching chair is placed across from him. The desktop is piled high with papers in mouldering brown sleeves tied with red cord and stamped with various official seals.

'Kage,' the Colonel says, looking up from the sheaf of parchments in his hand. 'Sit down.'

I walk across and lower myself into the chair, which makes squeaking protests from its legs as I settle into it. The Colonel has turned his attention back to studying the documents he is holding. I wait there patiently. Locked up in that cell, patience was something I learned quite a bit about. The sort of patience I imagine a hunter has, waiting for his prey, sitting or lying there immobile for hours on end. The sort of patience that tests your sanity, the slow drifting of the hours and days threatening to unravel your mind. But I learnt. I learnt how to settle my thoughts, focussing them inwards: counting my heartbeats; counting my breaths; mentally going over a hundred rituals of weapons preparation and maintenance; fighting armed and unarmed combats with different opponents in the confines of my own head while my arms and legs were chained to the wall.

I realise I've drifted into the well-practiced trance state when the Colonel coughs purposefully, and I blink and focus on him. He hasn't changed a bit, though I didn't really expect he would have. Still that strong, clean shaven jaw, sharp cheek bones and the piercing glare of his ice-blue eyes. Eyes that can bore into your soul and burn through you sharper than a lascutter.

'There is another mission,' he begins, sitting back and crossing his arms.

'I figured as much,' I reply, keeping my back straight, my expression attentive.

'There is not much time, relatively speaking,' he continues, his gaze constant. 'You will assemble and train a team to assassinate an alien military commander.'

This surprises me. Last time out, he was very defensive about revealing the mission objectives. I guess things are different this time.

'As you are probably expecting, the selection process will be more directed and focussed than last time,' he says, as if he can read my mind. 'I cannot afford the luxury of the time required to repeat the procedure you underwent before.'

I bet, I think to myself. It took four thousand soldiers and two and a half years to 'select' the Last Chancers when the Colonel last led me in battle.

Other than the Colonel himself, I was the only survivor.

'This prison contains some of the most specialised soldiers in this sector of the Imperium. I have had them incarcerated here for just this purpose, gathered here in one place where I have easy access to them rather than scattered across the stars. It makes assembling a team much more straightforward, with the additional benefit that few people know they are here, and I can maintain absolute secrecy,' he tells me, indicating the records on the desk with a sweep of his hand. 'You will go through these files and choose those you deem most appropriate for the mission. You will then train them in the skills they do not possess while I prepare the final details of the mission itself. I will then lead the Last Chancers on that mission. Is that understood?'

'Perfectly, sir,' I answer carefully, mulling his words over in my head. 'If I'm gonna choose, I'll need to know a little more about what you're planning.'

'For the moment you do not. I would rather you choose men and women whose skills you value regardless of the exact situation we might face,' he says with a shake of his head. 'Our choice of personnel will, to some degree, inform the plan of attack that I will devise. Flexibility will be the key to success.'

'I think I get you,' I tell him, leaning forward and resting my hands on the desk. 'Pick a team that'll be able to do what we need, whatever that is.'

'Once again, your ability to grasp complex issues astounds me,' the Colonel replies sarcastically. 'That is what I said, is it not?'

'Almost,' I answer with a grin. Something then occurs to me. 'Colonel, why use penal troops? I mean, I'm pretty sure you could have your pick of guard regiments across the segmentum.'

'You yourself once told me the answer to that, if you can remember,' Schaeffer replies after a moment's thought. 'I can bark orders, I can make men do what I want, but for my missions that is not enough.'

'I remember now,' I say when the Colonel pauses. 'You want a team that has nothing else to live for except succeeding in the mission. It was in Deliverance, wasn't it? Yeah, I remember: give men nothing except life itself to fight for and they'll be the best fighters ever.'

'You learnt that well,' Schaeffer says pointedly.

'Well, I'm still here,' I reply with a bitter smile.

THERE ARE TWO hundred and seventy-six military personnel in the prison. It takes me just over a week to go through their records, sitting down with one of the vincularum scribes to read me out their details. I never did learn my letters, there wasn't really any need for it. I see the Colonel once in that time, to tell me that I've got three more days to make my choices. To begin with, I didn't know where to start. The Colonel's briefing was so vague, I found it difficult to picture what we could be doing. I spent the first day just sitting and thinking, something I've had plenty of opportunity to do in recent months. I figure that about ten or so good fighters will be enough. My experience from Coritanorum tells me that on the Colonel's missions, if you can't do it with a few well-trained men, then an army isn't going to help.

So I go through all the records with the adept, trying to make some more sense by dividing them up by expertise, previous combat experience and, almost as important, why they're in this prison. There's all kinds of dregs in here, but all of them are ex-military. That's not too surprising, considering the Colonel's purpose in life. But there's something particular about this bunch of convicts. They're all specialists of one kind or another. There's pilots, snipers, infiltration experts, saboteurs, engineers, jungle fighters and cityfighters, tank crews, artillery men, storm troopers, pioneers and drop troops. Like the Colonel said, he's gathered together some of the best soldiers from across the segmentum, and they're all here for me to choose from. So what am I looking for? How do you pick a team of expert soldiers when I've got a whole company of them to choose from? What could I look for that would set some of them apart from the others?

With only two days left to decide, my frustration is beginning to build. I need an angle, some way of picking out the best of the best. I begin to appreciate more why the Colonel did what he did for the last mission. I start to understand that perhaps dragging four thousand men and women through hell and back and seeing who survives is the only way you can really find out who has that warrior instinct; who the fighters and survivors are, and which ones are just cannon fodder, destined for a bullet to save the life of a better soldier. Perhaps I should just get them to fight it out, pit them against each other and see who walks out.

Then I have a flash of inspiration from the Emperor. Perhaps I can't put them through a few battles to see who comes out on top, but I don't have to physically eliminate the weak links. It's halfway through the night when I send the guards to rouse the adept. I pull on my new uniform, kindly supplied by the Colonel. I slip into the plain olive shirt and dark green trousers, pulling the belt nice and tight then step into my boots. I can't tell you how good it feels to wear tight, solid combat boots on my feet after months of being barefoot. It makes me feel like a soldier again, not a prisoner.

I make my way to where the Colonel outlined my task and wait for the adept. A few minutes pass before he gets brought into the audience chamber, sleepy and confused.

'We're going to talk to all of the prisoners,' I tell him, grabbing the first couple of dozen folders from the desk and thrusting the pile of records into his arms.

'All of them?' he asks wearily, eyes bleary, suppressing a yawn.

'Yes, all of them,' I snap back, pushing him tottering towards the door. 'Who's first?'

Juggling awkwardly with the shifting pile of paperwork, he looks at the name on the top folder.

'Prisoner 1242, Aphren,' he tells me as we wait for the elevator. 'Cell thirteen-twelve.'

* * *

THE GUARD IS asleep on his feet when we step out of the lift onto the thirteenth floor, leaning against the wall. I give him a push and he falls to the ground, a startled yelp escaping his lips as he bangs his head on the floor.

'Wake up, warden!' I shout at him, dragging him to his feet.

'What's going on?' he asks dizzily, rubbing his eyes.

'Open cell twelve,' I tell him, grabbing his collar and dragging him towards the cell door. 'And you will address me as lieutenant or sir, I am an officer!'

'Sorry, sir,' he mumbles, the keys jangling in his shaking hand as he puts them in the lock. As he swings the door open I push him to one side.

'You, in here,' I snarl at the clericus as I step into the cell. He follows cautiously. The room is just like all the others, cramped and bare with a pallet on the ground along the wall opposite the door. The man inside is already on his feet, fists balled and raised. If ever a man could be described as big, it's this guy. He's easily half my height again, with shoulders like an ogryn's and biceps bigger than most men's thighs. He's wearing just his prison trousers and muscles ripple across his chest as he clenches and unclenches his hands. He's got a broad face and small eyes that are too close together under a heavy brow. I doubt he could count to ten, even using his fingers.

'You gonna try and hit me?' I ask casually, closing the door behind me and leaning back against it with my arms crossed.

'Where did you just drop out of the warp?' Aphren snarls back, taking a step forward. The adept makes a panicked squeak and backs into the corner. 'You can't just barge in here, I'm entitled to six hours sleep a night. Prison regulations say so.'

'Prison regulations say I'm not allowed to kill anyone here as well, but that didn't stop me,' I tell him in the same off-hand tone.'

'You're Kage, aren't you?' he asks, suddenly less sure of himself. 'I heard about you, you're fragged in the head.'

'I am Lieutenant Kage of the 13th Penal Legion, the Last Chancers, and you better remember that when you address me, soldier,' I remind him. The Colonel told me he had reinstated my rank when he gave me the uniform, which was kind of nice of him.

'Do you expect me to salute?' the prisoner replies with a sneer.

'Read it,' I say to the clericus, ignoring Aphren. The adept visibly pulls himself together and clears his throat in a pompous manner.

'Kolan Aphren, ex-drill sergeant of the 12th Jericho Rangers,' he begins in a monotonous drone. 'Seven years' service. Three campaigns. Arrested and court-martialled for brutality of recruits. Sentenced to dishonourable discharge and five years' hard labour. Sentence converted to life imprisonment, order of Colonel Schaeffer, 13th Penal Legion.'

'A drill sergeant? I could've guessed,' I say to him, meeting his angry gaze with a cold stare of my own. 'Like beating up on the new guys, eh? You're no good to me, I need a real soldier, not some training camp bully. Someone who's fought in a battle.'

'Why you little runt!' he bellows, hurling himself headlong at me. I side-step his clumsy charge and ram his face into the metal cell door. He drops like a stone. I pluck the record from the adept's grip, smiling inwardly at the look of horror on his face, and toss it onto the bed. 'You can pick that up later when we're done,' I tell him, rolling the unconscious Aphren out of the way with my foot and opening the door. 'One down, two hundred and seventy-five to go.'

'ERIK KORLBEN,' THE clericus reads out in his monotone voice. 'Ex-master sergeant, 4th Asgardian regiment. Three years' service. One campaign. Arrested and court-martialled for insubordination on the field of battle. Sentenced to thirty-five lashes, dishonourable discharge and ten years' imprisonment. Sentence extended to life imprisonment by order of Colonel Schaeffer, 13th Penal Legion.'

Korlben is short and stocky, with a thick mop of red hair and bushy eyebrows. He sits on the edge of his bed, gazing blankly at the floor, hands in his lap. Everything about him says dejected and broken, but I give him a chance to prove himself useful.

'So you don't like taking orders, Korlben?' I say, scratching my head. 'Bit of an odd choice, joining the Imperial Guard.'

'I didn't ask to join,' he mumbles back, not looking up.

'Oh, a draftee,' I reply slowly. 'I bet you must be plenty fragged then. Dragged into an army you don't want to fight in. Then slammed up in here to rot for the rest of your life. I guess the Emperor really doesn't like you, Korlben.'

'I guess he doesn't,' he agrees, meeting my gaze for the first time with a bitter smile.

'How'd you like to get out of here, maybe even go back to what you did before?' I offer, studying his reaction. 'It'll mean following more orders though.'

'I would like that a lot,' he nods slowly. 'I don't mind following orders – unless it's on a suicide charge to storm an enemy bunker.'

'Well, Korlben, that was the wrong answer,' I tell him viciously, slapping his record out of the adept's hands. 'You won't be seeing me again.'

'GAVRIUS TENAAN,' THE adept mumbles sleepily, barely able to keep his eyes open. We've been at it solid for the last thirty-six hours straight, going back to the Colonel's audience chamber and picking up more records when we run out, stopping only twice in that time to grab something to eat and drink. He's swaying on his feet, on his last reserves of energy. Weakling. Just like most of the inmates here.

Only about half a dozen or so have impressed me so far, the rest have got serious discipline problems, or are cowards, or would probably kill me as soon as look at me. 'Ex-marksman, Tobrian Consuls. Thirteen years… service. Six campaigns. Arrested and court-martialled for firing on Imperial citizens without orders. Sentenced to hanging. Sentence… sentence overturned to life imprisonment by order… order of Colonel Schaeffer, 13th Penal Legion.'

Tenaan is a wiry man, in his early forties I'd guess. He has a grizzled, thin face and a cold, distant edge to his eyes, like he's not really looking at me. He's sloppily stood to attention, fingers fidgeting with the seam of his fatigues.

'You like the killing don't you?' I say to him, cocking my head to one side and giving him the once over. 'I bet you used to be a hunter, before joining up.'

'That I was, sir,' he drawls back. 'Used to hunt deer an' such in the mountains. Then they came an' said that I could shoot orks if I wanted to, and that seemed like a good offer.'

'So how come you shot non-combatants?' I ask, wanting to hear the story in his own words.

'They was in my way, sir,' he replies in a matter-of-fact tone and a slight shrug. 'They shouldn't a been there.'

'How many?' I prompt, knowing the answer was in the records, but wanting to keep him talking. This guy had some potential.

'I don't remember exactly, sir,' he replies slowly. 'I think that time it was a dozen or so, I think.'

'That time?' I ask, surprised at this admission. 'How many civilians have you shot?'

'About fifty odd, by my reckoning, sir, mebbe a few more,' he nods, inwardly confirming this tally.

'Fifty?' I say incredulously. Okay, so my bodycount makes that look like spit in the sea, but at least I was under orders. 'You're too trigger happy, even for me.'

'Sorry to hear that, sir,' he apologises and gives another slight shrug.

With a grateful sigh, the adept drops the file and stumbles out of the cell and I follow him out.

'How many does that leave us with?' I ask him as we walk back to the elevator. He glances down at the small sheaf of papers left in his hands.

'Eight, lieutenant, there's eight you haven't rejected,' he tells me wearily, handing the documents to me.

'You'll be needing those,' I tell him, tossing the records back as I step into the lift. 'Have them mustered in the audience room tomorrow after breakfast, and inform Colonel Schaeffer that I will meet him there. I'm off for some sleep.'

MY EIGHT 'RECRUITS' are lined up in the chamber, standing at ease, each of them with their eyes fixed on me. All of them are curious, it didn't take long for the rumour to spread that psycho Kage was talking to everyone and offering a way to get out of prison. But other than that, they don't have a clue what's going on. One or two of them shuffle nervously under my gaze. The door swings open and the Colonel strides in, wearing his full dress uniform as always.

'Attention!' I bark and they respond sharply enough. It's one of the reasons they're here, they've still got some measure of discipline left in them.

'What have you got for me, Kage?' the Colonel asks, walking slowly up the line and eyeing each of them in turn.

We start at the left of the line, with Moerck. He's tall, well proportioned, handsome and smart. His blond hair is cropped short, his face clean-shaven, his eyes bright. He stands rigidly to attention, not a single muscle twitching, his gaze levelled straight ahead.

'Ex-Commissar Moerck, sir,' I introduce the Colonel and he nods, as if remembering something. 'An odd one, I'm sure you'll agree. Commissar to a storm trooper company, Moerck here has an exemplary history. He left the Schola Progenium with a perfect record. He has been cited for acts of bravery ten times. After five campaigns, he spent three years on attachment to the Schola Progenium training commissar cadets before being granted his request to return to battlefield duty. He has been wounded in action seven times; on three occasions he refused the offer for honourable discharge and a return to training duties. In short, sir, he is a genuine hero.'

'Then remind me why he is in a military prison, lieutenant,' Schaeffer says sourly.

'The commissar and his storm trooper company were participating in a night drop attack, as part of an anti-insurrection operation on Seperia,' I tell the Colonel, dredging back the details I spent most of last night committing to memory. 'The attack was a complete success: the enemy camp was destroyed, all foes eliminated with no prisoners, as ordered. The problem was, they had the wrong target. Some departmento map maker had mixed up his co-ordinates and our hero here led his men on an attack into the command camp of the 25th Hoplites. They wiped out their entire general staff. Without loss, I should point out,' I smile at Moerck, who has remained dispassionate throughout the sorry tale. 'To cover their own hides, the departmento charged the entire company with failing to carry out orders, and they were drafted into the penal legions. That's when you came in and transferred the hero here. A genuine mistake, and probably the only innocent man in this whole prison.'

'You must hate him then, Kage,' the Colonel says, giving me an intent stare.

'Of course, sir,' I reply, tight-lipped.

'So why have you chosen him?' he asks, turning his attention to the ex-commissar. 'Some measure of revenge, perhaps?'

'Not at all, Colonel,' I reply with all honesty. 'This man will follow your orders to the letter, with no questions. He has almost unmatched combat experience, discipline and faith. He is entirely dedicated to the Emperor's cause and will do everything to ensure our mission is a success. I personally can't stand him, sir, you're right. But if I want someone watching my back, our hero here is the best for it.'

The Colonel just grunts and steps up to the next in line. He's short and wiry, bald as a cannonball but with a bushy beard so that you could be mistaken for thinking someone turned his face upside down.

'Hans Iyle,' I tell the Colonel, looking down on the little man's shiny scalp, puckered by a jagged scar just above his left ear. 'Formerly served in a recon platoon for eight years, Iyle here is the best scout I could find. He has actual combat experience in desert, forest, jungle and urban warzones. I think he likes the wilderness a bit too much though. He deserted whilst fighting on Tabrak II, slipping away while on picket duty. He survived out in the plains for eighteen weeks before the advance of the rest of the army caught up with him and he was captured. He's resourceful and has proven he can act on his initiative.'

'Any other reasons for choosing him?' Schaeffer asks, a slight scowl creasing his brows. 'I do not want another desertion halfway through a mission,' he adds pointedly, referring to my numerous escape attempts during the last tour of duty.

'Well, sir, because he hates being locked up in a cell even more than I do, and will do anything to get out of here,' I explain. I do have a slight doubt, but I think that Iyle would be more willing to see the mission out to the end than try to go it alone again. Of course, I don't say this to the Colonel. Schaeffer gives the man another hard stare before moving on.

'This is Paulo Regis,' I indicate the next man in line. He's about my height and build, a bit flabby around the waist and face, with pallid skin and a crooked nose. He's the most nervous of the bunch, his eyes flicking between me and the Colonel, fear mixed with flashes of hatred in them.

'A gunnery sergeant for seven years, our friend Paulo has extensive siege and bombardment experience,' I continue as the Colonel turns his ice-blue eyes on Regis. 'Our greedy gunnery sergeant was caught looting in the ruins of Bathsheman hive on Flander's World, against explicit orders from his captain.'

'A looter?' the Colonel exclaims with a grimace, eyes still fixed on Regis.

'One who was sentenced to hang for it, until your intervention, Colonel,' I point out. 'Not only that, there was a great deal of suspicion that looting wasn't all he did. Some might call it outright pillage or worse, but there was no way to prove it. He's unadulterated scum, sir, but I think he has learnt the importance of following orders.' Regis gives a grunt and a nod, and a look of irritation passes across Schaeffer's face.

'Did I say you could move, Regis?' I bellow at the prisoner in response.

'N-no, sir,' he stutters back, a panicked look in his eyes.

'Then you don't move!' I snarl, annoyed at being shown up like this in front of the Colonel. If it gets screwed up now, we'll all be enjoying the hospitality of this tower for the rest of our lives. That's something I definitely don't want. I glance at the Colonel to see his reaction, but he's now concentrating on the next soldier.

'Sniper first class, Tanya Stradinsk,' I announce as the Colonel looks her up and down, his face a mask. Tanya's not bad to look at, though I wouldn't go so far as to say she's pretty either. She has short cut, raven hair and soft brown eyes, full-lipped with prominent cheek bones. She's a few inches shorter than me, with the well-muscled build you'd expect a soldier to have.

'Without a doubt, she's the best shot in this prison, probably in the sector. Four hundred and fifty-six confirmed kills over nine years of service. Has won thirty-eight regimental and inter-regiment shooting medals, also awarded three medals for acts beyond the call of duty. She's in here for refusing to fire on the enemy, something which she did four times before being court-martialled. She was involved in an unfortunate incident that left the royal nurseries of Minos a flaming ruin and killed twenty children, including the Imperial commander's heir. She was exonerated of all blame by an investigation conducted by the Inquisition, but has since been unable to shoot except on a firing range. Don't let that fool you into thinking she's had it tough. There is a suspicion that she fired on that nursery on purpose.'

'You have brought me a sniper who refuses to shoot?' the Colonel asks doubtfully, one eyebrow raised. 'I fail to see your reasoning, Kage.'

'Well, sir, you must have thought she might be some use when you had her sent here for your collection,' I point out, my inescapable logic earning a scowl from Schaeffer. 'If nothing else, she knows more about shooting than either of us and has training experience. Anyway,' I add, giving Tanya my hardest stare, 'I will get her to shoot again.'

Colonel Schaeffer's expression remains doubtful, his eyes lingering on me for a few seconds. I hold up under his close scrutiny, meeting his gaze evenly. The expressionless mask the Colonel usually wears for a face drops back into place again and he moves along another place to Lowdon Strelli.

If ever a man looked shifty and untrustworthy, it's Strelli. Slim built and long-limbed, it's like he was stretched as a baby or something. Even his face is long, with a pointed chin and high forehead, separated by an arrowhead of a nose. He looks at me with narrowed eyes and clenched jaw, assessing me, trying to gauge what sort of man I am.

'Strelli here is the team's shuttle pilot, should we need one,' I explain to the Colonel. 'Originally a pirate from the Sanbastian mining asteroids, Pilot Strelli saw the error of his ways when orks invaded that system eight years ago. Until his court-martial, he served as a shuttle pilot, and then later on Thunderbolt interceptors. It was during this time, and despite becoming a widely-known and respected fighter ace, that he took the rivalry between the guard and navy a little too far by strafing an armoured infantry column belonging to the Fighting First of Tethis. The colonel of the Tethis First demanded that the navy turn Strelli over to them and be subject to their justice and he was duly convicted and sentenced to death by hanging. Your intervention saved him.'

This time the Colonel says nothing, staring long and hard at Strelli, as if trying to pin him to the wall with his stare. The pilot shifts uncomfortably under the unremitting icy gaze and I notice his long fingers beginning to tap nervously on his thighs. As the Colonel's harsh scrutiny continues, Strelli's eyes begin looking towards the door and I think he's going to bolt. At that moment the Colonel turns his attention away and steps on. Strelli darts a quizzical look at me, his earlier cockiness gone. I ignore him.

'Next we have Trooper Quidlon, formerly of the New Bastion 18th regiment, who is here because of his inability to curb his curiosity and pay attention to the warnings of his superiors.' The first thing that springs to mind when looking at Quidlon is 'square'. He's short, has broad, straight shoulders, a lantern jaw and a flat head. Even his ears are almost square. Standing to attention, perfectly immobile, you might think he was a sculpture by an apprentice who hasn't worked out the finer points of the human form yet.

'It seems he can't stop messing about with machinery,' I continue hastily at the Colonel's prompting stare, pulling my thoughts away from the young soldier's strange appearance. 'Following several complaints from servants of the Adeptus Mechanicus and despite reprimands from his senior officers, Quidlon here continued to make unauthorised alterations to the weapons and vehicles of his tank platoon. Fed up with him, and wisely not wanting to start a feud with the tech-priests, his superiors eventually charged him with insubordination.'

'Why did you not heed the warnings you were given?' the Colonel asks Quidlon, the first time he's spoken directly to any of the prisoners since he came in.

'I like to know how things work, sir, and the changes I made didn't do any harm, they made the engines and guns work better,' the trooper replies quickly, the words coming out in tumbled bursts, like a stubber firing on semi-auto.

'And why do you think you are here, trooper?' the Colonel continues his questioning.

'Here, now, in this line with the others and you and the lieutenant, or here in this prison, sir?' I was amazed by the speed of his talking when we first met, but I soon realised it was because his brain works that fast. It does have the unfortunate effect of making a very smart man sound very stupid though, and I can imagine why his talents have been overlooked by others who might not have realised this.

'In this chamber now,' the Colonel confirms, 'with these other prisoners.'

'Well, sir, I don't know for sure why I'm here but I might hazard a guess, considering everything I've heard so far, and my conversation with the lieutenant yesterday, that perhaps I might be useful to you, sir, because I know how to fix things,' Quidlon blurts back, looking up at Schaeffer.

'You might be,' agrees the Colonel with a nod before taking a couple more paces along the line.

'I've no idea what rock you turned over to find this next one,' I say, looking at him. The man appears unremarkable in every way. Average height, average build, dark brown hair, grey eyes, plain-looking face with no distinguishing features. His record was strangely short as well, and those bits that were in it were vague. But what was there made interesting reading. Well, interesting listening as it turned out, but that's not the point.

'Oynas Trost, a former expert in sabotage and terrorism,' I announce to Schaeffer.

'I'm still an expert,' Trost growls beside me.

'Did I tell you to open your mouth?' I snarl back, face inches from his. His eyes meet mine and a shiver runs down my spine. They're dead. I mean absolutely emotionless, flat like they're painted on. It's a look that tells me I could be on fire or bleeding to death and he would just walk past without a second glance.

'Try me. I'll show you what cold-blooded is,' I whisper in his ear, regaining my composure.

'I remember this one,' the Colonel says, pushing me to one side and squaring off against Trost. 'I remember this one very well. Trost, covert agent of the Officio Sabatorum. He has probably killed more people than everyone in this tower put together, including you and me, Kage. I remember that he made a mistake and ended up poisoning three admirals and their families.'

Trost is still trying to stare me down, but I'm not giving him an inch. If I show weakness now, he'll know it and I'll have a hard time imposing my authority later if I need to.

'Who is this final one?' the Colonel asks, pointing to the last man in the line.

'This is Pieter Stroniberg, field surgeon of the 21st Coporan Armoured Cavalry, sir,' I tell Schaeffer, tearing my eyes away from Trost. The chirurgeon is gaunt, dark-skinned with thinning black hair and a nervous tic in his right eye. He looks at the Colonel with tired, bloodshot eyes. 'While on campaign in Filius Sekunda, he became addicted to a strange cocktail of stimms and pain suppressants of his own making. Not only did this affect his performance, losing five times more patients than he saved by the end of the campaign, he began to distribute this substance to the troopers in return for favours and money.'

'And you think that his medical expertise will prove useful on this mission?' the Colonel says derisively. 'He looks dead on his feet, I would not trust him to open a pill bottle, and would never consider letting him near me with a cauteriser.'

'He's been here three years, Colonel, and cannot sleep more than four hours a night due to his long-term addiction,' I explain. 'However, he has acted as prison doctor for the last year to the satisfaction of the governor.'

'Hmm, we will see about that,' the Colonel grunts, darting a glance back at me.

The Colonel clasps his hands behind his back and turns on the spot, striding to stand in the middle of the room in front of the 'recruits'. I walk over to stand just behind and to his left. He looks up and down the line a couple more times, weighing up the merits of each of them in his head. I'm not sure whether it's them he's judging, or me for choosing them.

'They all seem satisfactory, Kage,' he says quietly to me, not turning around. 'But we must see which of them passes the final test and which will fail.'

'Final test, sir?' I ask worriedly. I can't think what the Colonel has in mind, I thought I'd covered every angle.

'My name is Colonel Schaeffer,' he barks out, his strong voice filling the chamber. 'I am the commanding officer of the 13th Penal Legion,' he glances towards me for a second, 'which some of you may have heard being called the Last Chancers. It was I who brought you all to this prison, and I now stand before you to offer you a choice. I need soldiers, fighters like you, to take part in a dangerous mission. It is likely that many of you, perhaps even all of you, will not survive this mission. You will be subjected to the most ruthless training that Lieutenant Kage here can devise, and I will expect total obedience. In return for your dedication to this duty, I offer you a full pardon for the crimes for which you have been convicted. Survive my mission and you will be free to pursue whatever lives you can. If you do not survive, then you will be pardoned posthumously, so that your souls may be cleansed of your sins and ascend to join the Emperor. Remember that a life not spent in the service of the Emperor is a life doubly wasted, in this world and the next. I also remind you that you all swore oaths of loyalty and service to the Emperor and the Imperium that serves him, and I again offer you the opportunity to fulfil those oaths.'

I look at the Colonel. He's stood there, ramrod straight, hands held easily in the small of his back. I can't see his face, but I remember the last time he gave that speech, to me and nearly four thousand others over three years ago. It wasn't exactly the same speech, but I recall his face. It radiates confidence and sincerity, those blue eyes shining with pride. He truly believes he is here to save our souls from damnation. And maybe he is. My old friend, Franx, certainly believed so, and after what I went through in the Last Chancers I'm damn sure I earnt myself some redemption.

'Moerck,' he says, looking towards the ex-commissar. 'Do you volunteer for this duty?'

'I do, sir!' he booms back, and I can picture him now, striding through the bullets and las-bolts, his voice like a clarion call to the soldiers around him. 'It will be an honour and a privilege to serve the Emperor again.'

'Iyle,' the Colonel calls out. 'Do you volunteer for this duty?'

'If it means staying out of that cell, then yes I do,' the recon man replies with an emphatic nod of the head.

'Regis, do you volunteer for this duty?' the Colonel asks the gunnery sergeant. Regis hesitates, glancing along the line to his left and right, and then back at the Colonel.

'I don't want to die,' he mumbles, eyes cast downwards as he says it. 'I would rather stay here, sir.'

I see the Colonel stiffen, as if Regis just insulted his mother or something.

'I offer you one last chance, Regis,' Schaeffer says, his voice dropping low, a sure sign that he's angry. 'Do you volunteer for this duty?'

'You fraggers can go to hell,' answers Regis, his sadness suddenly replaced by rage, lunging towards the bolt pistol hanging from the Colonel's belt. 'I'm not going anywhere with you madmen, I'll kill the fragging lot of you!'

Schaeffer steps into his rush, brings the heel of his hand into Regis's jaw and hurls him backwards to the ground with a single blow. He scrabbles to his feet and takes a swing at the Colonel, but I get there first, smacking a solid punch across his nose, spraying blood everywhere and spinning him to the floor again.

'I am truly sorry to hear that,' the Colonel replies solemnly, unmoved by the attack. 'By failing to volunteer you have proven to me and the Emperor that you are no longer a faithful and useful servant. Your presence in this facility is no longer warranted. By the authority invested in me as a commanding officer of the Emperor's judiciary, your sentence of life imprisonment is revoked,' the Colonel continues. A smile creeps across Regis's face. When the Colonel unbuckles the flap on his bolt pistol holster, the smile fades, replaced with a look of horror. 'I hereby sentence you to death, to be carried out immediately. Lieutenant Kage, do your duty.'

He pulls out his bolt pistol and holds it out for me to take. It feels heavy in my hands, smelling of fresh gun oil. It's the first time I've held a gun in months and its weight is reassuring.

'Don't move, and it'll be quick,' I tell Regis, aiming the pistol at his head. Regis ignores me and leaps to his feet, sprinting towards the chamber door. I head after him, but Trost intervenes, tackling him to the ground. The two roll across the floor, scuffling and exchanging short punches with each other as Regis tries to break free. I catch up with them and bring the butt of the pistol across Regis's forehead, stunning him. Pushing Trost aside, I place a booted foot across Regis's throat, pinning him in place. He tries to struggle a moment longer, hurling threats at me before going limp. Tears stream down his face, a dark patch spreading from the crotch of his grey fatigues.

'Take your punishment like a soldier,' I hiss at him, sickened, levelling the bolt pistol at his left eye. One smooth pull of the trigger is all it takes, the crack of the bolt's detonation ringing off the walls as the explosive round blows Regis's skull apart, spattering my legs with blood and shards of bone. I step back, the pistol smoking slightly, and look at the others. Quidlon looks aghast; Strelli wears a savage grin; Moerck is still standing to attention, eyes fixed straight ahead. The others look at me with blank expressions. Death is no stranger to them. Good, because before this mission is out, I'm sure they'll see plenty more.

I return the Colonel's pistol to him and shout at the others to fall in line again. Schaeffer continues as if there had been no distraction at all, asking each in turn if they volunteer for the duty he has for them.

They all say yes.

THE CRACKLING FLAMES in the grate blazed with a shower of sparks as the room's occupant dropped another log onto the fire. Rubbing his hands together, he returned to the low, leather covered armchair at one side of the fireplace. He was lean, with hooded eyes, his dark hair slicked back, a perfectly groomed goatee beard adorning his chin. He was wearing a heavy shirt of dark blue wool, tied at the collarless neck with golden cord, with which he fidgeted as he sat waiting. His long legs were stretched out in front of him, clad in tight trousers made from the same material as the shirt. He gazed interestedly around the room: at the red lacquered panelling on the walls, and the ceiling-high bookshelf that stretched several metres along the entire length of one wall. A clock stood upon the mantle, apparently carved from ivory or bone, ticking methodically above the sound of the fire. Turning his attention back to the bookshelf, the man stood and slowly walked over to study the assembled volumes. He ran his fingers along their spines, head cocked to one side to read their titles.

At that moment the door behind him opened with the clicking of a latch. Turning, he greeted his host with a smile. The other man was much older, his face creased like a crumpled

parchment, but his eyes were bright and clear. A few wisps of
white were all that remained of his hair and he leant heavily on
a walking cane.

'Gestimor, it is so long since we last met,' the younger man
said stepping forward and laying an affectionate hand on the
old man's shoulder.

'It is,' Gestimor replied shortly, his voice firm and strong. 'I
fear that both of us pay more attention to our duties than to
our friendship.'

'It cannot be any other way,' the visitor said matter-of-factly,
helping the ageing man to the chair. 'Come, sit and we will
talk.'

The younger man took a straight-backed chair from in front
of the study's desk and sat opposite Gestimor, leaning forward
with his arms on his knees, hands clasped together.

'You look even older than I imagined,' he said sadly.

'Yes, Lucius, I am old,' Gestimor agreed, nodding his head
slowly. 'But I still have a few more years of grace left to me, and
my mind is as sharp as ever.' He tapped at his temple in illustration.

'Why do you submit yourself to this? You know there are
ways to remedy your ageing,' asked Lucius.

'To be human is to be mortal,' the ageing man replied philosophically. 'To deny that is to invite thoughts of immortality,
which is the province of the blessed Emperor alone. That or the
gift of the Dark Powers we must thwart. To deny my mortality
is to deny my humanity and all that I have fought hard to protect in others.'

The two sat in silence for a few minutes, the comfortable
silence allowed by many years of familiarity. It was Gestimor
who spoke next, turning his gaze from the flames in the grate
to look at Lucius.

'You didn't travel across seven sectors to inquire after my
health,' he pointed out, his face serious.

'You received the data I sent?' Lucius asked, sitting back, his
expression businesslike.

'I did, and I say you are playing with fire,' Gestimor answered
sternly. 'But you will have whatever aid you need from me.'

'It is advice that I need more than anything, old friend,'
Lucius explained. 'You are right, the endeavour is risky, but the
potential rewards are well worth the hazards. For all that, I

would prefer some more surety than I currently have. I may need to act swiftly and strongly and decisively, and I am not sure that the men I have are equal to the demand.'

'Ach, that is simple,' Gestimor dismissed his comrade's worries with a wave of his veiny hand. 'Invoke the old oaths, rouse the brotherhood to duty once more.'

'Such things should not be done lightly,' Lucius replied with caution. 'The brotherhood is intended for use in extreme cases. Besides which, subterfuge and stealth are my weapons, as ever.'

'If you need their intervention, then the time for deception and intrigue will have long passed,' Gestimor countered, rubbing a hand over his bald head. 'Take just a single brother. For surety, as you said.'

'I will consider your advice,' Lucius said thoughtfully, looking into the flames and remembering the battles of the past.

THREE
LAURELS OF GLORY

+++*The target is ignorant and proceeding without thought. We have their total trust*+++

+++*Beware of underestimating them. They must remain unaware of our plans*+++

'YOUR ADDITIONAL TRAINING begins immediately,' announces the Colonel as we board the shuttle, the wind whipping across the landing pad while we make our way across the gantry. 'Lieutenant Kage has my full authority when I am not present. You will do exactly as he tells you. Your lives will depend on you maintaining discipline and learning everything you and he have to teach each other.'

The interior of the shuttle is better furnished than those I'm used to. In place of long wooden benches, the main compartment has individual seats, six rows of three each side of a central aisle. Upholstered with black padded leather, pillow-like headrests, hung with thick safety restraints with gilded buckles and clasps, the luxurious seats are obviously for the comfort of more important Imperial servants than us. Still, it's ours for the moment, and I settle into one of the seats near the back, enjoying the sensation after five months of being mana-cled to a wall. To my surprise, the Colonel comes and sits next to me.

'You do understand your position, Kage?' he asks, strapping himself into the harness.

'I think so, sir,' I answer after a moment's thought. 'I have to turn this bunch of misfits into a fighting team.'

'I mean, that I only offer one last chance,' Schaeffer says. 'You have already squandered that. There is no pardon for you this time.'

I had suspected as much, though it's still a blow hearing it stated so bluntly. So, this is it. There is no pardon, no end to the fighting except death.

I'm surprised by my own feelings, I find myself strangely calm. I get the weirdest sense of detachment, of someone else taking control of my life. It's an odd feeling, hard to explain.

My whole life I've fought against everything. I fought to get out of the hives on Olympas. I fought boredom on the world of Stygies, and ended up in the Last Chancers. I fought for two and a half years to escape the Colonel and the death I was sure he had waiting for me. I fought against the guilt and depression of being the only survivor from Coritanorum and failed. And for the last six months I fought to get out of prison, and against the growing madness that all the fighting had been building in my head.

I realise that, as last time, even if I was free, I would still be fighting. I don't know how to do anything else. Call it my destiny, my fate, if you like. Perhaps it's some part of the Emperor's scheme for me to fight until I die. Maybe that's all I have to offer Him.

It's then that I'm struck by a revelation, astounded that it didn't occur to me earlier. That's why I am here, why the Colonel has chosen me, and why I survived when thousands of others died. I fight. It's what I *do*. Perhaps I might have been able to change given the chance, but the Colonel made sure that never happened, with two and a half years of constant bloodshed and battle. I have become his creature. Now I really am his type of scum.

'I understand, sir,' I tell Schaeffer, looking at him sat next to me. Oh yes, I understand exactly what he's done to me, what he's turned me into. Like I said, given a chance I might have changed, but my last chance was just to keep on living, not to have a normal life. This existence is the only one that's left for me now, thanks to Schaeffer.

'Good,' he replies shortly, leaning his head back.

'There's one other thing, Colonel,' I say through gritted teeth. He looks over at me out of the corner of his eye. 'I hate you for what you've done to me. And one day I'll kill you for it.'

'But not today, Kage,' he replies with a grim smile. 'Not today.'

'No, sir, not today,' I agree, leaning my head back too. I close my eyes and picture my hands around his throat, as I drift off into a contented sleep.

THE DAY CYCLE begins with the glowstrips in my room flickering to life. I push myself out of my bunk and dress quickly, pulling on my new uniform. Stepping through the door that links my chamber to the team's dormitory, I see that most of them are still asleep; only Stroniberg looks in my direction as I walk in.

'Wake up you lazy, fat, useless sacks of sump filth!' I bellow at them, walking along the room and kicking at their beds. 'You are supposed to be soldiers, not babies!'

'Drop dead, soldier-boy,' snarls Strelli, swinging out from his bunk and landing on his feet in front of me. 'You may think you're the man in charge because the Colonel says so, but you push me and I'll kick the living hell out of you.'

I hear Trost step up behind me and I turn slightly and take a step back to keep both him and the pilot in view.

'I'm with the navy man on this one,' Trost says hoarsely, his dead eyes meeting my gaze. 'You know how many people I've killed. Adding you to the list won't even make me blink.'

I say nothing, keeping my face impassive. I look at the others. Moerck is ignoring me, pulling on his prison fatigues, his back to me. Tanya sits on the edge of her bunk, swinging her feet, not joining in but certainly not leaping to my defence. Quidlon looks a bit confused, his eyes shifting between me, Strelli and Trost, trying to judge which side to be on. If he has any sense, it'll be my side. Iyle is still lying on his bunk, arms behind his head, looking blankly up at the ceiling and pretending nothing is happening.

Finally, I look back at Strelli.

'I think a little discipline is needed around here,' I say to him, crossing my arms.

'What are you going to do?' he taunts me. 'Put us in explosive collars?'

'I don't need to,' I tell him quietly. He smirks, just a moment before my fist thunders into his face, smashing a tooth free and slamming him into one of the metal bed posts. Quick as lightning I spin on Trost, who's stood with a dumbfounded expression, which turns to one of intense agony as I drive my boot up into his groin, crumpling him to the floor.

'You could have done this the easy way,' I say to all of them as Trost squirms about on the floor and Strelli pushes himself upright, keeping his distance. 'You're Last Chancers now. That means that you're the lowest scum in the galaxy. That means that you're going to wish that you were dead. It also means that if you go up against me, I will break you into little pieces and shove the leftovers out of an airlock. And if any of you think

you can take me out, then please, have a go. But make sure you
do it right, because if I survive, you won't.'

'WHAT IS THIS?' I ask Stroniberg, holding my knife up in front of
his face. It's the first day of real training, aboard the ship *Laurels
of Glory*. A fine vessel, and no mistaking. Purpose built for
storm troopers, the Colonel informs me, the *Laurels of Glory* has
got just about everything you might want. Right now, we're
stood in one of the combat bays. The ship has fourteen, each
of them rigged out to represent all sorts of warzones and maintained by a veritable army of tech-priests. There's a jungle bay,
a city bay, a desert bay, a nightworld bay, shooting ranges, drill
quadrants, even a beach in one of them. I've not actually seen
any of them yet, so I'm kind of curious to see how you can
make a jungle on a spaceship. Trees made out of planks, perhaps? The best thing is that there's an armoury you could
overthrow a hive city with, housing all kinds of lethal kit that
I'm just itching to get my hands on. But that's for later; for now
we start with the basics.

'It's a knife,' he replies bluntly, a dumb look on his face.

'Do I have a rank, Trooper Stroniberg?' I rasp at him.

'You're a lieutenant,' he answers quickly. 'I mean, you're a
lieutenant, sir.'

'That's better,' I say, stepping back, brandishing the knife
towards him. 'What is this?'

'It's a knife, sir!' he replies sharply.

'Wrong!' I bark back. 'What is this?'

'I don't understand, sir…' he answers hesitantly, looking at
the others gathered around me. This bay is just an exercise hall,
a wide open space for running, close combat training, rope
climbing and such. We're stood in the middle of the chamber,
the others forming a circle around me. I hold the knife up above
my head, and turn around slowly, looking at each of them.

'Can any of you tell me what this is?' I ask them, spinning the
knife between my fingers.

'It's a Cervates pattern general issue combat knife, sir,' answers
Quidlon. 'Standard close combat armament for many Imperial
Guard regiments, originating from the Cervates forge world.'

'Is that a fact, brains?' I ask, looking at the knife in mock
amazement. 'I suspect you could tell me all sorts of interesting
things about this knife, couldn't you?'

'That knife in particular, sir, or that kind of knife?' he asks innocently.

'What?' I reply, startled. 'Emperor's blood, you think too much, Quidlon.'

I take a moment to gather my thoughts again, closing my eyes and trying to put Quidlon out of my mind. Taking a deep breath I open my eyes and look around the circle once more. A couple of them are exchanging glances with each other. Trost looks bored, standing with his arms crossed, his gaze on the ceiling.

'This is not a knife that I hold,' I bark at them, my voice ringing off the distant bulkheads of the training bay. 'I hold a weapon in my hand. The only purpose of a weapon is to inflict injury and death. This is a man's death.'

They look at me with more interest now, intrigued to know where my speech is going.

'Hey, Trost, what is the purpose of a weapon?' I snap at the saboteur, who is still looking around the hall.

'Mmm?' he glances at me. 'The purpose of a weapon is to inflict injury and death. Sir.' His voice is flat, emotionless, his expression vague.

'What is so fraggin' interesting that you think you can ignore me, Trooper Trost?' I shout at him, dropping the knife and striding up to him.

'Am I boring you, Trost?'

'I was working out how many thermal charges would be needed to blast through one of these bulkheads,' he replies, meeting my gaze finally.

'A real demolition man, aren't you?' I say, squaring up to Trost. He smirks at me. My fist smashes into his jaw before he realises I'm even swinging at him, knocking him to his knees. He tries to fend off my next blow with a waved arm so I grab his left wrist in both hands, twisting it forward and pitching him face first into the floor. Putting one foot on his shoulder, I wrench on his arm and the joint pops like a cork, Trost spitting through gritted teeth. 'Your thermal charges didn't help much then, did they demolition man? Try setting one of your bombs now.'

I step back, letting his dislocated arm drop to the floor. He pushes himself to his knees with his good arm, groaning and darting murderous looks at me.

'Stroniberg, fix that,' I tell the surgeon, pointing to where Trost is knelt cradling his injured shoulder, gasping, his face twisted with pain.

'This'll hurt,' the medico warns Trost, taking a tight grip of his arm and twisting it back into place with an audible click, making him cry out.

'Right, everyone will pay attention to what I have to say, is that understood?' I ask them, daring them with my stare. Stroniberg helps Trost to his feet before taking his place in the circle again. 'I don't give a frag whether any of you live or die, you can be sure of that. I do care whether I live or die, and that means I have to rely on scum like you. Make no bones about it, if the Colonel thinks any of us are not shaping up, the chances are he'll put a bolt into all of us and start afresh, so you best start acting like you care. Listen to me, and we'll all live. Ignore me, and we're all fraggin' shafted.'

Iyle raises a hand and I give him the nod to speak.

'Who the hell are you, sir?' he asks.

'I am the man the Colonel visited a dozen kinds of hell upon and survived,' I reply slowly, gesturing for the others to gather in front of me so I don't have to keep turning around to look at them all. 'I am the man who helped the Colonel kill three million people. I am the only man to survive when four thousand others died on the battlefield. I have killed men in their sleep. I have shot them. I have stabbed them. I have strangled them. I've even beaten them to death with my hands and fists. I've fought tyranids and orks, I've marched across searing deserts and frozen wastelands. I've nearly died six times. My own men have tried to kill me on more than one occasion. I've fought things you don't even know exist. And I killed them.'

Every word of it is true as well, and they can tell it by the look in my eye, even Trost, who shows the first sign of any feelings at all, a glimmer of respect.

'But none of that matters,' I carry on, walking up and down in front of them, looking at each of them in turn. 'I am Lieutenant Kage, your training officer. I will do what the hell I like, to who the hell I like, when and where the hell I like, and there's nothing in the Emperor's wide galaxy you can do or say to stop me. And it will be the worst, the very worst, time of your life. But, as the Colonel said, if you want that pardon and live to hold it, hold it in your hand and walk free, then you will listen to what I say, and do exactly what I tell you to do. If just one of you messes up, I will frag you all.'

I leave them with that thought for a while, picking up the knife as I walk to the far end of the training hall. I smile to myself. I once said I'd be a great training instructor if it wasn't for my lousy temper. Now I'm here, I figure my lousy temper is the best weapon in my arsenal. That and the knowledge that my own life depends on these boneheads shaping up to the Colonel's satisfaction.

I look back at them and can hear them talking amongst themselves. They're a long way from becoming a fighting team, but their mutual hatred of me will bring them together. That's the way I plan it, anyway. It worked for me. My loathing of the Colonel and everything he stands for gave me the determination to survive. I'll dare them to die on me, prove to me how weak they really are. I'll break them and put them back together, and to be honest, I'll enjoy every minute of it. Why? Because other than actual battle, it's the only thing left in my life to take pleasure in.

I toy with the knife in my hands, standing there looking at them. They're all veterans, they all think they're special. It's an illusion. I've seen first-timers walk through a battle with honours, while old campaigners got blown to bits or broke down and cried. Time served means nothing to me, I don't care how good they think they are, what they think they are capable of. I've seen men pushed to their limits of sanity and endurance. I was one of them. The Colonel tells me I've got about two months to work on them. Two months to turn them into a fighting force he's willing to lead into battle.

And there's an odd thing. Why is the Colonel leaving this to me? Why did he leave me in the vincularum with the others, to be dragged out again later, like an old sword handed down from father to son? It's a trend that started when he put me in charge last time around, just before False Hope and the horrors of the god-plant. Even back then, did he have something like this in mind? I'm certain he knew I'd be fighting for him again if I survived Coritanorum. The fact that he caught up with me so quickly proved that.

I give myself a mental slap. All this thinking and pondering is a symptom of the prison we've left behind. I don't have time to stand around and think. I have work to do. I realise that I'm going to have to train myself too. Six months in that cell may have sharpened my philosophy skills, but they've blunted my battle readiness. Idly tossing the knife from hand to hand, I walk back to the group.

'What is the purpose of a soldier?' I call out to them as I approach. They answer with shrugs and shaking heads.

'To follow orders and fight for the Emperor, sir?' suggests Iyle, hand half-raised like a child.

'Pretty close,' I agree, looking at the knife before turning my gaze on them. 'The purpose of a soldier is to kill for the Emperor. Any fool can fight, but a true soldier kills. He kills whoever he's told to kill, whenever he's told to. Battles are not won by fighting, they are won by killing. An enemy who can fight you is not a problem. An enemy who can kill you, there you have a threat. Which of you claims to be a soldier?'

'I've killed more men than can be counted. Sir.' Trost steps forward. 'By your reckoning, that makes me a soldier.'

'How did you kill them?' I ask, setting the knife spinning on its pommel on the tip of my index finger. 'Did you stab any of them?'

'No, I've never had to stab a man,' he admits. 'I use explosives, gas and poison. If I had to fight man-to-man that meant I'd been discovered, which meant my mission had failed. I never failed a mission.'

'I'm sure those three admirals thought highly of you as they died,' I sneer.

'The mission was still completed. Normally a few additional deaths are allowed,' he states coldly. I focus my attention on Strelli and point the knife at him.

'Are you a soldier, flyboy?' I ask him. He opens his mouth to reply, but at that moment I whip round and hurl the knife into Trost's left foot, pinning it to the floor. He shrieks and keels over. Pulling the knife free with both hands, he lets it clatter to the floor in a bloody puddle. 'You forget to call me "sir" one more time, demolition man, and I will do a whole lot worse to you!' I growl at Trost.

'Well, Strelli?' I ask, turning back to the pilot. 'Are you a soldier?'

'Not by your definition, sir,' he tells me, glancing at Trost squirming on the floor, hands clutched around his bleeding foot. 'I flew shuttles and fighters, I've never fought face-to-face with an enemy.'

'Do you want to become a soldier now, flyboy?' I challenge him.

'Not with you, sir,' he smiles back cockily. 'You'll cut me to pieces.'

'Yes, I will,' I assure him with a grim smile.

'Sir?' I hear Stroniberg ask from my right. I don't turn around, I already know what he's going to ask.

'Nobody gets treatment until I say so,' I tell him, still looking at Strelli. I hear a grunt and the thud of feet and spin to my left. Trost plunges the knife down at my face, but I catch the blade on the outside of my left forearm and deflect it away. Even as he tumbles off balance, my right foot connects with the outside of his left knee, buckling his leg and pitching him into the floor.

'I'd wait until I've taught you how to use a knife properly before doing that again,' I tell him, pulling the blade from his blood-coated fingers. The others are all staring at me. At my arm to be precise. Blood is dripping from my finger tips onto the clean wooden planks of the floor. I check out the wound. It isn't severe, not much more than a layer of skin taken off.

'If this is the most blood you see in the next couple of months, I'm going too easy on you,' I tell them with a grin. 'Enough of the theory for today. I'm going to show you how to use this knife like a soldier.'

I SPEND THE rest of the week teaching them knife-fighting. Proper knife-fighting, hive fashion, including every dirty trick I've learnt over the hard years. We all get a few more cuts and bruises, but I allow no one to go to the infirmary until the end of the day. Each morning after breakfast, I give them a sermon on what it means to be a soldier. One day it is about following orders. The next it's on the nature of victory. I tell them about teamwork and trust. Other times I regale them on the uses of fear as a weapon.

There's no pattern to my teachings, just stuff that's come to me the night before as I lie on my small cot in the officer's room adjacent to the dormitory they share with each other. It's all stuff that I know in my heart is true, but finding the words to explain it to them is difficult. How can I teach them something which I just know inside me?

I have no doubt that what I have to say is just as important as knife-fighting, marksmanship, wilderness survival, camouflage techniques, field navigation and all the other stuff they can fill your head with, but I can't quite figure it out just yet. I sit on my bunk at the end of the first week trying to get it all straight, trying to work out exactly what it is they need to know if they're going to survive. On my own in that small room, with just a bunk and a small locker, I feel like I've just swapped one cell for another. I hear a laugh through the connecting door, and my heart sinks. I'm not one of them this time around. I'm the officer in more than just title. I can't sit in there and swap stories with them. They are not my friends.

I slouch there wishing more than ever that Gappo or Franx were still alive. Even better, that Lorii wasn't a scattering of ash on Typhos Prime. It all seems unreal to me, like it was all a dream or something and I've just woken up in this bed, half-remembering it. Why was I the only one who survived? What is it about me that I can pass on to these others, so that perhaps they'll live as well?

It's with a start that the answer comes to me, and I almost bang my head back against the wall as I sit up. It was more than plain determination, more than just skill and luck. You can leave destiny hanging for all I care, I've been thinking about this the wrong way around. It's not why I survived, it's why the others didn't. They didn't really want to. Not as much as I did. Never once did I truly think that I was going to die. I never really believed anyone could kill me. Except perhaps the tyranids, but even they didn't manage it.

The Emperor helps those who help themselves, one of the old sayings tells us. Everything I've been struggling to understand starts to come together. This isn't about building a team, training soldiers, passing on skills. It's about giving each of them the same indestructible belief in themselves that I have. Tonight's the night for realisations I guess, because it's then that I see how the Colonel can walk through the bloodiest battles in the galaxy without a scratch. He's got even more belief in himself than I have. It protects him almost like a shield. The only problem left is how do I get the others to create their own shields, to think they're invincible?

A plan begins to form in my mind.

* * *

THE NEXT MORNING I appear in the mess room with a pile of grey and black uniforms in my arms. While the others settled into bed last night, I took a trip to the store rooms with a special request. The hall itself is about thirty metres long, fifteen wide, with six wide tables arrayed in two rows along the length. The bare, unpainted metal of the walls is polished and pristine, the result of the team's labours yesterday before I allowed them their evening meal.

Well, discipline isn't just about being calm under fire, or following orders, it's also about being able to do the dull, lousy jobs and still stay sharp. Like sentry duty, or cleaning the mess hall.

'Form up!' I shout and they push themselves to their feet, standing at ease behind their places at the long bench.

'This morning I have something different to show you,' I announce, placing the uniforms at the end of the table. 'You will not become true soldiers until you think like true soldiers. You will not think like true soldiers until you understand what it means to be true soldiers. You will not understand what it means to be true soldiers while you think you are something else. The logical conclusion of this is that while you think you are something else you will never be true soldiers.'

They look at me with dumbfounded expressions. I don't expect them to understand, it only became clear to me last night. I look at the name tag sewn on to the breast pocket of the first uniform.

'Who are you?' I ask, pointing at Stradinsk.

'Tanya Stradinsk, sir!' she replies, standing to attention.

'No you are not,' I tell her with a shake of my head, picking up the top uniform. 'Who are you?' She thinks for a moment before replying.

'Trooper Stradinsk, 13th Penal Legion, the Last Chancers, sir!' she answers with a look of triumph.

'Nice try, but still not right,' I say, looking at all of them. 'A true soldier does not know who they are because of their name. You,' I say, pointing at Moerck. 'How does a true soldier know who they are?'

'I do not know the answer to that, sir!' he barks back, snapping to attention as well.

'Can anyone here tell me how a true soldier knows who they are?' I cast my gaze around as I'm speaking.

'By knowing his purpose in the eyes of the Emperor, Lieutenant Kage!' a voice bellows like a thunderclap behind me, causing us all to jump to attention. The Colonel strides up and stands beside me, glancing down over my shoulder at the uniforms. 'Am I correct, Lieutenant Kage?'

'Yes, Colonel, you are,' I say. His eyes meet mine and his ice-blue stare holds me for a second. He gives an approving nod.

'Carry on, Lieutenant Kage,' he tells me, stepping back a couple of paces. I try to block his presence from my mind, replaying the last minute or so in my head to catch up with where I had got to in the little mental script I devised for myself instead of sleeping last night.

'A true soldier does not know himself by his name, where he is from, even who he fights for,' I tell them, the words coming back to me. I can feel the Colonel's eyes on me and my throat goes dry. I cover my discomfort by beckoning Tanya over with a finger, before continuing. 'A true soldier knows himself by what he does.'

I turn to Stradinsk, and hand her the uniform.

'You are not Tanya Stradinsk, you are not Trooper Stradinsk,' I tell her. 'Who are you?'

'I still don't know, sir,' she says apologetically, glancing at the others for help, or maybe just support.

'What does your name badge say?' I ask softly, indicating the uniform in her hands.

'It says "Sharpshooter", sir,' she replies after glancing down.

'Who are you?' I ask her again, my voice firm.

'Sharpshooter, sir?' she answers hesitantly.

'Why are you asking me?' I say, voice dripping with scorn. 'Do I know you better than you know yourself?'

She stands there for a few heartbeats, looking at me, then the uniform, then back at me. Her jaw sets tight and her eyes go hard as she realises the full truth.

'I am Sharpshooter, sir!' Her voice can't hide the bitterness she feels, her new name a constant reminder of the guilt she feels.

'Return to your position, Sharpshooter!' I command her, picking up the next uniform. One by one I call them over, give them their fatigues and send them back. When they're all back in line again, each holding their uniforms in front of them, I walk to the opposite side of the table. Out of the corner of my eye I can still see the Colonel, watching everything, studying me and the other Last Chancers.

'Sound off!' I bark, looking at Strelli at the left of the line.

'Flyboy, sir!' he shouts.

'Demolition Man, sir!' Trost calls out next.

'Sharpshooter, sir,' Stradinsk tells me again.

'Hero, sir!' comes Moerck's parade ground bellow.

'Brains, sir!' Quidlon replies.

'Eyes, sir!' shouts Iyle.

'Stitcher, sir!' Stroniberg finishes the roll call.

'From now on, those are your names,' I tell them harshly. 'You will use those names all the time. Every time your name is spoken, you will hear it well and know who you are. Anyone forgets this rule, and you'll all be punished. Is that clear?'

'Yes, sir!' they chorus.

I'm about to dismiss them to get ready for the morning's training when the Colonel interrupts.

'What is your name?' he asks.

'My... My name, sir?' I ask, taken aback. I turn and look directly at him. 'I hadn't thought of a name for myself.' He seems to think for a moment, before the corner of his lip turns up into the slightest of smiles.

'You are Last Chance,' he says with a nod. As he strides out of the mess hall, he looks back over his shoulder at me. 'I expect to see you in uniform in the future.'

THE TRAINING CONTINUES steadily for another two weeks, as I work on the Last Chancers' fitness and marksmanship. It almost settles into a routine, so halfway through the second week, I speak to the ship's officers and arrange for the day/night lighting cycle to be adjusted in our quarters. Sometimes we'll have the equivalent to a twenty hour day, followed by just a few hours' sleep, other times I let them rest for half a day before rousing them. I'm still worried about their alertness, though; I need them to be as sharp as knives when we arrive at wherever we're going. So I organise a little exercise to test them.

It's midway through the twenty-first night, and I creep into their dorm. The room is filled with heavy breathing and gentle snores, the Last Chancers worn out from a day of training wearing heavy packs the whole time. In my hand I have some small slips of parchment used for identifying corpses, that I had a scribe write on, 'You were killed in your sleep'. The first bunk is Trost's, curled up with his face to the wall, hands holding his blanket tight around him. Barely breathing, I lean over him and place the first piece of paper on the pillow next to him. On the bed above Stroniberg lies stretched out on his back, his blanket down to his waist, mouth open, his breathing punctuated by a nasal whistling. I lay the parchment slip across his throat. I continue like this around the dormitory, easing myself from one bunk to the next in the dim night lighting. There's only Moerck left, the most likely to wake up, when a murmuring causes me to freeze. I stay like that, breath held, for a few seconds trying to identify where the noise is coming from. It's to my left, and I cautiously follow the mumbling to its source. It's Stradinsk, talking in her sleep. She's restless, plagued by her dreams.

Satisfied she's asleep, I creep back to Moerck's bunk and slide the parchment under his blanket. I then sit myself down by the door to my room, back against the wall, and wait for the morning.

It was far too easy for me, and that's worrying. I have to work out how to punish them so that they'll learn never to be so complacent again. I can't be too hard on them though, who would think they have to set a watch aboard a friendly starship? Something short and sharp should do the trick. If they don't learn this time, I'll have to come up with something more serious.

I sit there watching them. So quiet. So vulnerable. Two and a half years sharing a hall-sized cell with hundreds of murderers, thieves and rapists taught me how to sleep lightly. I listen to their slow breathing, imagining the blood bubbling into their lungs if I'd been a real enemy. I hear Stradinsk give a short gasp before rolling over. I filter out the noises: the breathing, Tanya's mumbling, Stroniberg's light snoring, and listen to the sounds of the ship around me. The walls hum slightly; energy conduits coursing with plasma run underneath the floor. I can hear a faint clank-clank-clank of heavy machinery operating in the distance. There's the sound of the armsmen patrolling the corridor outside, their boots clumping along the metal decking. The calm is a long way from the thunder of shells, the crack of lasguns and the boom of grenades that I'm more used to. I concentrate on the sounds, picking out different ones in the music being played out by the ship, to keep myself awake.

It's Stroniberg who wakes first, his withdrawal-induced sleep-lessness rousing him only a couple of hours after midnight. I watch him from the darkness, sitting up in bed, startled by the fluttering paper that drops to his lap. He picks it up and turns it to the faint light from the dimmed glowglobes above, trying to see what it is. He slides his feet out of bed and sits on the edge. I don't move a muscle, I just look at him. He must have noticed me out of the corner of his eye, because he twists sharply to look at me, alarm on his face. I raise my finger to my lips to keep him silent and then point at his bed. He gets the message, lying back down again, the parchment crumpled in one hand.

The others rouse themselves when the lights flicker into day-time brightness at the end of the eight-hour sleep cycle. One by one they wake, making confused exclamations or just scratch-ing their heads upon finding their mortuary tags.

'Form up!' I shout, pushing myself to my feet. They fall and scramble out of their beds, standing to attention in front of their bunks.

'So now I'm leading a squad of corpses,' I tell them scorn-fully, walking the length of the dormitory. 'Well, that's the mission fragged good and proper, isn't it?'

None of them reply, they all look straight ahead, not meet-ing my gaze as I walk past them. I walk back again slowly, deliberately, teasing out the suspense, aggravating their anxi-eties. Stopping at my door again, I spin on the spot to face them, hands behind my back.

'Next time I shall use a knife,' I warn them, meaning every word of it. 'And I won't think twice about cutting you. As for your embarrassing performance last night, I have this to say: you are all corpses, and as we all know, corpses don't eat, so there will be no meals today and battlefield water rations only. Do any of you have a question?'

Tanya steps forward, concern on her face.

'Yes, Sharpshooter?' I say.

'You were in here last night, Last Chance?' she asks worriedly.

'Almost the whole night, Sharpshooter,' I tell her with a smile. 'Does that worry you? Don't you trust your training lieu-tenant, Sharpshooter?'

'I trust my training lieutenant, Last Chance!' she replies quickly.

'Then you're an idiot, Sharpshooter,' I snarl at her, striding
down the room towards her. She flinches as I stop in front of
her. 'There's not one person in the Emperor's dark galaxy that I
would trust, least of all me. I am not here to be nice to you,
Sharpshooter. I am not here to look after you.' I round on the
rest of them and bellow at them. 'I am here to make sure that
when the time comes you can look after yourself, and me, and
the rest of your squad!' I whirl on her again. 'I'll break you in
half on a whim, Sharpshooter, so don't ever trust me unless I
tell you to. Is that clear?'

'No, Last Chance, it isn't,' Quidlon replies, stepping forward.
'If we can't trust you, then how are we supposed to trust you
when you say that we can, given that you may be lying to us
about trusting you?'

'Exactly my point, Brains,' I tell him with a grin. 'Now, all of
you get cleaned up. Breakfast time will be spent in the armoury
doing weapons maintenance drill. I will join you at the normal
time for today's new adventure. In the meantime, I believe
there is still some fresh meat left in the officers' kitchen, which
I shall be enjoying.'

They break ranks and busy themselves with getting ready. I
turn to walk out when something occurs to me.

'Oh, one more thing,' I say to them, causing them to pause in
their preparations. 'If any of you can tag me with one of those,
you all earn one day's rest and recuperation. However, if any of
you try and fail, then it'll be another day without food. That
sounds fair, doesn't it?'

'Yes, Last Chance!' they reply in unison.

'Good. I'll be seeing you shortly,' I tell them, whistling a
jaunty tune that my dead comrade Pohl taught me a couple of
years ago. I won't bore you with the bawdy lyrics, but suffice to
say it's called the Hangman's Five Daughters.

THE NEXT DAY, and the day after that, they all look exhausted.
None of them have got any sleep as far as I can tell. I suspect
they're having disturbing dreams of me sneaking around with
my knife. Good, that was the point. I overheard them this
morning discussing a watch rota. That should be interesting to
see in action, considering the variable length of the nights that
I've requested. I've decided to give them another week before I
try anything again. That'll show whether they can keep their

guard up night after night, or whether they lapse into a false sense of security again.

I think it's time to start doing some squad-based training now. After breakfast on day twenty-four I lead them to training bay six. We're kitted out with full equipment; we'll be spending the next several days in there without coming out. I've issued everyone with lasguns, the standard Imperial Guard armament, as well as knives, ammunition for a hundred shots each, rations, water canteens, bedrolls and everything else. I also gave them new uniforms, with a common brown and green camo scheme. They don't have name badges to remind them who they are now. Not one of them has slipped up so far on that front, but I'm waiting for it. They're starting to get tired. Weary from irregular sleep and day after day of me bawling them out, pushing them hard, relentlessly driving them on.

It's for their own good. If they can't take the training, how in the Emperor's name are they going to fare in real combat? Like I said, their pasts mean nothing to me, all of their previous achievements count for nothing. Here, and on the mission, is where they'll prove themselves to the Colonel. And prove themselves to me, as well. I'm spending a lot of energy myself, doing this for them.

It's been tiring work for me too. Somehow, I doubt they appreciate the effort I've put in on their behalf.

When it comes down to it, I'm starting to feel responsible for them, like I've never felt responsible for anyone else before. I tell myself that if they get themselves killed, if they foul up and the mission goes up like a photon flash flare, ultimately it'll be their own fault. But inside, I know that isn't one hundred per cent true. I know that if I miss something out, if I take anything for granted, if I go easy on them for just a moment, I will have failed them, and through them the Colonel.

Anyway, we're all decked out in battledress and heading into the training bay. We pass through a couple of airlocks monitored by white-robed tech-priests, whose job it is to maintain the stable environments inside each of the bays. At the end of it a large double-doored portal rolls open.

It's amazing. On one side of the door is metal mesh decking. On the other side steps lead down into rolling hills and fields. I can see a small pre-fabricated farmhouse a few hundred metres to my left, smoke drifting lazily out of its chimney. We walk down the wide stairwell on to the grass, gazing around us like first-timers in a brothel. With a clang, the doors slam closed behind us.

I assume the walls have some kind of image painted on to them, because the agri-world landscape stretches as far as the eye can see. Above our heads, small puffy clouds dot a deep blue sky. I blink in disbelief as I notice the clouds are drifting across the ceiling.

'Last Chance...' Iyle whispers in awe. 'Sorceries of the machine god.'

He's looking behind me and I turn to see what he's staring at. The doors have disappeared, as have the steps. As in every other direction, the hills stretch as far as the horizon. In the far distance I can just make out the purple slopes of a mountain range, topped with snow. The others are murmuring suspiciously, shrinking back from the open sky above.

'Yes, magic, the most powerful techno-magic,' I say quietly in agreement, awed and afraid at the nature of our surroundings.

'This is unbelievable...' gasps Quidlon, dropping to his knees and running his fingers through the grass. 'It feels real, and even smells real.'

I notice that he's right. It smells like an agri-world. There's even a faint breeze blowing from our left. Fresh air, on a ship where the air gets constantly cycled through great big refiners, breathed millions and millions of times before until it's almost thick with age. I was expecting something pretty special, after the Colonel told me there were only a couple of dozen of these ships in the entire navy, but nothing as extravagant as this. His powerful contacts have been working hard for him again.

'It is real,' I say ominously, a sudden shiver of unnatural fear coursing through me. 'I think it's been grown here by the tech-priests.'

This is wrong, a voice at the back of my mind tells me. Ships don't have woods and meadows on board them. They have engines, and guns, and they're built out of metal, not dirt. At that point a voice blares out, seemingly from the air itself, shattering the illusion.

'This is Warrant Officer Campbell,' the heavenly voice tells us. 'Tech-priest Almarex will be monitoring you in training bay six. If you need to contact him, adjust your comm-sets to shipboard frequency seventy-three. When you wish to leave, return to this point and transmit a signal on shipboard frequency seventy-four and the doors will open. Oh, and a word of warning. Our climate regulators predict rainfall for most of the night, so set up a good camp. Good luck with your training.'

'Rainfall?' Tanya laughs nervously. 'We're going to get rained on aboard a starship? There's a first.'

'No fauna though,' Quidlon continues, looking around.

'No what, Brains?' asks Trost, who's sat on his pack, tossing a grenade from hand to hand.

'No fauna,' Quidlon repeats himself, squinting up into the sky.

'What Brains means is there aren't any animals here,' Stroniberg explains, squatting down next to the ex-Officio Sabatorum agent. 'No birds, no animals, no insects. Only vegetation.'

'Why didn't he just say that!' complains Trost, ripping up a handful of grass and letting it scatter between his fingers.

'Okay everyone, daydreams in paradise time is over!' I snap at them. 'We are here to work, not rest. Flyboy, you have the map, find out where we are.'

Strelli pulls off his pack and starts to rummage through it, looking for the chart one of the tech-priests handed to me as we passed through the bay entryway.

'Emperor's blood, Flyboy,' Iyle swears at Strelli, pulling the pack from him and tipping its contents on to the ground. He finds the chart and waves it angrily under the pilot's nose. 'What in hell's use is a map that you can't find?'

'Well, you take care of the map then, Eyes,' Strelli snaps back, gathering together his stuff and piling it back into his backpack.

'Flyboy keeps the map,' I tell them, snatching it off Iyle and handing it to Strelli.

'Why, Last Chance?' asks Iyle. 'I was in recon, remember. I can find places with my eyes closed.'

'That's why you don't need to learn how to use a map, you stupid son-of-an-ork!' I shout at him, pushing him onto his backside. I glare at the others.' And that's why Flyboy here is in charge of the map! When Eyes gets killed, who else is going to know what to do?'

'Don't you mean if *I* get killed, Last Chance?' says Iyle defensively. I round on him and kick him in the chest, flattening him again.

'The way you're going, Eyes, it's most definitely "when", not "if",' I spit at him. 'When everyone has finished arguing, we might carry on. Right, our mission for today is to take and attempt to hold that farmstead.' I point at the clutch of buildings about half a kilometre away.

'This whole area is to be considered hostile. We're expecting the place to be reinforced at dusk, so we have to be in by then. There will be targets appearing during the course of the day, and our progress will be monitored by the tech-priests. This evening we will set camp and have a full debriefing. Now, Flyboy, show me that map.'

The others gather round as I spread the chart onto the grass. It shows that the farm is in the cleft of a shallow valley between two hills. We have no way of knowing how accurate the map is though, but there appears to be a road or track of some kind, leading in from what I reckon to be the north.

'How would you attack, Demolition Man?' I prod Trost in the arm.

'Wait for cover of darkness, then sneak in, Last Chance,' he tells me. 'I could rig something up with the squad's grenades, blow the whole thing to tinder.'

'Great, then we get to defend a pile of sticks,' Strelli points out. 'Listen to the orders, fraghead. Take and hold, not level the place.'

'Well, the orders are stupid,' Trost huffs, stepping away from the group.

'Flyboy's right, Demolition Man,' I say, standing up and dragging him back to the map. 'When we find out whatever it is we've got to do, there'll be a plan, and everybody has to stick to the plan. You may be used to working on your own, but unless you want a bolt pistol pointed between your eyes, you better start learning to share.'

'So what would you do, Last Chance?' Stradinsk asks, squatting down and looking at the map again before turning her eyes on me.

'I want to hear what you meatheads come up with first, and then you get a chance to shoot holes in my plan,' I tell them, pulling my pack off and sitting down on it. 'Come on, Sharpshooter, let's hear what you've got to say.'

So we spend an hour or so discussing different ways of taking that farm. We go over frontal assaults, flank attacks, diversionary feints, fusillade and half a dozen other ways of kicking a potential enemy out. As the time passes, I let them get on with it more and more, and soon they're discussing the good points and the pitfalls without any intervention or prompting from me.

I let them think that they're going to have their say, although I decided straight away what we're going to do. It's best to let them get it out of their system first before I start giving them orders. Hopefully, they'll learn a thing or two, including following the man in charge. One of them distracts me from my thoughts. 'What was that?' I ask, looking around. 'Someone say something?'

'I asked what type of support we can expect, Last Chance,' Quidlon tells me. 'You know, air support, artillery, tanks, that sort of thing.'

I just laugh. I laugh until I'm red in the face. They look at me like I've gone insane, which to them probably isn't too far from the truth.

'You got sod all, Brains,' I say, grinning like a fool. 'This is it. No planes. No tanks. No artillery. Just the eight of us, with our lasguns and frag grenades and our heads switched on.' I rein myself in and get serious. 'I'm training you for a real mission, when all we're gonna have is us. Forget about support and what you don't have, that's how dead men think. True soldiers think about themselves and what they can do, without help from anyone else. So, have you agreed on a plan yet?'

'We think we have one that will work, Last Chance,' Stroniberg informs me solemnly.

'Good, now forget it,' I tell them. My statement is answered with objections and confusion, and they start to try and tell me anyway, arguing that it'll work. Trost hurls abuse and stomps away angrily.

'I don't give a frag about your plan, I'm in charge,' I tell them harshly, slapping away Stroniberg's hand, which he laid on my arm when he was arguing with me. 'I never said we'd use your plan for the actual attack, I just asked how you would do it. Now, shut the frag up, and listen to what I'm going to tell you. If we don't take this farmstead, nobody eats tonight and we try again tomorrow, is that clear?'

They answer sullenly, like children who've been told that they can't play. Tough.

'This is the plan. Any of you fail to follow orders, it'll be bad for all of you,' I tell them. They gather around the map while I point out the various locations.

'Demolition Man, Eyes, Hero and myself will infiltrate the farm and sneak into this building,' I point to a barn-like structure within the compound, about twenty metres from the main house. 'If we encounter any resistance we take them out quickly and silently, using knives only.'

I glare at them to make my point. If this was a real fight, any noise would probably bring down all kinds of crap onto us before we even got started.

'Sharpshooter and Stitcher will take up positions on this ridge,' I point to the slope to the east of the objective. 'Find some good cover with flexible firing positions. Your job is to bring fire down onto the farmhouse before our assault begins, and to cover our backs when we go in. We die, it's your fault.'

The pair of them nod seriously, understanding the importance of their role. The only way to take that building is to get someone actually in there and clear it room by room. However, that would be worthless if reinforcements came in behind us or surrounded us before the others could bolster any defence we might muster.

'You two,' I say, looking at Strelli and Quidlon, 'will move into position once the others begin their fusillade. Get on to the roof of this outhouse,' I indicate a large building just behind and to the left of the one we plan to assault from, 'and provide covering fire on the target as we move in. Once we're inside, take over our position ready to follow us in quick when I give the shout.'

Quidlon is studying the map intently, a slight frown creasing his flat forehead.

'You have something to say, Brains?' I ask, turning my gaze on him.

'The attack is all centred on the south and east, Last Chance,' he points out, drawing an arc around the farm with his finger. 'You've got nothing to protect you from the north and west.'

'We can't spread ourselves too thin,' I reply patiently. 'Any less in the assault team and we risk getting kicked out straight away. One person on the ridge won't be enough to keep any enemy heads down before we go, and won't be able to cover their own back. The same goes for you two inside the compound with us.

The main road comes in from the southwest.' I trace the point of my dagger along its length on the map. 'So we'll have run into anything along there. The objective itself will shield us from any counter-attack from the opposite direction, 'cos the enemy will have to either enter from the opposite side of the building, which puts them in front of us, or circle round to where we go in and get caught in a crossfire by you guys and the team on the hill.'

'You talk about enemy moving round and encircling, but aren't these just pop-up targets like on the shooting ranges, Last Chance?' asks Trost.

'I've got two answers to that,' I snap at him. 'First, this whole area is littered with those targets and the tech-priests in control can raise and lower them in sequence to simulate movement. Second, and more importantly, this is a battle. Don't think of this as an exercise, something to pass the time. When we're on the mission, we'll be fighting real bastards who will want to kill us, and I don't want any of you getting into a routine where the enemy stays in one place. A soldier who sits still too long is a dead soldier, and useless to me and the Emperor, or an easy target if he's fighting for the other side.'

'That's true,' agrees Stradinsk. 'First rule of the sniper is to take a shot and then move on.'

'Well, thanks for your support, Sharpshooter,' I say sourly before getting back to the attack. 'This has to be timed right, everyone needs to act when and how I tell you. Eyes goes in first and scouts around, and reports back to me. We'll make any changes then, and after that you follow your orders no matter what happens. Is that understood?'

They all nod, although Quidlon and Trost seem doubtful.

'Once we have a clear route, Stitcher and Sharpshooter get into position on the ridge,' I continue, 'I'll give you half an hour to make your way there. You can see the whole thing from where you'll be, or you should be able to if you get in the right place. Sharpshooter, once you're up there point out a few good places for Stitcher to settle.'

'I'll pick a couple of good spots, Last Chance, don't worry,' she assures me with a tight-lipped smile.

'I bet you will,' I agree, remembering her lethal record. 'When you see everyone else in position, open fire on the building. The covering team in the compound,' I look at Strelli and

Quidlon, 'will open fire only when the assault teams fire. Direct
your shots at other parts of the building to the ones we're firing
at. When we get inside, get off the roof, don't waste any time at
all, and then get into where we were. Don't anyone even think
about firing into the farm once we've gone in, you're there to
keep the grounds clear. Anyone shoots me, I'll come back and
haunt you for the rest of your fraggin' lives and make you even
more miserable than you are now.'

'No firing on the building once you are inside, I can remember that,' says Quidlon with a nervous nod.

'Relax, Brains,' I tell him. 'I've been through more blood and
guts fighting than you could imagine, and I know what I'm
doing. Now, everyone tell me what the plan is.'

I make them repeat it to me three times each, first all of the
attack in the order I explained it. I then get them to tell me their
own parts, pointing at them each in turn, then doing the same
again but picking on them randomly. Satisfied they understand
what's expected of them I wave them away to get their kit
together.

We move out some time in what I guess to be mid-afternoon.
I forgot to ask how long the 'day' was supposed to last in here.
That said, I don't know how much information we'll have on
the actual mission so some flexibility and adaptation won't be
out of order. I mean, the Colonel and Inquisitor Oriel had
been planning Coritanorum for years and we still had to make
it up as we went along at some points. For all I know, we might
just get dropped into a big mess and be forced to improvise the
whole thing from the start. It's too much to expect this bunch
to be able to do that at the moment, though. I'd rather they
learnt how to follow orders to the exact letter, and can get their
heads around a plan without it taking hours to explain.

Everyone is lined up with their kit on, and I shoulder my
own pack and join them.

'Right, we'll move out in single file, ten paces apart, Eyes goes
on point thirty paces ahead,' I tell them, waving the recon spe-
cialist on with my lasgun. 'Everyone keeps their eyes and ears
open and their mouths shut, I don't know what surprises this
place has got in store for us. You see the enemy, hit the dirt and
wave everyone else down. Don't fire until I give you the order.
I want this to be disciplined and calm, no mad firefights unless
I say so.'

'Yes, Last Chance!' they chorus back.

'Right, let's move out,' I give the order, and we set off across the field.

MARCHING ACROSS THE fields of the training bay brings back some memories. Memories I'm not sure I want. While half my brain scans the surrounding grasslands, the other begins to wander, remembering the faces of all those comrades left broken and bleeding on a dozen battlefields. I look at the others in front of me, fanning out to sweep a track ahead, and wonder how many of them are going to die. And then I get to wondering how much of it will be my fault if they do. I picked them. I plucked them out of their cells and held the gun to their heads, so to speak. I'm also the one who's training them, teaching them what they'll need to know to survive. If I fail them, if they die, then some of it must be down to me, mustn't it? All those other bodies, all those dead faces that haunt my dreams, they weren't my fault, I'm sure of that. I wasn't the one who put them there, I wasn't the one who was responsible for them. But these Last Chancers, these are my team. Chosen by me, trained by me, and I suppose led by me when the time comes.

The weight of that dawns on me and my hands begin to tremble. I've faced horrors blade to blade and gun to gun that you wouldn't dream of in your worst nightmares and not given it a second thought, and here I am shaking like a new recruit in their first firefight. I drop back a bit so that the others won't notice, pulling the map out of my leg pocket to make out I'm checking something. The paper shakes in my hand and I feel my heart flutter. There's something wrong. This doesn't happen to me, I've killed more people then most have met. So why am I getting a massive attack of the jitters in an Emperor-damned training bay?

'Okay, rest up for a few minutes while I check something,' I call to the others just as the first of them, Iyle, reaches a hedge-line across our advance.

They drop into the grass and I walk off a little ways, down into a shallow hollow, and dump my gun on the ground. Spots start dancing in front of my eyes and my whole body is trembling now. I sit down heavily, my legs pretty much buckling under me. The straps of my pack are tightening across my chest and I wrench them off and let it fall behind me. Every muscle

in my body seems to be in spasm at once. I can't stop clenching and unclenching my fists.

This isn't just nerves! I scream at myself. This is some kind of
pox I've caught, perhaps in that Emperor-forsaken prison. My
breathing is ragged, my head swimming. A shadowy figure
wavers in front of me and I can just about hear what they're
saying over the hissing and pounding in my ears. I wonder
vaguely why the sky's behind them.

'Are you okay, sir?' I dimly recognise Tanya's voice.

'Name's Last Chance,' I slur back, trying to focus on her face,
which sways from side to side. 'No rations for anyone this
evening.'

I feel someone grabbing my shoulders firmly and a face leers
into mine, making me recoil with surprise.

'Hold him still,' snaps Stroniberg and hands clamp on my
legs and arms, pinning me down in the grass. I taste something
metallic in my mouth and gag.

There's an explosion to my left, and I hear screaming. It
sounds like Quidlon, or maybe Franx. It's all a bit unclear. My
eyes are playing up: one moment I'm lying there on the grass
in the field, the next I'm in some kind of ruined building, bullets tearing the place up around me. I get dizzier, and a surge of
frustration fuels my anger, threatening to rip me apart from the
inside.

'Open your mouth, Kage, open your mouth!' Stroniberg
shouts at me, and I feel his fingers on my jaw, and realise my
teeth are welded together. 'Dolan's blood, somebody take that
knife off him before he does any more damage!' he snaps to
the others, who I can just about see around me in between
flickers of the dark, ruined city. One of them pulls it from the
cramped fingers of my right hand. I didn't even realise I was
holding one. Something wet is dribbling down my throat and
chest, and I try to reach up to touch it, but my arm is held firm.

'What the frag is he screaming about?' I hear Strelli asking.

I don't know who he's talking about, I can't hear any screaming. I try to sit up and look around to find out who it is. For
Emperor's sake, we're supposed to be in the middle of a battle
here, if someone's making that much racket, they'll have hell to
pay when I'm feeling a bit better.

I feel a sharp stinging pain in my face that brings tears to my
eyes and makes my ears ring.

'This is just getting better and better!' I hear Trost shouting. What's he talking about? I'm just feeling a bit ill, that's all. If they'd just give me some room, I'll be alright. I try to wave them away, to give me some air. Something heavy lands on my chest, pinning me down. I try to heave it off, but a stabbing pain in my leg distracts me.

Suddenly all the strength leaves me. I can feel it seeping out, starting at my fingers and toes and spreading up my body. A wave of panic hits me as I can no longer feel my heart beat and a moment later everything goes black.

WHEN I OPEN my eyes, it's to a vision of insanity. Right in front of my face are dozens of glass lenses, clicking in and out of an arrangement of tubes, a bright light shining through, almost blinding me. Tiny chains and gears spin back and forth rhythmically, accompanied by a low humming. Little cantilevers wobble erratically, pumping a dark green fluid through a maze of transparent tubes. My nostrils catch a mix of oil and soap, along with the distinctive smell of blood.

I try to turn my head, but I can't. I feel something hard and cold around my face, like bars running across my chin and forehead and down my cheeks to a block under my jaw. As sensation slowly returns I can feel more restraints. Glancing down past my chin, I can see heavy metal clamps across my chest and legs, held in place with serious-looking padlocks. I can feel things in my arms and throat, piercing the flesh in half a dozen places. I turn my attention back to the apparatus around my head, my eyes tracing cords and cables that disappear into the mass of the machinery. My ears catch the squeaking of a badly-oiled wheel somewhere in the mechanism.

I open my mouth to say something, but my jaw can't move and it just ends up as a cross between a growl and a moan. The lights in the machine flicker and go off, leaving me bathed in a lambent yellow glow. With a whirr the apparatus pulls back from my face, its lenses and levers folding in on themselves, retracting into a small cube that disappears from view above my head. I can see the ceiling and far wall: brick painted in a light grey.

I hear a door latch and then the sound of a door closing to my right, and a tech-priest enters my field of vision. He wears light green robes, spattered with dark patches of what looks

like blood. A heavy cog-and-skull sigil hangs from a silver
chain about his neck. His face is old and lined, creased heavily
like a discarded shirt. A variety of tubes and wires sprout from
his neck and head, lost from view over his shoulders. In his
hands he carries what looks like a gun with a needle instead of
a barrel.

'Am I audible to you?' he asks, his voice a hoarse whisper.
'Blink your eyes for an affirmative.'

It takes me a moment to realise he wants to know if I can
hear him. I blink once for yes.

'Am I visible to you?' he asks next, moving to the left side of
the bed I'm bound to.

Another blink. I hear the door opening and closing again,
and I see Stroniberg walk to the other side of me. He exchanges
a look with the tech-priest, who nods once and then turns his
attention back to me, his dark brown eyes regarding me clini-
cally.

'So it is mental, not physical,' Stroniberg says, as much to
himself as me and the tech-priest. He still hasn't looked at me,
busying himself instead with a sheaf of papers hanging from a
hook at the foot of the bed.

I lie there, helpless as a new-born, my mind starting to race
as I recover my wits. What the hell has happened to me? What
did Stroniberg mean by 'mental, not physical'? Surely I've just
caught a dose of something? All I did was get a bit shaky and
dizzy, nothing too serious about that.

I want to ask him what the frag is going on, but as before it
just comes out as a meaningless mumble between my teeth. It
attracts his attention though and he comes and stands by my
left arm.

'There's no point trying to speak, Kage,' he tells me, not
unkindly. 'You're in a restraint harness for your own safety. And
ours. You really are a good fighter, aren't you.'

One blink. Yes I am.

'No one on board fully understands what happened to you.
We don't have anyone who has done much more than a cursory
study of this area of madness,' he continues, turning and pulling
a chair to the bedside before sitting down. I can just about still
see him out of the corner of my eye. 'You are suffering from
some kind of battle-induced vapours leading to a self-destruc-
tive trauma. Do you understand what I'm saying, Kage?'

No blink. He could be speaking in foul ork speak for all I know what he's on about. He chews his lip for a moment, obviously in thought, choosing his words.

'Okay, I'll start with the basics,' he says with a sigh. 'You are insane, Kage.'

I try to laugh, but the jaw restraint constricts my throat, making me cough instead. When I recover, I direct a vicious frown at Stroniberg.

'Your years of intense fighting have allowed dangerous amounts of ill vapours to build up in certain parts of your brain, affecting your mental state,' he carries on explaining, patiently and slowly. 'Something that happened in the training bay triggered another release of these vapours, which have begun eroding your senses of judgement, conscience and self-preservation. Are you following me?'

No blink. I never did know much about medicine, and all this mad talk of vapours eating my brain sounds like grox crap. I mean, I'd feel it if my brain was melting.

'The symptoms you displayed in the training bay all point towards a serious battle-psychosis developing, hence your suicide attempt,' he tells me.

Suicide attempt? What the frag is he talking about? I've never even thought about killing myself, not in all those long months and years of fighting and locked alone in that cell. Suicide is for the weak, the ones who have nothing useful left to offer. I'd never kill myself! Emperor, what kind of soldier does he take me for?

'You tried to slit your own throat,' he confirms, seeing the disbelief in my eyes. 'Luckily, the madness vapours had also affected your ability to control your muscles so you just ended up slashing your jaw. You severed a tendon, which is why we've had to bind your jaw shut until the muscles knit together again.'

In a flash of memory, I recall the metallic taste of blood in my mouth during the seizure, and my teeth locking in place.

'I think we caught this before too much damage could be done to your brain, and Biologis Alanthrax,' he indicates the other man, who is still regarding me dispassionately, much as he might look at an interesting specimen, 'was able to perform the surgery and release the vapours before they became fatal.'

Surgery? What in the Emperor's name have these blood fiends done to me? I guess my expression must show what's passing through my mind, as Stroniberg lays a hand on my arm, to try and comfort me I guess. I flick it irritably away with my fingers, one of the few parts of me that I can actually move.

'It is a fairly standard practice, though not common,' he tries to reassure me. 'Biologis Alanthrax has performed it several times before, with almost fifty per cent of his charges making full recoveries. It is a simple matter of temporarily removing a portion of your skull, making an incision into the affected area to release the vapours and then bone-welding the cranium back in place.'

You stuck a knife in my brain! I want to scream at him. For Emperor's sake, you bastard, you stuck a knife in my brain! I'd rather take my chance with the madness than have these saw-bones chopping me to bits. I try to push myself up, but there's no give in the restraints at all. Pain shoots through my face as I clench my teeth and snarl at Stroniberg. Emperor damn it, I didn't go through hell and back with the Colonel to die on some damn surgery table under the knife of a jumped-up tech-priest who's got more in common with the knife in his hand than me.

How could the Colonel let them do this to me? He can't believe in all this garbled nonsense. What the hell does he think he's doing, putting me under the knife? Mother of Dolan, I've seen as many men die at the hands of cretins like these as from bullets and blades. I've seen men dying in agony from rotting wounds, cut into them by these sadistic bloodmongers.

'You need to remain calm, Kage,' Stroniberg tells me, standing up, concern written all across his face. 'You need to allow your body to heal.' He glances across at Alanthrax, who steps forward with the gun-like needle. I try to spit a curse at the Emperor-damned pair of them as he pushes it into my forearm and squeezes down on the trigger. As before, sleep washes gently over me.

I SPEND ANOTHER week in the infirmary, locked down on to that table. To make matters worse, we must have dropped into the warp because my nightmares start again. Pumped up on Alanthrax's witches' brew, my dreams are plagued by the dead from my past, just like last time. Men and women missing limbs, their heads sheared in half, entrails open to the world, wandering aimlessly around my bed, staring at me with accusing eyes. I feel like I'm in a waking nightmare, strapped up tight with those creatures circling around and around me. All the time, the two small children I saw in Coritanorum stand at the foot of the bed and just stare at me. Their eyes say it all. You killed us, they say. You burnt us.

I want to scream at them to leave me alone, that I was just following orders, it was them or me, but the lock on my jaw stops me. Not once does the Colonel visit me. Not while I'm awake, at least.

For that whole week it seems like I've died and gone to hell.

THERE'S SUSPICION AND fear in the eyes of the team when I next meet them. It's just before lights-down; they're sprawled in their bunks chatting when I walk in to the dormitory. None of them says a thing and I stand there, feeling their eyes upon me. I look at Stroniberg, who meets my hard gaze without a trace of guilt.

I feel like an invader, such is their hostility.

'Training will resume tomorrow,' I tell them. None of them replies. I don't blame them, I wouldn't know what to say either. I turn and take a step towards the door to my chamber.

'Excuse me, Last Chance,' I hear Quidlon blurt from behind me. 'Colonel Schaeffer said we were to assemble in the briefing room after breakfast tomorrow.'

'The Colonel?' I ask, turning around.

'He carried on with the training while you were…' Iyle leaves it unsaid. Strapped to a bed in case you turned into a raving lunatic and tried to kill yourself or someone else, is what he doesn't say.

'And what did Colonel Schaeffer have to say about me?' I ask, suddenly worried. What's to become of me, if the Colonel is taking direct control of the training again? I feel the horrid sensation of failure begin to well up inside me. He can't have me shipped back to vincularum, not now we're in the warp and underway I don't think. But there's bound to be a brig aboard the *Laurels of Glory* and he could just as easily have me banged up in there for the duration. Or perhaps he'll just finish it, put a bolt through my head as an example to the others. They shake their heads or shrug in response.

'Nothing, Last Chance,' Tanya tells me. 'He said nothing about you.'

'Very well,' I reply, keeping my voice level. 'I want you all looking sharp tomorrow morning, now is the time we have to stay focussed and disciplined.'

I walk out and into my room. I hear them start to chatter again and I'm about to close the door when a random thought occurs to me. I stick my head around the doorframe.

'Does Schaeffer have a name?' I ask them. 'Like the ones I gave you?' They exchange glances, half-smiles on their lips.

'Yes, Last Chance, he does,' Quidlon tells me. 'He said he is Colonel.'

Figures, I think to myself, nodding and closing the door. As I do so, I catch a snippet of what Trost says next.

'We set a double watch tonight,' he says to the others. 'That psycho's not coming anywhere near me while I'm asleep.'

At first I'm tempted to wrench the door open and pound the mouthy meathead into the deck for saying that, but I stop short. I sit down on my bunk and I can't stop a smile creeping across my face. That's one lesson they'll never forget, I reckon. I lie down on my bunk and close my eyes, waiting for sleep and the nightmares to come again.

THE NEXT MORNING, the Colonel sends an armsman to wake me up early. I dress hurriedly and follow him up to Schaeffer's chamber. He's there waiting for me, immaculately dressed despite the early hour, clean shaven and bright-eyed. The armsman closes the door behind me without a further word.

The Colonel looks at me for a long, long time, his eyes unwavering, stripping away layer after layer of my soul. I begin to fidget under his gaze. The circular scar on the side of my head itches like mad and it's all I can do to keep myself standing at attention and not scratch at it.

'One more mistake, Kage,' he says slowly, 'and I am finished with you.'

I say nothing. There's nothing to say.

'I am watching you more closely than ever,' he warns me, eyes not moving. 'I will not tolerate the slightest slip-up on your part, nor the merest hint that your treatment was unsuccessful. Do I make myself clear, Kage?'

'Perfectly, sir,' I answer quietly, dread knotting my stomach. Now the pressure's really on.

* * *

THE BRIEFING ROOM is shaped like half an amphitheatre. Thirty metres across, it has a hundred stepped benches descending to a semicircular floor with a similarly shaped dais on it. There's a table on the dais, a lumped cloth covering whatever is on it. The Colonel seems to fill the room with his presence as we enter, all of us focussing our attention on him as we walk down the steps to the lowest benches. The others stand to attention in front of their places, me to one side. The Colonel waves us to sit down and begins to pace up and down.

'So far you have been training blind,' he tells us, scanning his ice-cold eyes along the line. 'Now we begin to prepare for the mission in earnest. It is our task to assassinate an alien commander who has been causing the Emperor's servants considerable pain, and his own rulers at the same time. With their collaboration we will infiltrate his base and kill him.'

He pulls the cloth back off the table to reveal a scale model of a bizarre looking building. I've never seen anything so odd in my life. If I guess the scale correctly from the size of details like doors and windows, it's a massive dome, probably big enough to house a small town. The Colonel removes the dome and places it to one side, revealing an open plan of the interior, divided into numerous large chambers, and beckons us over to look inside. The chambers look remarkably similar to the training bays. Some of them have small model jungle trees inside, one has a little replica of a beach, another what looks to be the outskirts of an Imperial city.

'This is the target area,' the Colonel explains. 'The alien we are hunting is from a race who call themselves the tau. He has some unpronounceable heathen name, which I am assured by a lexist translates to something equivalent to Commander Brightsword. Now, this Brightsword virtually rules one of the tau worlds only a few weeks' travel from the Sarcassa system that falls within the Emperor's dominions. Over several years, Brightsword has been very aggressively sending colonising fleets into the wilderness space surrounding Sarcassa. We believe it is his intent to invade this system within the next two to three months. His superiors, the rulers of the so-called Tau Empire, very wisely wish to avoid a bloody and costly war with our forces and have agreed to this co-operative strike.'

He pauses to let the full weight of this settle in. These aliens, these tau, are helping us to kill one of their own commanders.

Either they must be really scared of what we'll do to their little empire if Brightsword goes ahead with his mad plan, or they really don't have much sense of loyalty to their own people.

'Excuse me, Colonel?' Quidlon raises his hand slightly. 'Why are the tau engaging in this mission with us, rather than simply removing Commander Brightsword from office, or perhaps covertly removing him themselves by other means?'

The Colonel waits a moment, probably while his brain catches up with Quidlon's quickfire way of speaking.

'Unlike our own great Imperium, the tau have no great Emperor to bind them together,' the Colonel explains, lip curled in distaste. 'They are godless, as far as we can tell, and have this strange concept which the tau call the "greater good". Their empire supposedly sustains itself through harmony between all of its subjects, rather than by making the supreme sacrifices the Emperor asks of us.

'As you might understand, with no such guiding hand, their empire is very fragile. Any hint that there are those not working towards this fictitious greater good undermines the whole basis for their society. They cannot admit to their citizens that one of their commanders is, in essence, a renegade. Similarly, they cannot risk being uncovered trying to assassinate that commander, for the same reasons. Thus, we have constructed a subterfuge that allows us, as outsiders, to kill Brightsword, posing as renegades rather than Imperial servants. We can show them official records and provide witnesses if necessary that will show that you are all military criminals.

'That is another reason why I am using scum like you. A half-truth is always better than an outright lie. All of this means there will be no call for a response against our forces. No blame will be traceable to either the tau government nor the Emperor's loyal subjects.'

'Very neat,' I mutter, not realising I've spoken out loud until the Colonel darts me an evil glare.

'You have something to say, Last Chance?' he asks scornfully, hands on his hips.

'Yes, Colonel,' I tell him, standing up straight and looking him in the eye. 'Aliens killing aliens I can live with. Us killing aliens, I can live with. Aliens helping us to kill aliens makes me suspicious. Besides, Colonel, this whole thing reminds me of Coritanorum too much. All this infighting, I mean.'

'Believe me when I say that this whole mission has been examined from every angle, by myself and others,' he retorts, looking around at all of us. 'We would be fools to trust the tau, you can be sure of that. However, the opportunity presented to end the threat posed by Brightsword, whom we believe is fully intent on and capable of taking Sarcassa, is too good to pass up. Therefore we will proceed, but with caution.'

He directs his attention back to the miniature building on the table and we close in again.

'This is a barracks and training area, what the tau refer to as a battle dome,' he informs us, leaning forward with his hands on the table. 'It also serves as the headquarters of Commander Brightsword. Currently he is reviewing his forces on the newly colonised worlds around Sarcassa but he will be performing an inspection of his troops at this battle dome before he leaves to rejoin his fleet for the invasion. Before and after the parade he will be beyond the reach of both us and our tau allies, so we will strike when he arrives to perform the inspection.'

I, and a couple of the others, nod approvingly. Any kind of hit like this, and believe me I did a few back on Olympas during the trade wars, relies on surprise. I don't know how paranoid and security conscious these tau are, but if we have people on the inside it shouldn't be too difficult.

'What are all these different areas, Colonel?' asks Tanya, pointing at the various chambers.

'The battle dome is a training facility, Sharpshooter,' he replies. 'Just as on this ship, each of these training areas represents a different type of locale, and can be modified to represent specific targets and objectives for an upcoming campaign. After our first diplomatic envoys to the tau reported on the efficiency of their tactics, we sent agents to observe their military facilities. On this vessel, and her sister ships, we have replicated the more laudable and practical aspects of their training methods. The tau have a somewhat lax attitude to the perils presented by over-reliance on technology, so the Adeptus Mechanicus have been unable to duplicate the more arcane and blasphemous systems employed by the tau. However, these ships represent the best training facilities we have currently at our disposal. Our tech-priests are currently reconstructing three of the training bays to represent the battle zone where we are planning to trap and kill Brightsword.'

He points towards an area at the centre of the battle dome which seems to be some kind of power system terminal surrounded by a wide concourse, perhaps a parade ground or embarkation level.

'When the new training bay is complete, we will begin operational training,' he continues, standing up straight. 'Until then, we will go over the exact particulars of the mission using this scale representation of the combat zone and continue with your general training. Now, pay attention to the plan.'

FLASH FLARES AND detonations explode across the pale yellow floors and walls, blinding in their intensity and billowing a cloud of acrid black smoke through the doorway where I'm crouched, an autogun gripped in my hands. As I've done a dozen times before over the last two weeks, I dive forward into the gloom, rolling through the smoke to the other side of the corridor.

I ripple off a burst of fire down the smoke-filled tunnel, covering for Quidlon and Stradinsk as they dive after me, heading for the gateway a few metres behind me. I work my way towards them crouched on my haunches, emptying the rest of the magazine with short bursts of fire at the silhouettes of possible targets moving backwards and forwards through the smoke. Sheltering in the gateway, I pull out the mag and toss it away, smoothly pulling another from my weapons belt and slamming it home.

I begin to count in my head. After I reach twenty, I give the nod to Quidlon, who pulls a las-cutter from his pack and begins to burn his way through the armoured gate. Sparks dance around the gate alcove, falling onto my left arm and leg and spilling onto the floor. Rivulets of molten metal pour down the doorway and pool on the floor, cooling with a cloud of steam. I count to another twenty before leaning out of my cover and firing off on semi-auto for another five counts. I watch as Trost emerges from a doorway in front of me and dashes past, throwing himself in behind Tanya.

'The door is open,' Quidlon informs us, stepping back and delivering a sharp kick, knocking out a section of metal and leaving a space just high and wide enough to crawl through. Trost pokes his head through and then wriggles out of sight.

'Clear on the other side,' he calls back after a few seconds. I fire another burst down the corridor while Quidlon, then Tanya, follow the bomb expert, before turning and diving through myself. Pulling myself up on the other side, I glance around to check the concourse is clear of targets.

'Cover smoke, Demolition Man!' I snap to Trost, who pulls a grenade from the bandoleer across his chest, primes it with a thumb and then hurls it into the centre of the parade ground. It clatters to a stop almost exactly halfway between our position and the door to the control chamber of the travel station. A moment later bluish smoke gouts forth, quickly spilling across the wide area and obscuring visibility in every direction.

'Let's move,' I say to Tanya and Quidlon, dashing out from the gateway, the others pounding across the floor behind me. Trost stays behind to cover the hole in the gate.

'Movement, get down!' screams Tanya, diving to the floor beside me. I drop and roll, noticing something moving in the smoke out of the corner of my eye. I hear the sharp crack of Stradinsk's marksman's rifle, followed by a scream of agony.

'What the frag?' I hear Trost shout.

'Since when do targets scream?' asks Quidlon from behind me. I get to my feet and dash over, keeping low, Quidlon just behind me. As I run through the smoke, I see something lying on the ground, a lumpen shape. As I get closer, I see it's Stroniberg, laid flat out, legs and arms splayed wide. A puddle of blood oozes from under him. Bending over him, I see the bullet hole in his left cheek. I roll his head to the side and half his skull comes away in fragments. I feel something pluck weakly at my arm. He's still alive!

'H... hel... help me...' pleads Stroniberg, eyes wide, tears streaming down his face and mixing with the blood seeping from his cheek. He coughs and spits, pieces of shattered tooth spraying bloodily onto his tunic.

Quidlon is on his knees, fumbling for the medi-pak strapped to Stroniberg's left thigh.

'It'll be okay, Stitcher, it'll be okay,' Quidlon says, pulling his knife out and cutting the medi-pak strap and tugging the bulky pouch free.

I look at the side of Stroniberg's face, or more precisely the gory, ragged remnants of it, and wonder what was going through his mind as he stood and watched that damn tech-priest digging around in my brain with a scalpel. Almost transfixed by the bubbling fluid spilling from the wound, I reach forward tentatively with a finger, and I'm about to prod the grey and crimson mess when Trost appears and grabs my wrist, pulling me away.

'What the frag are you doing, Last Chance?' he snarls at me, hate in his eyes. 'You are seriously cracking up. You need to be put out of your misery!'

I slap his hand away and push him back, snapping out of the trance. I turn back to Stroniberg and crouch over him.

'What should we do? Tell me what to do, Stitcher,' Quidlon asks desperately, spilling bandages, needles, tourniquets and stimms from the medi-pak across the floor. 'Stitcher, you have to tell me what to do, I don't know what any of this stuff is for.'

'G... green phial,' the chirurgeon replies, blood leaking from the corner of his mouth. 'Need to... to drink it...'

Quidlon finds the phial and pulls the stopper out, pouring the contents into Stroniberg's gaping mouth. The physician gags and chokes before swallowing it, frothy blood now leaking from his nose as well.

'Pad... and bandage,' Stroniberg gasps next, his hand flapping through the pile of stuff on the floor, using his touch to identify what he's after.

'We don't have time for this,' I say suddenly, standing up and pulling Quidlon with me.

'What do you mean?' Trost snarls hoarsely, a hand on my shoulder twisting me to face him.

'We only have roughly five minutes before the target will appear,' I tell him calmly. 'Quidlon needs to lock down the rail carriage and Tanya needs to be in the observation tower for her shot.'

'Stitcher will die if we leave him,' moans Quidlon, looking back at Stroniberg who is staring up at me with a glazed expression.

'You can't save him,' I say, staring back at him. 'Let the butcher die.'

Quidlon stands there stunned; Trost looks like I shot Stroniberg myself.

'We have to call off the exercise,' he growls.

'Oh right,' I snarl back. 'Like we'd call off the attack if this happens on the real mission. Don't be so fraggin' stupid. Now, get back to covering that gateway before I put a bullet through your head! And get Sharpshooter to shift her arse over her, we need to get moving. You,' I turn to Quidlon. 'Get into that control room and shut down the transport power.'

They all stand there like statues.

'Emperor damn it,' I curse, punching Trost square across the jaw and buckling him at the knees. 'Emperor so help me if you don't get moving now I will break every bone in your fraggin' bodies!'

He stumbles away, cursing like a navy rating, and Quidlon hovers for a moment before seeing the look in my eye. He grabs his gun from the floor and sprints over towards the entranceway. The smoke is beginning to thin and I see Trost bent over, talking to Stradinsk, who's sat on the ground by the looks of it. I run over to them and catch the end of what Trost is saying.

'...will kill you if you don't get moving,' he's telling her, shaking her by the shoulder. He sees me approaching and legs it for the gateway, unslinging his gun from his shoulder as he runs through the smoke.

Tanya is sat cross-legged on the hard floor, staring straight ahead, her gun lying next to her.

'On your feet, Sharpshooter,' I shout at her. 'Grab your weapon and come with me.'

She doesn't move a muscle, doesn't even blink. I snatch up her rifle and thrust it towards her, but it just falls out of her limp hands into her lap. Snarling, I grab a handful of tunic and drag her to her feet, where she stands swaying slightly, eyes still unfocussed.

'Pick up your rifle, Sharpshooter,' I say to her slowly and deliberately. 'That is an order, soldier!'

She doesn't move. I stare down at her, right in the eye, my face nearly touching hers. There's nothing there at all, her eyes staring through me at something in the distance I suspect only she can see.

'Never mind about me,' I say to her softly, calming myself down at the same time. 'If the Colonel sees this, we will both get shot. Don't you understand? You have to pick up your rifle.'

I grab the weapon and slowly ease it into her unresisting hands, before closing her fingers around the stock. She stands there doing nothing, absolutely out of touch with everything around her. The gun clatters to the ground again as I let go of her hand.

'Emperor damn you, snap out of it!' I scream at her, smashing the back of my hand across her face, splitting her top lip.
She sways and staggers for a second before righting herself. I
see a glimmer of life in her eyes then, a moment too late as her
boot smashes up between my thighs and knocks me to the
ground.

'Bastard!' she screams, kicking me in the midriff as I roll
around the floor. I think I feel a rib crack under the blow. 'I
don't want to shoot anyone again. Don't you understand? I'm
not a killer, I'm not this true soldier you keep talking about. I'm
never picking up a gun again. You can't turn me into a murderer!'

I sit up, clutching my ribs and wincing. Slowly I push myself
to my feet. I stare at Stradinsk for a long, long time, my face
expressionless. With a deliberate slowness, I reach down and
pick up her sniper rifle. She eyes it with disgust, barely able to
bring herself to look at it. I pull the slide and eject the spent
casing.

'Why didn't you say we had live ammunition?' she asks quietly, looking at the cartridge on the floor.

'What did you expect?' I answer calmly. 'This is not some
kind of game we're playing here. We're not doing this for fun,
Sharpshooter.'

'Don't call me that!' she snaps, recoiling away from me. 'I
hate that name.'

'It's who you are,' I tell her viciously. 'That or a corpse, like
Stroniberg.'

'Don't you mean Stitcher?' she replies sourly.

'When he was alive, and he was useful, he was Stitcher,' I say,
glancing over my shoulder at his cooling corpse. 'Now he's just
a useless dead lump of meat.'

'I'm not Sharpshooter, my name is Tanya Stradinsk,' she
argues. 'Do what you like to me, I'm not firing a gun again.'

I toss the rifle at her and she catches it easily. Her grip is loose
and sure, used to handling the weapon without thinking. She
looks down at it and then drops it to the ground with a clatter.
I pull the short stub gun out from the belt of my fatigues and
cock it in front of her face. I point it at her, right between the
eyes and move my finger onto the trigger.

'Pick up your gun, Sharpshooter,' I warn her. She shakes her
head. 'Pick it up, damn you, I don't want to kill you!'

'I'd rather be dead,' she tells me defiantly.

'Is that right?' I ask, uncocking the stubber and thrusting it back into my belt. I grab Tanya and drag her across the concourse to where Stroniberg lies in a pool of deep red.

'That's what you'll look like, that's all you'll be,' I snarl at her. She tries to look away, tears in her eyes. I grab her by the hair and push her to her knees next to Stroniberg. She gives a whimper as I pull out the stubber again and place it to the back of her head. 'Is this really what you want?' I demand.

'I can't fire a gun again,' she pleads, looking up over her shoulder at me, her cheeks streaked with tears.

'I'm not asking you to fire it, Tanya,' I say softly, lifting the gun away. 'I just need you to pick it up.'

She hesitates for a moment, wiping the back of her hand across her face, and then gets to her feet. She glances at me and I nod towards the rifle. I follow her as she walks over to it. She bends down, her hand hovering above it.

'Just pick it up,' I prompt her, my voice level. Her hand closes around the barrel and she pulls it to her. She stands there for a second, holding it away from her like it's a poisonous snake or something.

With an anguished cry, she falls to her knees, cradling the rifle to her chest.

'What have I done?' she asks between sobs.

'You killed a man,' I answer bluntly, turning away from her. The sight of her sickens me to the pit of my stomach. I'm gonna have hell to pay with the Colonel over this whole fragged up mess. 'You killed a man,' I say again. 'It's what we do.'

As I EXPECTED, the Colonel is less than happy with the day's events. I'm in his cabin, which looks surprisingly familiar to the one he had aboard the *Pride of Lothos*. I guess he has his own furniture or something and brings it with him. The walls are panelled in a deep red wood, behind him is a glass-fronted bookshelf with a handful of books on the top shelf. His plain desk and chair sit in the middle of the room, a pile of papers neatly stacked in one corner. Schaeffer himself is pacing up and down behind the desk, his hands balled into fists behind his back.

'This was a simple training exercise, Kage,' he growls at me, not even looking in my direction but pouring his scorn onto the universe in general. 'Now my team has a dead medic and a sniper who can barely bring herself to hold a gun.'

He rounds on me at that point, and I can see that he is really, really angry. His eyes are like shards of glittering ice, his jaw is tight and his whole body tensed.

'Stroniberg I can live without,' he admits angrily. 'But Stradinsk? The whole plan we have devised relies on her making that shot. She will only get one chance at it, one chance. You promised me you could get her to fire that shot. And you? Collapsing in the middle of an exercise and trying to kill yourself! What happened to the Kage that was with me on Ichar IV? Where's the hardened killer that watched my back on False Hope? Where's the good soldier that was with me in Coritanorum? Now, only weeks away, am I going to have to inform my superiors that the whole mission has to be abandoned?'

He stops in his tirade and takes a deep breath, turning away from me. I just stand there at attention, waiting for it to start again. My mind is reeling, I've got no idea what he's going to do next. Is he really going to call off the assassination? Is it his decision, or someone else's? If he does, what happens to me and the Last Chancers? What happens to him? As these thoughts fly through my head, he turns back to me.

'I am very disappointed in you, Kage,' he says solemnly, shaking his head. 'Very disappointed indeed.'

His words cut me more than any knife can, and all I can do is hang my head in shame, because he's right to be disappointed. I've failed.

'CLIMB FASTER!' I bellow at Stradinsk, standing at the bottom of the travel terminal's command tower in the mock-up battle dome. She's hauling herself up the side of the building on a rope, painfully slowly in my eyes. 'You've got thirty seconds to reach the top, from start to finish. Climb faster!'

She glances back down over her shoulder at me before renewing her efforts, her tired arms dragging her slowly, metre by metre up towards the observation chamber.

'I can't see why this is so necessary, Last Chance, considering there are stairways inside the tower,' Quidlon says, standing next to me and looking up. 'Is this supposed to be some kind of punishment, perhaps?'

'No, this isn't a punishment, Brains,' I reply, keeping my eyes on Tanya. 'This is called playing it safe. If something goes wrong and you can't open the doors to the terminal for some reason, I want there to be a back-up plan. Sharpshooter has to be in position for that kill, whatever happens to the rest of us.'

Tanya's only a couple of metres from the top now, but slowing badly. All it needs is one final effort and she'll be up, but she just hangs there, exhausted. Okay, this is the tenth time she's made that climb in the last hour, but she needs to build up the right muscles.

Moerck is standing beside me on the other side, intently looking at the climbing figure.

'She'll fall,' he says simply, glancing at me out of the corner of her eye. 'I think losing our sniper now would be a bad thing.'

He's right, the rope is swaying badly, and it looks as if she can only just about hang on, never mind climb any further.

'Motivate her,' I tell Moerck, crossing my arms. He pulls out his laspistol and readies it, the gun emitting a short, high-pitched whine as the power cell warms up.

'Sharpshooter, listen to me!' he bellows, deafening me. His voice could carry through an artillery barrage in a thunder-storm. 'I am going to count to three and then I'm going to shoot you if you're still hanging on that rope!'

She glances back again and sees him turn side on and raise his pistol towards her, assuming a duelling stance and sighting down the length of his arm. He stands as still as a rock, attention fixed on the struggling woman.

'One!' he shouts out. Tanya begins to haul herself up once more, reaching deep into her reserves of energy, dragging herself painfully up the rope.

'Two!' he continues, not moving a muscle except to adjust his aim higher. Tanya gets a hand to the rim around the top of the building, then the other. She pulls herself up onto the edge and then rolls over, disappearing from view. I turn to Moerck and nod appreciatively. Tanya pops her head back over and hurls abuse down at us, waving an angry fist.

'And you all think I'm a cruel training officer,' I comment to Quidlon, shouldering my autogun and heading off towards the tower door.

'The difference is, I wouldn't have fired,' Moerck calls out as I walk away. 'You would have.'

I stop and turn back towards them, looking at Quidlon then Moerck. 'That's true,' I agree with a nonchalant shrug.

STRELLI LUNGES AT me with the knife, making a jab towards my midriff. The attack is low and fast, but I manage to step back, using the outside of my right arm to deflect his hand away before stepping back in and driving my fingers towards his throat. He sways back, the blow falling just short, and tries to chop down on my wrist with his left hand. I roll my wrist over his and grab his arm, dragging him forward onto my knee, but he jumps at the last second, performing a forward tumble and rolling to his feet.

We stand there panting for a few seconds, eyeing each other warily.

'Okay, that's good,' I tell him, stepping away and wiping sweat from my forehead with the sleeve of my tunic. 'Quidlon and Iyle, you're next.'

The two of them circle each other, blades held back, away from the enemy until they're ready to strike. Iyle feints to the left and slips round to the right, but Quidlon's not fooled and meets the move, dropping low and driving his foot into Iyle's left knee. The scout stumbles but recovers quickly enough to leap aside as Quidlon lunges for him. Iyle rams his fist into the small of Quidlon's back, knocking him forward, but Quidlon turns the blow into a roll, rising up and spinning on the spot with an easy motion, a grimace on his face. The mechanic tosses the knife into his left hand and makes a slash at Iyle, who is forced to dance back a couple of steps. Quidlon follows up immediately, switching hands again. Iyle tries to take the initiative back and makes a sloppy stab. Quidlon easily avoids it, trapping Iyle's knife arm against his body and dragging him forward onto his own blade. Iyle gives a startled cry and flops sideways, pulling the blade out of Quidlon's hand. He sits there on the mat, legs out in front of him, blood pouring down his stomach and pooling in his lap.

'Good blow, Brains, now finish him,' I say, my voice quiet. Quidlon glances back at me, a confused look on his face. Iyle pulls the knife free and lets it drops through blood-slicked fingers.

'Last Chance?' Quidlon asks, taking a step towards me. I toss him my own knife, which he catches easily, and point at Iyle.

'Finish him,' I say with a shallow nod towards the wounded man.

Iyle stares up at me with a look of fear, still holding his guts. He tries to say something, but just croaks hoarsely, glancing between me and Quidlon. I see understanding dawn on him, and a look of determination crosses his face.

'Do it, Brains,' hisses Trost from my left, eager for blood.

'Leave him be!' Tanya argues from the other side, darting a murderous look at me. 'Don't do it, Brains!'

'He won't,' I hear Strelli mutter, standing to one side, arms casually crossed. 'He hasn't got the instinct for it.'

Quidlon's still looking at me, a shallow frown creasing his brow. He looks back at Iyle and then at me. I just nod. He turns away and takes a step towards Iyle.

'I'll make you eat the fragging thing!' Iyle gasps, trying to push himself to his feet. It's a good attempt, I'll give him that, but with that wound he'll get nowhere. Quidlon takes a running step and kicks Iyle square in the face, smashing him to his back. He leaps on top of him, driving a blocky fist into the scout's nose. Winded and concussed, Iyle can do nothing as Quidlon forces his head to the ground and pushes the knife point up under his chin. Quidlon closes his eyes and thrusts, sliding the blade up through Iyle's mouth and into his brain. Just as slowly, he pulls it out and stands up, facing away from me, the bloodied dagger in his hand.

'I can't believe he actually did it,' exclaims Strelli in astonishment. 'Maybe brains aren't all you've got.'

I look at Iyle's corpse and nod to myself. He died like a soldier. He died fighting for his life, not begging for it. I can respect that.

'You just murdered Eyes, you scum!' Tanya shrieks at Quidlon, turning away in disgust.

'No,' Quidlon replies slowly, turning around to face us, a splash of blood across his face. His voice is flat, his expression blank. 'I was just following orders.'

'Welcome to be being a true soldier, Brains,' I say to him, stepping forward and clapping him on the shoulder.

'THIS SEEMS LIKE a damn fool way to get a lot of men killed, if you excuse my plain speaking, lord,' the Imperial Guard captain proclaimed. He was standing with the robed inquisitor in the shuttle bay of the Imperial transport *Pride of Lothos*. His bullet-head and broad shoulders gave him a brutal look, but his soft spoken burr and quick eyes betrayed the fact that he was far smarter than he looked. Dressed in a simple uniform of black and grey camouflage, Captain Destrien was a tall, imposing figure. Yet the elderly man with whom he was speaking seemed to command much more attention. The black robes that he wore were a mark of the Adeptus Terra, the priesthood of Earth, yet Destrien was not fooled. This was no Administratum bureaucrat.

No adept of Terra carried themselves with such authority and confidence, yet with no hint of pompousness or pride.

No, though he chose to act as something else, the captain knew full well that he spoke to a member of the Inquisition, and the inquisitor knew it too.

'I agree that your orders are highly irregular, captain; one might even say unorthodox,' the inquisitor said with a smile, leaning heavily on his cane. 'Be that as it may, they are your orders and have been countersigned by your superiors, including Warmaster Bane himself.'

Destrien stiffened at the mention of Bane, Warmaster and overall commander of the Imperial forces in the Sarcassa region. This inquisitor wasn't playing around. He had organised this thoroughly, from the top down.

'You're right, those are my orders, and I'll follow 'em, but don't expect me to like it,' complained Destrien, knowing that any argument was useless, but wishing to make his protest all the same. 'We'll be here for another week at least, while we resupply.'

'I believe there are several lighters currently waiting to dock as we speak,' the inquisitor countered, still with the same polite smile on his face. 'I thought it would be necessary to resolve this matter as expeditiously as possible, and brought some of my… influence to bear on the Departmento Munitorum on your behalf. I believe the new uniforms and equipment specified in your orders are aboard. See that they are issued to your men in due course.'

'I just bet you could nail a fog cloud to a wall, couldn't you, lord?' Destrien answered grumpily. He was well and truly cornered here. He'd been hoping to use the week to get in contact with Warmaster Bane and try to get this assignment shoved onto someone else, but the inquisitor was one step ahead of him all the way.

'Yes, and tiptoe along the threads of a spider web as well, captain,' the inquisitor replied, his voice suddenly harsh and ominous, no trace of the previous smile. He pointed his cane at Destrien. 'Remember that you are not to speak of the detail of your orders to anyone, anyone at all, until you are en route to the target. Once there, you will open the second set of sealed orders and follow them to the letter. Is that absolutely clear?'

'To the letter, lord,' Destrien parroted heavily.

'Good.' The inquisitor's smile had returned as easily as it had disappeared. 'Now, I must be on my way. I wish you Emperor's speed and good luck, captain.'

FOUR
RETURN

+++*The signs are clear, the Blade inverted is revealed*+++

+++*It is imperative that he arrive. He is the key*+++

THE COLONEL WATCHES us impassively as we file into the briefing auditorium, standing behind the model of the tau battle dome, arms crossed. We stand to attention by the lowest bench and wait for him. With a nod he directs us to sit down and begins to pace back and forth across the dais, hands behind his back.

'As you are no doubt aware, we left warp space yesterday,' he announces, glancing at us from time to time as he strides to and fro. I had noticed that my warp dreams didn't come last night, and I'd guessed that was the reason. 'We are here to rendezvous with the vessel that will take us into tau-controlled space. This vessel is a tau warship, and under the guise of a diplomatic mission we will enter the Tau Empire and make contact with our allies in the tau government. Whilst aboard the tau ship we must, at all times, be on our guard. The crew of the ship are not privy to our scheme and must totally believe our subterfuge. If they become suspicious of our motives, then the whole mission is placed in jeopardy. I will give you each individual briefings as to your assumed identities before we embark the shuttle for transfer.'

He pauses for a moment, scratching his ear with a thoughtful expression and looking at us sternly.

'The tau will be watching us closely,' he warns us. 'Firstly, even if they believe everything they have been told, I am sure they will be under standing orders to study and observe us at every opportunity. Secondly, the growing tension around Sarcassa, and the rebellion of another renegade called Farsight, mean that the tau are very much on their guard at the moment. They are expecting an escalation of hostilities between their empire and the Emperor's servants soon, but we must do nothing to precipitate that. You will be on your best behaviour and act according to your roles as members of a peaceful delegation.'

I smile inwardly at the irony of this statement. I've spent the last few months training these people to be the hardest, most ruthless killers they can be, and now we have to try and hide that from the tau. It won't be easy. I've done a fair amount of this sneaking around in the past, and the Colonel's right. One slip up and your days are numbered. The fact that it's a tau ship picking us up is also an eye-opener. It shows that our accomplices within the Tau Empire must be pretty important. I don't know whether that's good or bad. On the plus side, they should have the muscle to make sure we can get everything done. On the down side, I've never known such people to fire straight. There's always a hidden motive somewhere.

The whole deal smells a little too clean for my liking. I'll be keeping my eyes and ears open, make no mistake. So will the Colonel, I'd happily bet. He's no stranger to this type of thing either. I mean, the whole Coritanorum mission was us fighting for the Inquisition, and a more slippery, manipulative and untrustworthy bunch doesn't exist. That said, I'd rather have them on our side, all things considered.

'Kage, I will be speaking to you first. Report at the start of the next watch,' the Colonel tells me, interrupting my thoughts. I guess he wants to give me the low-down on the others, as well as my own story.

I KNOCK AT the door and hear Schaeffer call me in. As I step inside, I'm surprised to see two armsmen flanking the Colonel's desk. Eyeing them suspiciously, I step inside and close the door behind me. They look like standard armsmen, carrying shotguns and wearing their black uniforms and dark-visored helmets. I have no idea why they are here though. The Colonel seems to read my thoughts.

'They are here to make sure you do not do anything rash,' he explains, glancing to his left then right and then looking back directly at me.

'Why would I do that, Colonel?' I ask hesitantly, totally confused.

'You are not going on the mission, Kage,' he tells me bluntly.

'Not… not going?' I stammer, my mind whirling. 'I don't understand, sir.'

'It is obvious that you are no longer mentally capable of performing in the mission I have planned,' he states coldly.

'Another episode like the one in the training bay would destroy any cover story we may be travelling under. You are too much of a risk.'

'No, this isn't right,' I say back to him. 'I can do this, better than any of the rest. You can't just get rid of me!'

'I can and I will,' he says calmly. 'The penal colony Destitution lies in the system where we are meeting the tau. You will be transferred by shuttle to an intrasystem vessel and be incarcerated there until such time as I need you again.'

'You can't do this!' I scream at him, taking a step forward. The armsmen take a protective step towards me, raising their shotguns and I back off. 'You can't lock me up again! If I've got problems in my head, it's because of what you've done to me! You're the one who's been fraggin' with my brains for the last three years. I don't deserve this, I've worked fraggin' hard whipping that bunch out there into shape. Emperor damn it, you know I can do this, and you know what going back to a cell will do to me!'

'I have made my decision, Kage,' he says sternly, standing up. 'Either you accompany these armsmen to the shuttle bay, or I will have them shoot you right here and now. Which is it to be, lieutenant?'

I stand there, my emotions swaying between murderous anger and crushing sorrow. How could he do this to me? How long has he intended this to happen? A thought strikes me, making the blood boil in my veins.

'You organised the meeting with the tau in a penal colony system,' I snarl at the Colonel, pointing an accusing finger at him. 'You planned this all along. Drag me along for the training and then dump me. You ungrateful bastard, don't you care at all?'

'I never once said that you were going to participate in the actual mission,' the Colonel replies evenly, like that's all the justification he needs.

'I bet you didn't,' I hiss.

'Now, Kage, do you walk out of that door, or do these men open fire?' he says, locking his gaze to mine. Without a word I spin on my heel and slam open the door. I turn back just before I'm outside.

'This mission will fail,' I tell him slowly. 'It will fail because I'm not there to pull you out of the fire, and not one of the scum that'll be with you gives a damn.'

The armsmen swiftly follow me out as I stalk down the corridor. The anger is welling up inside me, I want to lash out. I want to hit someone, something. What I really want is the Colonel's throat in my grip as I squeeze the last breath out of him. The desire to kill burns through me; I'm actually gnashing my teeth in frustration. It's all I can think about, every muscle in my body is tensed. Six months I was in that cell. Another three months I've been on this ship, sweating blood to train that team. And for what? To rot in another jail somewhere? To slowly go mad with it, to know that I was almost there, fighting again, doing my part for the Emperor. And Schaeffer just snatches it away from me, just takes it away like he had planned all along.

He said he needed me, but that was just a lie, wasn't it? He didn't need me, I was just useful. I just saved him the hard work. Now that's done, he doesn't give a damn, doesn't care a bit that I'm gonna end up clawing my own eyes out or smashing my brains out on a cell wall, cursing his name with my final breath. And all the while, he's off on the mission getting the glory that should be mine.

I can't let him get away with this, it just isn't right. I stop, panting heavily and balling my hands into fists.

'Keep moving, Kage,' one of the armsmen tells me, his voice muffled by his helmet. I round on him, ready to punch his lights out, but the other reacts quickly, smashing the butt of the shotgun into my midriff. His second blow smashes across my forehead and I spin dizzily to the floor.

'Said we shoulda done this straight off,' the other says, clubbing me in the back of the neck.

I COME TO my senses inside the shuttle. Not the plush shuttle we were on earlier, but a standard transport with wooden benches and canvas harnesses lashed to the ceiling. My wrists are manacled together by a length of chain, which passes through an eyebolt obviously recently welded to the decking. My legs are secured the same way, the heavy locks weighing down my ankles. The safety harness is strapped across me as well, pulled painfully tight across my shoulders, groin and stomach. My head pounds and my gut is sore, and I can feel dried blood just above my right eye. Sitting opposite me are the two armsmen, their shotguns held across their laps. They've got their helmets off and are chatting quietly. The one on the left is quite old, his short cropped brown hair greying at the temples, his face lined by the hard years in the navy. He'll be the tough bastard who knocked me out. The other is younger, perhaps in his mid-twenties, with the same short crop style to his blond hair, and clean shaven cheeks. His blue eyes dart back and forth between me and his shipmate, and it's him who notices I'm awake. He gives a nod to the other guy who looks over at me.

'Awake now, prison boy?' the older one says with a gruff laugh. 'Shoulda come quietly, boy.'

I just stare sullenly at him and he shrugs. I sit there in silence while they continue talking about their stupid little lives, my mind beginning to tick over. There's absolutely no way I'm going back to prison. It really would be the death of me, and I'd rather die trying to get out than spend another day alone in a cell.

But even if I could somehow escape, and that's a bloody big if, where would I go, what would I do? I'm stuck on a shuttle heading for another ship which is heading to a penal colony. Somehow I think freedom would be short lived down that route. And even if that wasn't the case, and I could go anywhere I wanted to, I still don't know what I would do. Go to an agri-world and raise crops or grox herds? I don't think so. Become a preacher in the Ecclesiarchy like my dead comrade Gappo? I reckon a month of listening to the monotonous dronings of some fat cardinal would be enough to make me want to crack some heads.

I could hire myself out as a bodyguard, join some pirates perhaps, or become a mercenary. That wouldn't be so bad, in itself, but what would be the point? Hijacking freighters and kidnapping are low, even for me, especially since I should be on a mission that's vitally important to the defence of the Emperor's realm. Emperor damn it, I saved an entire sector, I'm a fragging war hero by all rights, and now the Colonel is just shipping me off and forgetting about me.

My anger starts to rise again, thinking about the cold-heartedness of it all. The Colonel betrayed me, good and simple. But there's a part of me, a part that's growing bigger the more I think about it, that says I should prove the Colonel wrong. It's the same part that made me go back for him in Coritanorum. I've never told him that I was just seconds away from leaving him to roast in that fireball, but he must've guessed as much, he's a shrewd character. What thanks do I get for it? None at all. But it's not about getting thanks, is it? I knew he wouldn't be grateful when I did it, but I still did. And it's not about being a hero. I'll leave that to the likes of Macharius and Yarrick and Stugen Deathwalker. I'm not a hero, I'm just a soldier.

That's the whole point, though, isn't it? I'm just a soldier, and the Colonel isn't even giving me that. Well, damn it, I'll show him the kind of soldier he's created. A resolution begins to build inside me, a cool determination that's totally different from the burning anger I felt earlier. I'm going to prove to the Colonel just how good a soldier I am, and just how valuable I am to him.

A plan begins to form in my mind.

I'VE BEEN AWAKE for a couple of hours when the opportunity presents itself. I've spent all that time going over what I have to do in my mind. Using the techniques I learnt in that cell, I focus my thoughts on every part of the plan in turn, analysing it, trying to see what will go wrong, coming up with answers to questions that crop up in my mental dry run. There's still a few details which I'll have to improvise, but I figure if I can take over the shuttle and get it back to the *Laurels of Glory* and demand that the Colonel takes me on the mission, he can't fail to see how good I am.

So when the younger of the two armsmen pulls off his restraints and leaves the room, I put my plan into action. It'll be easier this way round, I reckon, so at least that's a break to start with.

'Hey, navy boy!' I say to the older guy left. 'Your company so dull, you're driving your shipmates away?'

'Shut your mouth, guardsman,' he mutters back, trying to ignore me.

'You know, I once gutted an ork who looked a bit like you,' I carry on with a laugh. 'Except the ork was better looking and smarter. Smelled better too, I reckon.'

'You talk a lot for a boy strapped to a bench, soldier,' the armsman says threateningly. 'Perhaps I should just push your teeth in right now.'

'Nah,' I sneer back. 'You better wait for your friend to get back first. You'll need his help like you did back on the ship. I would have kicked your face in so far you'd be able to see out your arse.'

That gets the best reaction yet, his face going a livid red.

'Unless you want to be eating soup for the rest of your short, sorry life, you shut your damn mouth, boy!' he shouts at me.

'I've heard about you navy boys,' I carry on relentless, smiling like an ethershark. 'You couldn't break wind, let alone my face. The only reason you made armsman is that you enjoy slapping other men around. Happens a lot, I hear.'

'Why you...' He's speechless now and rises to the bait like a dream. He puts the shotgun to one side and unstraps himself, before snatching it up again and stomping over in front of me. He pulls back for a swing, but as it comes in, I sway to my left, avoiding it thanks to spending the last hour gradually loosening my harness. It clangs against the bulkhead behind me and jars his arms. There's enough play in the chain around my legs to get a good kick in behind his left knee, causing him to buckle. As he stumbles forward, I grab the shotgun in both hands and ram it back into his face, smashing his nose to a pulp and loosening his grip on it. A quick twist crashes the butt into his cheek and sends him tumbling to the deck. I stamp my foot on his neck to trap him there and wedge the barrel of the shotgun between my legs, up against the side of his face. Now all I have to do is wait.

'What's your name?' I ask him conversationally, trying to avoid thinking too much about how hopeless this whole situation probably is. I keep the shotgun pressed to his face with one hand while I unstrap my harness.

'Frag you,' he curses out of the corner of his mouth.

'Listen,' I tell him. 'I don't really want to blow your brains out, and if you're smart you'll just do what you're told and you'll live to tell your shipmates about how the psycho Kage hijacked a shuttle you were on. You can leave out the part that has me overpowering you while chained down, if you like.'

'You're a really funny guy, do you know that?' he replies sarcastically. 'No way are you gonna take over this shuttle, there's another six armsmen on board, plus the pilot and co-pilot.'

'You don't think I can do it?' I say, giving him a prod with the shotgun. 'If you behave yourself, you might live to eat those words rather than a mouthful of shotgun shell.'

'Killing me won't help you escape,' he says defiantly.

'Not yet, but it would make me feel a hell of a lot better about myself,' I laugh back.

'Just where do you think you're gonna go with the shuttle, even if you do pull this off?' he asks. I reckon he's talking to try and keep me distracted, so I humour him.

'Well, I figured on going back to the Colonel and giving him another chance,' I tell him in all seriousness.

'Hah!' he sneers. 'Schaeffer's gonna have you shot as soon as he sets eyes on you. You're a hell of a lot dumber than even I thought.'

'So dumb I'm the one sitting here with the gun pointed at you, instead of the other way round,' I point out, pressing down on his neck with my foot and making him wince. 'I guess that really puts you far down on the brain scale.'

'You got lucky, that's all,' he replies, meaning it.

'Funny, the more fights I get into, the luckier I get,' I laugh, bending forward and patting him on the head in a patronising fashion. 'You'd have thought it'd have run out by now.'

'It's about to…' the armsman crows as the clump of boots resounds from the adjoining corridor. I sit back and look towards the doorway. A moment later, the young armsman enters, and the astonished look on his face is so funny I grin.

'Back so soon?' I ask pleasantly. He glances at me, then his shotgun lying on the bench opposite, a good five or six strides from where he is. 'Even the Emperor's vengeance doesn't act that fast,' I warn him.

'Wh… what do you want?' he asks, taking a step back.

'First off, you're gonna take two steps towards me away from that door,' I tell him flatly. 'Then you're going to take the keys off your belt and toss them over to me.'

'What if I don't?' he asks, one eye on the corridor behind him.

'First I shoot this fella here,' I give the armsman under my boot a nudge with my foot. 'Then I shoot you.'

'You wouldn't kill him just like that!' his voice rings with disbelief.

'He bloody well will!' my hostage spits out hurriedly. 'Just do what he bloody well says, Langsturm, just do what he says!'

'You heard your friend, Langsturm, shift yourself,' I tell the younger guy, gesturing him into the room with my head. He takes two hesitant steps in, eyes flickering between me and the other man.

'Now the keys, nice and slowly,' I order him, keeping my voice calm and even, though my heart is actually racing. This looks like it might just work. Might. He unhooks the ring of keys from his belt and holds them up for me to see. Then he gets stupid.

He tosses the keys full speed towards my face. My finger tightens on the trigger and something wet splashes up my leg. I bring the shotgun up and pump another shell into the chamber as he makes a dive for his gun, my ears ringing from the first shot. He grabs the gun and blasts one-handed at me, sending splinters from the bulkhead spinning into my left shoulder. My return shot catches him low in the right leg, blowing the limb off below the knee and sending him spinning, the shotgun whirling from his grasp as he pirouettes to the ground, the stump spraying crimson across the decking. Gunsmoke drifts up my nostrils, an acrid stench mixing with the tang of fresh blood.

'You… you shot my leg off, you idiot!' he screams at me, making me laugh out loud.

'Looks like I did,' I agree, still chuckling. 'I did warn you.'

'But… But… You shot my leg off, you bastard!' he yells at me, seeming more angry than in pain. I put it down to shock. The body does a wonderful job of shutting off anything too nasty for your head to sort out. Like the burning pain in my shoulder. I check out the wound: it's not too bad, slivers of metal imbedded in the muscle but not bleeding too badly. I'll live, that's for sure. Langsturm sits up on the deck, leaning back against the bench, looking at the shattered end of his leg in disbelief.

'Hey, a navy boy with a pegleg, who'd have thought it, eh?' I joke to him, but he doesn't smile. He keeps staring at the gunshot wound. I look around for the keys, but they're out of reach, a metre to my left. I try dragging them closer with the shotgun but no matter how much I stretch and wriggle I can't quite get far enough over. I have to act quick, if the dead guy was telling the truth and there are more armsmen aboard. They must have heard the shots, I suspect they're trying to decide what to do. Am I dead? Am I free and coming for them right now? It won't take them long to get their act together though, and if I'm still sat here like a firing range target when they arrive, I can pretty much kiss my life farewell.

'Langsturm,' I say to the wounded armsman. He glances up at me vacantly and I point the shotgun at him. 'That was a really stupid thing to do, so do something clever now and toss me those keys.'

'Forget that,' he spits back, his voice growing weaker.

'You're losing blood. I can sort that for you if I can get out of these chains,' I promise, giving him an earnest look. 'Otherwise I'll blow your other leg to bits,' I add in an offhand manner.

He looks at the spreading pool of blood he's sitting in and then at the keys. With a grimace he flops forward and drags himself across the decking. With his arm at full stretch he knocks the ring of keys close enough for me to bend down and pick them up. As I fumble through them someone shouts from outside the door.

'What in the Emperor's name is going on in there?' a deep voice calls out.

'You got a dead man and one on his way,' I shout back. 'You so much as stick your head through that door and you're gonna lose it!'

With my left hand I try the keys on my ankle locks, keeping the shotgun trained on the corridor, quickly swapping my attention back and forth between the two. I find the key to my left foot and the manacle drops away. The next key opens the lock on my right wrist, allowing me to drag the chain through the eye hole and stand up.

'I'll let one unarmed man in to get the wounded guy,' I shout to them, releasing the other locks and dropping the chains to the floor. I work my way along the bench towards the door, keeping my eye on Langsturm at the same time.

'What promises do we have?' their impromptu negotiator calls back.

'None!' I spit, rounding the doorway and blasting off a shot before ducking back. I didn't see if I hit anything, but that doesn't matter, they get the message. I hear Langsturm behind me grunt in pain and turn to see him swinging the discarded shotgun up towards me. I dive to my left and the shot slams into the bulkhead where I was standing.

I roll to a crouch and pump another round into the chamber, firing low, catching the armsman in the guts and hurling him backwards. At that moment someone else bursts through the doorway, firing on full with an autogun, wildly spraying bullets at the far end of the room. I react without thinking, leaping at him and smashing the barrel of the shotgun into his face. Stupid idiot had his visor up. I let go with one hand and rip the autogun from his grip before driving an elbow into his throat. He drops, gasping madly, hands clasped to his throat. Using the sling on the autogun, I hang it over my shoulder and with my free hand grab the collar of the guy's dark suit and drag him further from the door.

'Thanks for the new hostage and spare gun!' I call out, answered by an assortment of harsh curses involving my immediate ancestry.

I stand there, shotgun in one hand, dazed armsman in the other, and assess the situation. It's not going as well as could be hoped, but it's salvageable. They'll be trigger happy by now, as soon as they see me so much as put a toe outside this room I'm going to get filled with bullets. That's when a thought occurs to me. They won't if they think I'm already dead. My blood's pumping fast, my brain working at full speed. I look down at the armsman half-unconscious next to me, noticing his uniform, including that dark-visored helmet. The earlier thought begins to develop into a plan, all I need is for the others to leave me alone for a while.

I pull the helmet off the armsman and he looks up at me groggily before I smack his head back against the bulkhead, knocking him out cold. Stripping off his uniform is tricky, using one hand only as I cover the doorway with the shotgun, but after much wrestling with his inert form I have his clothes piled behind me. My uniform, complete with the Last Chance nametag, is next. I struggle to pull on his jump-suit and eventually have to leave the shotgun propped up against the wall, within easy reach, while I get dressed. I bundle his inert form into my uniform, a task as laborious as getting him out of his own clothes, one eye on the corridor all the while just in case. I finish by putting on his helmet, turning Kage the escaped prisoner into Kage the faceless armsman. I heft the guy up, a hand under each armpit, and then slam him hard against the wall, shouting incoherently as I do so. Holding him against the wall in one hand, I snatch up the autogun and put it against his chest. I pull the trigger for a quick burst as I let go, the bullets' impacts sending the ragged corpse flying out across the doorway.

'He's down!' I yell out, trying to disguise my voice and hoping the helmet muffles it enough to convince them. Apparently they buy it as three pound into the room. I fire high, spraying bullets into their helmeted heads, kicking all three off their feet in a single quick salvo. Without pausing I leap into the corridor, slap bang into the next one. He gives a startled yell as my fist drives into his unarmoured gut. As he doubles over I see another one behind him bringing up a shotgun and I drop and roll, pulling the armsman down with me. He kicks as the shotgun blast hits him in the back and vomits blood over me. One-handed, I fire the autogun down the corridor and hear a cry of pain. Glancing over the armsman's corpse, I see the other guy leant back against the wall, red holes stitched across his chest and abdomen.

I flick the autogun to single shot and walk up to him, casually putting a bullet through his facemask as I walk past. The corridor's short, about five metres, ending in the entry bay, the walls to either side of me unbroken, the engine housings behind them. The entry bay door is open and I can't see any movement beyond it.

As far as I remember, across the docking hall is another room like the one I've just been in, with a doorway through to the cockpit. This is where it's going to get really tricky. I need to get into the cockpit without getting killed and leaving either the pilot or his co-pilot alive. And there's another armsman or two somewhere, I feel pretty sure of that. I have to be on my toes, my whole body ready to react in an instant. The rush is great, I can tell you; there's no feeling like real combat. I take a step down the corridor and suddenly there's a stabbing pain right inside my head. I whirl round, trying to see if I've been hit, but I don't remember hearing a shot. The pain intensifies, making me cry out despite every effort not to, and dropping me to my knees. It's like a red hot coal has been driven into my left eye and it's smouldering through my brain.

Kneeling on the decking, my vision swims madly. The shuttle disappears and I'm suddenly swept up by the feeling that there's someone standing over me. It's like there's a massive shadowy figure towering above me, intent on killing me. All around me are gunshots and explosions, battering my swirling senses. My heart hammers in my chest, needles of pain shooting through my head and eyes. I feel like vomiting, my stomach churning as the attack begins to subside, until I'm back on the shuttle, my whole body wracked with pain.

I kneel there for a few seconds, teeth clenched against the agony, trying to keep my eyes focussed along the corridor, but my vision spins again for a moment. Then, as suddenly as it came, the pain disappears. Not even a dull ache left. Panic envelops me. What the hell is happening to me? Just what did those butchers do to my head while I was asleep?

Blinking away the tears of pain from my eyes I haul myself to my feet and stalk towards the landing bay. I pull off the helmet. I can't hear anything with it on and I need all my senses operating at full. I pause a couple of metres short of the doorway and listen, blocking out the sound of my own heavy breathing, the rush of blood in my ears and the hammering of my heart in my chest. There's no sign of movement, but just to be sure, I toss the helmet through first. It clatters noisily across the mesh decking of the stowed boarding ramps, but other than that nothing happens.

I edge out cautiously into the loading bay. It's about ten metres square, heavy exterior airlock gates to either side, the door to the far room shut. No cover at all and no other way through except that door, which they're bound to be covering. As I stand there pondering my options an unwelcome thought occurs to me. I have no idea how long this shuttle run is supposed to take. For all I know we could be just minutes away from the penal ship and getting ready to dock. I have to take charge now, because once we're onboard the other ship, there's going to be no way out. But how to do it? How can I get through this door and out the other side in one piece? Even if they don't blast me straight off, I have to enter the far chamber some way or another to get to the pilots.

I'm at a complete loss. I try to remember what I'd figured out earlier if this happened, but my mind has gone hazy. A throbbing pain has started in my head as well, not like the sharp stabbing agony of earlier, but in the same place, making it difficult to think straight. I sit myself down against the wall opposite the door, autogun in my lap and ready to go, but I can't wait them out. I toy with the idea of opening up the tech-priest access panels and messing with one of the engines but dismiss the idea almost straight away. For a start it's as good a way as any to get myself fried, poking about with things I've got no clue about. Secondly, there's no guarantee that whatever I did would be fixable, and we'd all be left drifting out here, waiting for the air to run out. I've almost gone that way before and I've no desire to repeat the experience.

A wave of depression hits me as I sit there. There's no way they're going to let me just give myself up now. Not with a handful of dead armsmen. Besides, I just can't go back to a cell, not yet, not without a fight. It's too much like giving up. Again, I feel so alone, so cut off from everything that's happened. As usual, it's me against the galaxy with no one on my side to back me up. How in all that's holy did I get into this situation? The Emperor must surely have it in for me, the amount of utter crap he's put me through these past few years. Is it some kind of test? I must have proved my faith countless times in my life, from when I first saw one of my family die to right now, fighting for the right to go on some completely mad suicide mission. Just what in hell am I doing? Do I really miss the fighting that much?

The truth is, I do. I'm beginning to calm down from killing my guards, but it was such a good feeling, being right there in the thick of it. The sheer sense of achievement I felt as I pulled the trigger and watched them die instead of me. Emperor, it was exciting! I never feel like that any other time, only when the bullets are flying and my life is in the lap of the Emperor.

Which is why I've got to keep fighting, why I have to take over this shuttle, turn it round and get back to the Colonel before he leaves the *Laurels of Glory*. I push myself to my feet and try to get my brain working at full speed again, ignoring the dull ache inside my head. I look around the loading chamber, seeking inspiration. There's a ventilation grille in the ceiling, but far too small for me to get through. There are a couple of panels set into the far wall. Weapons lockers perhaps? I step over to the one opposite to investigate. It's flush with the wall with no handle to open it, and there's a keyhole, so I figure it's locked. I try to open it with a finger but there's no give in it. Perhaps one of the armsmen was carrying a knife…

I go back to the bodies to check this, but come up empty-handed. In total, I have three shotguns and four autoguns, with about twenty shotgun shells and a hundred rounds of autogun ammo. I could try firing blind through the other door and hope I hit something, but it's quite thick. And even then, there's nothing to stop them trying the same against me as soon as I open fire. No, brains rather than guns are going to sort this one out. I look around for anything else I might be able to use, and notice the safety harnesses with their metal buckles. If I rip them out, there's a makeshift rope there. What can I use a rope for? Well, opening the other door from a distance, for a start. So, I start thinking it through one step at a time. I can get the door open without getting shot on the spot. So, I have a fire corridor if I need it. There's no point starting a firefight through the door, they can just keep out of the way and wait to dock before calling in some help. For all I know, they've already called ahead to report something's wrong and there's a welcome committee all ready and waiting for me.

So I need something that will allow me to attack. I could just rush them, take them by surprise and hope I shoot them first. That's too much like fifty-fifty odds for my liking. They could be waiting for that. So, a distraction of some kind perhaps? A fake hostage maybe, I think, looking at the scattering of bodies around me. They'd be suspicious though, and there's no telling whether they'd give a damn anyway.

Is there some other way I could trick them? I doubt it. If I was them I wouldn't be trusting anything right about now. And this fella, or fellas, is the smart one, he stayed out of trouble when the others dashed in. Maybe he's a coward, then? Maybe I can cut a deal – tell him to come quietly before he gets the same as his friends.

No, all this thinking about tricks and cunning ploys is getting me nowhere. I need to come up with a way that's going to take out whoever's in that room, once and for all. All I need are some bullets that fire round corners, I joke bitterly with myself. My wry smile disappears as I carry on thinking. Maybe I do have some bullets that fire around corners. I could rig up something with the magazines and shotgun shells. Something that'd go off like a grenade if I shot it. Yeah, a few magazines tied together, with cartridges wedged in for good measure. Open the door with a rope, toss the thing in and then set it off with a burst of semi-auto. While they're still reeling, assuming they're still standing at all, I rush in and finish the job. It's a one-shot plan, because it'll use most of my ammo to get a nice big bomb. What the hell, I tell myself, one shot's better than no shot, which is the alternative.

I set to work with a vengeance, conscious of every second ticking past bringing me closer and closer to the penal ship and swift execution. Straining every muscle, I manage to pull out one of the harnesses, and laboriously saw my way through some of the stitching with a jagged key left by Langsturm. With one strap I bind three magazines to each other in a kind of triangle, poking eight shells into the gaps left. A further refinement occurs to me and I strip off one of the buckles and put it into the pocket of the armsman fatigues I'm still wearing. I carry my hand-made grenade back into the docking area and place it carefully on the floor within easy reach. The door is on a latch and I gently turn the handle until it clicks off, pulling the door open by a fraction. I loop another strap around the handle, ready to tug it open. Using the butt of a shotgun, I smash open the ventilation grille. As I suspected, there's a conduit running back and forward towards the tail and nose of the shuttle.

With the door rope in one hand, and my grenade close by, I take the harness buckle out of my pocket and toss it through the opening, listening to it clatter towards the front of the craft. With a single motion, I yank the door open and sweep up the bomb, leaping past the open doorway and hurling the explosive inside. I drop to my belly and roll back to the doorway, autogun at the ready. I wait for a couple of seconds to see if anyone tries to pick up the grenade, then open fire. With a series of cracking detonations, the shotgun shells explode, shattering the magazines which go up half a second later, showering the room with small pieces of shrapnel, some of it clattering around me. I roll forward, and fire blindly to the left and right and then dive for the cover of the central bench. There's no return fire and the silence is almost deafening after the bomb explosion. I strain my ears but can't hear a thing. I move up to a crouch and glance around.

The room's totally empty.

All of that for no fragging reason at all. I'm actually disappointed for a moment.

I stand up slowly, scratching my head. Was the armsman lying, or are there more in the cockpit? I'm starting to get fed up with this messing about. At that moment the comm panel set into the wall next to the cockpit door crackles into life, and a tinny voice reverberates around the chamber.

'Was that an explosion we heard?' it asks. I stride across the room and press down on the reply switch.

'Yes, the prisoner rigged up some kind of bomb which went off,' I tell them, smiling to myself. 'I need some help out here clearing up this mess.'

'Who am I talking to?' the man on the other end asks, suspicious.

'He's still alive, I think,' I answer hurriedly. 'Give me a hand and stop asking stupid questions. He'll blow us all up, he's mad enough to do it.'

'Right,' the guy replies, the comm unit not masking the concern in his voice.

A second or two later, the door wheel to the cockpit spins and it opens into the room hesitantly. I grab the edge and wrench it open, barrelling through, ramming into the armsman on the other side and smashing him to the deck. I smack him across the head with the butt of the autogun and look up. The pilot and his co-pilot are looking round at me over the backs of their seats, horrified. I point the gun casually at them.

'Change of plan,' I tell them, stepping over the unconscious armsman towards them. 'Do exactly what I say and everything will be fine.'

'What are you going to do?' the co-pilot asks, eyes fearful.

'I'm not gonna do anything,' I say with a grin. 'But you're gonna turn this shuttle around and head back to the *Laurels of Glory* right now.'

'But we're locked into our landing approach,' argues the pilot, pointing out of the window. I look through the cockpit screen and see the penal ship, pretty close now. It's long and grey and almost featureless. Just like you'd expect a prison ship to look.

'Now, that's not the sort of answer I'm looking for here,' I warn them, the smile disappearing. 'Abort the landing and turn around.'

'If we break from the landing pattern they'll know something is wrong,' the co-pilot informs me. 'They'll open fire.'

'Well, give them a reason for turning around then,' I reply in exasperation. 'Tell him one of the engines is in danger of going critical or something.'

'They already know you've broken free,' the pilot admits heavily. 'We called that in over the comm a few minutes ago. If they think you've taken over the shuttle they'll assume we're dead too and blast us all to pieces.'

'Then you better save your own hides too,' I say menacingly, waving the gun at them to prove my point. 'Because if you try and land on that ship I'll kill you both where you're sitting.'

The pilot looks at me and then at his co-pilot. He sags in his seat a little more and turns back to the flight controls. He throws a few switches, and then nods to the co-pilot, who does the same on his end of the panel. There's a shrill tone sounding from a grille in the ceiling and a yellow light begins to flash. The pilot glances at my annoyed expression and punches a few more keys, turning off the alarm. Another light begins to pulse in the middle of the controls.

'That's the comm,' the co-pilot explains, leaning forward and pulling free a handset which he holds up to his ear. 'They're asking why we've disengaged the landing tracker.'

'Sod 'em,' I say harshly. 'Turn this crate around and hit the throttle, I'm going back to see the Colonel.'

'They will shoot us,' the pilot warns me earnestly. 'You have to believe me.'

'Then you better start praying that this shuttle can dodge and weave like a fighter,' I answer matter-of-factly. He scowls at me and then grabs the control column. The co-pilot makes some adjustments and my ears catch a change in the sound of the engines vibrating through the whole shuttle. The pilot banks us to the left, the prison vessel sliding out of view and then settles us on a new course.

The co-pilot ramps up the engines again, and the floor starts juddering underneath my boots.

'They're telling us to turn back to our original heading or they'll open fire,' wails the co-pilot, hand clamping the comm set to his ear.

I stand there saying nothing. A few seconds pass without a comment from either of them.

'Here it comes,' mutters the co-pilot, dropping the handset and gripping the arms of his seat tightly.

Something streaks past my field of vision, a tiny yellow spark, that erupts into a massive plume of red a moment later. The pilot dives the shuttle underneath the plasma burst, swearing under his breath. Thrown backwards, I curse as my body smashes into the door wheel.

'They missed,' says the co-pilot, relief and disbelief fighting within him.

'Just a warning shot across the bows, you idiot,' I say to him and he withers under my glare. 'Pay attention to flying this thing.'

More detonations soon follow, and I fix my attention on the pilot as he smoothly moves the controls from side to side and up and down, erratically pulling corkscrews and climbs, dives and spins. Suddenly the shuttle lurches and begins to shake. Half a dozen red lights spring into life along a display at the same time as a klaxon begins sounding.

'Shut the door! We've got a hull breach!' snaps the pilot, and I turn and slam the cockpit door shut with a clang, dropping the autogun so I can spin the wheel on it until it's locked tight. Just as I turn back, the co-pilot launches himself at me, but I swing into the attack, driving my fist hard into his right eye, hurling him from his feet.

'Don't be a hero,' I warn him, leaning over and punching him again, this time splitting his lip. 'If you promise to behave, I'll stop hitting you,' I add, smacking him between the eyes and breaking his nose. He whimpers and tries to roll away from me, but a boot to the stomach stops him. I drag him up and dump him back in his chair, where he sits stunned.

'Just do what you're told in future,' I hiss at him, but he's too dazed to hear me.

'You're going to have to help me,' the pilot says ominously. 'He's in no condition to.'

'Yeah, like I know how,' I reply sarcastically, looking at the pilot with a doubtful expression.

'Just do what I say, and we'll be fine,' the pilot assures me, his words given meaning by another detonation close by clanging along the length of the hull. I push the co-pilot back to the floor.

'Any red light, just flick the switch beneath it, okay?' the pilot instructs me, glancing across at me before concentrating ahead of him again.

'Okay,' I answer calmly, working my way along the display and flicking all the switches beneath the red lights. This isn't too difficult.

'There's three red levers just to your right,' the pilot continues, not looking at me. I can see them, right next to each other.

'They're the engine controls. From your left to right, they are larboard, main and starboard engines. Got that?'

'Larboard, main, starboard,' I repeat, touching each one in turn. 'Got it.'

'Adjust the throttles when I tell...' His last words are lost as an explosion bursts into life right in front of us, showering fragments of shell over the shuttle. A crack appears on the main window, causing a knot of fear to tighten in my chest. I don't want to get sucked out into space. That's a really grim way of dying. Not that dying any other way isn't pretty grim to me either.

'Pull all three back to seventy-five per cent power, at the same time,' the pilot instructs me.

I lean over and grip all three levers in my hand and pull them slowly towards me. They lock into place next to a notch with a label that reads 75%, and I leave them there.

'Now move the main engine back up to full,' the pilot says slowly, making sure I don't misunderstand him. I follow his instructions, pushing the lever back up.

'That's it, we're cruising now, soon be out of range,' the pilot sighs, leaning back.

'This isn't so bad after all,' I chuckle to myself, looking at the other controls. 'I thought flying a shuttle was difficult.'

'It's easier without a gun pointing at your head,' the pilot replies sourly.

'What's this one do?' I ask, pointing at a dial set above my head, its needle wavering about in a red section. The pilot glances over.

'Emperor's mother!' he curses, leaning forward for a closer look. 'We're leaking plasma from the main engine. Shut it down and eject the core before the whole shuttle explodes!'

'Like I know how to do that,' I snap back. The pilot unbuckles himself and pushes me out of the way, sitting down in the co-pilot's seat. His hands move quickly over the controls, finishing by stabbing a finger into a red-flashing rune near the top of the panel. The hull shivers with the sound of four successive detonations, there's a pause for a couple of seconds and then a final explosion which sets my ears ringing. The pilot gives me a relieved look and takes his own place. I hear a groan from the co-pilot, and look at him. He's recovering his senses, so I grab a handful of hair and ram his forehead down into the decking, knocking him out cold. I can't be bothered with him any more, he's obviously not that essential.

* * *

MOST OF THE flight passes without event, the pilot seeming content to do what he's told. I have to knock out the armsman in the cockpit again when he starts to come round after about an hour, but apart from that, I just sit in the co-pilot's chair, asking what the different controls mean. You never know, it might come in handy one day.

That all changes when we get back within comms range of the *Laurels of Glory*. I hear a buzzing from the handset, still hanging from its cord from the panel, and lift it to my ear.

'*Alphranon*, this is *Laurels of Glory*, what is your situation?' the voice asks. 'Repeat, shuttle *Alphranon*, please report your condition.'

I press down on the transmit stud.

'*Laurels of Glory*, this is Lieutenant Kage of the 13th Penal Legion,' I report, a grin creeping across my face. 'Requesting permission to land.'

'Who the hell?' the comms officer on the other end exclaims. 'What is going on?'

'Ah, *Laurels of Glory*, this is Lieutenant Kage of the 13th Penal Legion,' I repeat. 'I've, er, commandeered this shuttle for important military reasons. Please contact my commanding officer, Colonel Schaeffer.'

'Someone get Schaeffer up here at the double!' I hear the officer calling off the link, before he talks back to me directly.

'Who is piloting that shuttle?' he asks me hesitantly. I look over towards the pilot.

'What's your name?' I ask him, realising I don't know it yet.

'Karandon, Lucas Karandon,' he answers, looking confused.

'Pilot Karandon is in control, with my assistance,' I report back, giving the pilot a wink. 'We've suffered some damage, had to jettison the main engine.'

I glance over at Lucas, letting go of the transmit switch.

'Anything else they should know about?' I ask, waving the link at him in explanation.

'Ah, tell them we have a possible hull breach as well,' he tells me after a moment's thought.

'We also have a hull breach, not sure where,' I pass the message on, holding the link back up to my mouth.

'Kage, just what do you think you are doing!' the Colonel barks back at me, making me almost drop the comm set. I start to reply but fall silent, confused suddenly. What *am* I doing? It all seemed perfectly clear a couple of hours ago, but in all the excitement I've kind of forgotten.

'Give me one good reason not to order the crew to destroy you and that shuttle,' Schaeffer continues, and I can hear the anger in his voice. Perhaps this wasn't such a good idea, I begin to think. Maybe I was being a little optimistic.

'Well, I've got three good reasons here in the cockpit with me,' I reply, trying to keep the doubt from my voice, a little unsuccessfully. 'Plus there may be some others left alive.'

'Allowing their shuttle to be taken over does not particularly endear them to me, Kage,' he says heavily.

'Don't send me back to prison, Colonel,' I suddenly blurt out. 'Take me with you! At least let us land and I'll explain everything.'

'I will get you permission to land, but no other promises,' he tells me, and I hear the comm link click off.

The next half an hour is a nerve-wracking affair for me. I sit there, making the few adjustments Lucas suggests, as I try to sort out my thoughts. The Colonel doesn't sound too pleased, to put it lightly, and is going to take some convincing. Plus, what's to say he won't shoot me on the spot as soon as I step off board? Actually, that's more likely than anything else. Still, I've got three hostages. Despite what the Colonel says, that must give me some leverage. Well, if the navy have anything to say about it, at least. If it was just up to the Colonel, he'd sooner see them all dead than bargain with me, I reckon.

IT'S WITH A trembling heart that I stand in the docking bay and pull the lever that lowers the door ramp. I've got Lucas with me, shaking like a leaf. Not surprising, I'm holding him in front of me, arm round his throat, the autogun pressed to the back of his head. The shuttle's a complete mess. I did a quick inspection after we landed. There's a hole you could crawl through in the rear chamber, the benches are all ripped up and there's no sign of the other armsmen, I guess they got blown out into space.

With a clang the ramp touches down on the deck and I look out.

There's a line of twenty or more armsmen, all with shotguns. At their centre stands the Colonel and a couple of naval officers. I stand at the top of the ramp and stare back at them.

'Give yourself up, Kage,' bellows the Colonel. 'Otherwise I will have you shot where you stand.'

'I just want to talk to you, Colonel,' I call back. 'Just listen to what I have to say.'

'No deals, Kage,' he answers curtly. 'Unhand that man and step out of the shuttle, otherwise I will give the order to fire.'

The two navy guys exchange glances at that, but don't say anything.

The Colonel's stare is fixed on me, unwavering and hard as steel. I stand there and stare back at him.

'Aim!' he commands, and the armsmen follow the order, bringing up their weapons.

'Oh frag!' I curse, pushing Lucas forward and diving clear just as the Colonel shouts the order. Lucas's ragged body is flung back across the bay as I scramble into the aft seating chamber.

'For Emperor's sake, Colonel!' I shout out, cradling the auto-gun to my chest. 'I'll kill all of them if you come in after me, I swear!'

'You're not going to kill anyone else, Lieutenant Kage,' calls out a voice that sends a shiver down my spine. 'Step out where I can see you.'

It's the voice of a man I thought dead for the past year and a half. A man I left to die in a fireball that wiped out an entire city. A man who has absolutely no reasons to want me still breathing. It's the voice of Inquisitor Oriel.

I resist the urge to call back, but something in his voice nags at my mind and makes me stand up and walk back to the loading ramp. I stand there for a moment before throwing the gun away.

I was right, it is Oriel. He's stood next to the Colonel now, dressed in a long blue coat, trimmed with gold thread. He's grown a short-cropped goatee beard, making him look even more sinister than he did last time. He stands there casually, arms crossed, looking at me.

With a gesture he gets the armsmen to lower their weapons and strides towards me.

'Surprised, Lieutenant Kage?' he asks, walking up the ramp and stopping a couple of paces in front of me.

'I guess I shouldn't be. There was a second shuttle, after all,' I reply slowly, looking over his shoulder at the Colonel. 'And you've pulled the Colonel's strings before.'

'Yes, there was a second shuttle,' he smiles coldly, ignoring my other comment. 'Tell me why you've come back here, Kage.'

'I need to go on the mission,' I explain, speaking slowly, emphasising the words. 'It'll kill me if I have to go back to prison.'

'Coming back may kill you as well,' he answers after a moment. 'Going on the mission might kill you.'

'I'm prepared to risk it,' I reply evenly, finally looking into his dark eyes. 'I'd rather take my chances here or with the tau than in a prison cell rotting away.'

'Yes, you would, wouldn't you,' he says, eyes narrowing.

We both stand there facing each other for what seems like an eternity, Oriel slowly sizing me up. I'm convinced he's going to walk away and give the order to open fire, but he just stands there, watching me with those wise eyes of his, weighing his options. I say nothing, realising now that there is nothing I could actually say. It's up to this man, and this man alone, what happens to me next. This man who I pretty much tried to kill. A feeling of dread fills me.

'I'm impressed by your resilience, Kage. You refuse to die, don't you?' he says suddenly, breaking the heavy silence.

'I'll never die easily, that's for sure,' I tell him, feeling hope beginning to grow in my chest, like the first sparks of a fire.

'Very well,' he nods. 'You come with us on the mission. You give me any reason to doubt you, though, and I will have you killed.'

My reply is a sigh of relief and a wide grin.

'You won't have any need for that,' I say, feeling very tired all of a sudden. 'I'll do whatever's necessary, whatever you ask me to do.'

Oriel sat in front of the low desk, a single candle guttering on a silver stand over his right shoulder. He pulled the deck of Imperial tarot cards from a small drawer concealed within the desk itself, and fanned them across the table. Each crystalline sliver glittered in the candlelight, making the holographic images impregnated into them dance and judder. Scooping them back together, he cut the deck into three piles, and then into six, before gathering the cards back together, following the proscribed ritual. He performed this twice more, muttering a prayer to the Emperor as he did so.

He closed his eyes for a moment, focussing his thoughts and prayers on to the cards. Opening his eyes again, he placed the top card in front of him. Above that he placed the next, and then two more cards at right angles between them.

He turned the top card over, end-to-end away from himself and looked at it. A stylised grim reaper, complete with skull face and black robes, swiped its long scythe at him.

'Death,' he said aloud.

He then turned the right card over, revealing a swirling, gaping maw. 'The Abyss,' he stated to the galaxy in general, another important part of the ritual.

The left card turned out to be a many-tentacled beast, with eyes on stalks that wobbled around within the hologram.

'The Fiend.'

Lastly, with just the briefest of hesitations, Oriel slowly revealed the card nearest to him. It was upside down, and the holo-picture was of an ornate looking sabre, slicked with blood.

'The Blade, inverted.'

Oriel stroked his chin and looked at the cards, his eyebrows coming together in a slight frown of concern.

'Always Death and the Blade inverted,' he muttered to himself, picking up the Blade card and examining it closely. 'I was right about you, Kage. I was right.'

FIVE
ME'LEK

+++Contact made+++

+++The fly approaches the web+++

THE OTHERS STEER clear of me while we wait for the tau ship, which is due to arrive soon. They're not sure what my role is now, and to be honest, neither am I. The Colonel hasn't spoken to me since I came back, he just stalked off angrily when Inquisitor Oriel told him I was coming along. It's Oriel who summons me a little while later, after I've had a chance to clean myself up from the fighting during my hijack. He's taken up office in one of the state rooms aboard the *Laurels of Glory*, and I'm escorted there by a sullen armsman. I probably killed some of his friends, for all I know. Not that I care. There's nothing anyone can tell me about losing comrades in battle, because I've lost them all. It's one of the reasons I feel I have to carry on with life, so that someone remembers them and the sacrifices they made so that others would be safe. They'll never be commemorated, never be heroes except as I remember them. I can see their faces as I walk along the corridor behind the armsman. Good memories. That might seem strange, and I never would have considered it at the time, but there's not a bunch of people I would rather go through hell with than them. But they're not here this time, so it's just up to me now.

Oriel calls me after I knock, and I step into the state room. It's richly furnished, with five deep leather armchairs, a few low tables and cabinets neatly arranged along the walls. Oriel is sitting in the chair furthest from the door, and he beckons me over to the chair opposite with a wave.

'Sit down Kage,' he prompts me. 'You have some catching up to do.'

I do as he says, sitting on the edge of the chair, feeling uncomfortable under his gaze.

'Colonel Schaeffer has briefly explained the situation, I believe,' he carries on when he's decided I'm settled.

'Yeah, there's a tau ship coming to pick us up,' I say, trying to recall what the Colonel said earlier. It seems unbelievable that it was only a few hours ago; it seems like days. 'We pretend to be a diplomatic mission while on board, go to some tau world and meet up with the guys on the inside who are helping us out.'

'Yes, it's something like that,' agrees Oriel, leaning forward and resting his arms across his knees. 'I will be masquerading as an Imperial commander of one of the worlds close by the tau territories. You and the others are supposedly my counsellors, my advisors as it were.'

'That should be fun,' I say impulsively and he gives me a quizzical look. 'Giving advice to an inquisitor, I mean.'

'Well, you forget all of that as of now,' he says sternly. 'Even our contacts do not realise who I truly am, they believe in my part of the subterfuge. If they even get a sniff that the Inquisition is involved, they'll get scared off. They don't know too much about us, but they've heard enough stories to make them suspicious of anything that involves the Inquisition.'

I can't think why, I say to myself. Not that I think they're a bunch of underhand, murderous, double-dealing torturers and witch hunters, you understand. Or that my previous experiences with Oriel have left me with the certain knowledge that they consider everyone expendable to their cause, including themselves. Now, I don't mind that so much, after all I've sacrificed a few bodies for my own ends myself, but at least I don't claim the Emperor gives me the right to do it.

'Now, I and Colonel Schaeffer will do any talking when necessary,' he continues, not noticing my distraction. 'If you are asked any direct questions by anyone, then simply reply that you don't know the answer, or that you're not in a position to comment.'

'Play dumb, you mean?' I summarise in my own charming style.

'Yes, play dumb,' agrees Oriel patiently, tapping his fingers together slowly, as if counting something. 'Remember to refer to me as either "sire" or "Imperial commander", and don't call Schaeffer "Colonel" or "sir", none of us are supposedly military rank. Obviously, the tau don't believe that for a moment, but we have to play the game called diplomacy, which means at least pretending we're not on a military mission to spy on them. That's exactly what they're expecting us to be doing, and they will also be continuously trying to get what information they can from us.'

'Excuse me, but why exactly would we be sending diplomats to an alien world?' I ask, a thought occurring to me. 'And why are we bothering with the mission at all? Why not just assemble a war fleet and blast this traitor commander back under the stone he crawled out from.'

'Let me explain it in simple terms,' the inquisitor replies calmly, no hint of annoyance or impatience over my interruption. He's a cool character, and no mistaking. 'Our relationship with the tau is delicately balanced. At the present time, their empire is slowly expanding into the Emperor's domains, and contest for worlds has occurred. However, they are not overtly hostile to mankind, they merely see us as being in the way. Unlike, for example, the tyranids, who would wipe us out. In fact, with the massive tyranid threat posed by their latest hive fleets, in this area of the galaxy we cannot afford to start a long and costly war with the tau without weakening our defences in other sectors. Therefore, for the moment we try to keep our approach as peaceful as possible. Soon, some time in the future, the tau will need dealing with. But not yet. The Emperor has ruled the galaxy for ten thousand years; there's no need to be hasty.'

I sit there nodding, absorbing this piece of information. So what he's saying is there's no point starting a fight we don't need, not when there's plenty of other battles to win first. I can see the sense in that, after all only an idiot picks to fight more than one guy at a time. And, like he says, there'll be plenty of time later to sort out the tau, once we've dealt with the tyranids.

He spends the next hour or so explaining the various details of the cover stories, emphasising again and again how important it is that we don't raise any suspicions amongst the tau. He lays it on pretty thick, but this is his mission so I guess he has the right to. I take it all in, the name of the world we're from, why we're supposedly visiting the tau, what to keep my eyes out for, what we can learn about these aliens for the future, as well as completing the mission itself.

As I said, I'll do what I'm told. I'm just a soldier, and I'll follow my orders, I'm not really worried about the reasons. That kind of thinking is for those who might question their orders, and I've got no time for them. I broke my oath once, and look where it got me. This time out I'm doing things the right way, even though the Colonel tried to stop me. When he finishes, Oriel asks if I have any questions.

'How come you didn't back up the Colonel?' I say.

'Why didn't you just have me shot?'

'Because any man desperate enough to take over a shuttle and fly back to take part in a suicide mission is desperate enough to do whatever's necessary,' he answers with a smile. 'I know from your past that I can rely on you, Kage. So does Colonel Schaeffer, but he can't be seen to bargain with you, he can't allow the others to think that there's some kind of weakness in him. And to be honest, there isn't. I can be more flexible. I don't need to maintain my authority; I have absolute authority.'

'Guess being an inquisitor answers that question, eh?' I reply, matching Oriel's smile. His fades.

'I have a sacred duty, just as Colonel Schaeffer has,' he tells me sternly. 'I have absolute authority because I have absolute responsibility. All means are at my disposal, but all threats to the Emperor and his servants are mine to combat. I'm allowing you on this mission because I think you'll contribute and help me in my cause. I will use you any way I please and as soon as I stop finding you useful, Colonel Schaeffer can do what he likes with you. Is that clear?'

'Perfectly,' I answer quietly, feeling like I've been slapped in my face. 'But I'm not a tool, I'm a weapon, and they can go off in your hand.'

'Yes they can,' laughs Oriel. 'Just don't self destruct on me until the mission is over.'

He dismisses me with a wave of his hand, and I feel his eyes on me as I leave the room. The armsman takes me back through the ship to our quarters, leaving me outside the door to my room. I watch him walk away before opening the door and stepping inside.

SOMETHING SMASHES INTO my face, dropping me to my knees. Through watery eyes I look up and see Moerck standing over me, the others behind him. I put an arm out to push myself up and Trost steps forward and kicks me in the ribs, knocking the wind out of me.

'Just stay there and listen for a moment, Kage,' Strelli says, walking up and pushing me over with his foot on my wounded shoulder.

'The Colonel wasn't too impressed with you coming back, Kage,' Trost snarls. 'You're like a gun with a hangfire, could go off at any moment. We're keeping an eye on you. You so much as breathe out of turn, we're going to enjoy putting you in a bodybag.'

Quick as a sump snake, I roll over, wrapping my arm around Strelli's leg and wrenching him to the ground, twisting his knee viciously. Trost tries to kick me but I sweep his legs out from underneath him with a kick to his knee. Moerck throws a strong punch at me, but I turn and take it on my shoulder, rolling to my feet in one move. Strelli launches himself up at me from the floor, but I bring my knee up and smash it into his face as he tries to wrap his arms around my waist and bear me down. His momentum knocks me back a step, and Moerck wraps an arm around my throat, squeezing tight. I ram an elbow back into his ribs and he grunts, but doesn't let go. Trost has recovered and pushes himself to his feet as I try to wriggle free, slamming my elbow repeatedly into Moerck's body, weakening his grip enough that I burst free and drive my fist straight into Trost's face, spinning him down to the ground.

Moerck kicks me in the guts and then grabs me by the throat, heaving me off my feet and hurling me backwards into the wall, smashing my head against the bulkhead. Stunned, I just manage to dodge as he thunders a right hand at me, but duck into Strelli's fist, which catches me on the right cheek, stinging like mad. My vision whirls, and I see the others standing there watching impassively as Moerck drives one of his massive fists into my guts again and again, bruising the ribs and knocking all of the breath out of me.

'This is just so you don't forget, Kage,' he says, no trace of anger in his voice. Like a machine he grabs my throat in his left hands and holds me back against the wall before delivering a short jab with his right that crashes my head back, pain flaring through my brain at the impact. He lets go and I drop to the floor, gasping for breath and bleeding from my mouth and nose.

Trost makes to lay into me some more, but Moerck steps in and shoves him away.

'I think he's got the message,' the ex-commissar says, holding Trost back.

I dart them all a murderous look as I lie there, every part of me aching painfully. They file out through the door connecting my room to their dorm, contempt in their eyes. My ribs are really sore and pain flashes through me as I push myself to my feet. I reckon one of them's bruised, or maybe even cracked. My bottom lip is beginning to swell and dried blood is clogging up my nose as I slump down on my bed with a groan.

I've taught them well, I think. They're the sort of soldiers the Colonel needs, the ones who understand about fighting and power, and how to use it. I start to chuckle but stop abruptly as my ribs send stabs of pain through me again. I lie there looking at the ceiling, feeling the bruises growing across me. They've proved they have what it takes, that they'll kill when they need to. They're my true soldiers, alright. I close my eyes and let sleep take away the pain.

It's THREE MORE days of training in the firing range, on the combat mats and in the mock-up of the tau battle dome before the Colonel informs us that contact has been made with the alien vessel. We assemble in the briefing auditorium, where the Colonel issues us with clothes chests with our disguises. We lug them back to the rooms and prepare for the shuttle. In my trunk are four brown robes, typical of an Administratum flunky. I understand the choice when I put it on and pull the hood up – it hides my face in complete shadow, obscuring the tapestry of scars that covers my face and head. I'll be Brother Kage then, I tell myself with a bitter smile. Probably the only scribe who can't read or write in the Imperium.

There are amused looks from the others as we assemble in the docking bay. Oriel is dressed in a very grandiose and over the top dress uniform, hung with gold cording and medals. The red jacket is almost painfully bright, crossed by a garish yellow sash. Just the sort of pompous and totally meaningless display of opulence you might expect from one of the Imperium's ruling elite. The Colonel wears a severe black suit, with a long-tailed coat draped over one arm. Tanya wears a long dress of deep blue, tight at the waist and high at the neck, her hair cropped really short. Oriel explained that she's posing as a member of the Sisters Famulous, a branch of the Ecclesiarchy that provides housekeepers and chatelaines to the Imperial nobility. Trost, Strelli and Quidlon wear less extravagant versions of Oriel's uniform, while Moerck is dressed in plain white leggings and a white shirt with a soft leather jerkin over the top, looking every bit the gentleman. Oriel walks over to us and gives us each the once over.

'Will you all relax and try not to look like soldiers?' he says with an annoyed scowl. 'This isn't going to work if you keep standing at ease like that and quick march everywhere. Remember, you're civilians!'

We look at each other, and I see that it's true. I try to purposefully slouch a bit more, as do the others. I cross my arms and hide my hands in the sleeves of my robes, as I've seen various Departmento Munitorum scribes and their like do over the years. It's kind of uncomfortable really, and I walk back and forth a bit, trying to get it to feel natural. I feel horribly vulnerable without my arms free and the hood obscuring most of my arc of vision.

'Take shorter strides, Kage, you are not on a cross-country march!' the Colonel calls out to me, from where he's stood at the ramp to the shuttle. I look over at him and he nods, gesturing for me to try it out. I pace the length of the shuttle bay, some two hundred metres each way, keeping my steps half what I'm used to, and I feel like I'm tottering about like a small child. I bend my back a bit more, leaning my chin down into my chest and try it again and it feels a bit more natural, my gait more like the image I have in my head of Clericus Amadiel, the Colonel's scribe on the last mission.

When Oriel is satisfied that we don't stand out like a squad of highly trained soldiers pretending to be diplomats, we get all of our kit on board the shuttle and settle in for the ride. The mood is tense and nervous. None of us have any weapons. If the tau take a disliking to us, there's not a thing we can do to stop them killing us out of hand. I can understand why, though: if this is a peaceful delegation, it'll raise a few eyebrows if we turn up with a small arsenal. That's if the tau have eyebrows, I suddenly think to myself, making myself smile. We've not seen a single picture of them. They could be big bags of gas or tentacled squidgy blobs for all I know. I guess from the fake battle dome that they can't be too different from us, physically I mean. The doors were sort of human sized, the steps built for just two legs, so I guess that rules out floating gasbags. I let my mind wander with thoughts like these, preferring to put any thought of the upcoming mission out of my mind.

A couple of the others seem worried and I tell them to relax. There's no sense worrying now. The plan is in motion and it'll lead us wherever the Emperor cares. Personally, I try not to worry about anything. There's two things people worry about. There's things they have no control of and they're worried how it'll affect them. Then there's the things they worry about doing or not doing. Either way, it's a waste of time. If it's something you can't do anything about, then all of the worrying in the galaxy isn't going to change what will happen one bit. And if you can do something about it, then do something, don't just sit around and worry, take your destiny in your hands. It's that kind of thinking that's kept me alive and sane all these years.

Sane. I'm beginning to have my doubts about that, which I guess proves that I'm not mad yet, at least I don't think so. Do you have to be sane to wonder if you are; do lunatics just assume they are sane and not question it? I know what the others think, Oriel included, despite his choice to bring me along. They think my mind's more twisted than a rock drill head. I don't see it that way, it's not bent at all. In fact, it's so straight, so focussed on what I am that it might seem mad to other people. They like to clutter themselves up with all sorts of little illusions about who they are, what they're here for. Not me. I worked it all out in the stinking prison cell.

As I said to Oriel, I'm a weapon, nothing more. Point me at the enemy, and let me go. That sort of clarity is more comforting than worrying about if I'm doing the right thing, wasting time and energy agonising with my conscience and my morals. My conscience is the orders I'm given; my morals are the ones I'm told to have. Somebody else can have that responsibility, someone like the Colonel or Oriel. I just don't care any more.

We've been travelling for a couple of hours when the Colonel enters from the adjacent room.

'Here is your chance to get a first look at the enemy,' he tells us, pointing towards one of the wide viewing windows. I unbuckle myself along with the others, and we gather around the thick pane and look out into the stars. It's out there, the tau ship, and we get a good view of it as the shuttle circles, losing momentum to start its landing pattern. It's long and sleek, almost pure white. The main hull is like a slightly flattened cylinder, with a cluster of pods at the back, glowing faintly, so I guess they're the engines. The front end gets flatter and wider, a bit like a subtly squared-off snake's head. There are several outlandish Tau symbols emblazoned in massive lettering along the side, but I can't make out any sign of ports, docking entries or any other openings. I can't see any gun decks either.

'Is this a warship?' I ask Schaeffer.

'I believe it is non-military in its normal duties,' the Colonel replies.

As we approach, a section of the hull disappears from view, revealing the interior in a blaze of yellow light. It's not like a door slid back or opened, the section of ship seemed to roll out of the way, leaving a perfectly circular opening. We return to our seats and buckle down for landing, the blast shutters grinding up over the windows. It's a few more minutes, which pass with tortuous slowness as we sit there not knowing what's going to happen, until I feel and hear the shuttle landing. With a whine the engines power down, and the Colonel tells us to get to our feet.

'First impressions last,' he tells us ominously. 'From the second we step off this craft we'll be under close scrutiny. Right from this moment, you have to think and act exactly like the people you're supposed to be. We'll try to keep ourselves out of the way as much as possible, but there will be a number of official engagements on board while we are in transit, which good manners dictate we will have to attend. Be on your guard at all times, though. The tau will give us a certain amount of leeway, I hope; after all, we are placing a lot of trust in them not to hold us hostage. Now, move out and act casual!'

We troop after him and the Colonel as they make their way along to the docking chamber. We stand there, Oriel in front, us lined up behind him, and wait for the ramp to lower. My first view of the tau is like nothing I've seen before.

The shuttle bay is flooded with light, and the air is dry and warm, much hotter than I'm used to aboard ship. As we walk down the ramp, I look around, trying hard not to stare. The chamber is like a large oval shape, the floors and ceilings melding with the walls in a continuous line. Everything is a cool pale yellow colour. There's no sign of any hard edges anywhere, no supporting beams, no criss-cross of girders and cranes for manoeuvring shuttles into position. The space is cavernous in its emptiness and I feel swallowed up by it and yet horribly exposed at the same time.

A small delegation waits for us at the bottom of the ramp. There's no guards, no guns in sight. They either really trust us, or they have some other way of dealing with us if we start to cause trouble. Three tau dressed in thin, pale robes stand patiently as we gaze around, studying us with interest.

I was right, they're basically humanoid. All three are at least a head shorter than me, and they have delicate, thin limbs. Their greyish-blue skin seems to glisten with some kind of oil, and as the middle one steps forward and bows to one knee in greeting, I catch a sweet scent. I look at his flat face and bald head, noting the yellow eyes and slit-like nose, noticing his lip-less mouth and rounded teeth. He stands and opens his arms in greeting, revealing a flap of skin that stretches from his waist to his upper arm, like deformed wings. I suppress a shudder. Nobody mentioned these... these things might be able to fly!

The one to the leader's right steps forward then, mouth curling in a poor imitation of a human smile.

'Welcome to this vessel, one of our newest, the *Sha'korar Aslo*,' he greets us, beckoning us down with a long-fingered hand. His voice blurs the words together slightly, his pronunciation tinted by a husky accent. 'We extend the hand of friendship to our human allies.'

Oriel replies in stilted gibberish, which I reckon to be some kind of formal greeting he's learned for the occasion. This seems to please the tau, who look at each other and nod.

'This is Kor'el'kais'savon, who you may simply address as captain or El'savon if you wish,' the interpreter continues, indicating the tau who had bowed earlier.

'I do not speak well your words,' the captain explains apologetically, bowing his head slightly but keeping his gaze on Oriel.

'This is Kor'vre'anuk,' the tau nods a head towards the third member of the delegation, who stands watching us impassively. 'I am Por'la'kunas, and will be your voice while on board the *Sha'korar Aslo*.'

'Please tell Captain El'savon that his hospitality does him credit,' Oriel replies with an officious manner. 'I and my advisors would appreciate some time to rest from our journey before conducting a tour of this fine vessel.'

Por'la'kunas says something to the captain in Tau, who replies with a single word and a glance at Oriel. All this gibbering in Tau is making me nervous. It doesn't seem like Oriel's command of the language is particularly great, and I haven't got a clue what they're saying. They could all be plotting against us, laughing right in our faces, for all I know. Just another factor of this mission that makes my spine crawl.

'Of course, we have rooms prepared for you,' the translator assures us. 'If you would follow me, please.'

Without a further word, he turns and begins to walk away from the shuttle. Looking ahead, I can see no sign of a door out, the wall continues unbroken all round us. When we're a few metres from the wall, a swirl of small lines appears, making a series of spirals which swiftly expand as a portal opens up in front of us, vanishing seemingly into the fabric of the wall. I glance over at Oriel, but he's maintaining an air of disinterest, gazing about him in a bored fashion.

The others shuffle about nervously, and I can understand their unease. The whole ship stinks of technology gone wild. I glance at the doorway as I walk through and see that the wall is in fact hollow and the segments of the iris-door have simply slipped between the two bulkheads. Still, it's not that reassuring.

The corridor outside is just as featureless as the docking bay, and as empty of people. As with the shuttle chamber, small curved corners seamlessly connect the walls with the floor and ceiling, the pale yellow surrounding us without any other decoration. Or source of light, for that matter. I haven't seen a single glow globe or lighting strip. The more I think about it, the more disconcerting I find the sensation. How can they create light in the air itself? It's not even as if the walls are glowing, it's like the air is charged with light. Just what kind of creatures are we dealing with here? How in the Emperor's name can we trust them on a mission like this?

With a start I realise I've almost broken into a parade ground stride whilst I was thinking about other things. I glance at the others, who walk along in silence, subdued by our strange surroundings. I suspect they're just as nervous as me, even Oriel and the Colonel. I focus my attention back on myself, shortening my step, pulling my head further back into the hood. The air is dry and warm as well, making my throat and nose tight.

I turn and look back, and the loading bay has disappeared, the door shutting silently behind us. I feel isolated and vulnerable, stuck on this alien ship with no weapons other than my bare hands.

We follow our interpreter along the corridor and I notice something else. Or rather, it's something I don't notice. The whole ship seems to be still: there's no vibration, no noise, nothing. The ship was most definitely moving when we docked, I saw that as we came in to land. Inside, though, we could be in an underground bunker somewhere.

Walking further along the corridor, my disorientation grows. There's not a single door to either side, though a few side corridors branch off along the way, melding seamlessly with the one we're walking along. Our guide has remained speechless since leaving the shuttle area, walking ahead of us with effortless steps. I take some time to look at him. He doesn't have the membranes under his arms that the captain has, and is even more slightly built. His robes are light and airy, wafting around him as he walks, like a breeze given shape. Like the rest of the ship, he is surrounded by an air of calm and stillness. Every movement is slight and efficient, he barely swings his arms as he walks, his face set straight ahead without a moment's distraction.

I try to work out what the ship is made from, but it's impossible. There's no welding that might indicate metal; the coloration seems to be part of the material itself, no brushstrokes or drips from paint. I wander along one wall and let my hand briefly brush along it, feeling a slight sensation of warmth from the wall itself.

I watch the others from within the folds of my hood, which is beginning to get uncomfortably hot. I have to resist the temptation to pull it back for some fresher air. That makes me realise that there are no air currents, no artificial winds from cooling vents and air purifier ducts. But the air doesn't taste stale, it's just hot and has no moisture to it. Oriel strolls along behind Por'la'kunas with a languid, rolling gait, the Colonel stepping beside him with a more stiff stride, his attention focussed on the tau in front. Quidlon keeps looking around him, staring intently at the walls and floor, probably trying to figure out how this all works. It could be witchcraft for all I know, like the accursed eldar technology. That gives me a sudden bout of anxiety. These tau are obviously decadent enough to blatantly use such strange technology – perhaps they put up with psykers as well? Maybe this guide is not what he seems, maybe he can read minds. This could all be some elaborate ruse to lull us into a false sense of security. I try to think like a scribe, just in case, but my thoughts soon begin to wander.

I wonder if they'll torture us for information, trying to find out the full extent of our plot. What will be their reaction when they find out we're collaborating with their own kind? Or perhaps they'll just kill us out of hand. I know nothing about these tau, nothing useful. I can't work out how they think, how they'll react, what their motivation really is. How predictable are they in combat? How disciplined?

All of these thoughts fill my brain as we carry on walking down this Emperor-forsaken corridor that seems to stretch on forever, unending and unbroken. If they get suspicious there's absolutely nothing we could do, nothing at all. We're in the middle of their ship with no weapons whatsoever. And Oriel said they would be wary. They're probably watching our every move even now, waiting for us to slip up, ready to pounce on any opportunity to unmask us and interrogate us for everything we know about the Emperor's domains and armies. For all I know, this could be some elaborate plot by them, manipulating Oriel so that he's brought us all here, some of the finest soldiers in the Imperial Guard, just so that they can get their hands on what we know.

I start to feel tense, and the pain behind my eyes returns. I begin to sweat even more heavily, glad my discomfort is concealed by the heavy robes. That's just the sort of nervousness that they'll be looking for. If I have another attack here, we're all dead. Perhaps the Colonel was right, perhaps I am too much of a liability.

My mouth gets even drier as the pain in my head increases. I think I can hear the others talking, slightly panicked themselves, but I pay them no heed, concentrating on my own private agony as my heart starts to beat faster.

It must be obvious by now. I feel as if I'm panting like a dog, clenching and unclenching my fists inside the folds of my sleeves. If the translator turns and looks at me now, he'll see something's wrong. He'll either guess we're up to no good, or he'll fetch medical help. Then they'll be able to separate us, get me on my own and go to work on me. Will it be torturers or mind-readers?

I blink heavily as I catch up with someone. Biting my tongue in panic, I glance up. It's the Colonel, who looks across at me, his face expressionless, except for a slight tightness to his cheeks which I know means he's either angry or slightly worried.

'Control yourself, Kage,' he whispers harshly at me. 'Try to relax. The tau expect us to be a bit tense and uneasy, but you look more guilty than a man with a smoking gun standing over a corpse. Remember to breathe in through your nose, it'll help calm you down.'

With that, he quickens his pace again to catch up with Oriel, who glances at him and receives a nod of reassurance in return. I wish I was as confident. I try to distract myself by looking at the others again, but that brings little comfort. Strelli, normally so cocky and confident, gnaws on the nail of his left thumb, darting glances at the interpreter every now and then. Tanya walks along with her head bowed, staring resolutely at her feet, not meeting anyone's gaze. Moerck is the most obvious, in my opinion. He just strides along, his disgust barely concealed as he scowls at the back of our guide. I see his fingers twitch spasmodically, like he's itching to get a hold of Por'la'kunas's neck and squeeze the life out of him.

Por'la'kunas takes us down a right turn, then a left, and then two more turns which I would swear took us around in circles but there's no way of telling. He then stops abruptly and faces the wall to the right. He reaches out his frail-looking hand and touches the wall and a moment later another of the strange portals opens up, revealing a room beyond where moments before there had been nothing. I look at the wall closely and see that there's actually some discoloration there, almost like runes or switches manufactured into the material of the wall itself.

'These are your quarters,' our interpreter says, indicating the room with his hand. At that moment, another tau steps from an unseen side corridor and walks up to us. He doesn't say a word, simply stands next to the door, back to the wall, his face set. This one is dressed in more workmanlike clothes, a tight-fitting blue bodysuit that is ribbed across the waist and joints, his hands and feet bare, the suit drawn tightly around his neck.

As he moves there appears to be no wrinkling or gathering, as if the material is stretching and contracting around him.

'If you require anything at all, please inform me at once,' Por'la'kunas tells us, stepping inside the room, and we follow him in. We are in what appears to be the main living space, a rounded square about ten metres across. A low circular cushion seems to be the only furniture, set into a hollow in the centre of the room and taking up most of the space. Thankfully the adjoining rooms are reached through curved arches rather than the odd disc-doors. There are ten of them: in eight I can see low, broad beds, without any kind of sheets or blankets, which is strange. From what I can see, the other two rooms appear to be washing areas of some kind, I can just make out a basin-like fixture through the arches.

'Some refreshments, if you please,' Oriel says, not looking at the interpreter but strolling through into one of the bedrooms.

'How do we contact you?' the Colonel asks, leaning forward towards the short alien.

'If you say my name, the ship will inform me,' he replies, taking a couple of quick paces back from the imposing figure of Schaeffer.

'The ship will inform you?' Quidlon says, obviously intrigued by this magic. Out of the corner of my eye I see Moerck make a protective gesture, the sign of the eagle, with his hands. It's the first time I've seen him do anything like that. I suspect it's not part of his commissariat training. I wonder if he's holding up that well. He's not mentally prepared for this kind of action. He's an officer and a leader. His place is in the midst of the bullets and las-bolts, shouting speeches, shooting deserters and leading the glorious charge.

'Yes, of course,' Por'la'kunas replies with a little surprise, totally oblivious to my thoughts on Moerck. 'I will be able to attend to your needs immediately.'

Quidlon looks as if he's going to ask something else but Schaeffer waves him away irritably.

'Is that a guard on our door?' the Colonel asks gruffly, pointing towards the corridor.

'We have found that humans sometimes become lost on our vessels and he is there to ensure that should you wish to leave the room you will have an appropriate escort,' the tau replies smoothly. 'You are, of course, our guests, not our prisoners.

While on the ship you may roam almost where you wish, We ask that you only enter certain areas with an escort as they may present a danger or disturb the crew in delicate duties. A full tour will be provided for you when you are rested.'

The Colonel just grunts and darts a look at me. I stand there dumb for a couple of seconds until I remember that I'm supposed to be the menial. I shuffle forward, trying not to walk with too much swagger.

'Bring food and drink, please,' I say, as politely as I can manage, the words almost catching in my dry throat. 'And, is there any way you can make it cooler in here, it's like a bl... like a desert.' I stop myself swearing just in time, and avoid the tau's gaze.

'Of course, forgive my inattention,' Por'la'kunas apologises. 'I shall endeavour to make the environment within your chambers closer to your normal climate.' The tau nods to the Colonel and leaves, the door swirling back into place behind him.

'Isn't this place amazing?' blurts out Quidlon as soon as the door is closed. 'Can you imagine what sorts of things these people are capable of, considering just what we've seen so far about their ship, about the way they conduct themselves. It's so fascinating.'

'They're not people, they're aliens, don't forget it,' Trost grumbles, lowering himself cautiously onto the cushion, as if expecting it to swallow him up.

'I could do with some freshening up,' says Strelli, wandering over to one of the rooms I'd identified earlier as an ablution chamber. He walks in and then comes out a moment later, scratching his head in confusion. 'There's no pipes, no taps, nothing. How does any of this stuff work?'

'It senses your presence,' Oriel says, appearing at the doorway to his room. 'I've made sure we can talk freely here in these rooms, but once we step outside the door, guard your tongues.'

'What makes you so sure?' Tanya asks. We all fall silent as the door opens soundlessly and our guide returns. Behind him hover five trays, bobbing along on their own as if they were alive. I hear an involuntary hiss escape Trost, who springs to his feet. The tau seems to be bemused at this reaction, and I realise we're all staring at the food with wide eyes.

'The food is not to your liking?' he asks innocently, what I take to be concern on his face.

We exchange incredulous looks, and it's Quidlon who recovers first.

'Ah no, the food will be fine, we were not expecting it to be delivered so, um, swiftly,' he says quickly, a brief smile flashing across his lips. 'If you would like to, um, leave the food with us we have some matters we wish to, um, discuss amongst ourselves, if that would not be impolite of us.'

'Of course, I understand,' the tau replies evenly with a bow of his head. 'Please take as long as you require.'

He bows again as he leaves, the trays floating across the room to hover about knee height over the communal cushion. Moerck leans over and peers underneath one of the floating trays, scowling like a cudbear with a sore head.

'How does it stay up?' he asks, straightening stiffly and looking at Oriel.

'I should have expected this,' he sighs, rubbing at his forehead and walking further into the room. 'The tau employ a great many of these things, which I believe are called drones. I've never seen one working before. It must be some kind of anti-gravity technology. You'll have to get used to them, apparently they're all over the place on the tau planets, running errands, taking messages and such. Think of them as odd looking servo-skulls, mindless but capable of following simple orders and performing basic tasks. Of course, these are merely constructs, they have never had a soul like a servo-skull. One reason the tau must halt their expansion into our space. Who could tell what mad, heretical notions might grip the populace if they heard of such abominations?'

A growl in my stomach reminds me that I've not eaten yet today and I walk over to the food and plonk myself down onto the cushion. The nearest servitor-plate appears to be carrying some kind of fruit, a garish yellow thing that smells sweet. I take a small bite and its juice runs down my chin. It's like honey, with a tang of something else I can't identify. The others stare at me, waiting to see if I keel over and go blue or something. I nod to them and point to the trays.

'Tastes pretty good, tuck in,' I tell them, picking up a star-shaped green thing and giving it a nibble. It's smoky, with a bitter aftertaste like hot caff or chocolate. There's some dishes of blue-coloured rice. The only utensils provided for eating are some spindly paddles which appear to be no use at all as far as

I can tell, so I use my fingers instead. The others settle down as well, and we compare the various foodstuffs, passing our own judgements on the fruits and vegetables on offer.

As I chew on a bread-like stick the size of my finger, a thought occurs to me.

'None of this is meat,' I say to the others and they agree after a moment's thought.

'The tau do not eat flesh apparently,' confirms Oriel. 'I don't know if it's a biological thing, or maybe religious. There's not much data on that aspect of their culture.'

'I think it's time you tell us some more,' Strelli says to Oriel. 'What other surprises are there?'

'Are you sure it is safe to talk here?' the Colonel asks, eyes narrowed as he looks around the room.

'Perfectly sure,' confirms the inquisitor leaning back on one elbow, his other hand clasping a shallow dish of grape-like juice. 'Alright, I'll give you a broad overview of what we've found out in the last couple of hundred years. For a start, the Tau race is lucky to be here at all. Extensive research into some of our oldest records has recently shown that several thousand years ago, we almost wiped them out. Luckily for them, warp storms prevented the colonisation fleet reaching their home world. In the last six thousand years they've grown into the civilisation we will be seeing shortly.'

He downs the rest of his drink and places the glass back on the nearest tray, which drifts off towards Tanya with its load.

'As you have already seen, they have no respect at all for the limitations of technology,' he continues, using a fingertip to wipe some food debris from his beard. 'As far as we know they are utterly heathen, with no kind of formal religion. The closest they have are the ethereals, their ruling class. The ethereals are in charge of everything supposedly, but it's the other castes who do all the work. The air caste, for example, are our hosts at the moment. They run the ships. Then there's the water caste, like our friend Por'la'kunas, who do all the diplomacy and bureaucracy. We'll being seeing more of them when we arrive on Me'lek.'

'Sorry, Me'lek?' I interrupt. 'What's a Me'lek?'

'Me'lek is the tau name for the Kobold system, where they have a colony on one of the worlds,' explains Oriel. 'That is where we are heading.'

'That's where this Brightsword fella is?' asks Strelli, stretched out on the far side of the cushion-seat.

'No, he is on Es'tau, one of their more recent outposts, where we will be going once arrangements have been made with our contacts,' Oriel answers slowly. 'It's a lot less developed, only a single city, if my information is correct. We are going to Me'lek first so that I can update my intelligence with the contact I have inside the water caste. Speaking of Commander Brightsword, he is a high-ranking member of the fire caste, who are the fighters of the Tau empire. You've seen what the battle domes are like, and now you've got some idea of the technology we're up against, so you can understand why we wish to avoid a widespread conflict with the tau if possible. In the main, the fire caste are still kept in check by the ethereals though, even if some like Brightsword and the renegade Farsight are straining at the leash.'

'I would guess the other caste is the earth caste, since you've talked about the fire, water and air castes. It seems their society is based around the elements,' says Quidlon, who's sat cross-legged listening attentively to everything Oriel has to say.

'Yes, the workers of the earth caste are the last ones,' confirms Oriel. 'They are the builders, the farmers, the engineers and the like.'

'Sounds like they get the rough end of the deal,' I say. 'I mean, the others get to be warriors and pilots and such, they do all the labouring.'

'The tau don't see it that way at all,' counters Oriel, leaning over and dragging one of the food trays closer, making its engines whine in protest for a moment before it complies and glides next to him. 'This notion of the greater good which they believe in binds them together. It teaches them from birth that everyone has their place, and that the survival of the Tau empire is more important than any individual.'

'That's not too different from the oaths we swore when we joined up,' comments Tanya.

'This is nothing like dedication to the Emperor,' Moerck argues angrily. 'Mankind would never survive without the Emperor to protect us, no matter how many sacrifices were made. These tau are heathen creatures, devoid of any spiritual guidance. They will fall prey to their own selfishness and base desires in time.'

'Yes, in time they may well do that,' agrees Oriel, plucking another starfruit from the tray. 'There are already indications that the further they expand and the more contact they have with other races, the more stretched this ideal of the greater good becomes. We need only look at what is happening with Brightsword and his kind.

'At the present they are expanding rapidly, dominating what-ever races they meet and incorporating them into their empire or expelling them. Yet, when they run into serious opposition, it remains to be seen how much sacrifice the castes are willing to make for the greater good. And we will do what we can to hasten that day. Until then, however, they are a highly moti-vated, united society which presents a significant problem in this area of the galaxy, and we should not underestimate them just because their society is spiritually and philosophically flawed.'

'So why are we helping them with their Brightsword prob-lem?' I ask, swilling down another mouthful of fruit juice to try and ease the dryness in my throat. 'Surely it would be better to wait for him to attack and then crush him. That would give them far more to think about, a real display of our strength that would make them think twice.'

'Do you not listen at all, Kage?' snaps the Colonel. 'We do not have any strength in the Sarcassa system to display. If Commander Brightsword is allowed to attack, he will be victo-rious if all things remain as they are. We will not be able to respond, and this will further bolster the tau's courage and resolve, believing us to be weak.'

'As the Colonel says, it is better to strike now and prevent a war than try to win it,' Oriel says sternly. 'Rest assured, by the time we have finished, the tau will be in no doubt the foe they face is equal to what they might throw at us. We will be teach-ing them a singular lesson in interplanetary manners, make no mistake.'

'Well, I wouldn't mind giving that jumped-up interpreter a slap, that's for sure,' laughs Strelli.'

'You will do nothing of the kind,' snarls Schaeffer angrily. 'We will do nothing to provoke the tau, or that might indicate we are anything other than what we appear to be.'

'I was only joking,' grumbles Strelli. 'Do you think I'm stu-pid?'

'Do you really want an answer to that?' I butt in before the Colonel can reply.

'Shut your damn mouth!' Strelli snaps back at me, clambering to his feet.

'Behave, all of you!' snarls the Colonel. 'I will not tolerate any kind of bickering or lack of discipline, no matter how unfamiliar and unsettling our surroundings. When we are in the battle dome, there will be no time for this kind of behaviour.'

Strelli shrugs expansively, darting a look at me and I give him a slight nod of apology.

'I think it is time we saw some more of this vessel,' announces Oriel, standing up and walking carefully across the soft floor. He looks around and then up at the ceiling before giving a shrug. 'Por'la'kunas? I would like to have a tour now, if you please.'

We all stand up and wait there, wondering if this is some kind of alien joke. However, a couple of minutes pass and then the door opens, revealing Por'la'kunas standing there. As soon as the tau enters, I can feel everyone stiffen slightly, on their guard again. I don't know why we're so nervous just because he's actually here – after all we only have Oriel's word for it that the tau haven't been listening in to everything we've being saying whilst in the room. Still, Oriel is an inquisitor and should know what he's talking about, and on top of that he does seem to have a naturally persuasive manner.

'I hope that everything was to your satisfaction,' the tau guide says, stepping lightly into the room.

'It was,' Oriel replies shortly, strolling out past the interpreter, who remains unflustered at this arrogant display.

We file out into the corridor after our guide, and I note that our guard is still standing there, I could swear he hasn't moved a muscle since we entered. Perhaps he hasn't. Perhaps he's a different one; they all look pretty much the same to me. Por'la'kunas leads us back to the main corridor we came along before and then through a door into a high-ceilinged chamber, which rather oddly has a set of steps in the middle leading up to nowhere. It all becomes clear though when a portal opens to our left and a long, silvery, bullet-shaped vehicle glides into view and stops next to the steps.

'If you would follow me on to the transport, please,' our guide says, walking slowly up the steps.

We follow him cautiously – there are no hand rails on the narrow steps – eyeing the vehicle with suspicion. At our approach, the vehicle changes, like it's sloughing its skin, revealing a door which opens upwards and over the transport. A row of large windows shifts into view as plates rearrange themselves underneath the vehicle, and a ramp silently extends down from the door to meet perfectly with the small landing at the top of the steps. Por'la'kunas bows and extends a hand to invite us to enter first and we troop in, looking at each other hesitantly and gazing around us like children.

The interior is a crisp white, like the outside of the ship itself. The seats are arranged down the middle, with an aisle either side, in rows of four. They look to be made of some kind of hard material, but as I sit down, the seat shifts underneath me and moulds to my backside. It's a rather unpleasant sensation, actually, making me want to squirm and fidget but I force myself to sit still and gaze out of the windows at the blank wall beyond.

When everyone's settled in – I note there's no kind of safety harnesses – Por'la'kunas stands up at the front of the carriage. I take a tight grip of the arm rests either side of the seat.

'The captain is pleased you wish to view his ship and has allowed me to take you wherever you wish,' he announces. 'Is there any part of the vessel in particular that you wish to view first?'

'Not really,' replies Oriel with a vacuous smile. His persona as the Imperial commander is so different from the intense, serious inquisitor, it makes me wonder if that isn't just an act as well. I doubt we'll ever know what he's really like or really thinking. 'If anything occurs to me, I'll be sure to let you know.'

'Very well,' Por'la'kunas replies unperturbed. 'In which case, we shall start with the power plant and move forward to conclude at the control bridge.'

The tau touches a panel on the wall behind him, revealing a screen. He touches his finger to one of the boxes on the screen and then turns back to us. Without any warning, and as silently as it arrived, the carriage begins to rapidly accelerate. My grip on the arm rests tightens more, and my stomach begins to shrink and tie itself in knots. We flash through an opening in the wall into a dark tunnel, although the inside of the transport remains lit, again with no sign of any light source that I can make out. It's only about half a minute before we emerge back into open space again, the vehicle smoothly decelerating to a halt next to another set of steps. I realise my fingernails are dug into the slightly soft covering of the chair, leaving crescent-shaped indents. The Colonel's right, I have to try and relax more.

We disembark on slightly wobbly legs, and stumble down the steps into a room that looks exactly like the one we boarded in. Por'la'kunas shows us through another hidden door, into a truly enormous chamber. It rises in a dome about forty, fifty metres above our heads. The centre of the chamber is dominated by a large structure which stretches from floor to ceiling, roughly cylindrical but with outcrops and radial spars that link it to the walls at regular intervals. I can see various panels cut into its otherwise unbroken surface, and as with the rest of the ship there's no evidence of welding joins, bolts, rivets or any other means of construction. For the first time since boarding, I can detect the slightest hint of noise. It's a deep humming that obviously emanates from the power plant in the middle of the room, making the floor vibrate just enough to feel. A group of half a dozen tau are gathered around the base of the engine, inspecting flickering green windows, which I assume to be display screens of some kind.

This is like no engine I've ever seen before. Where are the cables and pipes? There seem to be no moving parts at all, no pistons, no cams or gears, nothing to indicate the roaring energies this thing must have to produce to keep a ship this size functioning. The calmness of the ship is very unsettling, when you're used to the bangs, grinding noises, rattles and hums of an Imperial starship.

'Here is our primary power plant,' Por'la'kunas announces with just a hint of pride. 'There are two sub-stations on the lower levels in case of emergency or battle, but this plant provides enough power for normal usage.'

'Battle?' the Colonel asks, too quickly to be entirely casual.

'As your own Imperial Navy is no doubt aware, this area of space is plagued by roaming bands of pirates,' the translator replies smoothly. 'Of course, such considerations are not an issue within our own empire.'

I bet, I think bitterly. These tau think they're so clever, I'm going to enjoy knocking off one of their top leaders.

Oriel wanders closer and looks over the shoulder of one of the tau, who's dressed in a similar tight-fitting garment as our guard back at the living quarters, except his is dark grey. The tau bows his head and steps aside for us to crowd around the screen. Only, it isn't a screen as far as I can tell, it really is a window. I gaze into the green glow, my eyes adjusting to the brightness, and realise I'm looking into the heart of the reactor itself. It's full of something like a gas or fluid, with strange eddies and currents merging and breaking apart in a constant flow. It's quite entrancing actually, looking at the ever-shifting shapes coalesce and disappear. Bright, star-like points dip and weave in the energy currents, like tiny suns caught in a storm.

'What is it?' Quidlon asks in a hushed tone.

'We call it sho'aun'or'es, I am not sure there is a human word or phrase which would equate,' explains Por'la'kunas apologetically. 'I would hazard that it translates simply as "source of power" which I am afraid is not very helpful. The fio'vre would perhaps be able to explain better, but I am afraid that their expertise is not in languages.'

'The fio'vre?' asks Oriel suddenly interested, though whether genuinely or part of his act, I'm not sure.

'Ah, yes, I am sorry,' the interpreter apologises again with a bow of his head. He indicates the other tau with a sweep of his arm. 'The fio'vre attend to the smooth operation of the power plant.'

'Just the six of them?' Trost suddenly speaks up. 'What if something goes wrong?'

'I am afraid I do not understand,' Por'la'kunas replies, turning his attention to Trost. 'The monitoring is merely a sensible precaution. There have been no incidents concerning a power plant of this type for hundreds of years. It is quite safe and stable.'

Trost looks doubtful and turns to peer back through the viewing window. I can just imagine what he's thinking. He's wondering how much it would take to shatter one of those panes and unleash the raging energy contained within the reactor. It's the sort of thing he thinks about too much. I also suspect, from what I've seen of the tau so far, that it would take a direct hit from some pretty heavy weaponry to so much as chip that screen, never mind break it open. I wouldn't say the tau are afraid, but they are certainly cautious and in control at all times. That could prove a useful piece of knowledge later. Sometimes our rashness and emotion is what makes us strong. I don't know if the tau are genuinely passionless or if it's driven out of them and suppressed by their dedication to their ideal of a greater good, but either way it makes them more predictable.

We move back to the transport and the tour continues for another hour or so. Everywhere is pretty much the same – large chambers, mostly empty except for a few panels or viewscreens, very few of the tau around. We see more of the drones in other parts of the ship, flitting around on their various errands. It's all very strange, but a little underwhelming really. Everything is the same, there's little decoration or individuality. In a few places there are some symbols on the walls, which appear to be strange writing, but other than that there's nothing. No paintings, no patterns, it's all rather bland. It just makes the ship feel even more impersonal, and makes me feel even more like an unwanted visitor.

As I follow the others silently around, keeping to my role as the unimportant scribe, I start to realise just how different the tau are. They look a bit like us but they certainly don't think like us. They don't have any individuality as far as I can tell. They're so wrapped up in their greater good that they've pushed out any scope for individual achievement.

That's the big difference between their beliefs and ours. I've been to over a dozen worlds in the Imperium, and they've all been different in some way or another. We've changed and adapted to live on ice worlds, in the depths of jungles, on airless moons and on board space stations, yet everyone is still human in some deep down way. The tau on the other hand are just repeating themselves, trying to turn the galaxy into their vision. That's what will kill them off in the end, I reckon. Life will throw all sorts of different challenges your way, and sometimes you have to go around them, while I think the tau will just try to ride straight through it all, driven on by their stupid idea that the greater good will see them through.

We finally end up at the front end of the ship and enter the bridge. This is a bit more familiar, or at least more like I imagine a ship's bridge to be since I've never actually been on one. Like the rest of the ship, the room is a broad dome, though less high than the other chambers. An elliptical viewing screen dominates the front of the chamber, and arrayed around the floor in a circular pattern are various consoles and displays, each with a tau air caste member standing at them. Seeing this brings home something else as well. Through the engine room, the gun decks – very disappointing, identical sealed-in modules, not a sign of anything gun-looking in the slightest – the surveyor arrays and all the other places we've been, I don't recall seeing a normal seat anywhere. They all seem to stand up on the job, as it were. Even the captain, who's standing in the centre of the room watching everything carefully, is dressed in a similar outfit to the others. Obviously the robe he wore earlier was purely for the welcome ceremonial rather than his regular uniform.

He turns to us as we walk in and the iris-like door closes, and says something in Tau.

'El'savon welcomes you to the control centre of his vessel,' translates Por'la'kunas with a slight bow of the head. 'If you have any questions, please do not hesitate in directing them to me and I shall inquire on your behalf.'

WE WATCH AS a small opening appears in the floor and a drone drifts up into sight, the aperture closing behind it. It hovers over to the captain and warbles something in Tau before disappearing back the way it came. He turns to our interpreter and says something long-winded, looking occasionally at us as he does so. Por'la'kunas replies in length, also looking at us, and the captain nods in agreement.

'It appears you have arrived on the bridge at a fortuitous time,' he tells us with a slight nod. 'Shortly we will undergo the transition into vash'aun'an, which I believe you call "warp space".'

He directs our attention to the large screen, which pans across the stars before settling on a reddish blob. As the ship powers closer, the blob expands into a spiral pattern erratically expanding and contracting in on itself. It shifts colour too, and sometimes disappears from sight altogether. The captain explains something to Por'la'kunas.

'Ahead is the sho'kara,' the water caste tau informs us with due grandeur. 'Which you might called the lens or window, perhaps. We will pass through the sho'kara into warp space and ride the currents within.'

'You have to use these warp holes, or lenses or whatever, to enter the warp?' asks Oriel, feigning only slight interest.

'The fio have yet to find a successful method of creating an artificial sho'kara,' admits Por'la'kunas sheepishly. However, he rallies well. 'It will only be a matter of time before the problems they have so far encountered are resolved.'

'And when inside the warp, you navigate how?' Schaeffer asks.

'I am unsure of the details, I will confer with El'savon,' he answers slowly, obviously a little put out by this sudden line of questioning. I guess warp travel isn't one of the things they've mastered yet, not that anyone can really master it if you ask me. However, it's obvious from Por'la'kunas's reaction that he'd rather not discuss this shortcoming. After a long discussion with the captain, during which the interpreter does most of the talking, Por'la'kunas turns back to us. He pauses for a couple of seconds, obviously collecting his thoughts and working out what to say.

'The captain informs me that the ship navigates along an extensive network of pre-designated pathways,' he announces, not quite hiding his faltering confidence. He glances back at the captain once before continuing. 'El'savon says that powerful beacons allow him to travel between our planetary systems with great speed and accuracy. For instance, we shall be arriving at Me'lek, our destination, within six rot'aa. From what I know of your time partitioning, that will be approximately four of your human days.'

'And these beacons allow you to talk to the other worlds whilst travelling perhaps?' the Colonel presses on. 'I only ask so that Imperial Commander Oriel's arrival be properly announced and anticipated.'

Sly bastard, I think to myself. Por'la'kunas is in a really difficult position now. He either has to tell us whether they can communicate whilst in warp space, a handy piece of information to know, or risk offending his honoured guest by not answering. In the end, after another brief talk with El'savon, he opts to answer, though whether truthfully or not I can't tell.

'A kor'vesa-piloted vessel is used for communication between ships in transit and our worlds, and also for the sending of messages to the widespread outposts of our sizeable empire,' Por'la'kunas duly informs us, using the opportunity to try and scare us away by talking about the size of the Tau Empire. I remain unimpressed though. Given time and no distractions, I haven't got a doubt that, should the Emperor will it, we could snuff out this jumped up species. They're just lucky we have to deal with the tyranids. I suspect their empire would be swarming with Navy warships and Imperial Guard regiments otherwise. Enjoy your lives while they last, I think to myself, glad that in some small way I might be playing my part in their downfall. It also shows up how little they know about the Imperium if they think they can threaten us by talking about numbers. I bet there's more of us on a single hive world than they've got in their whole empire.

As I ponder this, I watch the warp hole growing larger on the screen and I have to admit it starts to worry me. The warp's an uncontrollable beast, which can tear ships apart or fling them off route to wander lost between the stars. The idea of diving in through this opening and drifting along the currents of the immaterium doesn't fill me with joy. I don't even like the idea of a ship with proper warp engines and navigators on board, and all this reliance on spiritless technology, in a place where souls can be given form, makes me shudder. The others are fidgeting a bit as well, attention fixed on the screen. I spare them only the briefest of glances as I concentrate on the whorl of power that's sucking us into the dimension of nightmares and Abyssal Chaos.

The small warp tempest swirls ever closer and closer, distorting the appearance of the stars behind it, twisting them and stretching them into swirls and lines of light. I feel like we're going faster and faster, being relentlessly sucked in, and a brief panic begins to grip me until I realise that we're just approaching at the same pace and it was all my mind playing tricks on me. I'm glad for the heavy cowl concealing my face as my nerves fray just a little bit more.

Another minute or so passes until the warp hole is filling the entire screen, and its outer edges disappear from view. The shifting colours are dizzying to watch as is the rhythmic pulsing that can now be made out at its centre.

I actually feel sick looking at it, the mesmerising effect of the sight combining with my nervousness to make my stomach lurch a couple of times. I'm glad when the screen goes blank for a moment, the nauseating view replaced by a schematic of obscure symbols and ever-changing Tau writing. An alien standing at a panel to our left calls something out and the captain nods once.

'We are entering the sho'kara now,' Por'la'kunas announces, totally at ease again now that we've stopped bugging him with questions.

I would have expected some hectic activity, messages being sent from different parts of the ship, officers bustling around busily. It's not like that at all. The tau stand at their posts in silence, monitoring their positions without a word being spoken. Everything is conducted in the same calm, ordered manner the tau seem to employ in everything they do. They've obviously done this many times before, and such is their faith in their machines, however misplaced that may be, they have no thoughts of failure.

Another tau speaks up next, and the captain says something to our guide, bowing his head in Oriel's direction.

'El'savon wishes to inform you that we have safely navigated the sho'kara and now that his duties are complete for the day he would be honoured for you to be guests at his dining table this evening,' Por'la'kunas translates for us.

Oriel nods to Schaeffer, who turns and looks at the captain.

'Please convey Imperial Commander Oriel's thanks for El'savon's gracious invitation, which he will of course accept,' the Colonel says, addressing the captain directly. Por'la'kunas repeats the fanciful acceptance speech in Tau and the captain nods again before turning and leaving through a side door.

'I shall escort you back to your quarters now, if that is acceptable to the Imperial commander,' Por'la'kunas says stiffly, keeping his gaze on Oriel. There's something going on here, some petty etiquette or diplomatic statement being made which I'm not aware of. Oriel just nods and starts to walk out, forcing Por'la'kunas to hurry forward to keep pace with him. The Colonel watches us all file past, and I hang back and fall into step beside him before I realise I'm almost marching alongside. I shorten my paces like I'd practised and hope nobody noticed.

'What was that about?' I ask the Colonel in a hushed voice, not turning my head towards him.

'Word games,' he says curtly, glancing across at me. 'The kind of banter that rulers and politicians seem to crave. Imperial

Commander Oriel has demonstrated that he too can talk through an intermediary.'

'So what does that mean?' I say, still keeping my voice low.

'It means nothing, except that our translator is more confused about his honoured guest than he was when we arrived on board,' the Colonel explains. 'There are rules governing how to behave in certain situations like this, and I suspect the tau take them very seriously. At least tau from the water caste like Por'la'kunas. Imperial Commander Oriel is trying to break a few of them to see what happens.'

Hearing the Colonel's rough pronunciation of the tau's name makes me smile, luckily concealed within my hood. It makes me wonder about all those scribes I've seen before, busily doing their jobs, probably secretly smirking at us and pulling faces all the time, unseen by everyone else.

'If everything goes to plan, this verbal fencing will be the only combat we will see before the mission starts,' the Colonel adds.

'I've never been on a mission when everything went to plan,' I reply, serious again.

'Neither have I,' Schaeffer admits ominously.

POR'LA'KUNAS LEAVES US saying that he will return when it is time for us to join the captain. Our kit has been transferred from the shuttle and we pick our rooms. I notice the rooms are cooler than they were before, verging on being cold now, rather than hot.

We sort out an order to use the ablution rooms, and while we scrub up in pairs the rest of us congregate on the floor-cushion again. I must admit, it takes some getting used to, but it is actually quite comfortable and forces us either to sit together or spend our time isolated in our rooms. It is also a great leveller, since no one can look too dignified slouching about on the floor, and as it's circular there's a kind of equality because nobody can sit higher or further towards the head of the table. Something tells me the tau don't need seating orders and bigger chairs to indicate who's in charge; they just know it.

'We have to be careful what we say while outside this room,' Oriel reminds us sternly, pulling off his boots and settling on to the cushion. 'The captain for sure speaks Low Gothic, and I

suspect more of the crew than Por'la'kunas says also understand us.'

'How can you know that?' Trost asks. The inquisitor is about
to reply when a shriek from Tanya in one of the washing rooms
makes us all jump. Moerck is on his feet and dashes to the
door, asking if everything is all right.

We gather behind him and peer into the room. At the far end
is a shallow bowl-like depression, filled with water that quickly
drains away through a small hole at its centre. Tanya is backed
up against the wall looking at the floor in horror, arms hugging
herself across her bare chest. Her legs are trembling and she
glances up at us with a start as we enter. Seeing her naked is
nothing new for any of us after the communal washrooms
aboard the *Laurels of Glory*.

'What's the matter?' demands Oriel, pushing to the front and
darting a look around the room.

'I'm sorry, it st-startled me,' Tanya replies, clearly put out, her
teeth chattering.

'What startled you?' the Colonel asks, peering suspiciously
around the room as well. We all look around too, backing
towards the door again. All I can see is the sink and the bare
walls.

'Watch,' she tells us, and steps gingerly into the depression,
shoulders hunched. Water begins to spray down from the ceiling, and I see that tiny holes have appeared where there weren't
any before.

'And it's cold!' she adds, prancing back out again, causing the
downpour to stop immediately. 'And there's nothing to dry
myself on, and the hole in the floor just opened up underneath
me. I just wasn't expecting it,' she finishes lamely, recovering
from the shock and now beginning to feel embarrassed.

Quidlon takes a couple of steps towards the showering area
and then quickly backtracks as a panel appears at waist height
in the wall next to him and slides out of view into the ceiling.
As he moves away, the panel reappears and then slots back into
place, leaving only the faintest of lines, so thin you wouldn't
see them if you didn't know they were there. He takes another
cautious step forward and the alcove reappears.

'Be careful,' Moerck warns him, stepping away from Quidlon.

'I hardly think there will be anything too dangerous in a
bathroom,' the Colonel says crossly. 'What is inside?'

Quidlon bends down and looks into the hole before laughing nervously.

'It's a garderobe,' he says, chuckling to himself, turning to us with a relieved expression on his face. 'Everything must be activated by proximity detectors. Just back yourself up against it and... Well, I don't have to explain the details, I guess. There might be some other things around here. Let's investigate.'

We look totally ridiculous for the next minute or so as we cautiously wander back and forth across the room, waving our hands at the walls and floor, seeing what else appears. If you look closely, you can see faint panel lines and the same kind of discoloration that activate the doors. Trost gets subjected to a blast of hot air from a hidden nozzle just to the right of the sink, next to the showering receptacle, while Oriel works out that the sink is activated just by putting your hands inside.

'Right, do you think we can leave Tanya to finish her ablutions without supervision?' Oriel says bitterly, drying his hands under the blower before herding us outside. 'If you're all going to react like this every time something odd happens, this is going to be a very irritating and short-lived mission.'

We exchange nervous glances as everyone drifts back to the communal seat. I never thought having a wash could be such a frightening and interesting experience, and I have a moment's trepidation when I think what other strangeness we might encounter on this trip.

The more I learn about the tau, the more I'm glad to be human. I never thought I'd ever appreciate the simplicity of taps and towels, but the episode with the shower room brings home to me just how lucky we are that the tech-priests keep control of the wild excesses of techno-magic.

'As I was saying before our little excursion,' Oriel says harshly, focussing our attention on him, 'we must not assume that the tau who are with us cannot understand what we are saying.'

'How can you be so sure it's safe to talk here?' Strelli asks, looking meaningfully around the open room.

'You'll just have to trust me on that,' Oriel answers with a tight-lipped, humourless smile. 'Now, it has become obvious to me that the tau are willing to share most of what they know with us. In fact, I haven't learnt anything so far that I did not know before from other sources. Also, they are still slightly suspicious of our motives, especially Por'la'kunas. At this formal engagement with the captain, we must be a bit more free and easy, it's all been far too tense and official so far. Have a drink, enjoy the food, but don't let your tongues wag too much. Ask any questions you wish, and if you're asked anything that won't directly show up our real plans then answer them honestly.'

At that moment, Tanya exits the bathroom and gives me a nod, since I'm up next. I miss the next part of the conversation as I hurriedly duck under the chill waterfall. I look around for soap, but realise there's actually some kind of cleanser in the water itself. Shivering, I step out in front of the dryer mechanism, which blasts me from head to toe with warm air, a matter of a few seconds. I pad through to my bedroom and pull a clean robe from my chest, tossing the dirty one haphazardly over the bed. I feel slightly more refreshed for a little while, but by the time I return to the others, the constant heat of my thick garments has sweat prickling all over my body again, making the heavy robe chafe painfully in places.

'We may not actually be a genuine diplomatic mission,' Oriel is saying, 'but that doesn't mean we can't cause a serious mess if we do things wrong. That said, the tau already look down on us, so they'll forgive most of our indiscretions, and the more they believe we're a stupid and short-sighted race, the more they'll underestimate us in the future, so don't hide your ignorance under a bushel.'

'Shouldn't be too difficult for you, Demolition Man,' Strelli jokes, without thinking what he's saying. I cringe, because I know what's going to happen next.

'What did you call him?' snaps Oriel, jumping to his feet and glaring at Strelli.

'I, ah, it's his name,' Strelli replies lamely, looking over at me. I glance horrified at the Colonel.

'It is part of Lieutenant Kage's training regime,' Schaeffer explains to Oriel. 'One which I fully authorised.'

'So you've all got jolly nicknames?' Oriel's voice drips with scorn. 'Emperor protect us! A slip like that in front of the tau will raise all kinds of questions. What did you think you were doing?'

'I was training soldiers for a military mission,' I butt in quickly, my anger rising. 'You wanted trained soldiers, and that's what I've given you. You want spies to be sneaking around pretending to be people they aren't, you can sort it out yourself.'

'Did it not occur to you that a degree of subterfuge would be involved?' Oriel replies testily. 'Or did you not think at all?'

'If I'd been told you wanted a bunch of brain-dead nobility for the mission, I might have done things different,' I snarl back, rising to my feet, my hands balling into fists by my side. 'What you've got is a squad of the best-trained soldiers the Imperial Guard can provide, and when we get down to the meat of this mission, you'll be thanking me you have, because these mind-games aren't what we're here for.'

Oriel stares at me angrily, gritting his teeth.

I knew it wouldn't be long before he showed his true colours. That he's out to get me one way or another. I match his venomous stare, daring him to carry on. He takes a deep breath and looks around at the others, visibly calming down.

'Thank you, Kage,' he says finally. 'We are all on edge here, understandably so, so your aggression will be overlooked this time. It was also an oversight on my part, I realise now. I should have briefed Colonel Schaeffer more fully. You are right, we must not lose sight of our true mission here. Your focus on the military aspects is commendable. Now, if you would like to tell your men that the next one who so much as thinks about using one of your names will be shot by me.'

He stalks from the room, leaving us looking at each other.

'What other "oversights" has he made?' Trost growls, scratching his stubbled chin and looking at the Colonel.

'Keep your opinion to yourself, Trost,' Schaeffer tells him coldly, walking off into his own room.

'Did you mean that?' asks Tanya when the Colonel's disappeared. 'About us being the best the Imperial Guard can provide.'

I look at her and the others, who are watching me like hawks.

'Yes I did,' I tell them, pulling up the hood of my robe and walking out.

AFTER ORIEL'S WARNING, we're all a bit jittery at the captain's dinner. We were escorted here by Por'la'kunas as usual, and brought into a wide, oval room not far from the bridge. Well, I think we're not far from the bridge, I still haven't got myself fully orientated, but I think I've managed to work out which way is the prow and which way is aft. The ceiling is quite low and flat, compared to the high, dome-like structures of the other rooms. The main chamber is the dining area. To one side are rows of shelves, the first I've seen, being laden down with food by a small army of drones that glide back and forth through a hatchway in the opposite wall. I watch in horror as one floats up to the shelf, a tray on its upper surface. The tray then rises up, a flickering blue mist around it, and is deposited on the shelf. How can food be surrounded by something like that and not be contaminated? Emperor knows what pollutants could be leaking out of those drones! And these tau expect us to eat this stuff after they've been messing with it? Not only that, they could have put Emperor-knows-what in there. Narcs to drug us to get us to tell the truth, perhaps? Then I remember the Colonel's words and calm myself down a little. If the tau wanted to do anything like that, there's nothing we could do to prevent them.

At the centre of the room is a large round table surrounded by backless stools, which seem to be moulded up from the floor itself. As I look closely at the floor, I see a slight patterning there. It's very subtle indeed, almost unnoticeable, but actually in the spread of white are different hues of green and blue.

Por'la'kunas notices my gaze and detaches himself from the Colonel and Oriel and walks over.

'Is it not beautiful?' he says, looking across the floor himself. I squirm uncomfortably inside my heavy robes, not happy that I have his undivided attention for the first time.

'But you can hardly see it,' I say, shifting my weight slightly so that I'm further away from the alien.

'It is a particularly celebrated school of art within our empire,' the guide explains. 'It demands that one pay attention to it and examine it carefully. It aids contemplation and is calming to the nerves.'

It's not calming my bloody nerves, I think to myself, darting a pleading glance behind Por'la'kunas's back at Oriel and the Colonel. The inquisitor gives a brief frown before calling the interpreter's name. The tau gives me a slight bow and then heads back to talk to the pair of them. I breathe a sigh of relief and smile my thanks to them.

'I don't trust that creepy bastard one bit,' Trost whispers to me, standing with his back turned slightly towards me, keeping his eye on the tau.

'Me neither,' I agree. 'Don't start anything, just keep your mouth shut and your ears open.'

'Nothing in the Emperor's galaxy could get me to talk to these freaks willingly,' he tells me with feeling.

A chime sounds from nowhere, startling everyone except Por'la'kunas. The door cycles open, and El'savon, the captain, appears with four other tau. They are dressed in similar flowing garments to the ones they wore at the welcoming ceremony. Por'la'kunas makes the introduction – more bizarre, unpronounceable names – and we all sit down at the table, in no particular order.

Por'la'kunas translates a few pleasantries from the captain, who informs us the journey through the warp is progressing to schedule, and that a drone-controlled pod has been despatched to Me'lek to ensure our arrival is anticipated. He asks if the conditions of our quarters are satisfactory, and so on. As he speaks, one of the other tau gets up and strolls over to the food, and begins filling up an oval plate with various fruits. We all give him a surly look.

'Is something amiss?' Por'la'kunas asks, noticing our displeasure.

'We were expecting something a little more, well, formal,' Tanya says, remembering that she's supposed to be the chatelaine of the group. 'The Imperial commander is not used to inferiors dining before him.'

The interpreter looks at us blankly for a moment, and El'savon speaks in Tau to him. An alien conversation ensues, and they talk right over us, almost forgetting we're here in the room with them. They all give a start when the Colonel pointedly clears his throat.

'Would you mind explaining what you are talking about?' he asks, no hint of aggression in his voice.

'My apologies,' the interpreter says, apparently sincere, turning his attention back to Oriel. 'No disrespect was intended. We are all equal in our labours for the greater good. Such enforcement of hierarchy is unnecessary within our society. We were just discussing how to resolve this situation. As I'm sure you understand, this is El'savon's vessel and therefore he has greatest authority amongst us, yet you are a planetary ruler and so may see yourself as his superior. We are unsure how to proceed. Perhaps you could advise us?'

Oriel seems momentarily taken aback by the tau's candour, but rallies quickly.

'Well, when on Terra, do as the Terrans do, as we say,' he says casually, waving a hand towards the shelf. The gathered tau look at Por'la'kunas and he translates. They look quizzically at each other and then at Oriel.

'We shall follow your example,' Tanya explains after a surreptitious gesture from the Colonel. 'For, we are as united and equal in our dedication to the great Emperor of the Galaxy as you are to your cause.'

Nicely done, I think to myself, catching her eye and giving her a wink. Let's not allow them to forget who they're dealing with here. Por'la'kunas has been a condescending little scumbag since we arrived, it's about time these upstarts were put in their place. I suppress the urge to remind them that they're only around now because a warp storm stopped us wiping them out in their racial infancy. Anyway, the reply seems to satisfy everyone. Oriel smiles at Tanya; the tau nod approvingly. I feel someone kick me under the table, and glance to my right to see Strelli looking at me.

'I believe it would be a fitting gesture for our scribe, as the lowest and most humble Imperial servant present, to demonstrate our willingness to embrace this wonderfully liberal ideal,' he says smoothly. All eyes turn to me when Por'la'kunas translates, and I stand up, my flesh prickling under their scrutiny.

'You're dead,' I silently mouth to Strelli from the confines of my hood, darting him a murderous glance as I walk past him. The tau standing by the shelves gives me a pleasant nod. I hesitantly take a plate he proffers towards me, and walk up and down the shelves, looking at the trays of food. There's forty dishes on the four shelves, and I glance at the tau's plate to see what he's taken, trying to identify the same foodstuffs on the loaded platters in front of me. They come from different shelves, all over the place, so I guess there's no formal order to what should be eaten when, as far as I can tell anyway.

I load up my plate, grabbing different fruits and vegetables at random, a couple from each shelf, spooning various hot sauces over the top. There's what sounds like amused muttering from behind me and I turn around. The tau are looking at me, slightly incredulous expressions on their faces. Por'la'kunas says something sternly to them, and they avert their gazes, before saying something at length to the tau standing next to me. He gently, but firmly, takes my plate from me and says something in Tau. A drone glides into the room through the hatchway and extends its green mists, plucking the plate from the tau's hands before drifting off again. The tau says something to me, and then points towards the shelves, and his plate, indicating each food in turn. It's only when he does this that it becomes clear he has taken from every eighth dish. With this in mind, I realise one of the things that's been nagging at me all day, and it's hammered home when the tau passes me a fresh plate. They only have one thumb and three fingers on each hand. Of course they would count in eights, and it makes some sense. If you're a fragged up alien that is.

I look at the food for a short while before grabbing a couple of the starfruit I had earlier, since I know they're quite tasty. I then count eight along. I look at the tau and he nods approvingly, moving away from me back to the table. I spoon a small pile of dark blue grains onto my plate, then count along again, arriving at a deep bowl with a brown gravy-like substance in it. I ladle some over my food, wondering why I'm putting gravy on fruit, and then get to the final plate. This is more familiar, it looks like bread, although there are striations of different colours – greens and greys – running through the loaf.

There's a small device next to the plate and I pick it up. Somebody appears next to me, and another tau is there, along with the Colonel. I ignore him and examine the device, seeing a small stud, which I press. A blade extends outwards, thankfully away from me, I could have slit my wrist by accident. It begins to shimmer. In fact, judging by the feel of it, it's vibrating rapidly. I use the knife to slice some bread for myself, and then press the stud again, turning the vibro-knife off. My hands are shaking and I hurry back to the table.

I sit down and then realise that I can't eat this with my fingers, not with gravy all over it. I look at the tau who started before me and see he's got some of the paddle-like utensils we found in our quarters. He has a pair in each hand, deftly using them to slice up the food, using one pair to hold it in place and the other to cut, before spooning the food into his lipless mouth. I look around for the utensils and Tanya catches my eye. She reaches under the table, pulls some out and waves them at me with a patronising smile. I look down, and see that there are small drawers in the outside of the table, with finger holes for handles. The tau have slender hands and only my little finger fits in the hole.

I pull the drawer out and find eight of the eating paddles, along with a silky, napkin-like cloth and a covered bowl of white crystals. I tentatively dab a finger into the bowl, using the long sleeves of my robe to conceal the action, and then cautiously taste it. I'm surprised to find it's just salt. Good old, familiar salt. I take some in my fingers and sprinkle it on my dish, before sorting myself out with the utensils.

It all takes some getting used to, and we spill quite a lot of the food on the table. Strelli almost takes Trost's eye out when he accidentally catapults a hot round piece of potato-like vegetable across the table, causing Tanya to stifle a laugh and the Colonel to scowl at him. Every now and then a drone buzzes in, extends its mist-field and clears up.

The tau don't seem to mind our amateurish attempts, one or two of them circling round the table, giving us some help with the positioning of our less articulate fingers. One of them says something and the others give little nods and make a tittering noise which I guess is laughter. Oriel raises an inquisitive eyebrow and asks what is funny, affecting a slightly offended tone.

'A joke, Imperial commander, which intended no insult,' Por'la'kunas responds good-naturedly.

'Perhaps you'd care to share it with us?' Strelli asks, sitting back and forgetting there's no chair back, so he has to lean forward hurriedly to stop himself falling off his stool. I give him a sneer which no one else can see thanks to my hood. Once again, I wonder just what all those adepts we see around the place are really up to when we're not looking at them.

'The Emperor loves you so much, he has gifted you with extra fingers,' the interpreter explains, nodding in amusement. He stops and looks slightly put out by our blank reaction. 'In the Tau tongue, it is quite a humorous play on words,' he assures us. 'Perhaps it does not translate very well.'

Por'la'kunas barely has time to eat, as the conversation begins again, with Quidlon plying the various tau with questions about their technology, the drones in particular, although the answers seem to baffle him even more. Moerck and Trost are steadfastly silent, only picking at their food and trying to ignore the tau as much as possible. Tanya asks about the various foodstuffs, and like Quidlon gets more and more confused by the explanations given to her.

Another drone swooshes gracefully through the hatch after about fifteen minutes or so, carrying a tray of drinks in long, slender goblets of pale blue ceramic. Por'la'kunas explains that it's a fine tau drink. Like wine, I suppose. We all take a glass, and Oriel stands up and raises his.

'I wish to toast El'savon,' he declares, looking at the captain. Both he and Por'la'kunas look shocked.

'You wish to do *what*, Imperial commander?' Por'la'kunas asks quickly.

'I propose a toast,' he repeats, turning his attention to the translator.

'You wish to immolate El'savon?' Por'la'kunas asks, horrified.

'I… What?' Oriel answers, glancing around the table, realising the misunderstanding. 'No, no! A toast is, ah, an act of appreciation.' He looks at the rest of us for support and we all stand and raise our glasses too. The tau chatter to each other for a second before copying us.

'To El'savon, may he live a long and healthy life,' declares Oriel, and we repeat it, drinking from our glasses. The wine isn't really wine at all, it tastes almost salty rather than fruity, and is a bit sour. I take only the smallest of sips and put the goblet down again. Por'la'kunas translates and the tau mimic us in their own language, taking deep draughts of the drink. El'savon speaks up, and the process is then repeated in reverse, with El'savon toasting Imperial Commander Oriel, and I'm forced to drink some more of the tau alcohol.

With no formal courses to follow, the meal drags on for what seems like hours and hours. Both sides are wary of making too many more social mistakes, and the conversation dies away to the odd question about the food, and polite inquiries regarding our destination, Me'lek. It seems the world is fairly well established, although not as old as much of the Tau Empire. Oriel deftly avoids some questions about his reasons for visiting and we finish eating in silence. Finally, after a short lifetime of worry and discomfort, El'savon bids us goodnight and the tau leave, except for Por'la'kunas who shows us back to our quarters.

Nobody says a word as we go to our beds, all too tired and wrapped up in our own perturbed thoughts for conversation.

* * *

WE PRETTY MUCH keep a low profile after that as the ship ploughs through the warp towards Me'lek. Back in the warp, my nightmares return, my nights filled with the living dead from my past. Combined with being constantly on my guard around the tau, the sleeplessness leaves me exhausted and feeling ancient. The others are just as ragged, and several times, there's close calls, when one or other of us almost trip up and blow our cover stories.

Oriel is withdrawn, the Colonel his usual uncommunicative self, so that leaves me to deal with the other Last Chancers. I gather them all together to go over the plan again, mentally praying to the Emperor that Oriel was right in saying we could talk freely inside our own chambers. If not, the tau will know exactly what we're up to. And perhaps that's their plan. To lull us into a false sense of security so that we'll open up and tell them everything they need to know.

But I can't just leave the Last Chancers alone, I have to get them doing something, and focussing them back on the mission seems like the perfect distraction from our unsettling surroundings.

The one sticking point is Tanya. When we reach the stage when it's time for her to make the shot she says the words, but there's no conviction in her eyes, no belief. I corner her the next morning as she wakes up.

'You realise this is all for nothing if you don't pull the trigger?' I quietly say to her, blocking her into the room by standing in the doorway.

'It's not that difficult a shot. You could make it, so could Hero,' she replies, not meeting my gaze.

'Possibly, but you're Sharpshooter, you make the shot,' I tell her, taking a step forward.

'I know, Last Chance,' she sighs, sitting back on the bed.

'You'll have to do better than that!' I snap at her, advancing across the room.

'What do you want me to say?' she replies hotly. 'That I don't want to take that shot, that I can't kill another person?'

'I'm not talking about a person, I'm talking about the target,' I snap back. 'It's just an alien, like an ork or an eldar or a hrud. It's not like I'm even asking you to kill a real person.'

'I don't think the tau will see it that way,' she counters, gazing at the floor.

'What's this crap?' I hiss, my voice dropping low. 'Feeling sorry for aliens? You disgust me, Tanya. How can you sit there and compare one of these stinking tau to a person, how can you pretend they're more important to you than me, or the Colonel, or your squad mates?'

She looks up at me then, brow knotted in confusion.

'I never said that,' she protests.

'It's what you were thinking, even if you didn't realise it,' I continue harshly, not letting up for a second. 'If you don't make that shot, this Brightsword scumbag is going to invade Sarcassa and butcher thousands of humans. They'll die because you think some damned alien has got more right to be alive than they have.'

'I don't think that at all!' she stands up, pushing me away. 'I don't want this mission! Why does it have to be me? Why do they have to rely on me?'

'Because you swore an oath to protect the Emperor and his domains,' I reply quietly, trying to calm things down. 'Look at it another way – why didn't you just turn down the Colonel back at the prison, and take a bolt to the head? You must have known you would be asked to kill someone.'

'I didn't think about it,' she says, shaking her head. I just didn't want to die.'

'So you're just a selfish bitch, is that it?' I'm getting angry again, I can feel my blood heating up inside me. I jab a finger into her chest. 'As long as you're still alive, all those innocent people on Sarcassa can just go to hell, murdered at the hands of the creature you refuse to kill?'

'I don't want that to happen!' she snaps back, slapping my hand away and giving me a shove. 'Get out of my face, Last Chance.'

'Not until you promise me you'll make that shot, not until you've thought long and hard about what it means if you don't pull the trigger,' I reply, stepping back in front of her again, glaring down at her.

'Yeah, well maybe it'll be you in the crosshairs straight after Brightsword,' she threatens me.

'If that's the way it's gotta be, I'm happy,' I admit, taking a pace back and giving her some room. 'If you want to see me in the crosshairs when you pull that trigger, that's just fine by me. Do whatever you like, as long as you nail that bastard dead.'

I look at her then, and she glares back at me, hatred in her eyes. Good. She'll make that shot, I'm pretty sure.

OUR RECEPTION ON Me'lek is more grandiose than the one on the ship. As the ramp touches down on the landing concourse, some kind of band strikes up, mostly composed of different drums, with a few tootling pipes thrown in seemingly just to add to the discordant noise. It's totally unlike the well-paced, rhythmic hymns and marches I'm used to, and starts to grate on my ears after just a couple of seconds. Two lines of large walking machines flank the route towards the space port building in front of us, which rears from the ground like a stylised mushroom, a broad dome atop a spindly-looking tower.

The machines are about three and a half, maybe four metres tall, and broadly humanoid in shape. Judging by their shape, and assuming they actually have pilots, I'd say the driver sits in the main body, the flat, many-lensed head atop the broad form just some kind of remote link. The arms are stocky and heavy-set, and armoured plates cover the shoulders and thighs. The lower legs are actually made of open struts, though everything else is encased in heavy-looking, gently faceted armour. Each machine also has an extended back pack from which protrude rows of nozzles, possibly some kind of jet device. They're obviously war machines of some sort; the devices mounted on their arms are unmistakably weapons of different designs. Several of the battle suits also have weapons mounted on one shoulder, long-barrelled guns and rocket pods in the same efficient clutterless design of all the tau machines I've seen so far. Several of them have drones hovering around them, which flicker with some kind of energy field.

Both the battle suits and drones are coloured in a jagged camouflage pattern of grey and orange, with Tau lettering and symbols written across them in various places. Possibly squad markings, maybe the pilot's name.

As one, accompanied by a whine of servo-motors, the twenty machines raise their right arms in a salute, forming an incomplete arch for us to walk through. If these are what the tau use to fight, I can suddenly understand why we need to stop them invading Sarcassa. They look unstoppable to me, walking tanks rather than heavy armour, from what I can tell. Almost like the massive Space Marine dreadnoughts that I heard about on

Ichar IV. I glance over at Oriel, who's standing just to my right, taking it all in.

'If we do this right, we won't have to fight against battle suits,' he whispers, giving me a meaningful look which says if we do this wrong, that's exactly what we'll be facing.

Oriel starts off down the ramp and we follow a respectful distance behind, masquerading as the dutiful entourage. As we walk down the aisle of battle suits, I'm even more intimidated by them up close. They tower over us, hulking things that could probably pound us to bloody pulps with their artificial muscles and impressive-looking weaponry. Each lowers its arm behind us as we pass, making me feel even more hemmed in and panicky.

At the end of the row is a small cluster of tau dignitaries, dressed in ceremonial robes similar to those worn by the captain and Por'la'kunas when we arrived on the tau ship. Behind them are ranked up another few dozen warriors, not in battle suits, but still well armed and armoured. Their uniforms are made from a light, billowing material, over which they've got plated carapace armour on their chest and thighs, and thick shoulder guards protecting their upper arms. All of them are wearing helmets, fully enclosed with a small cluster of different sized lenses instead of a proper visor. They too sport the grey and orange camo scheme, except for their helmeted heads which are different shades of blue, yellow and red, possibly to identify individual squads.

If this is supposed to be a show of strength, it's working on me. I certainly wouldn't want to face this lot. They're armed with long rifles, about two-thirds my height. I suspect those guns have got enough punch to put a hole in the back of a battle tank. I mentally kick myself then. I will be facing this lot, I tell myself, not long from now. Well, not this bunch exactly, but others like them. I pull myself together, telling myself that healthy respect for the enemy is one thing, but actually they're not so scary as say an ork or a tyranid. I'm almost convinced by my own arguments. Almost.

The band stops its banging and screeching and the tau in the centre of the group steps forward, bowing politely to Oriel, before addressing us all.

'Welcome, one and all, to the tau world of Me'lek,' he begins, his speech almost perfect, with no trace of the slurring and accent that Por'la'kunas had. 'I am called Por'o-Bork'an-Aloh-Sha'is. You may address me as Liaison Ambassador Coldwind if you so wish, or simply as ambassador; I will take no offence.'

His tone is pleasant and his eyes active, looking at each of us briefly as he speaks, making sure he has eye contact with us. There's a voice in my head that tells me he's our contact. I don't know how I can tell, perhaps just something about the way he looks at us, but I'm sure of it. He introduces the others, representatives from the water and earth castes whose names are just a jumble of meaningless sounds to me.

'May I add that it is an honour and a pleasure for me to welcome you to Me'lek,' he concludes. 'You are the first official visitors from His Holiness, the Emperor of Mankind to visit us, and I wish your stay to be pleasant and constructive.'

Once more, Oriel gives a stuttering speech in Tau, probably to say how happy we are to be here and all that, while I direct my gaze around the space port. The other buildings are a series of low, flat-topped domes linked by covered walkways along the ground and a few metres in the air. Most of the buildings are white, and like the ship everything is almost painfully bright. Also, the air is dry and the sun is warm on my back, which is pretty much how the tau like it, judging by conditions on the alien ship. When the formalities are over, Ambassador Coldwind tells us that he has a vehicle waiting to take us to our temporary quarters.

He leads us through the space port terminal, a white-walled building with high arches linking the domed chambers. It's here that we start to see just how many drones the tau have. They buzz about everywhere, some of them carrying boxes and bags, others without any visible purpose, although Coldwind informs us that many of them are messengers. For a busy space port, there seem to be relatively few of the actual tau themselves: there's the odd fire caste warrior, dressed like the others outside, standing at some of the doorways, stubby carbines in their hands. One or two of the robed water caste pass us by, giving respectful bows to Coldwind and Oriel as they walk past. Through a distant archway I catch a glimpse of a group of air caste, or so I assume since they seem to be wearing the same tight-fitting outfits the ships crew wore.

As we pass through a massive sliding glass door at the front of the terminal, we get to see the city proper. The space port is located on a hill overlooking the rest of the settlement, and the clear day allows us to see for many kilometres in every direction. Broad boulevards radiate out from the space port in every direction, lined by high-sided buildings of every shape you could imagine. Some are domes, others needle-like towers, while many have flat facades facing the streets which curve gently into spherical shapes or pyramids with rounded edges.

Most of the buildings are white, with the odd pale grey, yellow or blue mixed in at fairly regular intervals. It all gives the sense that everything has been put in its place quite deliberately. Numerous walkways and elevated roads criss-cross between the buildings, giving the city a busy appearance, although there's a feeling of space and calm I've never experienced in any Imperial town. The air above is a pale blue, with just a scattering of fluffy clouds drifting past, the Me'lek star a large, bright orb just below its zenith. Coldwind has the presence of mind to allow us to stand there for a few minutes, looking at the vista.

It then comes home to me. If we were hung out on a limb on the tau ship, we're right up to our necks in the sump water now. This is a fraggin' tau planet, for Emperor's sake! There's just a small group of us, and there's a massive army here. I suspect that even the detachment paraded at our reception would be enough to wipe us out several times over. If we thought we had to be careful aboard the ship, we're gonna have to be perfectly behaved here. The more it goes on, the less and less I like this whole mission. This sneaking around just reminds me of those spine-chilling moments in Coritanorum when we were almost caught. And of course, those innocent people we had to kill simply because there was a danger of them giving our position away.

Then again, that won't be a problem here, these are only aliens after all. The galaxy certainly won't miss them, and I'll miss them even less.

'They like to spread out a bit, don't they?' comments Strelli, shielding his eyes against the glare.

'Don't you find it all a bit soulless?' I ask the others, keeping my voice low enough for Coldwind not to hear.

'I don't get you,' says Tanya, turning towards me.

'It's all the same, wherever you look,' I complain, waving a hand to encompass the whole city. 'It hasn't grown, or changed, or anything. It's probably exactly how they intend it to look. There's nothing personal here, no distinctions between the different districts.'

'And I suppose you're used to that are you?' butts in Trost. 'You're just hive scum, what do you know about building cities?'

'At least in the hive you could tell where you were,' I answer him with a smile, remembering the dank, claustrophobic corridors and tunnels of my youth. 'Everywhere had a different light, a different smell. You could tell which of the levels were older, which of the habzones belonged to which of the clans. There was graffiti and totems to mark territory, and gang symbols painted on the floors and walls. It had a life to it. This place is dead.'

'I understand what you mean,' Moerck agrees with me, much to my surprise. 'I don't think the tau have any sense of history, or tradition. They seem so concerned with the greater good and building the empire, they ignore their past.'

'Perhaps they have reasons to forget,' Tanya muses, looking back over the city. 'Perhaps this is all a new beginning for them.'

Oriel coughs to attract our attention and with a nod of his head directs us towards a wide, shallow ramp leading down from the plaza where we're standing. We follow him and Coldwind down towards the street, where our vehicle is waiting for us. It's similar to the transport on the ship, in that it hovers above the ground, although only about half a metre up. It's made from the same silvery material, but is a lot less broad. Its blunt nose is rounded at the corners, the front curving up and blending seamlessly with a transparent windshield which extends another metre above the seating inside. The back end is open to the elements, a roughly oval cavity lined at the edges with padded seating, which we duly haul ourselves into when a section of the side drops to the ground to form a ramp.

Once we're settled, Coldwind seats himself as well, near the front, and then says something out loud in Tau. The vehicle rises up another half a metre and slowly accelerates. I glance towards the front, but can't see any driver. Quidlon asks the obvious question. You can always trust him to do that.

'Erm, excuse me ambassador, but how is the vehicle steered, I mean who is controlling it?' he says hesitantly, torn between looking at Coldwind and gaping at the buildings we go past.

'Thank you for asking that,' Coldwind replies with a slight nod, which I'm beginning to realise is actually not so much a sign of respect but one of pleasure, like a smile. 'This ground car, as you might call it, has a small artificial brain inside, much like the drones you have seen. It is not really sentient as such, but does know the layout of Me'lek City and can respond to simple verbal commands.'

'You just have to tell it where to go, and it takes you there?' Tanya checks, shifting uncomfortably in her seat. They are a little low, making you hunch up slightly. I guess they're more comfortable for the water caste members, who are shorter than us, and the fire warriors we saw at the space port. I then realise that it isn't the seat making her uncomfortable, it's the idea of some alien brain-device driving us around the city, taking us who knows where.

'That is correct,' confirms Coldwind. 'Rest assured that it is perfectly safe. In fact, I suspect it is safer than a vehicle driven by a sentient pilot. It cannot be distracted, nor does its mind wander and daydream. Its sensors are far more accurate and cover a much wider range of the spectrum than any living creature's.'

'Could you tell us a little about these buildings?' the Colonel asks after Oriel whispers something to him.

'Most certainly, chief advisor,' Coldwind replies, looking at the Colonel with his dark eyes. 'We have just left Me'lek space port, one of two such facilities on the planet. The geodesic structure approaching on our right,' he points to a faceted silver dome that reflects the light in a hundred different ways, creating a dappling sheen across its neighbours, 'contains the surface housing for members of the kor, whom you refer to as the air caste. Only a few of them can live planetside nowadays due to the depreciation of their muscles and skeletons caused by prolonged space flight over successive generations. The conditions inside are maintained at a lesser gravity than the rest of the city.'

'You're very forthcoming, ambassador,' comments Oriel, sitting forward suddenly. 'Any particular reason why?'

'There are two reasons, Imperial commander,' Coldwind replies smoothly. 'Firstly, I am of the highest rank of the por, the water caste in your tongue, and as such it is my duty to co-operate fully with such an important and honoured visitor. Secondly, I will be furnishing you and your team with much more confidential information before we depart for Es'tau.'

So he is our contact, I think triumphantly. None of the others seem surprised, least of all Oriel. It's good to have it said though.

'I assume that we can talk safely here?' Oriel asks, looking steadily at Coldwind.

'This vehicle has been secured against any kind of surveillance,' Coldwind assures him earnestly.

'Are you absolutely sure?' the inquisitor presses the matter.

'I would certainly not be engaging in this discussion if I did not believe that to be the case, Imperial commander,' Coldwind points out.

'Hmm, I suppose not,' Oriel concedes, leaning back again and relaxing slightly. 'Have you any update on Commander Brightsword's movements?'

'O'var, as we often refer to him, returned to Es'tau almost a kai'rotaa ago,' the ambassador replies without hesitation. He sees our confused looks. 'Sorry, that is almost two Terran months. He is expected to remain there for several more weeks, I believe. He is currently assembling sufficient transports and escorting warships for his army to move on the world you call Sarcassa.'

'What can you tell us about Brightsword himself?' the Colonel asks, leaning forward and resting one elbow on his knee, cupping his chin in his hand. His eyes are fixed on Coldwind, and the ambassador seems momentarily put out by his icy, penetrating gaze. I can't blame the tau; everybody I've met feels uncomfortable when they have Schaeffer's full attention. Even aliens, apparently.

With a look at Oriel, who nods in agreement, the tau delicately clears his throat before speaking.

'He is Shas'o-Tash'var-Ol'nan-B'kak,' he tells us, the Tau syllables almost blending into one long word. 'That is, he is a fire caste commander, from the world of Tash'var, who has earnt the honorary titles of Brightsword and Sandherder.'

'Sandherder?' laughs Trost. He has one arm hooked over the edge of the car and slaps his hand against the outside in amusement. 'What sort of name is that?'

'One of great value,' Coldwind replies, ignoring Trost's rudeness. 'It is a traditional title that dates back many generations. As a tau I find its origins intensely interesting, but I suspect that as outsiders the explanation may tax your powers of attention.'

'Yes, it will,' the Colonel says heavily, glaring at Trost for the interruption. 'Please continue telling us about O'var.'

'Like all members of the shas caste, O'var was born to be a warrior,' Coldwind tells us, looking at each of us rather than focussing his attention on one person. He's certainly used to speaking to groups, that's obvious, and his command of our language is better than most humans I've met. 'During his most formative years, the period sometimes referred to by the shas as 'on the line', O'var fought for the great military hero O'shovah for several years. During this time, O'shovah was impressed by O'var's skill at arms and tactical forethought and they conducted the ta'lissera together. This allowed O'var to join O'shovah's hunter cadre, as we know our military formations.'

'This ta'lissera is some kind of bonding ceremony isn't it?' Oriel interrupts. 'It's supposed to be a very grave undertaking.'

'Indeed it is, Imperial commander,' Coldwind answers, giving no hint of surprise that Oriel should know this. 'It is one of the most profound commitments that we can make to achieving the tau'va; the aim in life for all of our people, a complex concept which your translators interpret merely as the greater good. O'shovah became O'var's mentor, and taught him many battle skills and the intricacies of the art of war. In time, O'var rose to a position of authority which meant he could no longer remain in O'shovah's cadre. It was supposedly an emotional parting for both of them. It was also at this time that the seeds of dissent were sown in O'var, as the fio might say. O'shovah, once a brilliant and highly respected leader of our armies, has since turned his back on the greater good and shunned our ways. O'var, no doubt inspired by his mentor, has become an aggressive and headstrong leader. Although he still swears to uphold the ideals of the tau'va, his militaristic approach is increasingly becoming counter to our non-aggressive policies of colonisation.'

'You mean he's a gun that could go off any time,' Strelli states humourlessly. 'That must be a real headache for you.'

'What an evocative analogy,' Coldwind replies, again with that tiny nod of amusement.

'Sorry,' Tanya butts in. 'These names are confusing me, could you go over them again.'

Myself and Moerck both nod in agreement. The Tau syllables are all mixed up in my head, along with the translations.

'There's only one we need worry about,' Oriel replies. 'That is O'var. We call him Commander Brightsword. The other is O'shovah. That translates as Farsight. Farsight was Brightsword's commander in his early military career, that is all you need know about him. Please try to pay attention and keep up.'

'Well, I was getting confused,' snaps Tanya, crossing her arms. 'After all, I am supposed to kill this guy, I'd like to know I got his name right in my head when I pull the trigger.'

We all glance sharply at her.

'I would prefer you weren't so specific about our mission, especially out here in an open-topped car,' Oriel snarls at her. He turns his attention back to Coldwind. 'Not that I do not trust your assurances, ambassador. Now, about Brightsword?'

'He has, as you point out, become something of a problem, although not as much as O'shovah,' the tau diplomat continues. 'But as you say, O'shovah is not our concern for now. O'var's expansionist aggression will, if allowed to continue unchecked, inevitably lead to conflict with your people. Much more widespread conflict than the relatively small skirmishes that have so far been fought. And, of course, ignoring your somewhat premature and abortive crusade through the area you call the Damocles Gulf.'

'We're not here to rake over history or make a critique of the Imperium's military policy, Coldwind,' Oriel says sourly. None of us have a clue what they're talking about, I've never heard of any Damocles Gulf crusade. In fact, up until a couple of seconds ago, I'd never heard of the Damocles Gulf, wherever that may be.

'We, of course, wish to avoid all conflict where possible,' Coldwind smoothes over the tension. 'It is unproductive and counter to the needs of the greater good. Your officials,' he looks at Oriel then, 'also realise the folly of a war between our two states and wish to avoid conflict. Thus, we arrive here, conspiring together to rid us both of a problem.'

'So why can't you just depose him or something?' asks Tanya. 'Promote somebody else in his place?'

'I am afraid that would be contrary to the tau'va,' the ambassador explains. 'On appearances, O'var is doing nothing wrong. He is expanding our domains so that the tau'va may be spread to other races across the galaxy.'

'So why get us to kill him, why not do the dirty work your-selves?' Trost argues back. Oriel darts him another warning look about speaking too openly and the demolitions expert gives a surly grunt and folds his arms. I'm momentarily dis-tracted as we pass by a huge sphere supported on stilts, linked to the ground by spiralling moving stairways. I snap out of it and listen to what Coldwind is saying.

'The thought of killing another tau is absolutely horrific to us, except for certain shas ritual combats,' Coldwind is actually physically repelled at the thought, his skin blanching a paler blue. 'Even if such an individual could be found to perform the act, the risks are far too great. If it were ever discovered that we had done such a deed, it would cast doubt on the tau'va. Surely you understand that.'

'We don't really need to go into the whys, do we?' I say to the Colonel and Oriel, trying to keep the conversation relevant. 'What we need to know are the details of how, where and when.'

'Yes, of course,' Coldwind replies, glancing ahead of the car. 'Unfortunately, we have arrived at your residence for the evening and will be in company with others in a moment. Tonight there is a dinner in your honour, and we will not be able to talk then. Tomorrow morning I will be conducting you on a tour of the city, during which there will be periods when we can converse properly.'

The ground car slows to a halt outside a rearing edifice like an inverted cone, its levels splaying further and further out-wards as it reaches into the sky. I have no idea how it could stand up, it seems supported only by the linkways and bridges that connect it to the overhead roads and nearby buildings.

'If you would follow my aide, Vre'doran, he will show you to your chambers,' Coldwind says, indicating a shorter, skinny-looking tau waiting patiently by the flower-like doorway to the building. As we clamber out, he bows deeply and steps aside, allowing us to precede him as the 'petals' of the door open into the building to allow us access. I glance back and see the car disappearing back down the street, taking our ally with it.

OUR QUARTERS ARE a slightly more grandiose version of those aboard the ship. As before, there's a central chamber, this time with a large central cushion and three smaller ones in a trian-gle around it. There are ten bedrooms connected to the main

living area, each with its own showering room. We barely ha[ve]
time to wash and refresh ourselves before a chiming noise
attracts our attention to the door. Vre'doran is waiting for us on
the landing outside, and he asks us to accompany him to the
upper floor where the state dinner is being held.

'Are all the rooms like ours?' asks Tanya, though whether out
of curiosity or just trying to play her role, I'm not sure. 'Are
these normal quarters, or those specially prepared for offworld
visitors?' I think she almost said 'aliens' then, but realised that
they're still the aliens, even if we are on their world.

'They are similar in design to our own habitations,' Vre'doran
informs us, leading us along a hallway which is coloured a very
pale blue, decorated by a thin frieze of Tau lettering at about
head height. 'If they are not suitable, I can arrange for rooms to
be specially prepared that are more suitable. We are not fully
aware of all human needs.'

Tanya glances at Oriel, who shrugs.

'The quarters we have will be sufficient, thank you,' she tells
the tau graciously.

We follow the alien onto the moving ramp that serves instead
of a staircase, gently revolving around a central pillar that runs
the height of the building. The inside is hollow; the twelve
floors have circular landings with bridges that reach out from
the conveyor, the rooms radiating outwards from there. The
central column itself is startling – glass or some other transparent substance that contains an ever shifting mix of coloured
liquids that gently rise and fall along its length.

Like all of the stairwells I've seen, the mobile ramp has no
handrails, and we crowd into the centre near the column for
fear of plummeting to our deaths. It's obvious the tau don't lose
their footing very easily. I can see why, they seem a very leisurely
race, I've not seen anything except the drones hurrying around.
Like everything to do with the tau their pace of life is calm and
sedate as well.

We reach the final landing and are led into the banqueting
hall. It runs the entire circumference of the building, as far as I
can tell, its outside wall a continuous window allowing a magnificent view of the city in every direction. Low, wide circular
tables are arranged along the centre of the room, disappearing
to the left and right, each surrounded by the now familiar seating cushions. Me'lek's star is just setting, and as we wait for the

...ner guests to arrive, we stand at the window and look out over the settlement, bathed in the rosy glow of the coming twilight.

For the first time since we arrived, the city starts to come alive as darkness descends. The sunset casts a warm tint across the harsh white buildings, softening the glare, and lights from thousands of windows spring into life in the space of a few seconds. Strips of luminescence run the length of the roadways and bridges, adding to the spectacle, and as the star rapidly dips beneath the horizon, I'm amazed at the glorious array of twinkling starlight and iridescent rainbows that replace the severe whiteness of the city in daylight.

A steady stream of yellow and blue lights moves along the roadways as the vehicles build in number, soon forming an almost constant stream.

Looking to my right I can see the space port atop the hill, blazing with beacons and landing guides, geometric shapes shining in red, green, blue and white making an almost dizzying pattern from this angle. The bright landing jets of some starship erupt into life as it lifts off and I watch the white sparks ascend into the clouds, underlit by the last rays of the day.

'That's pretty impressive,' Strelli says casually. 'Can you imagine how much power it takes to run all of those lights?'

'Pretty lights and baubles,' snorts Moerck, turning away. 'Glittering decorations that impudently seek to outmatch the stars. Only a race so blind to the obscenities of technology would try and rival the beauty of the Emperor's heavens.'

'Beats living in the dark,' Tanya says pragmatically, gazing at the bright array blazoned across the land as far as we can see.

'No light can hide the darkness in an alien's soul,' Moerck sneers from behind us.

We turn as we hear others entering. Four fire warriors, fully armoured and armed, precede a young-looking tau wearing a robe of several differently coloured layers. In his hand he carries a short rod, a glittering gem at its tip. They pay no attention to us, but move out of sight around the bend. Ambassador Coldwind follows soon after and directs us towards a table a little way from the door, with a view of the space port out of the window. He follows our gazes outside.

'Magnificent, is it not?' he says, bobbing his head slightly. 'We adore the night, you see. When our ancestors were still young, we lived in the dry and arid heat of T'au, and spent living area, each with its own showering room. We barely have time to wash and refresh ourselves before a chiming noise attracts our attention to the door. Vre'doran is waiting for us on the landing outside, and he asks us to accompany him to the upper floor where the state dinner is being held.

'Are all the rooms like ours?' asks Tanya, though whether out of curiosity or just trying to play her role, I'm not sure. 'Are these normal quarters, or those specially prepared for offworld visitors?' I think she almost said 'aliens' then, but realised that they're still the aliens, even if we are on their world.

'They are similar in design to our own habitations,' Vre'doran informs us, leading us along a hallway which is coloured a very pale blue, decorated by a thin frieze of Tau lettering at about head height. 'If they are not suitable, I can arrange for rooms to be specially prepared that are more suitable. We are not fully aware of all human needs.'

Tanya glances at Oriel, who shrugs.

'The quarters we have will be sufficient, thank you,' she tells the tau graciously.

We follow the alien onto the moving ramp that serves instead of a staircase, gently revolving around a central pillar that runs the height of the building. The inside is hollow; the twelve floors have circular landings with bridges that reach out from the conveyor, the rooms radiating outwards from there. The central column itself is startling – glass or some other transparent substance that contains an ever shifting mix of coloured liquids that gently rise and fall along its length.

Like all of the stairwells I've seen, the mobile ramp has no handrails, and we crowd into the centre near the column for fear of plummeting to our deaths. It's obvious the tau don't lose their footing very easily. I can see why, they seem a very leisurely race, I've not seen anything except the drones hurrying around. Like everything to do with the tau their pace of life is calm and sedate as well.

We reach the final landing and are led into the banqueting hall. It runs the entire circumference of the building, as far as I can tell, its outside wall a continuous window allowing a magnificent view of the city in every direction. Low, wide circular tables are arranged along the centre of the room, disappearing to the left and right, each surrounded by the now familiar seating cushions. Me'lek's star is just setting, and as we wait for the other guests to arrive, we stand at the window and look out over the settlement, bathed in the rosy glow of the coming twilight.

For the first time since we arrived, the city starts to come alive as darkness descends. The sunset casts a warm tint across the harsh white buildings, softening the glare, and lights from thousands of windows spring into life in the space of a few seconds. Strips of luminescence run the length of the roadways and bridges, adding to the spectacle, and as the star rapidly dips beneath the horizon, I'm amazed at the glorious array of twinkling starlight and iridescent rainbows that replace the severe whiteness of the city in daylight.

A steady stream of yellow and blue lights moves along the roadways as the vehicles build in number, soon forming an almost constant stream.

Looking to my right I can see the space port atop the hill, blazing with beacons and landing guides, geometric shapes shining in red, green, blue and white making an almost dizzying pattern from this angle. The bright landing jets of some starship erupt into life as it lifts off and I watch the white sparks ascend into the clouds, underlit by the last rays of the day.

'That's pretty impressive,' Strelli says casually. 'Can you imagine how much power it takes to run all of those lights?'

'Pretty lights and baubles,' snorts Moerck, turning away. 'Glittering decorations that impudently seek to outmatch the stars. Only a race so blind to the obscenities of technology would try and rival the beauty of the Emperor's heavens.'

'Beats living in the dark,' Tanya says pragmatically, gazing at the bright array blazoned across the land as far as we can see.

'No light can hide the darkness in an alien's soul,' Moerck sneers from behind us.

We turn as we hear others entering. Four fire warriors, fully armoured and armed, precede a young-looking tau wearing a robe of several differently coloured layers. In his hand he carries a short rod, a glittering gem at its tip. They pay no attention to us, but move out of sight around the bend. Ambassador Coldwind follows soon after and directs us towards a table a little way from the door, with a view of the space port out of the window. He follows our gazes outside.

'Magnificent, is it not?' he says, bobbing his head slightly. 'We adore the night, you see. When our ancestors were still young, we lived in the dry and arid heat of T'au, and spent

Despite the unnatural but vaguely pleasant surroundings, I lose my appetite quickly, and I'm soon just picking at small titbits out of politeness.

As we eat, I watch Me'lek's twin moons rise across the night sky, and in the moonlight the city changes again. Most of the lights dim, leaving just the buildings glowing in a variety of colours, some looking silver or gold, others with a kind of pearly hue, yet others still dappled with glowing blues and purples.

'Our cities are planned and built so that they interact with the movement of the celestial bodies, taking their mood from the changing positions of the moons and stars,' Coldwind tells us, noticing the direction of my gaze. 'Do you have such spectacles on your worlds?'

I glance at the Colonel, who gives a shrug and a nod. I decide I can tell them the truth, there's no way Shas'elan could guess I wasn't a scribe just because of where I'm from.

'I come from a city that stretches three kilometres into the skies of Olympas,' I tell the tau, trying to make it sound as impressive as I can. There's no point letting them think they're the only ones who can build a fancy city. 'The lower levels are delved a similar distance into the rock. A billion humans live in that one city, and there are thirteen such cities on my world.'

'That cannot be,' argues Shas'elan. 'That is more humans on one world than there are tau in this sept!'

'We call them hive worlds, from the busy nests of insects,' explains Quidlon. 'There are many hive worlds in the Imperium, and other kinds of worlds too.'

'Many worlds with this many humans?' Shas'elan looks shocked and glares accusingly at Coldwind, muttering something in Tau. Coldwind answers back in a sharp fashion, as far as I can tell anyhow. The rest of the meal is eaten in uncomfortable silence.

IT IS COLDWIND who meets us the next morning. The day is already beginning to warm up as the ground car glides up onto one of the high aerial roads. I pay more attention to the journey this time, watching as other vehicles pass us in the opposite direction: floating cars like the ones we are in, long articulated transports, small pod-like conveyors carrying a single tau. I notice how many drones there are as well. They seem to be everywhere, flitting along the roads, skimming in and out of the buildings, weaving their way up through the bridges and walkways.

'We must leave tonight,' Coldwind says suddenly, drawing my attention back inside the vehicle. 'I have received word that O'var will be departing Es'tau very shortly. If we do not move as soon as possible, the opportunity may be missed.'

'You say "we", does that mean you are coming with us?' I ask, glancing at the Colonel.

'I shall meet you there,' he replies evenly. 'O'var is assembling many mercenaries to supplement his own fire warriors, and in the guise of mercenaries you will arrive on Es'tau and enter the employ of O'var. I have made this possible, and must travel to O'var to ensure that all of the necessary records are completed in a fashion that does not link you to me in any way.'

'Covering your back then?' Trost laughs. 'You seem to trust us not to give away your secret.'

'If you were to reveal the connection, the records will support my argument that such an arrangement did not exist,' the ambassador answers smoothly, not put out in the least. 'Also, you have nothing to gain from such a revelation, as popular opinion would be far more concerned with eliciting recompense from the Imperium than questioning my role in the affair.'

'Nobody is going to reveal anything to anyone,' Oriel says sternly, giving us each a hard look before turning to Coldwind. 'Has our starship arrived yet?'

'Several days ago, the vessel you described to me achieved orbit,' the ambassador confirms with a nod. 'I have also arranged for you to be conveyed by lifter to the outer regions of the system so that you may engage your warp engines as soon as possible.'

'What do you mean, conveyed?' Schaeffer asks suspiciously.

'Do not be alarmed, it is a standard procedure,' Coldwind assures us. 'Often when dealing with alien vessels, we use the superior acceleration capabilities of our own ships to give them a boost, as you would say.'

'So how long do you expect it will take us to reach Es'tau?' Strelli asks from the back end of the ground car.

'It is a short journey, relatively speaking. I would estimate three, perhaps four rot'aa,' he replies after a moment's thought.

'That's just over two days?' Oriel says, glancing over to Coldwind for confirmation, who gives a nod. 'Not long at all. We'll use the time to make our final preparations.'

'Good, I believe everything is in order then,' the ambassador seems pleased.

WE SPEND THE rest of the day going over the next part of the plan. The ambassador briefs us more as he escorts us around various local places of interest. We pass close to the palace of the ethereals, a towering edifice with dozens of skyways webbing out from the central spire, and have our first look at a real fire warrior battle dome, a huge building that can train thousands of warriors under its arching roof. Coldwind becomes particularly animated during our tour through the water caste district, going on at length about the dozens of domes and towers full of administrators collating information from all across the planet and the nearby worlds.

The stop-start nature of our conversations means we have to back-track a lot so that we're all clear about what's going on, but I think I get it all in the end. There's a decommissioned ex-navy transport in orbit, a small vessel barely capable of warp travel, which will take us to Es'tau and Brightsword. We will land, sign up for Brightsword's army and then keep out of trouble until it is time to strike. When the tau commander makes his final pre-invasion inspection, we hit hard and fast, shoot the bastard in the head and then leg it as quick as we can.

Coldwind assures us that in the mayhem and confusion we should be able to get away and into orbit without too much difficulty. I have my doubts. It was the same problem with Coritanorum – getting in was difficult enough, but it was getting out that nearly killed me. Midway through the afternoon, Coldwind returns us to our quarters and says that we have a few hours to make any final preparations before departing.

That evening just as the sun is dipping behind the tall domed buildings, Coldwind turns up yet again with the floating car to take us back to the space port.

'I've just had a thought,' Tanya says as we smoothly overtake a long tanker of some kind. 'What happens to you, Coldwind, when all this goes off? I mean, you won't be able to entirely deny any involvement with us.'

'Our story is that you are renegades, acting without authority,' the tau ambassador replies calmly. 'In the unfortunate event that I am somehow implicated I will of course support this story. Rather foolishly, I have trusted the evil humans, and O'var has paid the price.'

'So, you'll just look incompetent rather than treacherous?' I laugh harshly. 'That won't do your career much good.'

'If that comes to pass, it is almost certain that I will lose much prestige and rank,' Coldwind agrees with a nod, still seemingly at ease with the thought.

'However, my personal circumstances and career are secondary to the needs of the tau'va.'

'You would risk having your life ruined for this?' Tanya asks, leaning forward. 'This tau'va must be pretty important.'

'I certainly risk much for the tau'va, it is true,' answers Coldwind slowly. 'However, ask yourself this. Why do you all risk even more than I do, for your distant Emperor?'

Nobody replies, as we ponder this. I have the quick answer, though some would say it's avoiding the issue. I risk everything for the Emperor and mankind because it's better than any of the other options. I remember a preacher once, he came to the hive factories, and held a great mass. He wanted to bring together the different houses through the worship of the Emperor. It didn't work, the mass turned into a riot, then a battle, than a full scale trade war. I think he got shot by accident, though nobody wished him any harm really. Anyway, this preacher was extolling us to work for the Emperor, and to fight for the Emperor. He quoted from the Litanies of Faith, or perhaps some other holy book, I can't really remember, I was very young at the time. He said there were two types of people. There were those who worked and fought for mankind and the Emperor. They were the ones who dedicated themselves to an ideal bigger than them. They were the ones who would be gloried in the afterlife when the Emperor took them. Then there were the others, the leeches he called them, sucking life and blood from the rest of us. They had no purpose beyond themselves, and when they died there was only the Abyssal Chaos to greet them. It must have had an impression on me, though I didn't realise that until I was in the 13th Legion.

WE'RE ALL SHOCKED out of our thoughts when the front right-hand side of the groundcar explodes, sending silvery metal spinning in all directions and causing the vehicle to plough into the roadway, nearly spinning over and tossing us in all directions. I don't remember seeing a blast or missile, but I guess someone must have shot at us.

'What the frag?' I shout, jumping to my feet. I hear the ting of small arms fire rattling off the transport, and we all spill out of the carrying compartment to shelter behind the bulk of the ground car. I check out everyone to see if they're alright, but the padded seats and floor mean that none of us will have worse than bruises in a few hours.

'Where's it coming from?' shouts Tanya, scanning the buildings around us. There's a spire-like tower we were just passing, standing alone amongst the elegant tangle of roads and bridges. Behind us is a complex of interlocked domes around a central spherical hub, but with no visible windows. Further along the road is another building still being assembled. Gravcranes hover over it, winching in large slabs of whatever material it is that the tau use.

'The construction site!' I snap, just as Tanya says the same, and I point. It's about three hundred metres away, with plenty of cover, yet open routes of escape in every direction. I hurl myself to my feet again and I'm about to start towards the building when Oriel grabs my robe and flings me bodily to the floor.

'You're a scribe, you stupid idiot!' he hisses. 'Not a bloody Space Marine!'

'Sorry, I forgot...' I apologise as more bullets rattle into the roadway. I glance around, nobody seems to have been hit. My heart is pounding; the suddenness of the attack galvanising my body into action. I have to fight hard against the urge to get myself a weapon and go on the offensive.

'Who do you think is attacking us?' the Colonel bellows at Coldwind.

'There are some fundamentalists who believe we are too tolerant of other species, particularly humans,' Coldwind replies, cowering underneath the shattered remnants of the ground car. 'The shas hunt them down when they can, but there are always one or two who refuse to see the wisdom of our policies.'

It's at this point that the shas, the fire warriors, choose to make their entrance. Judging by the speed they've got here, I guess they've been following us around all day. Not that unexpected considering Oriel is supposed to be a very important dignitary. I don't know where they come from, but suddenly five battle suits are landing on the roadway in front of us, screaming groundwards on their jetpacks. As they land, their feet gouge holes into the surface of the road, their knee joints and lower leg structure compacting smoothly to absorb the landing impact. No sooner have they arrived on their feet than they open fire. As the hovering cranes lift themselves out of the line of fire, salvoes of missiles erupt from shoulder-mounted pods on two of the suits. The other three leap forwards, powering away into the air with hissing bounds, their multiple weapons spitting bullets and plasma bolts into the half-built dome. Something erupts over our heads and a massive blast of energy sails between the advancing battle suits, its detonation sending a massive fountain of debris into the air. A shadow passes over us and I glance up.

It's a tau tank, gliding above the roadway, passing overhead. It's big, bigger than any grav-vehicle I've ever seen, though that's not many to be fair. Like the space ship we travelled on, it flattens and widens at the front, almost like a hammer head. The expanded front houses two weapons pods, one on each side just forward of what looks to be a cockpit, fitted with the same multi-barrelled cannons that I noticed on the battle suits. The guns track left and right, seeking targets. The back end, flanked by heavy engines which are tilted slightly downwards at the moment to push the whole thing slowly forwards, is much blockier, topped by a turret with an offset cannon. The gun itself is huge, easily three or four metres long, and blocky. As it passes us by, the whine of its engines making my ears ring, the tank opens fire again, spitting a ball of energy into the target zone, its aim slightly adjusted from the previous shot.

'I think we should get out of here,' mumbles Strelli, glancing back along the road. Traffic from behind us has slowly started to snarl up, and many of the vehicles have settled on to the ground, out of the way of the advancing tank, providing cover for us to escape. I see tau abandoning their vehicles and fleeing away from the fight.

I look around and see the air caste dome nearby, and the shape of a craft lifting up into the air a short distance away.

'We're within walking distance of the space port. We should just head for the shuttle!' I say to the others, and Oriel nods.

'Yes, once we're there, Coldwind can get us clearance to leave and we can get out of here with the minimum of fuss,' the inquisitor agrees.

'Yes, they will send another vehicle for you soon,' Coldwind agrees. 'It may be wiser to avoid any escalation of the situation. Close scrutiny of your presence here would be undesirable.

'We can't carry all of our gear,' Strelli points out, nodding to the pile of bags and chests now spilled from the storage compartment of the wrecked groundcar.

'We don't need it any more,' I argue. 'Once we're out of here, our cover story changes and we have to dump it all anyway.'

'Very well, double back. The less official attention we get, the better,' Oriel says quickly, running past us in a stooped stance, keeping the smouldering wreck of the ground car between him and any attackers. We follow swiftly, and within a couple of minutes are out of the area and on our own, hidden in the shadows under a taut, blue awning that extends for several hundred metres from the side of one of the nearby domes.

'I must apologise for this attack,' Coldwind says to us as we catch our breath, his composure regained. 'I hope this does not compromise the mission any more than necessary.'

'Just get us to the space port and to our ship,' snaps Oriel, stalking away.

WE HEAD TO the shuttle, on foot this time, heading down fairly empty backstreets after Coldwind. The few tau we see give us odd looks, but we try to look as if we're out for a stroll rather than fleeing for our lives, and most of them only give us a glance before going past. Coldwind uses his position of authority to get us past the fire warrior security at the space port without any questions, but it's only once we're on the shuttle heading for orbit that we begin to relax a little.

Coldwind isn't with us; he'll be meeting us again at Es'tau. The ambassador is travelling on his own vessel, as it would appear very strange if he were to arrive there on a mercenary transport, so we're completely free to talk about him while he's not here.

'Well, the tau didn't take their time rescuing us,' Strelli says, slouching comfortably in his padded leather seat.

'I would like to know how they knew where we would be,' Moerck says, looking at Oriel. 'And if they knew that, what else might they have found out?'

'Imperial Commander Oriel has been under fire warrior protection since he first landed,' the Colonel says scornfully. 'If you had paid more attention, you would have noticed the transport craft that was shadowing us for the last two days, a few hundred metres up and about a kilometre behind us. But you were all too busy looking at the buildings and the tau.'

'I have never heard of tau dissidents before,' states Oriel, deep in thought. 'If such radicals did exist, then the whole subterfuge with Brightsword would be entirely unnecessary. No, Coldwind was lying to us about that, I could sense it. I also think Coldwind was anticipating the attack. He didn't seem to be as scared about it as you'd expect a non-combatant to be.'

'Perhaps he's just brave for his caste?' suggests Tanya, earning herself a withering look from Oriel.

'No, there's more going on here than we bargained for,' the inquisitor says slowly. 'The car was hit with the first shot, but in such a way that none of us were injured. After that, the shooting was pretty poor. If it was a shot at all. Did anyone see a muzzle flash before we were hit, or a rocket or shell?'

We all shake our heads.

'No, this seems to be orchestrated to me,' the inquisitor continues. 'He either thinks we are more stupid than we are, which I don't believe for a moment, or he's playing some kind of game which I don't quite understand yet.'

'Maybe it's part of his own cover story, so that he can explain why we left in such a hurry,' muses Tanya, and we all look at her in amazement. Her explanation does make some sense. 'Well, I know all about distractions, lures and false trails, so don't give me that funny look. There's more to being a sniper than just aiming straight,' she says petulantly, turning her head away to look out of the shuttle window.

'Well, whether it was for our benefit or his, I don't know what Coldwind is playing at, or what purpose the attack serves,' Oriel says, unbuckling his safety harness and standing up, 'but from now on, keep a close eye on our friendly ambassador.'

The inquisitor walks out into the front chamber, followed by the Colonel.

'I wouldn't trust the slimy cretin as far as I could throw him,' agrees Trost with a sneer.

'There is no such thing as a trustworthy alien,' Moerck says emphatically. We all nod in agreement.

THE CLUTTERED HOLD rumbled and rattled in time with the pulsing engines located nearby. A light strip flickered into life with an erratic buzzing, shedding a yellow glow across the stacked crates and metal boxes. Oriel strode through the open doorway, glancing back into the corridor briefly before closing the door. He walked quickly through the maze of piled cargo before entering a more open space near the centre of the hold.

'Where are you?' he asked, his voice low.

'I am in prayer, inquisitor,' a deep voice rumbled back from the gloom.

'This will be my last chance to talk to you. Come out where I can see you,' he told the hidden figure.

'Have you no respect for my traditions, inquisitor?' the deep voice answered.

'You have done little else but pray on this journey, Dionis, I am sure the Emperor will forgive this short interruption,' Oriel responded evenly, sitting down on a smaller carton.

A tall, broad figure emerged from the shadows, swathed in an armless, open-fronted robe, a hooded cowl over his face. The man was very large and towered over the inquisitor. His exposed arms and shoulders were corded with thick muscle,

rope-like veins pulsing beneath his deeply tanned skin. Across
his expansive chest muscles were numerous scar lines which
cut across an ornate tattoo of a double-headed eagle with its
wings spread. The face inside the cowl was similarly broad and
square-jawed, the lips set in a hard line.

'What else have you to tell me, inquisitor?' the man asked, no
hint of deference in his voice.

'We are underway again, heading for Es'tau and the final
stage of the mission,' Oriel told him, looking up at the giant.

'This much I have already observed, inquisitor,' he answered
curtly.

'I thought you would have,' Oriel replied quietly. 'I want to
check one last time that everything is understood.'

'Rest at ease, inquisitor,' Dionis told Oriel, crossing his thick
arms across his chest. 'I know that I am to act only when called
upon by you. I know that I am to remain covert until that time,
or until we return to the Emperor's realms if my prowess is not
needed. I also know that it is a dangerous game that you play,
and more likely than not I will be called upon to fight.'

'I understand this is not the dignified and glorious methods
of battle you are familiar with, and I thank you for your
patience, Dionis,' Oriel said smoothly. 'You understand why I
wish it to be this way.'

'I understood that well when I swore my oaths of obedience,'
acknowledged Dionis. 'I will start my battle-prayers and the
rites of honour. I shall also pray for you, inquisitor, that you do
not have need of me even as I pray for the battle I have been
born to fight.'

'Pray for us all, Dionis,' Oriel whispered, turning his gaze
away. 'Pray for us all.'

SIX
ES'TAU

+++*The playing pieces are ready for the end game*+++

+++*Then let us make our final moves*+++

LOOKING OUT OF the shuttle window as we descend towards Es'tau, I see that the planet is mostly desert. Ochre-coloured sands stretch as far as the eye can see once we're below the cloud layer. I see a blob of buildings far below us and guess that must be where we're heading, but it's still indistinct when the Colonel calls over the internal comm for us to unstrap and get our kit together. I cast one last glance out of the opposite port, wondering if this will be the last world I'll ever see.

Our reception on Es'tau is certainly not as ceremonial as the one on Me'lek, but no less military. That's to be expected, since we're now just another band of Imperial renegade mercenaries to them, rather than visiting officials. Fire warriors are everywhere, carrying their carbines and rifles and obviously not just for show. These ones wear a dark blue and grey camouflaged uniform, with red identification markings on their chests.

'Sarcassa is a night world,' Schaeffer murmurs to me as we pass by a squad. 'They are obviously almost ready to depart.'

Indeed, several tau craft sit on the landing apron, squads of fire warriors marching on board. I see three of the tanks, Hammerheads the Colonel calls them, gliding slowly on to a massive transport ship. The tau don't seem to pay us any more attention than anyone else around, so obviously our first appearances are convincing.

We're dressed in a ragtag collection of old uniforms, armed with a variety of different weapons. I've got an autogun and an old revolver, Tanya has her sniper rifle, Oriel and the Colonel carry stub pistols and chainswords, while the rest have lasguns. We've got an assortment of other bits and pieces like a few frag and smoke grenades, plus Trost has a pack full of demolition charges and fuses. A tau warrior sees us and holds up a hand to stop us.

'Warriors?' he asks, face hidden behind the viewing lenses of his helm, his strangely-accented voice emitted through a hidden speaker.

'Yes,' Oriel replies. 'Is there a problem, shas'vre?'

'All warriors checked,' the shas fighter replies, pointing to a temporary-looking dome beside the main space port complex.

'We have to go in there?' the Colonel asks, looking over towards the checking centre.

'Yes. All warriors checked,' the shas'vre repeats, more angrily this time, thrusting his finger towards the building.

'Alright, we're going,' Oriel placates him, giving us the nod to change course.

'What's going on?' I ask the Colonel as we make our way across the black-surfaced landing pad.

'I am not sure,' he replies, glancing around at all the fire warriors in the area. 'Maybe Brightsword has got wind of something, I do not know.'

As we make our way to the building the fire warrior indicated, I can see another group entering just in front of us. The mercenaries are a mix of races, mostly humans but with a couple of lanky, blue-skinned creatures with high crests over their heads and ridges down the centre of their faces. Inside the building is fairly open, with just a couple of archways to other rooms and a single door out on the opposite side.

Oriel tells us to wait and makes his way over to a small table to one side, behind which is sat a tau. Judging from his build and robes I'd say he was water caste, an observation which is proved correct when he pulls a sheaf of transparent sheets from a bag beside the table and begins writing.

He talks to the other sellswords first for a few minutes before directing them through into one of the side rooms, and then turns his attention to Oriel, who speaks at some length with him, the pair of them occasionally looking over in our direction.

I fidget nervously as we wait, keeping my gaze on the floor, trying not to catch the eye of the fire warriors passing through and stationed at the archways. I guess we're signing on for Brightsword's army. I hope Oriel's cover story is good, and that Coldwind has helped us out behind the scenes. I can't imagine Brightsword being too trusting at the moment, after all he's about to launch a major invasion and he must have some idea that not everyone in the Tau Empire is giving him their full support.

I snap out of my thoughts when Oriel comes back to us.

'Well, we've joined up,' he tells us with a grim smile. 'Coldwind's references smoothed the whole thing admirably. We should get out of here though and keep a low profile.'

As we turn to the exit we see three smaller figures standing close to the doorway.

'What the hell is this?' growls Trost uneasily.

'Psykers,' Oriel replies quietly, teeth gritted. 'Stay calm, we'll be fine.'

As we get closer I see that the figures are small aliens, nearly naked but for short skirts, grey-skinned with wide yellow eyes and completely devoid of hair. They look at us as we approach. I eye them back evilly.

'Think of something simple, something easy to remember,' I hear Oriel say. 'Like an old nursery rhyme, or a gun drill, or a marching chant. Repeat that in your head, just keep thinking it over and over again.'

As we pass between the aliens my skin crawls. I probably imagine it, but I swear I can feel something poking around in my head, like clawed hands turning my mind over and having a look. The sickening feeling carries on.

'Don't think about them, it will make it easier for them to read your mind,' warns Oriel. I try to remember the house anthem, but only get part way through the third verse, so I start again. That's when events catch up with me and I have to try hard not to stop dead in my tracks. It sounded just like Oriel was whispering in my ear, both times he spoke, but he's at least five paces ahead of me, in front of the others. He's a thaumist, just like these aliens!

'Keep singing that anthem, Kage,' Oriel's mind-voice tells me. 'I'll explain later, just don't think about me!'

I try to put all thoughts of Oriel and psykers from my mind and go over the lasgun maintenance drill I was taught back when I joined up. I used to pass hours going over and over that drill when I was in prison. I reckon I could do it with my eyes closed now. As I pass through the doorway, I try hard not to glance over my shoulder. Just ahead, Trost growls at one of the aliens, making it flinch, bringing a wolfish smile to his face. Gone is the cold-blooded mass murderer, now I think he enjoys it more than he's ever done. I'm not sure which one I find scarier.

Once we're outside, I see that this city is much less developed than the Me'lek capital. There are no sky-roads, no soaring towers, just many more low domes and spheres, all in a very regular radial pattern around the space port. Planned by a more military mind, is my first impression.

Oriel leads us left along the road outside the starship terminal, taking us towards one of the boulevards stretching outwards from the central hub created by the space port. None of us say anything as we walk for a couple of minutes, all of us wary of the mind-reading aliens we've just left behind.

'Okay, we're far enough away now,' Oriel tells us, glancing around to make sure there are no tau close by. He stops us at a junction with one of the radial roads, which is deserted at the moment.

The city seems very quiet, but perhaps that's just because there aren't many tau here who aren't fire caste, and they're all busy preparing for their invasion, I reckon. 'We need to contact Coldwind as soon as we can, and make a final survey of the battle dome to see if anything has changed.'

'Don't try and avoid the fact that you're a damned witch,' I snarl at the inquisitor. 'You've been messing with my head, haven't you?'

'I wouldn't know where to start,' he sneers back.

'What's this?' Tanya asks, and the others look accusingly at Oriel, except the Colonel who glares at me.

'He's a fraggin' psyker, that's what,' I hiss, pointing at the inquisitor. 'I bet he's been inside all of our heads.'

'This is none of your concern,' Oriel says sternly. 'You are in no position to judge me. Especially you, Kage, of everyone here. Others far more worthy have done so and declared me pure and strong. Do not forget that I am an agent of the Emperor's Holy Orders of Inquisition, and not answerable to the likes of you. If I have gifts that are useful to my vocation, I will use them. How do you think I knew El'savon could speak Gothic? How do you think I ensured our privacy aboard his ship? How do you think I know Coldwind was expecting us to be attacked, or that he's been hiding something ever since we met? If it wasn't for the protection I just gave you all, we would have never got past the telepaths. I am not prepared to discuss this matter.'

We look at each other and then back at Oriel, defiance in our eyes.

'We're on a Tau world, in Tau space,' Trost points out. 'All your authority counts for nothing here. What's to stop us just walking over to the next tau and turning you over to them. Damn, we could just as well be real mercenaries.'

'How dare you consider such a thing!' barks Moerck, stepping over to stand beside the Colonel. 'Any more talk like that, soldier, and I will kill you myself.'

'Looks like five against three, not too good odds,' Strelli laughs coldly.

'Four against four, actually,' I tell them, squaring off against Trost. 'I don't care much for mind-fraggers like Oriel, in fact I'd rather they were all dead. But I came here to kill an enemy of the Emperor and that's what we're gonna do. Any one of you want to dispute that with me, they're quite welcome to step up right now and give it their best shot.

'Any of you think you can take down Last Chance? What about you, Flyboy? Come on, Demolition Man, you've been wanting to do this ever since I put you on your backside that first day of training.'

No one moves. It's a stand-off, neither side ready to back down. We glare at each other, the tension thick enough to cut with a bayonet. It's the Colonel who breaks the deadlock.

'We should move on,' he says looking around. 'If the tau get suspicious we will all end up dead. Remember, we are just a mercenary company, and we need to act like it. Anything out of the ordinary might get noticed, and Brightsword doesn't seem to be taking any chances, so be careful.'

Reminded that we're in up to our necks together on this one, we grudgingly put aside our differences, warily stepping away from each other.

'What next then?' I ask.

'All the mercenaries can be found in the alien quarter,' the Colonel replies.

'Well, let's get something to eat,' suggests Tanya. 'And see what the locals are like.'

WE FIND THE alien quarter easily enough. It's the one with all the aliens in it. Oriel seems to know the layout of the area and it was only a few minutes' walk from the space port.

I've never seen so many freaky things in my life, and I've been around a bit. There are tall ones, short ones, fat ones, hairy ones, spiky little guys, things with more arms and eyes than is entirely necessary for any kind of lifeform. And all of them living together in the same part of the city. Since we're not far from the space port, I guess all the off-worlders have been gathering in this place over a few years, making it a real home from home.

The buildings are still tau construction, but heavily adapted, decorated and adorned by the local population. Banners and streamers flutter from food shop fronts, religious-looking icons on tall poles are stuck into the ground in front of other buildings. As we pass one in particular there's an unpleasant charnel house smell. We look at the building and see it's daubed in savage-looking alien runes and hurry on, not wanting to know what goes on inside. Fire smoke from different types of wood fills the air with a mix of sweet and acrid scents, which blend into each other to create a disturbing stench. There's sand and dust everywhere as well, blown in from the surrounding desert, and combined with the noise, smell and heat makes me feel sick.

There are market stalls selling anything and everything from clothes to guns and grenades. We take a look at one of the arms traders, a small green guy with a scaly skin and pale yellow eyes, who deftly picks through his wares with three-fingered hands.

'Interested in guns, yes?' he asks us as we stop next to his stand. His voice is kind of scratchy, more of a hiss than anything else. 'Lots of guns for brave fighters.'

He's right, there are lots of guns, and most of them seem to be Imperial in origin. There's lasguns, autoguns, a couple of bolters, some knives, a few grenades, plus what was once obviously an officer's power sword. I pick it up, and read the inscription on the hilt.

'Colonel Verand, 21st Hadrian Guard,' I tell the others, putting the sword down again. 'I guess he ran into some bad luck.'

'What's this one?' Quidlon asks, pointing at a bizarre pistol-shaped armament which looks more like it was grown than built. It's green and veiny, shining slickly in the bright light.

'Kathap pistol, you like?' the store owner says, picking it up and offering it to Quidlon. He reaches out for it, but Moerck's hand clamps down around his wrist.

'You do not want to touch that,' he warns the short man, dragging his arm away. 'It is not consecrated by the machine god. Its taint will spread to your other weapons. Best to leave it be.'

'Aah, machine god is it?' the gun-runner butts in. 'You humans all same. You idea that there be machine god, you make bad weapons.'

'You don't seem to be shy of a few,' Strelli argues, indicating the assorted Imperial weapons.

'That because only cheap humans buy bad work like this,' the dealer smiles. 'Proper fighters want proper weapons.'

'I'll give you proper fighters,' I snarl, taking a step towards the merchant, who hisses in fear and turns to scurry away.

'Leave him alone, Last Chance,' the Colonel says sternly, and I back off.

Nobody comments that we're using our mission names again. It seems natural now that we're allowed to be soldiers once more. That's good, it was why I did it. We may be undercover here, but we're a lot more natural when it comes to being fighters than we are at being an Imperial commander and his entourage. It'll hopefully make things easier than it was back on the ship and on Me'lek.

'Where's a good place to drink?' Oriel asks the arms dealer, proffering a small coin delved from one of his pockets.

'Two streets on, look for the skulls,' the green alien replies, hesitantly taking the money, glancing up at me as it does so. He points to show us the way and then impatiently waves us away.

THE DRINKING HOLE isn't hard to find. Like the dealer said, just look for the skulls. It's a small tau dome with the front of the bottom level missing, open to the street. Arranged over this is a line of spikes with skulls impaled on them, of different species. I recognise human, ork, a couple of tyranid creatures, a slender one that I guess to be eldar, plus four others which aren't familiar.

'Nice place,' mutters Tanya, eyeing the skulls.

'We need to maintain the masquerade. If we start acting suspiciously, someone may notice. If this is where mercenaries drink, it's where we'll drink,' Oriel tells us quietly before stepping into the shade inside.

There's a small counter just off the street with a burly-looking creature sat behind it. It's squat, its head sunk deep

beneath its broad shoulders, its three beady eyes peering at us
from beneath a heavy brow. Thick-fingered alien hands
beckon us over.

'No weapons inside,' the alien growls, standing up and dragging a crate from a pile behind it. 'In here till you leave.'

'You all seem to speak Gothic quite well,' Strelli remarks,
placing his lasgun carefully in the crate.

'You humans speak nothing else, and humans are trouble-
makers,' the security thing grunts back as we hand over our
guns and knives.

'Nice to know we're welcome,' Tanya says sarcastically as we
enter the main room.

The bar is quite dark, the few red lamps around the wall do
little to light the circular room. A round bar in the centre, similarly lit, appears like a red island in a sea of smoky darkness.
There are tables and chairs filling the rest of the space, of
assorted shapes and heights. Most of them are occupied. Many
sets of eyes, not all of them in the regular pair, regard us as we
walk in. I see more of the same species as the door warden
gathered around a circular table to my right, arguing heavily
with each other in guttural grunts. Most of the other aliens I
don't recognise.

'What are they?' Trost whispers to Oriel, looking over at a pair
of diminutive creatures swathed in rags in one of the darkest
areas. Small, clawed hands clasp their drinks tightly, long snouts
twitching in our direction. I catch the hint of a tail whipping
nervously under their table.

'Hrud,' the inquisitor replies. 'Scavengers and tunnel-dwellers
for the most part, you'll find them all over the galaxy, though
never in large numbers. They're pretty much parasites, if you
ask me.'

'What about those?' I ask next, indicating three multi-limbed
creatures splayed on a bench along one side of the bar. They
have no heads, but clusters of eye-like organs wave towards us,
like grass in a breeze. They have no arms or legs, just a set of six
tentacle limbs which I guess must serve them for both pur-
poses.

Oriel thinks for a moment before replying.

'I've never seen one before, but they match the description of
galgs,' he tells me as we stop by the drinks counter. 'I think their
world was conquered by the tau a few centuries ago. They're

not particularly warlike as far as I remember, and not too advanced technically either.'

'Emperor on his holy throne!' curses Tanya quietly. We all look at her with surprise and she surreptitiously nods towards the far side of the room. There, as unmistakable as my own face, sits a group of bloody orks. Five of them in fact, the burly greenskins ignoring us, concentrating instead on two of their number who are having some kind of contest. Born warriors, I've fought orks on a couple of occasions, and barely lived to tell the tale. They're big, though not massive, with powerful muscles and an ability to soak up injury and pain like nothing else I've seen.

The two orks have their hands locked behind each other's thick necks, and are grunting to each other in their crude language. It's like they're counting or something. When they reach three, they smash their heads together, with a crack I can hear across the room. They all burst into raucous laughter, grabbing jugs of thick-looking drink from the table and taking large swigs.

'Weak or strong drink?' says the bartender, dragging our attention away from the head-butting contest.

The owner is a gangly alien, with dark blue skin and no fat at all, just wiry sinews and taut muscle. Its face is pretty much one big mouth, with a single vertical slit for a nose and tiny white eyes.

Oriel replies in some gibberish language that sounds like coughs and splutters, gesturing for us to sit down at a nearby table. He joins us after a short conversation with the barkeep.

'We can have rooms here on the upper level,' he tells us. 'I don't want to stay on the shuttle if we have to go through a mind screen every time we go in and out of the space port.'

'Where did you learn to talk like that?' Trost asks, looking at the bartender. Oriel just gives him a patronising look, but Trost still doesn't get it.

'He's an inquisitor,' Tanya explains slowly, keeping her voice low. Trost gives a grunt, not entirely satisfied, and slouches back further in his chair.

The alien barman bring us over our drinks, eight large glasses of frothing blackness. I take a cautious sip first, the others waiting to see if I drop dead on the spot. I give them the all clear with a grin.

'It's just like ale, really,' I tell them, taking another mouthful. It's actually quite refreshing after the heat outside. The others start on their drinks, Quidlon giving an appreciative nod, Strelli drinking half of his in one long draught.

'Hey,' I say to the others when I realise what's just happened. 'How come I've become the official food tester? Why doesn't one of you eat or drink something before me for a change?'

'Because if you die, we don't have to change the mission plan,' Strelli points out. 'All of us have specific jobs to do. You're just hanging around to provide a bit of firepower.'

I'm about to give him an angry reply but stop short. He's got a point. We have Flyboy, Demolition Man, Sharpshooter, Brains. I'm just Last Chance; all I do is survive.

'So what do we do between now and the mission?' Tanya asks, wiping some froth from her top lip.

'Keep quiet, and don't attract any attention, strictly low profile activity,' Oriel answers, toying with his glass. 'This is the part that has the greatest chance of going wrong. I don't know how Coldwind is going to contact me. I don't know when Brightsword is going to do his inspection, or if he's done it already and left. I don't know exactly how tight security is going to be while he's back. The last thing we need is any trouble, so keep your lips tight and your eyes and ears open.'

With this in mind, we hunker down and try to look the other way as the orks leave their table and stride past. They dart us a few glances, joking with each other in their own guttural tongue, but nothing else happens. I breathe a bit easier knowing that they've left.

'You said the tau conquered these galg things?' asks Tanya, looking over at the blobby aliens.

'Conquered is not really the right word,' Oriel replies thoughtfully. 'Coerced them might be a bit better. You see, the tau'va, the greater good, isn't really a religious thing just for them. They believe it's a common destiny across the galaxy, and includes everyone. The tau would much rather prefer other races as allies, or really servants to be honest, than enemies. You see, they're not fighting a war against anyone really, but there are lots of races in their way that they need to deal with.'

'Sending an invasion fleet seems to be an odd way of not fighting a war,' says Strelli, and I nod in agreement.

'Well, for a start, that's Brightsword being overzealous,' counters Oriel, taking another sip of his drink. 'We sometimes have the same problem with Imperial commanders taking it on themselves to pick a fight with some other world which we don't need to fight just yet. Unlike the tau, we can remove them without worrying that it damages our beliefs. After all, the Emperor is infallible, not his servants.'

'Does that include inquisitors?' Trost asks slyly.

Oriel glares at him. 'We were talking about the tau, though, not mankind. The tau arrive at your world, with a fleet, tanks, attack craft, fire warriors and battle suits, and they ask if you want to join in their quest to achieve the greater good. Well, that's the way I think it happened with the galgs. The galgs were clever enough to say yes, but there are some records that show what happens to those worlds who say no. Sooner or later they either say yes, with their cities burning and their soldiers rotting in their open graves, or are in no position to say anything at all.'

'I guess there must be a lot of resentment then, all those conquered races, the tau obviously in charge, not everyone's going to be happy with that,' suggests Quidlon, looking around the tavern.

'Unfortunately, that isn't usually the case,' Oriel replies with a shake of his head. 'The tau are very magnanimous in victory. Those races that become a part of the Tau Empire aren't slaves, although they certainly aren't in charge either, as you say. The tau find out what they are able to do and then put them to good use. They don't always colonise the worlds they've conquered either, sometimes they just want to remove a strategic threat. As you've probably noticed, they favour very hot, dry worlds and there's usually not much competition in that regard.'

'Until they ran into mankind,' adds the Colonel. 'We can live on tau worlds just as well as they can, and occasionally the explorators will investigate a world at the same time as the tau colony fleet arrives. It does not always end in bloodshed, but frequently does.'

I'm about to add something when Moerck's look distracts me. I have my back to the door, sitting opposite him, and turn around to see what he is staring at. There is a small group at the door, humanoid in shape, talking with the guard.

'What's up?' I ask the ex-commissar.

'Traitors,' he says grimly, nodding back towards the outside. I look again and see that it's true: the newcomers are humans. As they enter, I can make them out better. Like us, they are wearing an assortment of different clothes, some of them obviously alien-made, and each of them wears a band of white, either as a bandanna, armband or around their waists. I've seen their kind before, professional mercenaries who'll sell to the highest bidder regardless of what they look like or who they have to fight. I've fought against them and I've fought alongside them, and I didn't like it either way.

They give us nods as they walk past into the bar, but there's an angry murmuring from our left. Looking that way, I see a group of tarellians walking in our direction. I saw tarellians on Epsion Octarius. Well, their corpses at least. Narrow-waisted and broad shouldered, the tarellians are a bit shorter than most people, with long canine-like faces, which is why we call them dog soldiers. There's six of them, and they growl to each other menacingly.

One of them steps forward from the group and snarls something at us in Tarellian. We look at Oriel, who shrugs and looks over at the bartender, saying something in the language he used earlier.

The barkeeper points at us, replying quickly, and then at the door. Oriel says something back, and the owner shakes his head.

'The tarellians say that we have to leave. They don't like us drinking here,' Oriel translates.

'I heard him,' says one of the mercenaries, who have stopped next to our table and are glaring at the tarellians. He makes a kind of barking noise at the aliens, adding emphasis by tapping himself on the chest. This doesn't please the tarellians, who snarl and bark something back.

'Oh, frag this,' I say, getting to my feet and walking over to the tarellian leader. I hear Oriel call my name but ignore him. The aliens gather round me, snapping their jaws, but I ignore the rest and focus on the spokesman. 'If you want to be able to ever drink again, leave now,' I say to the soldier, smiling. He looks over at the bartender, who gives a quick translation. The tarellian peers up at me, showing his long teeth. One way or another, these tarellians have got a real problem with us and I don't figure on them letting us just walk out of here.

If I remember my legends correctly, we virus-bombed a few of their worlds back when the Emperor was leading the Great Crusade. Guess they still haven't got over that after ten thousand years. The tarellian is snarling something to the barkeeper still, jabbing a clawed finger into my chest as he does so.

By the Emperor, this is the slowest-starting bar brawl I've ever been in and it's a while since I had a good fight, so I ball my fist and smash the stupid alien straight across the jaw, knocking him backwards into a table. 'One for the Emperor!' I spit, spinning on the spot and driving my boot into the stomach of another dog soldier.

As the tarellians jump on me, the other Last Chancers pile in, as well as the human mercenaries. The rest of the bar seems against us, though, as all manner of things crawl and jump out of the darkness. A tarellian tries to grab my throat but I sway back out of reach. As it steps forward, I take a stride as well, driving my knee into its ribs. I get it into a headlock, but something hits me in the back of my neck, causing me to lose my grip. Turning, I see one of the galgs launch itself at me, flailing with its limbs at my face. I react just in time, grabbing it in mid jump and spinning, hurling it across the room.

A tarellian tries to take my head off with a chair, but I duck, seeing Moerck hurling another of the dog soldiers bodily across the bar counter. Grinning like a fool, I drive my elbow into the tarellian's face and kick the chair out of its hands. It lunges at me, jaw snapping, and I jump to one side, rolling across a table. I land on my feet the other side, just as the galg recovers and propels itself towards me. I snatch up a stool and swing it, connecting heavily with the galg and sending it hurtling back again. A glass crashes across the back of my head, stunning me for a second. A green-scaled alien with a frog face and long arms swings at me, backhanding me across the chest and knocking the breath out of my lungs. I block the next attack with my arm, grabbing the thing's wrist and tossing it over my hip on to the table. I drive my fist towards its face but it rolls out of the way and my knuckles crash painfully into the unvarnished wood.

A tarellian kicks a chair at me, which I jump over, landing awkwardly as I bang my hip against the table. The tarellian snarls something and tries to grab my throat, but I bat its hand away and step back. It makes another lunge and I duck, spinning on my heel to deliver a sweeping kick to the tarellian's right knee and knocking it from its feet. There's no time to follow up though, as the frog-face is back on its feet, its webbed hands grabbing my arm and swinging me into an upturned bench, crashing me to the ground. I kick out hard, feeling my boot connect with something soft, and the creature staggers back, howling like mad. I take the quick break in fighting to look around.

Moerck is bashing a tarellian repeatedly against the wall, a galg latched onto his back, trying to wrap its tentacles around his throat. I see the Colonel deliver a neck-breaking punch to another greenie, smashing it into a back flip. Oriel is struggling with another tarellian: he has its neck in a lock, and is trying to smash its head against the bar. Tanya and a spiny-headed thing roll across the floor, each other's throats in their hands. I can't see Trost or Strelli, the press of bodies is too tight. One of the mercenaries is clubbing a tarellian on the floor with a stool, shouting something I can't understand. A second lies draped over a table, blood dribbling from a cut to his forehead. The two hrud are hiding in the shadows, hissing at each other in their strange language and pointing in my direction. It's then that I realise just how outnumbered we are. It's pretty much us against the whole bar.

The tarellian on the floor springs to its feet and charges me, driving its shoulder into my gut and slamming us both to the ground. I defend myself with my arms as it flails at my head with its fists, and then head butt it on the end of the snout, causing the dog soldier to recoil in pain. I drive my fist into its face, cracking it just below the right eye and forcing it back far enough to give me space to get to my feet.

Something lands on the bar, screeching like a bird of prey. Crouched on the counter, I can see that it's long-limbed and rangy. Its skin is a greenish-grey hue, patterned with body paint in zigzags and jagged lines. It doesn't appear to be wearing clothes as such, just a tight harness with various pouches and trinkets attached. Its face is beak-like and orange and red spines splay angrily from the back of its head. It puts its head back and shrieks across the bar, a piercing noise which causes everyone to pause for a moment. Unleashing the power of its whipcord muscles, the alien pounces a good five metres across the room, landing on the back of the creature strangling Tanya.

More of them appear, bounding swiftly from table to table, their long arms swinging as they join the fight. Their speed is amazing, and the way they hurl themselves around, you'd think they were built out of springs. One leaps long and high, rebounding off the wall and spearing into a tarellian. I see the first one wind up for a punch, its long arm swinging around in a wide arc before catching another tarellian full across the head and hurling it through the air to crash down through a table.

I redouble my own efforts, grabbing the face of one of the scaly green things and driving my knee up into its gut and then again into its chest. Dropping the frog-thing to the floor with a thud, I sprint across the bar, picking up the splintered remnants of a chair and bringing it full force onto one of the tarellians, smashing it clear of the human mercenary. The others are fighting back hard as well.

Put off by our surprise reinforcements, the tarellians and other aliens break off, heading for the door. Some of them stop on the threshold and turn to face us, calling out taunts and jibes in whatever language they're speaking. The quill-headed aliens all put their heads back and begin screeching, the sound filling the room and deafening to hear, putting the others to flight.

I stand there panting, leaning on my knees, and one of the aliens walks over to me in a low, sloping stoop.

'Well, that was fun,' I say to myself, standing up straight and meeting the gaze of the approaching creature.

'Yes, it was,' it replies to my amazement, in strangely good Gothic for something that looks so feral. 'But there's no profit in it.'

OUR UNLOOKED-FOR allies are kroot, an entire race of sellswords, most of them working for the tau. There are several hundred of them on Es'tau, in the employ of Commander Brightsword. They're organised into family groups which Oriel calls kindreds, and the one that came to our rescue is led by a kroot called Orak. There are thirty or so of them, and Orak invites us back to their camp after the fight in the bar. Oriel accepts, obviously he thinks that a refusal might displease our new-found allies and attract more unwanted attention, and we follow the tall, gangly aliens through the streets of the city.

On our way out we picked up our weapons, and I note the long rifles and power cartridge bandoleers that all the kroot carry. Although they look like guns, the longrifles also have lengthy stocks carved into vicious-looking blades, and curved bayonet-like attachments under the barrels.

The kroot walk easily and confidently through the throng in the streets, their rangy legs carrying them along quickly and effortlessly until I'm panting in the heat to keep up. They chatter to each other with clicks and whistles, and the crowds part before them to get out of their way.

A hrud bustles up to Orak and tries to sell him a jar of something. The kroot isn't interested, and as the exchange continues it seems to get more heated. Orak's quills quiver more and more, and with a final angry hiss, they stand out like spikes, a fearsome crest which sends the hrud scurrying into the gathering gloom.

'Problem?' I ask the kroot leader, who looks at me, his quills lowering again.

'Bad haggling,' Orak replies, clicking his beak, laughing I suspect. 'It was new here, it will learn.'

'So how long have you been a mercenary?' I ask as I half-jog alongside the tall alien, puffing to keep up, the arid air turning my mouth dry.

'All my life, of course,' Orak answers. 'I did not fight until I came of age, but always have been a fighter for the Tau empire. How long have you been fighting?'

'All my life as well,' I reply after a moment's thought. 'But for myself, never for anyone else.'

'Not even for family?' the Kroot asks, quills shaking in surprise.

'Not for a long time,' I tell him quietly. We carry on walking through the street as the sun dips towards the horizon, turning into a large, deep red disk just above the domes.

'You will be fighting for O'var?' Orak says after a while.

'When he's in battle, I'll be fighting for sure,' I reply, trying to think how to change the subject. 'Is your camp far?'

'No,' Orak answers abruptly. 'Why did you start the fight in the bar?'

'Someone was going to,' I tell him with a lopsided grin. 'I figured it'd be better if one of us did, than one of them. Always pays to get the jump on the other guy.'

'That makes sense,' Orak agrees. 'Still, it was a brave or stupid thing to do. If we had not come to your aid, they might have killed you.'

'It was just a bar fight. It would never have got that serious,' I say with a shake of my head.

'You forget, humans are despised by most races here,' the kroot disagrees, turning down a smaller street leading off the main thoroughfare. 'Nobody would have missed you.'

'Why such bad feeling?' I ask, wondering what we could have done that is so upsetting.

'You humans are everywhere, you spread across the stars like a swarm,' Orak tells me, with no hint of embarrassment. 'You invade worlds which are not yours, you are governed by fear and superstition.'

'We are led by a god, we have a divine right to conquer the galaxy,' I protest, earning more clicking laughter from the kroot leader. 'It is mankind's destiny to rule the stars, the Emperor has told us so.'

'Driven by fear and superstition, even worse than the tau and the tau'va,' the kroot says, his voice suggesting good humour rather than distaste.

'So what do you believe in?' I ask, wondering what makes the kroot think he's got all the answers.

'Change,' he says, looking at me with his piercing dark eyes. 'As we learn from our ancestors, we change and adapt. We learn from our prey and grow stronger. The future is uncertain, to stagnate is to die.'

'You worship change?' I ask incredulously.

'No, human,' he says, showing signs of irritation again. 'Unlike your kind, we simply accept it.'

As the stars begin to appear in the sky, the flames of the bonfire stretch higher into the air. We're seated outside a half-finished dome with Orak and his kindred, and I watch the flames crackling on the great pyre. Huge steaming chunks of meat on sharpened poles hiss and spit within the fire, bringing the smell of cooking flesh and smouldering fat.

I'm seated next to Oriel, who has been watching the kroot closely since our encounter.

'What do you know of these guys?' I ask him when we've got a bit of space to talk privately.

'Not too much, except that they are exceptional close combat fighters, but you know that already,' he tells me with a grim smile. 'The kroot have been hiring themselves out as mercenaries to other races for hundreds of years, the majority of them to the tau. They'll fight with or against anyone as long as the pay is right.'

'They don't look too rich to me,' I comment. 'They don't really wear ostentatious clothes, they don't have palaces or anything else like that. What do they take as pay?'

'It's rather grisly,' Oriel warns me with a distasteful look. 'They fight for technology, arms and ammunition, but also for the bodies of the slain.'

'What do they want them for?' I ask, intrigued at this somewhat morbid form of payment.

'They eat them,' the inquisitor replies curtly. 'They believe that by consuming slain foes, they can take the prowess and skills of their enemy. They also eat their own kind, supposedly to preserve their souls or something. It's a bit complicated really, but some magi amongst the tech-priests believe that the kroot may be actually capable of absorbing information from their food, and passing it on to future generations. I don't understand the details, and it seems highly implausible to me, but the kroot certainly believe it.'

'They're cannibals?' I say, gazing around with new found horror at the aliens around us. 'That's pretty sick.'

'To you or I, certainly,' Oriel agrees with a nod. 'To them it is perfectly natural.'

At that point Orak rejoins us, still with his rifle slung over his shoulder.

'The feasting shall begin soon,' he tells us with relish, his eyes reflecting the firelight.

'Is this some kind of celebration?' Tanya asks as drums and whistles begin to play somewhere in the darkness.

'Yes, it is,' affirms Orak, standing tall above us, looking proudly over his kindred. 'Tomorrow we go to fight once more. Some of us will not return. Some of us will kill many foes and take their essence and grow strong. Either way is unimportant as long as the kroot survive, and the dead are not allowed to waste their treasures.'

'Do you look forward to battle?' Strelli asks. 'Is it an honour and glory thing for you?'

'It is a necessity of evolution,' Orak says strangely, turning away and calling out something to the other kroot. Two of them appear carrying a rack of meat between them. It smells somewhat odd, but not unappetising. There are no plates, and the kroot just tuck in, using their sharp beaks to tear away strips of flesh, gulping them down with relish. I pull out my knife and hack off some meat for myself. I bite hard, but it is surprisingly tender, the hot juices running from the corner of my mouth down my chin. The others cut off chunks for themselves too, cradling the hot meat gingerly in their hands as they eat.

'We took these carcasses in our last campaign, and have preserved them for tonight, to bring luck to the coming battles,' Orak informs us, his thick tongue wiping solidifying fat from his beak. 'Hopefully we will feast on this sweet gift again during the coming war.'

'I thought that O'var was waging a war against humans?' Schaeffer says uneasily, looking hard at Orak.

'Yes, that is so,' the kroot confirms. I get a sick feeling in the pit of my stomach, and bile rises in my throat as I look at the cooling flesh in my hands. I remember Oriel's words.

Cannibals. The kroot are cannibals. It doesn't mean anything to them to eat their own kind. I look at the others, who are coming to the same conclusion. Trost's hands are trembling; Tanya clamps a hand over her mouth; Strelli hurls the hunk of meat away from him, earning him a puzzled look from some of the surrounding kroot. With a choke, Quidlon turns away and vomits onto the dusty ground, his retching punctuated by sobs.

'Is something wrong?' Orak asks, his quills rising slightly. Trost is about to say something but the Colonel cuts him off.

'I think perhaps the excitement of the brawl earlier has unsettled our stomachs,' Schaeffer says hurriedly, darting a venomous glare at all of us to contradict him.

'I understand,' the kroot accepts Schaeffer's explanation and his quills subside again. 'Perhaps the dish of honour will be more comfortable for you.'

He stands up and gestures to one of the other kroot, who disappears for a minute before bringing back a covered tray. I can't help but notice the distinctly Imperial look of the silver platter, probably looted from some noble's house.

'Together we share this morsel,' Orak tells us sincerely. 'Your kindred and mine will be linked, for we shall share the same essence of the foe. In eating together, we shall become a wider kindred. Never before have I allowed this with a human, but your actions impress me. You fight as brave warriors, and you sit with pride at the feast. Join me now.'

He lifts off the lid with his four-fingered hand to reveal what is unmistakably a raw brain. A human brain, by the look of it. In the firelight, the grey mass shines orange, and I can still see a piece of spinal cord dangling from it. I want to gag. Orak picks it up reverently in both hands and holds it above his head and declares something in his own tongue.

'Not for this feast the quick gorging of battle,' he tells us. 'With pride we eat the most precious of all flesh. This warrior was a great leader, he and his soldiers battled well against us. I have been saving this gift for only the most worthy to share with me, and now I offer it to you.'

He lowers the wobbling brain and his beak snaps forward, nimbly stripping away some of the rubbery flesh. He turns towards us and offers the brain forward. We just sit there dumbfounded and nauseous, looking at the quivering pile in Orak's hands.

'Who among you will share this treat with me?' he asks, looking at each of us. None of us move except to swap horrified glances. Even the Colonel looks pale.

'Who among you will share this treat with me?' the kroot leader asks again, his quills beginning to tremble. 'This is a great honour, and I do not offer it lightly.'

When none of us react, clicks and quiet squawks begin to sound around us, and the kroot I see are getting to their feet, their quills extending in anger. I look at Orak, who still holds the brain towards us like a medal. Fighting back the sickness threatening to swamp me, I stand up.

'I will share this treat with you,' I reply hoarsely, and I hear a hiss of breath from the other Last Chancers. I gulp hard. I can hardly believe I'm going to do this. If I don't though, it could be my brain on the platter next time. The kroot don't seem too pleased with us at the moment.

'Very well,' Orak says, proffering the human brain towards me. I take it gingerly, my hands trembling madly. The touch of it makes me want to hurl up the contents of my guts. It's soft and seems to slither around in my grasp as I lift it up above my head for the assembled kroot to see.

My body shaking, I slowly lower it again and look at the organ in my hands. I try not to think about the man this once belonged to. I try to pretend it's something else like grox brain which I've eaten before. It doesn't work. It's like it has eyes that stare accusingly at me.

Gulping again, I lift the brain to my lips and glance at Orak. He gives me a casual wave to proceed, leaning towards me eagerly.

My mouth is very dry and my throat feels like someone is choking me. I close my eyes and bite down on the brain. It doesn't come away easily, I have to gnaw a portion off. My gut rebels, but I choke back the bile in my throat. I swallow hard, not daring to chew, and that almost makes me vomit as well. Opening my eyes, I hand the rest back quickly. Orak lifts it up once more for all to see and we're surrounded by a sudden clamour of bird-like shrieks and stomping feet. I guess I passed the test, but I feel like fainting. I don't think I'll ever forget the taste.

Orak passes the honour dish to another kroot and gestures for me to accompany him slightly outside the circle.

'That was well done,' he tells me, bending down to talk quietly in my ear.

'Uh, thanks,' I reply, desperately trying to forget the last half minute of my life.

'I understand how difficult that was,' he confides in me, his black eyes gazing into mine.

'You do?' I ask, surprised at this comment.

'I am not stupid, human,' Orak assures me, laying a long-fingered hand on my shoulder. 'I know that you do not share our same beliefs and abilities.'

'You knew how disgusting I thought that was?' I say angrily, remembering at the last moment to keep my voice a whisper. 'Why the fraggin' hell did you do it then?'

'To see if you would,' Orak replies evenly. 'To see what kind of humans I would be fighting alongside. We go to fight against your own kind. What you have just done proves to me that when the fighting becomes fierce, you will not stay your hand. Now, return to your friends, and I will have you brought food that you will find more agreeable.'

I stumble back into the firelight and sit down heavily with the others.

'It was damn test,' I hiss to them. 'All along it was a damn test.'

'Well, we seem to have weathered that little storm at least,' Oriel says, lying back with his arms behind his head.

'Yeah,' I reply sourly. 'Next time you can eat the brains though.'

WE DECIDE NOT to return to the skull-laden bar and our rooms, after the trouble we caused our re-appearance might not be appreciated. Instead we make a rough camp not far from Orak's kindred. As we watch their fire dying a couple of hundred paces away, Oriel calls us all together.

'Orak said that they are leaving tomorrow,' he says. 'That doesn't give us much time I suspect. If they are leaving, Brightsword will be making his inspection soon. I still haven't been able to make contact with Coldwind, so we might have to play this by ear for a while. Wake up bright and early tomorrow, we could be forced to move at any moment.'

The night passes fitfully for me, close as we are to fighting the final part of the mission, and mixed with scattered nightmares of horrific feasts with the kroot. In one dream, I imagine devouring Brightsword's brains, even as the others point at me and hurl abuse. I wake just before dawn, caked in sweat and dust, and push myself tiredly to my feet. I see that the Colonel is awake already, standing looking at the coming sunrise with his hands behind his back.

'Do you think it will be today, sir?' I ask him, and he turns and glances at me across his shoulder. It's not often we talk, but sometimes we do, and sometimes it even makes me feel better.

'Perhaps not today,' he says, looking into the distance again. 'But if not today, then certainly tomorrow.'

'What if we can't talk to Coldwind? What do we do then?' I say, a slight doubt nagging at me.

'We will do what we can,' Schaeffer replies quietly. He spins on his heel suddenly and turns his ice-blue stare on me full force. 'Will Tanya make the killing shot?'

'Of course she will,' I answer hurriedly, taken aback by the surprise question.

'If she does not pull the trigger when needed,' the Colonel warns me, 'you will certainly not live to regret it.'

'If she doesn't pull the trigger,' I reply grimly, 'none of us will live to regret it.'

ORIEL STOOD IN the pre-dawn glow out in the desert a few kilometres from the city and watched the lightening sky. The wind,
chill at the moment, whipped up small sand devils around
him, and fluttered the long sand-coloured coat around his
shoulders. He was sure he was alone; there was no sentient
presence that he could detect. Removing a small wand-like
object from a pocket inside his coat, he placed it in the ground,
driving it into the sand with a thump. Fiddling with the instrument, he activated the beacon, which began to pulse with a
dim red light, barely visible to him, but he knew the keen
receptors of the craft it was intended for would pick it out as
brightly as a searchlight.

It was not long before a streak of light began to descend
through the sky like a shooting star. It arrowed down towards
Oriel, and then veered a thousand metres up, swinging into a
wide landing circle. As it grew closer, Oriel could make out the
white-hot pinpricks from the shuttle's plasma engines, though
the black hull was all but obscured from view by the darkness.
Another minute passed as Oriel waited, and the small shuttle
began to slow. With barely more than a whine, it descended,
sophisticated anti-grav motors kicking in rather than loud and

clumsy jets. The hull shimmered and rippled, the darkness around it distorted by an energy field which extended for several metres around it. Oriel gave a silent prayer to the machine god, hoping that the infernal tau surveyors had been fooled by the specially constructed stealth shield. The tech-priests had assured him this would be the case, but he was never one to rely heavily on the artifices of the Adeptus Mechanicus. Clawed landing feet extended from the hull and the shuttle touched down, taking a few seconds to settle into the soft sand. The whine of the engines died down almost immediately and a second later, the fore hatch opened with a short hiss of pressure.

The inquisitor watched impassively as Dionis walked down the ramp, the metal reverberating to his heavy tread, his helmet under one arm. As he stepped off the ramp, it hissed back into place and the shuttle shimmered, the cloaking field activating fully, causing the small craft to disappear from view. Within a few seconds the small transport, which was barely three metres high and five metres long, was invisible.

'Greetings, inquisitor,' the new arrival said, stopping in front of Oriel, his voice low but clearly audible.

'And greetings to you, brother,' Oriel responded formally, looking up into Dionis's broad face. 'You are prepared?'

'I am always prepared, inquisitor,' Dionis chided him slightly. 'Is it not my brotherhood's motto to stand ready at all times, to counter the threat when called upon?'

'So you have sung your battle hymns and made your offerings to the Emperor?' asked the inquisitor.

'I am ready to face the foe. My soul is pure and my weapons cleansed, inquisitor,' answered Dionis.

'May we not have need of them,' muttered Oriel, turning away.

'Praise the Emperor, inquisitor,' Dionis called out to Oriel as he plucked the portable beacon from its hole.

'Yes,' Oriel replied with feeling. 'Praise the Emperor indeed. Today, we may well copy his sacrifice for mankind.'

'It was what we were born for, inquisitor,' Dionis reminded him.

'Yes, sooner or later,' agreed Oriel with a grim smile to himself. 'Let's hope it's later though, there's lots more work to be done.'

SEVEN
ASSASSINS

+++Time to cast the final die+++
+++Fate and luck be with you+++

ORIEL WOKE UP not long after me and headed off without a word to either me or the Colonel. I guess he's gone looking for Coldwind. If Brightsword is making his inspection today, we could be fighting within hours. The thought that I'll be in battle again, real battle against enemies trying to kill me, sends a thrill through me. No more targets that don't shoot back. No endless drill and routine and theory. This is the real thing, and there's nothing like it.

As the sun begins to creep over the horizon, between two domes in the distance, I sit down and begin to strip down my autogun. My hands work automatically, allowing my mind to wander for a while. At first I run over the plan in my head, but that's so ingrained now, all of the possibilities looked at, that there's little diversion there.

I just want it to start. I want the bullets to start flying, the blood to pump through my veins, that feeling of life which I briefly grasped again during the shuttle hijack but which has otherwise been denied to me for over a year. I want to know if Tanya makes that shot, whether Trost will do his job properly, whether those months of hard training have been worthwhile. I want to know if I was right, and I deserve to be on this mission, or if the battle psychosis grips me again and the Colonel should have left me behind.

That part worries me more than anything else. I don't want to be the cause of the mission failing. It's odd, the mission for me isn't about stopping an alien commander invading a human world. The test has become much more personal, a challenge from the Colonel and Oriel. It's whether I picked and trained the team well enough to complete the mission. It's whether I can hold up under the pressure. For me, that'll be the victory, regardless of what the wider consequences are. This isn't a battle against the tau, it's a battle against Schaeffer and the inquisitor he serves.

'Thinking deep thoughts?' asks Tanya, standing behind where I'm sat and looking at the coming dawn.

'Yes,' I reply shortly, not feeling like sharing them with her. She's not my friend, there's nothing special between us. She's Sharpshooter, and my only concern is that she makes that shot so we can get the hell out of the firestorm that'll follow.

'What are you thinking about?' she asks again, sitting down beside me.

'You first,' I say, turning my head to look at her, my fingers still working over the mechanisms of the autogun.

'Whether I'm going to see another dawn,' she admits, not looking back at me. 'But I'm not scared, not really. I'm just curious.'

'Like this isn't you, that it's happening to someone else's life?' I suggest, knowing the feeling.

'Yeah, it's something like that,' she agrees, looking at me for the first time, understanding in her eyes. 'Is that how you feel?'

'All the time,' I admit, snapping the magazine of the autogun back in place and cocking the firing mechanism with a loud click. 'When the time comes, it's almost like the rapture some preachers talk about. It's like the Emperor enters me, takes me over, like I become his weapon and nothing more.'

She looks at me with curious eyes and I meet her gaze. Suddenly the detachment is gone, and I don't see Sharpshooter, I see Tanya Stradinsk. Possibly the last woman I'll ever see in this life. I stand up and look at the others, at Trost and Strelli, at Moerck and Quidlon.

For a moment I see them as people, looking past the names and labels I gave them. There's Tanya, strong and confident again, but still haunted by her guilt. Trost, a merciless killer who acknowledges the pleasure he has gained from his bloody work and now relishes it. Strelli, without a care about anyone or anything else, determined to survive. Like I was a couple of years ago, I suddenly realise. And Quidlon, more restrained, more awed by the wondrous and horrifying galaxy we live in, his eyes opened to the perils he has to face, but still determined to examine it, to try and understand it. And then there's Moerck, sanctimonious, unforgiving, unrelenting in his beliefs and morals. He sees himself as a rock amongst the effluence of the stars. I couldn't hope for a better team. Then the moment passes, the grim reality of what we have to do returns and they become names and labels again. Sharpshooter, Flyboy, Demolition Man, Brains and Hero. All of them part of an intricate plan, like a finely tuned clockwork device, that must work together perfectly or the whole system breaks down and we all die. And of course there's me, Last Chance. Will I turn out to be the weak link?

'Is this going to be the last sunrise I see?' Tanya asks from behind me.

'That's up to you,' I reply coldly. 'It depends how much you want to see another one.'

'I still don't know if I can take that shot,' she says quietly, and I spin on her, ready to bawl her out. But she's sat there, cross-legged, watching Es'tau's star rising in the distance, bathing her in a red glow, lost from the world in her own thoughts. She wasn't telling me; she was asking herself.

'Of course you'll make that shot,' I assure her, whispering in her ear. 'If you make that shot, you get to see another sunset and another sunrise.'

'Is that a threat?' she asks calmly.

'No,' I say with a smile she can't see. 'It's my promise. If you make that shot, I'll make sure you see another sunrise.'

'You said to never trust you,' Tanya points out. 'How do I know you won't abandon me?'

I don't answer straight away. I don't understand myself why I said it, it just came out. I stand there, looking at her, and then at the others, and it comes to me.

'You're one of my Last Chancers,' I say after a short while. 'You're my team, not the Colonel's. You're my Sharpshooter, and I picked you because you're the best. I picked all of you because you're all the best at what you do. I want to see you get those pardons and walk free, to do that thing which I can never do again. I want you to enjoy your next sunset, knowing you can enjoy them for the rest of your life. Most of all, I have a head full of memories which are all that are left of the Last Chancers my first time around. I don't want to add any more. There's enough dead folks in my dreams.'

But Tanya isn't really listening to me, caught up in her own thoughts.

* * *

IT'S QUIDLON WHO wakes up next, and following my talk with
Tanya, I decided to chat with him, to gauge how he's feeling.
It's not some notion that I want to see he's okay, but rather trying to figure out how he's going to act if we do end up fighting
today. Will he get over excited, will he be a coward, will he be
focussed on the mission or is he distracted? Knowing those
things, I can take them into account when the fighting starts.

'A bright and hot day,' I say to him conversationally as he
drinks from a canteen.

'They all are, aren't they?' he replies. 'The Tau home world is
dry like this, they settle more worlds like their own, so I guess
it's always going to be a bright and hot day.'

'I've been in prison, aboard ship and on these hot worlds for
almost a year now,' I tell him. 'I think I would like some rain.
To feel it falling down on me.'

'I've never liked rain, it's cold, it's wet, and it makes people
miserable,' argues Quidlon. 'Where I'm from it rains almost all
the time, a constant, demoralising drizzle that goes on and on
and on, and when it stops it's always cloudy. There's never any
light, it's always grey and overcast.'

'Don't you miss that then?' I ask him as we walk together
towards the shade offered by the looming dome between us
and the sunrise. 'Would you like to see those cloudy skies
again?'

'Not at all,' he says vehemently. 'I've been shown much more
than I would've ever seen at home. There's so much in the
galaxy I never knew about that I know about now. Every day
has opened my eyes to something else. I've met soldiers and
navy staff, I've talked to officers and commissars, I've seen sun-
rises on other worlds, and looked at different stars in the night
skies, and none of that would have happened if I hadn't joined
the Imperial Guard.'

'You realise that might all end today?' I say quietly as we
enter the shade and sit down. I look around. A few kroot are
walking past, one of them nods towards us and I wave back.
The sounds of the city waking up begin to grow in volume, the
clatter of stalls being set up, the alien traders' shouts increasing,
the murmur of life building around us.

'I could be dead, that's true, but I'm not really thinking about
it,' he replies.

'It doesn't worry you at all?' I probe, not believing him.

'I want to see more, but I've seen a hundred times the things most men see in a whole lifetime, more than I ever imagine existed when I was growing up,' he tells me earnestly. 'Who knows what'll happen when I'm dead? Perhaps that's the greatest thing of all, the experience of a lifetime so to speak.'

'Don't be too eager to enjoy it,' I warn him, remembering my own brushes with death. As I sit there, the pain behind my eyes starts again, a dull ache that spreads through my brain, not unbearable, but certainly uncomfortable. I get a glimpse in my mind's eye of bolts of lightning, and the stench of charred flesh. I try to ignore the thoughts and listen to Quidlon.

'Oh, Last Chance, I've got no intention of getting myself killed just to see what it's like,' he laughs back at me, not noticing my distraction. 'Like I said, there's so much more to see here in the mortal world before I pass over. I've met orks now, but I would like to see an eldar, to see if it's true that they walk without touching the ground, or perhaps to visit one of the great cathedrals, or make a pilgrimage to Holy Terra itself.'

'Is that what you'll do when you get your pardon?' I ask, pushing the strange vision out of my thoughts as much as possible.

'To travel more, oh certainly,' he tells me with a smile. 'I don't know how I'd do it. Perhaps I could continue working for Inquisitor Oriel, or maybe sign up as a crewman on a starship; after all I know a lot about mechanics.'

'I'd avoid the navy if I were you,' I caution him. 'You don't seem to mix well with the Adeptus Mechanicus, and there's hundreds of tech-priests aboard every vessel. As for Oriel, the sooner you're shot of him and his devious ways, the better. He's a schemer, and his schemes can backfire horribly. And it'll be you in the firing line when it happens, not him, he's got a habit of escaping. Believe me, I know that, I tried to blow him up once and that didn't work.'

'I never realised you'd worked with Oriel before. What was it like? I mean you haven't said much about the last mission you were on,' he points out.

'That's because I'd rather not talk about it,' I tell him, looking away. 'Too many memories, too many people died who shouldn't have done. I did things I'd never thought I would be able to do, and now I'll do them without a second thought. It killed me, but also showed me exactly who I am.'

'And who is that?' asks the Colonel, giving me a start. I see him standing behind me, watching me with those ice cold eyes of his.

'I'm Kage, lieutenant of the 13th Penal Legion Last Chancers,' I tell him, standing up. 'I'm Last Chance, like you said.'

'What does that mean?' he continues, gesturing Quidlon away with a flick of his head. The trooper gives me a glance and then walks off.

'It means I'm here to fight and die for the Emperor,' I explain bitterly, turning away from him and taking a step.

'Do not walk away from me, Kage,' he growls at me, and I turn back. 'What do you think you are doing, turning your back on an officer?'

'It's not like that any more,' I laugh coldly. 'It's all changed this time. I'm not just the lieutenant, you're not just the Colonel. This isn't about rank, this isn't about seniority. I've realised something. I've realised why you asked me to do the choosing and training. You can't do this on your own, can you? I know how much I've got bottled up inside me, all those memories, all that pain, all that blood on my hands. I can deal with it. You could deal with it as well, but how much more is there for you? I know you care, don't try to tell me you don't. It may only be for our souls, not our bodies, but you care, and you also give a damn about the mission, and you believe in the Emperor and everything else. You're not just a machine, you're a man just like me. Emperor knows, maybe you *were* me once, maybe you were just some poor grunt – or were you born to it? Were you raised on officer's milk as a babe?'

'You know nothing about me, Kage,' he says after a moment, his eyes boring into me. 'Yes, you are right, I needed your help. You showed something special in Coritanorum. I know you came back for me, and it was not just for some damned pardon in my pocket. You do understand some of what I am trying to do, but you don't have a clue about the wider picture. You do not know my past, and you do not know your future. I needed you, and I still need you, but that is all. I do not care about you, I made it clear that you only get one chance with me. You had that chance and you squandered it.'

'So why not just kill me now?' I dare him, holding up my hands like a hostage.

'Maybe I will,' he says, pulling his autopistol from its holster.

'Do it,' I snarl. 'Kill me, you don't need me for this mission, I'm just going to be babysitting Quidlon and Tanya, and they can take care of themselves. I've done my part. You could have had me killed any time over the last four years, any time at all. And you've had justification. You could have killed me after you caught up with me and the rookies on Typhos Prime, but you let them persuade you otherwise.'

'They were threatening to kill me if I did,' he tries to argue, but not too convincingly. The Colonel's never been too good at lying. Not telling the whole truth, he's got plenty of practice at that, but outright lies? No, he just can't pull it off.

'They wouldn't have, despite what they said,' I tell him, bringing my hands down and pointing accusingly at me. 'You could have killed me then, you could have left me for dead when we got lost in Coritanorum. You could have killed me after I murdered those Typhon officers and you found me drunk to the world, but no, you decided to wait until I woke up and then offer me another last chance, knowing I would take it.'

'What do you want me to say, Kage?' he asks, holstering the pistol. 'That I need you on this mission in case it all goes wrong? That is true, I do need you as my back-up. You are without doubt one of the best soldiers I have ever met. But that is not what you really need from me. You want me to carry on punishing you, because that is what you deserve. You know it is true. This is not about redemption, this is about punishment. You had your chance to get out of this forever, but you threw it away because you still feel guilty. You have felt guilty all of your life, Kage, and you want me to feel guilty for you. You want me to put you through hell so that you can hate me, so that you do not have to admit that everything you are trying to prove to me is in fact something you need to prove to yourself.'

'I'm a lying, cheating, murdering son of an ork,' I laugh at him. 'I was a bastard even before you got hold of me. What makes you think I feel guilty about anything I've done?'

'It is not what you have done that plagues you, it is what you did not do,' he says to me, striding up and standing full in my face. 'You are right, you do not give a damn about those people you have killed, you do not care about the misery you have brought others. But you do know that perhaps, if you had not been so selfish and obsessed with your own survival, more of the Last Chancers might have made it out of Coritanorum alive.'

'You never intended any of us to survive, you or Oriel,' I accuse him, stepping back from his intimidating presence.

'Where was your sacrifice when it was needed?' he continues relentlessly, stepping forward again, my personal judge and jury. 'Every night you ask yourself if you could have saved them. Do you think you could have saved Franx if you had not played dead in that air attack? Would you have steered Gappo away from that minefield if you had not been trying to desert? Why did you sweat blood on Kragmeer to save Franx? Was it because you felt he was better than you? Do you hate yourself because all of those people who died deserved to live more than you did? That is why you are Last Chance. That is why you need me to punish you, because yes, you are a loathsome, selfish, cowardly piece of filth who the Emperor should have killed. But for your life you do not know why he has not, and instead has taken away everyone you once knew, except me. I am the only thing you have left, Kage. I am not a memory and I am here to tell you that you do not walk away from me when I am talking to you. Nothing has changed, you are still scum and it is still my duty to save you from yourself.'

I just laugh out loud. A good hearty laugh from the gut, making my jaw ache. The Colonel stands there, looking at me with a quizzical stare, one eyebrow raised. I manage to get myself under control. A couple of the others start to come over, but when they see the Colonel, they back off again.

'Yes, Colonel,' I reply, saluting smartly, even as I try to stop smirking. 'If you have finished being a sanctimonious son of a bitch, sir, I would like my squad to fall in for inspection.'

'Carry on, Lieutenant Kage,' he says with a nod, the formality restored. My thoughts are jumbled as I walk away, feeling his piercing gaze on my back, but they soon clarify when I start shouting orders at the others.

ORIEL TURNS UP about midday and tells us to pack up and clear out. The mission is going ahead here and now. Without comment we get ready, do our last weapons checks, pack our ammo up and leave the rest. Having sleeping rolls and camp burners will only weigh us down, so we head off light. We exchange brief waves of farewell with the kroot, who are also getting ready to leave. Oriel leads us unerringly through the streets, avoiding the worst crowds of the alien quarter, taking us up past the space port. He points to a tau ship standing on the apron, a gleaming white shuttle decorated with large tau symbols in red. That's Brightsword's transport; he's already headed to the battle dome for the inspection.

The inquisitor leads us away from the space port and we see another dome, out in the desert, linked to the city by a single gleaming silver rail. As we get closer, I see bullet-shaped carriages slipping back and forth along the rail and realise it is some kind of locomotive.

'That is how we will gain access to the battle dome,' he tells us, pointing as one of the transports zooms past. 'The training drill you performed on the *Laurels of Glory* represents the zone of action once we are inside the dome. Trost's demolitions will provide the distraction we will need to infiltrate the central complex where the power relays are situated. Once there, Quidlon, Tanya and Kage, rejoined by Trost, will cut the power to the outer entryways and the rail system, cutting the dome off from the outside. The Colonel, Moerck and I will sweep O'var out of hiding, into Tanya's sights. She kills the commander, and we exit again through the rail terminal. Strelli, there is a shuttle some five kilometres or so to the sunward of the dome, out in the desert, which you will go to.'

'When you activate this you should be able to see the shuttle.' The inquisitor passes Strelli a small cylinder with a brass rune etched into its base. 'Fly back to the dome to pick us up. Once we're on board, we will return to our ship in orbit. I have spoken to Coldwind and he assures us that the chain of command will be uncertain for a while following Brightsword's death, and he will do what he can to increase that confusion.'

'That's all well and good,' says Tanya, watching another transport bullet speed out of sight, 'but how do we get on one of the trains?'

QUIDLON CURSES GENTLY and continuously under his breath as we lower him down into the hole. Oriel assures us that the power relays for the travel rail are buried here, and Quidlon simply needs to temporarily cut the power, bringing one of the carriages to a halt. We take the train, switch the power on and ride it all the way inside the fortified dome. Sounds good on paper, but judging from Quidlon's swearing the practice is a little more difficult. It also took us the best part of an hour to find one of the power conduits, sneaking amongst the desert dunes in case a fire warrior saw us from one of the passing carriages and became suspicious. After a while, he emerges, blinking in the bright light after spending several minutes in the small opening we found after levering up a panel situated a couple of hundred metres from the rail.

'I think the power will shut down for several minutes,' he tells us, dusting himself off and putting some oddly-shaped tools back into his pack.

'You think?' Moerck barks at him.

'I don't know how tau timing systems work, they don't even use seconds and minutes, so I'm having to guess,' he moans back, obviously aggravated. 'I couldn't even read the labels on all the switches and terminals, so think yourself lucky I'm not a fried mess right about now.'

'So we manage to stop one of the carriages. What then?' asks Trost.

'I say we kill everybody on board,' I tell them, looking around for disagreement.

'Last Chance is right,' Trost agrees. 'Half of us each side, attacking from the front and back. We storm the place, shoot anything that moves and then wait for the power to come back on. These things don't have drivers, it'll take us right in there.'

'Demolition Man, Kage and Sharpshooter are with me,' the Colonel orders us quickly, glancing down the line towards the city where a dazzle of sun on metal indicates the next transport. 'The rest of you with Oriel. Keep low, shoot at chest height, that way we should avoid killing each other.'

'First in, with a grenade,' I suggest, pulling a frag charge from my belt. 'That'll take most of them out in such a tight space.'

The Colonel nods and Trost chucks one of his frag grenades to Oriel, who passes it to Strelli.

'Why do I get to go in first?' he whines, holding out the grenade for someone else to take.

'Because we can always walk out of there if we need to, Flyboy,' I tell him bluntly.

'Oh, gonna walk up to orbit are we?' he says bitterly, spitting on the ground and stalking away.

Oriel and the others cross the rail and wait on the other side a couple of hundred metres further up the route. We don't try to hide; as far as I know, there's nothing the tau on board the fast-approaching land shuttle can do to stop even if they did see us.

'You are in first, Demolition Man,' the Colonel says, pointing at Trost. 'Then Last Chance and myself. Sharpshooter, you stay here and take out any targets that present themselves at the windows.'

I can see the carriage approaching now, slowing down as it nears us, carried forward by momentum rather than power now that it has moved onto the section cut off from the energy grid. Like I said, it's bullet-shaped, about twenty metres long, with a row of narrow windows roughly two thirds of the way up the side. There are no obvious wheels, it glides soundlessly above the rail. It goes past us still moving quite quickly but slowing, and as we run after it, it settles down onto the track, its lower parts carving furrows into the sand, braking it even more quickly.

At the back of the carriage is a small triangle of steps leading down to either side. I point Trost to the right hand flight and he nods, hefting a grenade in his hand. Tanya peels off to our left, diving prone and taking up a firing position along a sand drift. The hatchway at the top of the steps opens and the door hisses upwards. A tau in a fire warrior's uniform sticks his head out and the Colonel fires, the bullets impacting into the alien and flinging him backwards.

With a skill born of years of practice, Trost lobs a grenade straight through the opening and there's panicked shouting from inside. The detonation blasts out the back five windows and hurls a body out of the door. About two seconds later an accompanying explosion takes out the front half of the train. Trost reaches the steps first and throws himself up, firing with his lasgun as he jumps inside. I go in next, firing the autogun to the right, one-handed, pulling myself through the hatch with my spare hand. Glass crunches under my feet and I see tau bodies strewn all over the benches that run the length of each side of the transport. One or two move and we fire into them, and I hear the Colonel jump up behind me, his autopistol at the ready.

The others burst in from the front and we stand there looking at each other and the three dozen or so corpses lying between us. A few more start to come round so we begin the grisly job of executing them all, pulling off their helmets and putting a round into every single head. Tanya joins us, but keeps her finger away from the trigger of her sniper rifle.

'Let's clear some space,' I hear Oriel say, as he grabs a corpse by its legs and begins to drag it towards the door. As I grab another under the arms and heft it up, a humming begins beneath my feet and I feel the train start lifting off the ground again. Hurrying, we grab bodies and push them out of the doors, watching them tumble helplessly into the dust and sand as the train picks up speed.

'Won't someone see them?' Tanya asks, putting her hands under the armpits of one of the fire warriors.

'We will be inside and the alarm raised by the time that happens, Emperor willing,' Moerck points out.

'How long until we get there?' asks Strelli, helping Tanya lift up the body.

'Ten, fifteen minutes at most, judging by our acceleration and the time it'll take us to brake to a stop,' Quidlon says, peering through one of the shattered windows.

'Forget the rest, get ready,' Oriel says, slamming a fresh clip into his pistol and cocking it. It reminds me of the first time I saw him, in the plasma chamber of Coritanorum, two smoking autopistols in his hands. He's assumed the same cockiness, the same confidence and air of control. There's no doubt at all he knows what he is doing – that if any of us will get out of this alive, it's him.

'When we start to slow down, jump for it,' the Colonel tells Strelli, pushing him towards the back doorway. 'Head for the shuttle but give us at least one hour before you deactivate the stealth field, because when you do the tau will know it is there. After that, get to us as quickly as you can.'

'Where's Coldwind?' the pilot asks, a bit of a strange question at a time like this.

'His part in the mission is over. He's not even going to be at the battle dome,' Oriel replies from up front, waving Strelli to get out. I stand at the top of the steps as he climbs down towards the speeding ground. I give him a thumbs up and he lets go, pushing himself off to one side with his legs. I see him land and roll. A moment later and he's on his feet.

He stands there and waves. As we carry on, I watch him, still standing there, making no effort that I can see to get to the shuttle.

The next few minutes pass in silence as we all watch the battle dome rise further and further out of the sands as we get closer. It's big, bigger than I imagined it would be when we were training back aboard the *Laurels of Glory*. I reckon it must be as least three, maybe four kilometres across at the base, dwarfing anything we saw back near the space port. Even the battle dome on Me'lek was only half the size, though I guess they had a lot more of them there.

I feel the locomotive decelerating quickly now. The dome's just a few hundred metres away, and I get ready, crouching down by one of the broken windows, the autogun warm in my hands, all thoughts of Me'lek put to the back of my mind. Trost jumps for it a hundred metres shy of the black hole that swallows up the rail, and heads off to the right, pulling charges from his pack. I check the autogun one last time and rest it on the sill of the window.

'Last Chance,' Quidlon says to me, a worried expression on his face. 'I've been thinking: we're about to take on a whole army, just the handful of us I mean. How are we supposed to beat a whole army?'

'Inquisitor?' I call out to Oriel at the front of the coach. 'How many are we gonna be facing?'

'Coldwind says it's just Brightsword's own hunter cadre and one other cadre left here,' he tells me, looking back down the carriage at us. 'About a hundred, maybe a hundred and twenty warriors.'

'Small change, Brains,' I say to Quidlon, grinning. 'Coritanorum, now that was a real army we took down, thousands of them.'

'How did you do it?' he asks, subdued for a change.

'Short answer or long one?' I say to him, peering out of the window. The opening in the side of the dome gets closer and closer. The white dome itself gleams in the strong light, dazzling against a pure blue sky.

'I think we've only got time for the short answer, Last Chance,' Tanya says from the opposite side of the aisle.

'Take them on in small lumps,' I laugh, feeling very calm. The throbbing in my head begins to subside as I settle down. It's like everything from the last few months focussing in to me, that out-of-body feeling I've had before. The rapture I told Tanya about earlier, the feeling that something else is inside my body.

Everything goes dim for a second as we pass inside the dome, but I realise it isn't really dark, the yellow lighting is simply nowhere near as bright as the harsh glare outside. In a moment we're through the gateway and entering the terminal. Long boarding platforms run the length of the track on each side, with wide archways at regular intervals. There are a few tau fire warriors stationed there and I can imagine their surprise as the train glides gently to a halt, its windows smashed.

We don't give them a chance to react.

I rise up slightly, still with the autogun on the window frame, and open fire with a short burst, gunning down the nearest tau, the bullets kicking across his stomach and chest, ripping chunks out of his armoured breastplate. The Colonel aims low at another, the row of bullet impacts from his pistol stitching a line along the wall before kneecapping the warrior. Oriel is jumping through the door, firing as he leaps, scoring a cluster of perfect hits on the helmet of a third warrior.

I propel myself out of the back door and roll left to the opposite of the now-stationary carriage, using its back end for cover. A fire warrior turns to run through one of the archways, but I get a bead on him first, the shots taking him high in the back and pitching him forward. He rolls and clambers to his feet, still alive and kicking, and returns fire with his bulky carbine, chewing a massive chunk out of the side of the train and forcing me to duck back.

Glancing out, I see Quidlon fire from inside, his fusillade of las-bolts slamming into the fire warrior and spinning him down again.

Just then, a dull boom sounds from our right, Trost's charges going up. A piercing wail fills the air as warning sirens screech into life.

'Make for the power complex!' the Colonel bellows, following Oriel and Moerck out of the other side of the station in search of Brightsword. They have to flush the commander out into the open so that Tanya can get her shot. I silently wish them the protection of the Emperor.

Quidlon and Tanya join me in the nearest archway. It all springs back to life, the hours and days and weeks spent on the *Laurels of Glory*. It's just how the training bay was set up. We go through this arch, take the next doorway on the left, three doors to the right down the corridor and across a jungle arena.

On the other side are two more doors and then we're into the central plaza, the power facility and armoury entrance.

'Everyone knows the drill,' I say to the other two. 'Come on Last Chancers, time to die.'

With that I toss a smoke grenade through the arch, and follow it through a couple of seconds later. Shots detonate around me, too close for comfort, and I hit the ground, returning fire down the corridor. Tanya sprints across the tunnel and takes cover in the next door alcove, Quidlon following her, snapping off shots from the hip as he does so. I push myself to my feet, rattle off another burst of fire and follow them through. The magazine's empty so I pluck it out and discard it, slamming another one home with well-practiced ease. Another corridor and another smoke grenade, Quidlon firing back through the arch we just passed through, and I hear a shout of someone hit.

We get to a closed portal and I signal Quidlon to get it open. He searches around for an access panel and finds it just above the floor inside the archway.

'Come on, Brains, we haven't got all day,' I hiss at him, before firing at a glimpse of movement to my right. I glance back and see he has the panel open, an odd-looking instrument in his hands, like a pair of compasses made from crystal and wires. There's a hiss and the door slides open.

Tanya ducks through first and comes scurrying back a second later as explosions rock the room beyond.

'Grenades!' I tell them, and Quidlon tosses one through the doorway, followed a moment later by one from my belt. The twin detonations scatter shrapnel across a wide area, the smell of explosives hanging in the air. Another, much louder, explosion rocks the walls and I see debris pile up further down the tunnel. Trost comes bursting through the hole, firing blindly behind him with his lasgun.

I grab Tanya and force her forward, pushing her ahead of me until we reach the next alcove. The smoke, dust and yellow lighting makes everything look foggy and polluted, and it threatens to clog my mouth and nose. Tanya pulls out the lascutter and gets to work on the next door as we provide covering fire. Three more fire warriors go down further along the narrow corridor, and many more duck back out of sight. I can hear the hiss of the lasburner melting through the door, and a moment later Tanya calls out that she's through.

Crawling through the opening I find myself in the middle of a jungle, like I expected. The humidity and heat makes sweat jump out of my skin straight away, and it takes a while for my eyes to adjust to the relative darkness. Trost is rigging up a grenade and tripwire next to the opening as we take positions against the trunks of the trees, up to our waists in large fern leaves.

'Drones!' snaps Tanya, levelling her sniper rifle to the left.

I look that way, and half a dozen of the things come flitting down through the leaves. They're domed discs about a metre across, with thick aerials protruding from their curved tops, each underslung with a pair of linked guns that track and swivel as they scan the jungle for us. Tanya opens fire, plucking the closest out of the air with a single shot, its fractured casing spinning to the ground trailing sparks. Quidlon and I shoot next, a converging salvo of las-bolts and bullets that sends three more of the drones out of control, smashing into trees and plunging into the bushes.

The two that are left return fire and we duck for more cover as the shells smash fist-sized chunks from the tree trunks, hurling bark everywhere and spattering me with sweet-smelling sap. I roll sideways through the ferns, flattening leaves, and finish on my back, firing up. The shots ricochet off one of the drones, causing it to judder in its flight, but it recovers and dips down out of sight. Smart little beggar. A swathe of falling ferns is the only warning I get of the drone's shots and I roll to my feet and dive sideways, landing awkwardly behind a fallen log. The shells strip through the leaves at knee height, splintering along the log – the drone must be hovering just above the ground. One of them hits a more rotten patch of wood and passes straight through, scoring a bloody cut across the back of my right leg just below the knee, but missing the bone. I bite back the pain and fire back blindly, resting the autogun on the log and squeezing off the remainder of the magazine.

Banging more ammo home, I glance over the top of the fallen trunk, and see the drone gliding towards me, its guns tracking left and right, smoking gently. When it's just a couple of metres away, I burst out of my cover and leap at the thing, diving right on top of it.

It sways sideways trying to escape and I drop the autogun and grab its circular rim with both hands. My muscles strain against

its anti-gravity motors as I turn it vertical, its guns spinning
wildly, trying to point at me but instead just finding thin air.
With a shout I break into a headlong run at the nearest tree,
pushing the drone in front of me, and smash it against the
trunk, gouging a strip from the bark and causing one of the
guns to snap off its mounting. I smash it against the tree again
four more times, until the motors die and it suddenly becomes
heavy in my hands. I drop the drone to the ground, where it
wobbles uncertainly for a few seconds before falling still. I go
back and pick up my autogun and shout for the others.

Tanya appears first, her right cheek bloodied, splinters of
wood imbedded in her face.

'Any closer, I would have lost my eye,' she tells me, sitting
down against a tree and dabbing at the blood with her cuff.
Quidlon and Trost appear together, apparently unharmed.

'I think it's this way, but I got turned around in the fight and
it all looks the same, so maybe it isn't,' Quidlon says, pointing
up a trail to our left.

'Check your direction-finder, idiot,' I tell Quidlon, and he
pulls the magneto-compass from his belt, turning its dials to
align properly. He gives it a shake and adjusts it again.

'It's no use,' he says, shaking his head. 'I think the tau have
got some kind of interference generator, or perhaps just the
structure of the dome is jamming the scanning beams.'

'If you hadn't stabbed Eyes, we would know for sure,' snarls
Trost, inspecting the shot counter on his lasgun.

'Forget about the past, it's better to be moving than a sitting
target for more drones, or worse,' I snap at the pair of them,
slapping the compass from Quidlon's grasp. 'According to the
set-up on the *Laurels of Glory* there should only be one other
exit out of this area. We find that, we know where we are.'

'Oh, and the tau will just let us, will they, Last Chance?' spits
Trost, pulling Tanya to her feet.

'No, but we can make them think twice about stopping us,' I
tell them. 'Come on, less arguing, more moving.'

Progress through the jungle is slow, hampered by the under-
growth and the need to keep alert at all times. The arena is only
a few hundred metres across, but we take our time, not wanting to run into the tau without expecting it. After about ten
minutes, Trost hisses and hits the deck, the rest of us following
suit.

'Movement, twenty, maybe thirty metres to the left,' he whispers. I rise to a crouch and see he's right, I make out fire warriors advancing cautiously between the trees. I'm not sure how many, maybe half a dozen, perhaps more. I point upwards and they all nod, understanding the plan. Keeping the trunks between us and the tau, we shin up into the lower branches and wait for the enemy to pass beneath us. The first few walk by without noticing, but a drone buzzes past just below me and then stops.

'Now!' I shout, dropping down, the gun blazing in my hands. At this range I can't miss and the drone explodes into a shower of flaming shrapnel. The tau turn, but I'm on them, swinging the butt of the autogun into the helmeted face of the closest, smashing the small cluster of lenses that are where his eyes should be. The next in line raises his rifle to blast me apart but I kick the muzzle aside and the shot tears through his comrade, nearly slicing him in half. I reverse the kick and power my boot into the tau's chest, smashing him on to his back, and then leap on him, driving the autogun under his chin and pulling the trigger. The top of his helmet explodes across the ferns in a bloody spray.

I look up to see Quidlon driving his knife up into the groin of another fire warrior while Trost smashes a rock over the head of another. The two remaining aliens turn and flee, but Quidlon snatches up his lasgun and cuts them down with an intense salvo of bolts before they get out of sight. I take a pause to catch my breath, looking at the mutilated bodies. Rather them than me.

We head off in the direction the tau came from, figuring they must have entered through the doorway we're looking for. Another hundred metres or so, and there's a stream across our path, cutting through a wide clearing. It looks like a killing zone to me, good lines of fire from all around the perimeter, the stream to splash about and slip around in. But we're up against the clock here, no time to look for a better spot up or downstream. The drone attack has put us behind schedule already, we need to get out of here fast and into the central chamber.

Movement across the clearing catches my eye and I instinctively bring up the autogun, ready to fire. I look harder, but all I can see are leaves and branches. Then to my right, there's more movement, and I focus on the area quickly, but still there's nothing to be seen. I peer out through the foliage, keeping my head down, trying to see what's moving out there. I catch a glimpse now and then of something, but nothing I could definitely identify as a tau. It's then that my attention is drawn to the large bole of a tree pretty much directly opposite from where I'm crouched. I look at the deep score lines in the bark running up and down, and they bend and twist slightly. The strange thing is, the pattern of the lines is almost a perfect humanoid shape.

'Sneaky bastards,' I whisper to myself, lining up a shot on what I take to be the head of the near-invisible warrior. I pull the trigger softly, sending a single round cracking out across the clearing, it impacts on something in front of the tree and it's then that I see a figure thrashing to the ground, the light somehow bending around it, making it near impossible to see. Then all hell breaks loose. There's muzzle flashes from all around us, just within the far tree-line. There's incoming fire from every direction, a massive fusillade of bullets that converge on our position, shredding leaves and branches and punching into the thick trunks of the trees spraying iron-hard splinters around us, forcing us to hurriedly duck further back into cover.

'How do we get past?' asks Trost, leaning back against a tree, glancing back over his shoulder nervously. 'I can't even see them.'

'One of us draws their fire, the others shoot on the muzzle flashes,' I say.

'Great. Who gets the job of target?' Trost says, obviously not volunteering himself.

'I'll do it,' Tanya says, and before I can stop her she's heading out towards the clearing. Trost and me follow quickly after her, scanning the trees for signs of movement. Tanya breaks from cover for a couple of seconds and then dashes out of sight again, but not before the tau open fire. I see a blaze of light just to my left and fire quickly, emptying half a clip, before turning my aim on more movement to my right, using up the rest of the magazine. I pull it out and slam another one in. Three reloads to go, and there's still plenty of fighting to be done.

'Rush 'em!' I shout, ducking my head down and dashing out, firing wildly from the hip, before diving down into the cover offered by the shallow lip of the stream. There's more return fire, which kicks up dozens of impact splashes in the water around me, and I quickly wriggle my legs out of the way and fire back, targeting a cluster of bushes where I saw three or four flashes of light. There's a crackle of sparks and something crashes out of the bushes, flattening the leaves underneath it. I hear fire from my right and see Trost targeting the same spot, and open fire again, guessing that there's more than one of them there.

Something buzzes past my head and carves a furrow in the bank behind me before exploding, showering me with dirt.

'Demolition Man, show me some fireworks!' I shout out to Trost, who's now just upstream from me. He gives me a thumbs up and pulls a large canister from his pack, about the size of my forearm. Pulling the pin, he hefts it towards the far tree-line. I watch it spin through the air.

'Don't look!' Trost shouts, but too late. I'm just twisting my head away when the bomb explodes and a sheet of white fire erupts in a circle, searing my vision and causing spots to dance in front of my eyes. I feel someone grab me by the shoulder and haul me to my feet.

'Follow me,' I hear Tanya pant in my ear and I stumble into a run as she guides me across the clearing. All I can smell is burning, and I can feel the charred earth crunching under my step. Blinking my eyes rapidly, my vision starts to return, first a blur of yellow and green, but after a few more seconds hazy shapes of bushes, and a grey blob I take to be Quidlon or Trost.

'Door's not far,' I hear Quidlon say, and rubbing at my eyes, I can see him much more clearly.

'You got any more of those incendiaries, Demolition Man?' Tanya asks.

'Just one more,' he replies.

'Better save it,' I tell him. 'Use ordinary grenades.'

We charge the exit, which isn't that well held, the ten tau taken down with three simultaneous explosions.

'I thought it would be harder getting out,' Tanya admits as we pound down the corridor towards the entrance to the power chamber.

'A lot of them came after me,' Trost tells us. 'I caused a hell of a bang, nearly took down half the dome, I reckon.'

'And there's the Colonel causing mayhem as well,' I remind them as Tanya goes to work with the las-cutter again. 'We have to keep the advantage of surprise. I don't know how quick they can respond, but something tells me the tau are good at getting organised very quickly.'

'I'm through,' Tanya informs us, snapping closed the cutter and hanging it on one of her pack straps.

'Remember the plan,' I say, readying a smoke grenade. 'Cover the ground to the tower and get inside. Demolition Man and me hold off any attackers while Brains cuts the power and locks down the doors. Sharpshooter gets to the top of the tower ready to fire. Any trouble, just shout out and I'll come running.'

'Got it, Last Chance,' Tanya says with a nod, pulling out one of her own smoke grenades. 'See you at the top of the tower.'

We roll the grenades through the opening cut by Tanya, and I glance after them to see thick blue smoke spilling everywhere.

'Go!' I slap Tanya on the backside and she jumps through the hole, followed by Quidlon. I hear a burst of gunfire and follow through quickly, Trost bringing up the rear. I hurl myself through the smoke, not bothering trying to fire as shots whine and whistle around us, and nearly slam face first into the wall of the tower. Something explodes above my head and showers me with debris from the tower wall.

'Get inside, right now!' I bark at the others, and they head off in the direction of the door. I see shadowy shapes to the left and right and sight along the barrel of the autogun, picking my shots. I loose off one burst to the left and see a figure drop, then another to the right is kicked off their feet by the volley. I take a few steps along the wall to change my position, and return fire begins to send splinters up from the floor and wall where I was standing. I fire back at the muzzle flares and hear a muffled scream as my shots hit home. A few more steps and I can see Trost in the doorway, waving frantically at me.

'What's the matter?' I ask, hurrying over to him.

'Quidlon's gone awol, disappeared out the other side of the tower,' he tells me, pointing over his shoulder with his thumb.

'Okay, hold position here, I'll drag the stupid fragger back,' I tell the saboteur.

The inside of the tower is wide open, a single spiral staircase winding up to the other floors around a central pole, small landings at regular intervals going up towards the ceiling. I glance up and see Tanya still running up the stairs, her rifle over her back as she steadies herself against the central column, with no handrail to guide her.

Pulling myself back to the task in hand, I look across the circular hallway to the door opposite, where the door is still open. I dart a look outside: there's no tau in sight, but there is a line of five empty battle suits standing on the concourse, in front of a pair of heavy armour doors, and I see Quidlon over by them. The suits stand open, the front part of the bodies hinged up, the thigh panels lowered, showing the cockpit inside. Glancing around again, I sprint over the open ground to Quidlon.

'Hey, Brains, what the frag are you doing?' I shout at him.

'Magnificent, aren't they?' he says, grinning like a fool. 'Think, if we had one of these, there'd be no stopping us, we'd cut through the fire warriors with no problems.'

'If we don't get a fraggin' move on now, then a bunch of tau bastards in these suits are gonna come for us, and we're not gonna stand a chance,' I bark at him, spinning him round by the shoulder. 'Now shut the damn power off before more reinforcements arrive along the grav-rail!'

'I'll just take a quick look in one of them,' he says, pulling himself away and stepping towards the nearest battle suit.

'We have not got time for this crap!' I yell at him, grabbing his arm. He twists suddenly and drives his fist into my gut, knocking me to my knees.

'Back off, Last Chance,' he snaps. 'I might die here, and I want to have a look at one of these machines before I go.'

He climbs up onto the battle suit, but I jump after him, dragging him back to the ground. He rolls easily out of my grasp and swings a kick at my groin, which I barely deflect with my thigh. I guess I taught him well. His fist hammers into my right eye, faster than anything he ever threw at me in training. I fall back on my arse, dazed, and he climbs back up again.

With the fronts of the thighs lowered down for access, I can see that there's a seat inside, surrounded by display panels and rows of illuminated buttons. Hooking his leg inside, Quidlon drops into the seat, and I notice how his legs drop into the thighs of the suit. Bracing clamps close with a hiss around his legs, locking him in place.

As I push myself to my feet, clutching my gut, he stabs at one of the controls. There's a high-pitched tone and a tau voice says something.

'Get out of there. You don't know what you're doing!' I yell at him.

'Back off, Last Chance!' he shouts at me, a wild, possessed look in his eye. His left hand settles on a stubby control column while his right punches a few more buttons. 'I think I've got it, the controls are actually really simple, all in the right places.'

The thigh panels flip back up into place, sealing shut with a clang, and then with a whining of motors the main canopy drops down. The last I see of Quidlon is his wide grin. The suit sits there motionless for a moment, and I wonder if he really has worked it all out. Then the war machine begins to judder, shaking violently for a couple of seconds. With a hiss, the chest plate opens up again. The canopy hinges away to reveal a charred corpse in the seat, still smoking, burnt lips peeled back from grinning teeth. There's a few crackles of energy still playing around two rods inserted into either side of Quidlon's head. Silently, the rods withdraw back into the sides of the cockpit. The thighs peel downwards revealing his ravaged legs, pieces of material burnt onto the bone. The stench of burnt flesh fills my nostrils and I gag. I gulp heavily to stop myself throwing up.

'You stupid piece of sump filth!' I bellow at Quidlon's husk of a body. Losing my senses completely, I fire a few shots into the corpse, causing it to collapse into a pile of bones and ashes which spill out from the suit. I spit on the pile and then kick at it, scattering ashes and chunks of shattered bone around me. 'Stupid, fraggin', stupid, son of a bitch, stupid fragger!' I scream hoarsely, punctuating my shouting with kicks, before pulling myself together.

I stand there panting and look at the slightly smoking battle suit. I pull a grenade from my belt and toss it onto the seat, before stepping back. The explosion tears the cockpit apart, throwing out shattered glass and pieces of instrument panel that drop amongst Quidlon's burnt remains. Realising I haven't got too many grenades, I use my autogun on the other four, spraying short bursts of bullets into each one, my firing rewarded by sparks of electricity and small fires breaking out across the various control panels.

More gunfire draws my attention back to the tower, and I turn on my heel and leg it. Glancing to my left I see fire warriors coming into the surrounding chamber, and fire off a few bursts of shots, taking one of them down and forcing the others back out of sight. I reach the tower and Trost is there, firing from the other doorway. I look over his shoulder and see three more downed fire warriors sprawled halfway across the concourse.

'Keep it tight here, I'll check on Sharpshooter,' I tell him, before pounding up the steps two at a time, paying no heed to the fact that I could fall off and plummet to the ground below with a mis-step. It takes me some hard running to get to the top, passing rooms full of instruments and glowing control panels, but eventually I burst out onto an open platform.

Tanya is crouched behind the parapet, her sniper rifle clasped across her chest. Shots ring off the surrounding wall, and I duck and roll over to her.

'How's things?' I ask, pulling out the autogun magazine to check how many bullets are left. It's about half full.

'They know I'm up here. I can't prepare for a clean shot under this kind of fire,' she tells me with a grimace.

'Some hidden hunter you are,' I snap, worming my way forward as more shells kick chips off the edge of the parapet.

'They came in and started firing. They already knew I was here, they didn't see me,' she snarls back, giving me a sour look.

'We're gonna get surrounded pretty soon if we aren't careful,' I say, pushing the magazine back into the autogun.

I pop up out of the cover of the parapet and fire off three shots at a group of fire warriors crouched in one of the archways around the central chamber, causing them to duck back. Dropping back out of sight, I crawl across the platform to the opposite edge and peek a look over the top. Another seven fire warriors are closing in on our position from the other side. Again, I jump up, fire two quick bursts, catching one of the tau full on, before ducking down again.

Suddenly I hear someone bellowing in Tau, a much deeper voice than I've heard before. I scramble over to Tanya, and she nods. We both look down, and there we see a tall alien running amongst a group of fire warriors, wearing flowing red robes.

'That's Brightsword!' I hiss at her and she nods again, bringing her sniper rifle into position.

It's then that I hear another shout, this time in Gothic.

'He's heading for the armoury, stop him!' I hear Oriel's bellow, and see the inquisitor and the Colonel dashing into view from another archway, auto pistols spitting bullets, bloodied chainswords in their hands. Moerck follows them, firing shots at the fire warriors dashing across the chamber, taking a couple of them down. I join their fire for a couple of seconds, but can't get a clear shot on Brightsword. Another fire warrior squad intercepts Oriel and the others, cutting off their line of fire to the tau commander.

'Come on, Sharpshooter, take him down!' I snarl at Tanya, but she doesn't answer. As return fire makes me dive for cover again, I glance back at her. She's there, crouched over her rifle, taking aim. But she does nothing, she just slowly tracks him.

'Get a clear shot, Emperor damn you!' I snarl, but she ignores me. Then her hands begin to tremble, I see the muzzle of the rifle wobbling in her grip.

'Take it easy, relax, breathe, then plug the bastard,' I say, trying to keep myself calm. I crouch there staring at her, willing her to pull the trigger. *Now*, I try to mentally shout at her. *Now, damn it!* With a choked sob, she drops the rifle clattering to the platform and falls to the ground.

'Are you hit?' I yell at her, jumping over to her side. She balls herself up, arms over her head to protect herself, and I can hear her sobbing over the rattle of gunfire and the snap of lasguns.

'Tanya, are you hurt?' I demand, grabbing her shoulder. She's limp, and as I pull her arm away I see tears streaking down her face.

'I… I couldn't do it,' she sobs at me. 'I'm sorry, Kage.'

'Fraggin' stupid…' I lose the power of speech, I'm so incensed. I backhand her across the face. 'We are so dead now, you wouldn't believe it.'

'I'm sorry,' she apologises again, in between sobs and sniffs.

'It's too fraggin' late for that now,' I yell at her, dragging her up by the hair. 'Get your rifle, we have to get off this tower.'

She stands there dumbly for a second, staring blankly at me.

'Get your damn rifle, soldier, and move out!' I scream in her face. She seems to snap out of it, losing the glazed look in her eyes, and snatches up her rifle. She darts another look at me and then heads back towards the stairs. I take one last glance over the tower edge, just in time to see Brightsword and his bodyguard disappearing from view through the wide doorway just behind the damaged battle suits. I run after Tanya, changing the clip in the autogun, making an effort to slow myself as I dash down the treacherous spiral staircase. Tumbling down and breaking my neck would be such a stupid way to go. After all, I'm sure the tau are going to try pretty hard to kill me, I don't want to spoil their fun.

When I reach the bottom, Trost turns around to me.

'What's happening?' he asks, switching his attention back and forth between me and the fire warriors outside.

'Brightsword's escaped. We have to get out of here,' I say, heading for the other door. I see Oriel, Moerck and the Colonel fighting hand-to-hand with a squad of fire warriors. I'll say this, the tau have impressive guns, but they don't know the first thing about close combat. Schaeffer and the inquisitor easily cut them to bits with their chainswords and head our way.

More fire warriors appear behind them and I give them some covering fire, squeezing off just a few rounds at a time, knowing I've only got one magazine left. Moerck stops and turns, firing a few shots at the tau as well, driving them back into hiding again. Oriel's the first to reach the tower.

'Which way did he go?' the inquisitor demands, grabbing the collar of my camo shirt. I point at the doors, which have closed again now.

'He has got inside the armoury,' the Colonel says heavily, chest heaving from his recent exertions. 'That will make things more difficult.'

He and the inquisitor push past me, and Moerck jogs over, ejecting his lasgun's power pack.

'Sharpshooter failed us,' he says bitterly.

'Yep, she did,' I agree. 'Time for us to get the frag out.'

'The mission is not complete yet, Last Chance,' he says, sliding another power pack into place.

'In case you hadn't noticed, the mission has gone up like a demo charge, it's a fraggin' major catastrophe,' I snarl at him, trying to push past, but he grabs my arm. I wrench it free from his grip. 'It's over, we messed up, now it's time to cut and run!'

'Are you deserting, Lieutenant Kage?' he says ominously, the barrel of the lasgun swaying in my direction.

'Yes, I sodding well am deserting! You are not a commissar any more, Moerck!' I point out to him. 'You do not have to die here.'

'No, I am not a commissar,' he replies viciously. 'I am Hero. Do you remember that? *Hero*. Which is why I do not cut and run and I do not desert in the middle of the mission and that is why you are not going to take another step.'

'This is idiotic,' I snap back at him. 'Aren't there enough tau to fight without us gunning down each other? Today is a lost battle, but perhaps we've scared Brightsword enough that we'll win the war. Let's get on the shuttle and live to fight another day. Hell, I'm volunteering right now to join the defence of Sarcassa, but I am not staying here a second longer.'

'Hold your position, lieutenant,' I hear Schaeffer bark from inside. He steps through the doorway, and signals Moerck to get out of the way.

'Shoot me, cut me down, I really don't care any more!' I shout at the Colonel. 'I am getting out of here, and I'm not going to come back for you this time.'

The Colonel smiles then, a grim expression.

'Too late,' he replies simply, pointing over my shoulder. I look around. The armoury doors are sliding effortlessly open and I realise why Oriel was so confident that Brightsword would pass by Tanya's sniping position.

I FEEL THE ground tremble under my feet as the five battle suits advance, striding between the smoking wrecks of the ones in front of the doors. They pound straight towards us with their guns brought up. Brightsword's is easy to pick out: more decorated than the others, an intricate tau design on the front plate. A multi-barrelled cannon on his right arm swings in our direction, a missile pod mounted on his shoulder angling up towards the tower. On his left arm is a shield-like device which I can see crackling with energy. His bodyguard are armed with the same multi-barrelled guns, and a mix of other lethal-looking weaponry. I feel my legs buckle under me and I drop to my knees. Everything seems to slow down. I see the four barrels of Brightsword's gun begin to spin, building up speed, and then he opens fire with an explosive burst of light, the shells tearing into the wall just behind me.

I hear Schaeffer curse and dive back into the tower, and somebody calls my name, Moerck I think. Everything snaps back in my head, the roar of the guns is deafening and I dive to one side and roll, feeling the whip of bullets screaming around me. Something hot and painful catches my foot, sending me sprawling again, and I look down to see blood oozing out of a hole in my right boot. Biting back a shout of pain, I bring round my autogun and open fire, spraying bullets at

Brightsword. They ricochet harmlessly off his battle suit in a random pattern of sparks, leaving tiny little dents but having no other effect. One of the bodyguards peels off towards me, and points what is unmistakably a flamer in my direction. I hurl myself to my feet, ignoring the searing pain from my foot, and dive into cover behind the tower a moment before a jet of flame crackles past, spilling burning fuel across the concourse. The heat washes over me, stinging my eyes.

To my right I see the others sprinting from the tower. A couple of seconds later, a series of explosions wrecks the tower from inside, flames billowing out of the doorways. I try to stand, but my leg gives way, slumping me against the wall of the tower. The battle suit with the flamer stomps around the corner, weapons tracking from side to side seeking a target. It aims at the fleeing Last Chancers, not noticing me, and I open fire with the few bullets left in my magazine, aiming for the canister of flamer fuel on its left arm. The canister explodes, setting fire to the left side of the armoured suit and hurling molten shrapnel across the floor. The suit's pilot ignores the damage, turning on me with the cannon. I take the only route open and dive between the battle suit's legs, just as the gun opens fire.

The battle suit swings laboriously around to face me, forcing me to dodge aside again. I break for the cover of the smouldering tower and jump inside just as Brightsword turns and fires, the bullets tearing up great chunks of the floor behind me. Inside, the tower is littered with rubble from the destroyed steps, dirty great cracks in the walls. My foot has gone numb and I sprint lopsidedly out of the other door, limping heavily. The others are sheltering in one of the door alcoves on the far side of the concourse, shooting ineffectually at the battle suits as they split up and round the tower from each direction.

My foot slips on debris as I run out of the exit, twisting my tortured foot and sending me head first into the floor with a cry of pain. I look up and see the grey and black armour of Brightsword looming over me, one foot raised to stamp on me. I roll sideways under the foot, which smashes down just centimetres away from my leg, cracking the solid material of the concourse.

As I drag myself to my feet, Brightsword swings quickly, pivoting on one foot, the barrel of his cannon smashing into my chest and hurling me against the tower wall. I feel something break inside me, a couple of ribs probably, and my breathing becomes tight and short. The tau commander brings his arm back for another punch and I drop to one side, the blow smashing chips from the wall and showering me with dust.

The others direct their fire on Brightsword as he looms over me, las-bolts and bullets pinging around us. I get the strangest sensation that I've been here before. I then realise this is like the waking nightmare I had on the shuttle. In fact it's almost exactly the same – the gunfight around me, the massive figure looming over me. He turns, raising his shield arm, and the shots ricochet off it wildly, causing small crackles of energy to leap from the disc. His shield still locked in place, he swings at me again, nearly taking my head off.

Strangely, I don't feel so scared now though. It's like I know somehow that he's not going to kill me. Then I hear a sharper crack over the zip of lasguns and rattle of autoguns. Something slams into the shield, causing it to detonate in a bright shower of blue sparks, falling to the ground in three shattered pieces. More shots ring out, armour-piercing shells punching neatly through the battle suit in a tight cluster at the centre of the main chestplate.

The tau commander forgets me and turns on the others, swinging the burst cannon around to a firing position. The next incoming shot hits one of the barrels end on, causing it to split, and as he fires, the gun ruptures, shearing off the whole arm, which spins past and clangs to the ground just to my right. More shots in rapid succession cut through the struts of his right lower leg, causing it to buckle under the weight of the suit and toppling him down to one side.

There's a hiss from the battle suit, and a moment later a section of the body is punched away on four small jets, hurling Brightsword from the crippled machine. The four bodyguards are leaping towards the Last Chancers, who are heading for the far end of the chamber, propelling their battle suits forward in long leaps on their jump jets. I look back at the escape pod and see the hatch swinging open. The others are cut off, the bodyguard in between them and Brightsword.

'I'm coming for you, you alien meathead,' I snarl, propelling myself across the concourse, the other battle suits oblivious to my presence, leaving blood red footprints behind me.

I reach the escape pod as Brightsword pulls himself clear, bleeding profusely from a wound in his arm. He slumps to the ground and looks up at me, anger in his eyes. He mutters something in Tau and takes a deep breath. I heft the autogun in both hands, and he makes no attempt to block me as I swing the butt at his head, cracking his skull and causing him to scream out in pain.

I hear a screech of metal on metal and look around to see the battle suited bodyguard turning quickly in my direction. Wasting no time, I dash Brightsword's brains out across the floor with another two blows and then start hobbling back towards the tower.

'Run!' bellows Oriel, sprinting my way. One of the battle suits pivots in his direction and fires, a ball of white-hot plasma screaming past just behind the inquisitor to explode in a blinding flash on the distant dome wall.

'I can't!' I snarl back at him through gritted teeth, as he reaches my position.

The bodyguard have split up, two of them pursuing the other Last Chancers, the other pair, including the one-armed suit I'd tangled with earlier, heading back towards us to exact some vengeance for their dead commander.

'We have to rendezvous with the others back at the transport terminal,' Oriel tells me, putting one shoulder under my arm and lifting me to my feet. He drags me through into the tower just as a plume of explosions outside heralds a rocket attack, the shockwave hurling both of us into the rubble.

'Can you walk?' he asks me, standing unsteadily on the shifting debris.

'I'll bloody walk out of here if I need to!' I tell him with feeling, grabbing his arm and pulling myself up.

'Damn, more fire warriors,' Oriel curses, glancing out of the opposite door. 'There's too much open ground to get across.'

'Make a dash for it, leave me here,' I say to him, but he just laughs.

'Leave the heroics to Moerck,' he tells me.

'Sod the heroics, I'm hoping you'll draw them off,' I snap back, not at all amused. 'Can't you use some magic on them or something?'

'And do what?' he snarls, exasperated. 'Persuade them to go away? I don't think that will work.'

'Well, I don't know,' I shout back, getting angry. 'It's your frag-gin' power, not mine. Make 'em think we're dead or something, they'll go after the others then and we can make a break for it.'

A shadow looms in the doorway and we scuttle out of view as one of the tau thrusts through his burst cannon and lets rip, shredding the opposite wall and filling the air with dust and flying shards.

'Alright, I'll try it,' Oriel agrees. 'Lie down and play dead. At least if this doesn't work, we won't know about it.'

We sprawl ourselves on the rubble and wait. I try to make my breathing as shallow as possible. I feel the blood congealing in my boot, the dust settling in my mouth making me want to cough. I close my eyes so that I won't blink. Tau voices drift through the doorway behind us and I focus my attention on the sharp rubble under me, trying to act like I'm as dead as a stone. I can hear feet crunching, quite a few aliens by my judge-ment – inside now – and something prods at my back, the barrel of a rifle. There's more talking, and I hear the clump-clump of the heavy battle suits receding outside, followed by a burst of gunfire. The tau around us move out hurriedly, leaving us in peace. I lie there for a while longer.

'Sit tight, wait for them to leave the chamber,' I hear Oriel say, and then realise that he's inside my head again, rather than actually speaking. I count slowly to myself, picturing the tau running across the concourse after the others. When I've given them a couple of minutes to be well clear I sit up, and see Oriel is already by one of the doors, peering out.

'They've left a couple of guards at the far end,' he tells me, gesturing for me to look. I glance out and see two war drones hovering a hundred metres or so away.

'Guess you can't trick them Have to do it the traditional way,' I say, retrieving my autogun from where I'd discarded it on the floor.

'Take the one on the right, I'll take the left one,' Oriel says, moving over to the other doorway. 'On my count.'

I line up the shot, using the pitted and cracked edge of the door to help steady my aim. The drone is sat there, slowly rotat-ing, using its artificial eyes and ears to keep watch on the tower and doorways on its side of the chamber.

'One... two...' Oriel counts down, and then stops. 'Someone's coming!' he hisses to me, ducking back inside.

'Who?' I whisper back, moving around to get a clear shot out of the doorway.

'A tau, no armour,' he tells me. 'Perhaps come for O'var.'

I look out and see the tau picking his way cautiously towards the tower, glancing around every couple of seconds. He's dressed in layers of light green and blue robes which waft around him as he quickly walks our way.

'It's Coldwind,' I say, relaxing as he gets closer. I gesture to get his attention and he spots me, startled. He quickens his pace and hurries over.

'The shas think you are dead,' he says, gazing at us with astonishment.

'That's what I wanted them to think,' Oriel confirms, not giving any details. 'What are you doing here?'

'The others are in a safe place for the moment, but I wanted to check up on the reports that you had been killed,' he tells us, regaining his composure. 'It is rare for our warriors to make such a mistake.'

'Can you take us to the others?' I ask, glancing at the drones outside.

'Yes, follow me after I have dismissed the battle drones,' he replies immediately.

I watch him walk out again and say something to the drones in Tau. They bob in acknowledgement and then turn and zip out of one of the doorways to our left, moving at some speed. He waves for us to come out of hiding.

'Where are the others?' Oriel asks, helping me limp across the concourse. 'And just what the hell are you doing here?'

'Close by, in one of the urban training areas,' Coldwind tells us, pointing us the right way. 'They have doubled back and are now behind the firesweep the shas are currently performing. I will lead you to them and then you should be able to reach your shuttle without a serious encounter. I am here because I thought it might be prudent should something go amiss. It seems it was a wise decision.'

Oriel stares at Coldwind, his eyes narrowed.

'You're still holding something back,' the inquisitor snarls, stopping in his tracks. 'Tell me!'

The ambassador hesitates for a moment, and then sighs.

'Your shuttle has been detected and intercept craft have been despatched from orbit to prevent your escape,' he tells us, urging us to keep moving with a wave of his hands. 'I cannot guarantee you will reach your starship safely.'

'Is that all?' I ask. 'I never expected to get an easy ride out of here anyway.'

We follow the ambassador out into a corridor, which curves gently away to the left. We pass several open doors, one or two containing the corpses of fire warriors. The walls are scarred with the signs of battle, cracked and pitted from bullets, las shots and plasma impacts.

'In here,' Coldwind tells us as we reach a wide double door. 'They are in the two-storey building just beyond this doorway.'

He opens the door for us, and we step inside a small Imperial town, swathed in darkness. Two- and three-storey buildings loom up into a fake night sky around us, illuminated by two dully glowing moons. I load my last magazine into the autogun as we cross the deserted street, listening for any sign of the others.

We stop, and hear whispered voices from a building dead ahead.

'Yes, in there,' Coldwind tells us, pointing for us to precede him. We scuttle through the shadows, and Oriel calls out.

'Last Chancers?' he hisses.

'Inquisitor?' I hear the Colonel reply. The door opens on creaking hinges and we step inside. I look back, and see that Coldwind has disappeared. At that moment, blazing light like a sun breaks out everywhere, bathing the building in a white glare. Squinting out of one of the windows, I see the four battle suits standing in the square at the front of the building, searchlights springing from concealed lenses within their suits. I can also dimly make out other figures scurrying through the buildings, fire warriors hugging the plentiful cover.

'It's Brightsword's shas've. Coldwind has betrayed us,' snarls Oriel, ripping his pistol from its holster. He delves into a pocket in his coat and pulls out what looks to be a small globe. He whispers to it for a couple of seconds, before putting it away again.

I turn my attention back to the battle suits. With deliberate slowness, like a firing squad taking aim, the shas've angle their shoulder mounted rocket launchers at the building we're in.

'First rule of assassination. We should have realised,' I hear the Colonel say.

'What's that?' Tanya asks, loading large calibre bullets from her bandoleer into the sniper rifle in her hands.

'Kill the assassins,' I reply, cocking the autogun and taking aim at the lights.

'Your people will weep and your worlds will bleed!' a voice from one of the battle suits booms out, echoing off the surrounding buildings. 'You will not live to see the misery you have brought upon your people!'

This is it, we're all gonna die, I think to myself. Suddenly there's an explosion in one of the buildings to our right, and I see the bodies of tau warriors being hurled burning from the windows by the fireball. From out of the billowing smoke and flames strides a figure straight from legend. Something whispered about in military camps with awe. Something dreaded by all enemies of the Emperor. I feel goosebumps prickle across my body. An Angel of Death. A Space Marine.

'Emperor's blood,' curses Trost, eyes wide, his gun dropping from his fingers and clattering to the ground.

Even the Colonel darts a glance at Oriel, amazement in his eyes, before looking back at the advancing warrior.

Two and a half metres tall, and nearly a metre broad across the chest, the Space Marine towers over the burning bodies scattered around him. Clad head to foot in black power armour decoratively chased with metals that glint in the firelight, he advances on the battle suits. The red eyes of his helmet glow like a daemon's as he turns his head towards the aliens. He looks just like the pictures and woodcuts I've seen, only even more impressive in real life. I make out an Inquisition symbol on his left shoulder pad, an 'I' picked out in gleaming gold. In his left hand he carries a long power sword, gleaming blue in the darkness; in his right he raises a bolter and opens fire, the boom of the weapon resounding across the square.

I can just about make out the flickering trails of the bolts as they scream across the open ground, three of them impacting in quick succession on the closest of the battle suits, the one whose flamer I destroyed earlier, tearing great gouges out of the armour and knocking it backwards. Still advancing steadily, the Space Marine opens fire again, three more shots, three more perfect hits that set off a chain reaction in the suit, causing it to explode in a shower of shrapnel and burning body parts of the pilot.

The rest of the Last Chancers open fire on the tau furthest from the Space Marine, as the other two turn towards their attacker. Their cannon fire dims even the searchlights, and I see the shells converging on the Space Marine. Their impact would have shredded a normal man and hurled his bloody carcass a dozen metres, but the Space Marine is simply forced down on to one knee under the cannonade. Cracks and dents appear in his armour under the fusillade, and a shoulder pad goes spinning off, trailing sparks from its powered mounting. Unbelievably, the Space Marine pushes himself to his feet, ignoring the shells ripping up the ground around him and scoring across his breastplate, and returns fire, his bolts ripping through the burst cannon of one of the battle suits.

'For the Emperor!' I hear him bellow in a voice like a god's. He tosses away his bolter and grabs the power sword two-handed, breaking into a charge, his long strides covering over three metres every step, his boots cracking the concourse under his weight. The nearest battle suit, now one-armed, takes a step back, readying itself for a jump, but somehow the Space Marine gets there before the jets fire, swinging the sword in a crackling arc that severs one of the battle suit's legs and topples it to the ground. Without a pause, the Space Marine spins and delivers another blow, the glowing blade of his sword carving a massive rent in the body of the suit, shearing it wide open.

The battle suit the others are targeting launches itself into the air on a short trail of fire, its missile pod igniting as it does so, the salvo screaming towards us on smoky trails.

'Get down!' Moerck shouts and I hurl myself to the floor, hands clasped over my head. The front wall of the building implodes inwards in a shower of shattered bricks and mortar dust, lumps of debris landing heavily on my back. I glance up and see Tanya at one of the windows, kneeling on one leg, her sniper rifle tucked tight against her shoulder, aiming up into the air. Even as the dust settles around her, she fires a shot, ejects the spent casing, tracks further up and fires again. In all, she looses off five shots in the space of a few seconds.

Something heavy crashes into the floor above us, sending more rubble tumbling down the stairway that runs down the wall behind us. The floorboards above give an ominous creak and we scatter, seconds before the disabled tau battle suit comes plummeting down through the ceiling, trailing sparking wires and plaster. It lands with a heavy thump in a cloud of dust and twitches mechanically, one twisted leg juddering up and down, its rocket launcher erratically rotating left and right.

'I'm going after Coldwind,' I snarl, my blood up. Someone shouts for me to stay but I ignore them, running back out of the door, favouring my uninjured foot as the other drags along the ground slightly. I glance over my shoulder to see another battle suit lying blazing in the middle of the square, the other jetting away, firing salvoes of rockets at the Space Marine, who ducks down behind the cover of one of the ruined tau machines as explosions tear across the ground around him.

I scan the buildings left and right, illuminated by the burning battle suits, looking for some sign of Coldwind. Something tells me to move back the way we came in, and it's then that I hear a noise in the building to my left. I instinctively dive to the ground, a moment before a shot cracks out, the bullet punching cleanly through a wall just to my right. I roll onto my back and return fire, the autogun recoiling wildly in my hands as I blast at the dark windows. I half get to my feet and hurl myself bodily over the wall, slumping to the ground on the other side. I check to see what weapons I have. I've got about half a magazine left, one smoke grenade and two frag charges. What the hell was I thinking coming out here on my own?

I take a look over the wall, and can't see any movement in the darkened building. Something does catch my attention a little bit further away though, a wispy movement glimpsed down a narrow alley about thirty metres to my right. I head that way, keeping low behind the wall, ignoring the sharp stabs of pain from my foot every time I take a step. Getting to the end of the wall, about twenty metres from the alley, I vault over one-handed, the autogun in the other. Almost immediately, a ripple of fire from the building forces me into a sprint across the road, gritting my teeth to prevent a howl of pain escaping my lips. I slam into the wall of the alley and duck inside, panting heavily. It continues straight for another ten or twelve metres before turning sharply to the left around the back of a low building with a corrugated sheet metal roof.

I push myself onwards, burning with the desire to exact some revenge from Coldwind. My head is thumping, my leg feels like it's on fire, but the anger in my heart is fanned to new heights as I think about the slimy, double-crossing ambassador. All along, he intended for this to happen. Of course, I would have done the same, but I would have made sure of it. Now he's going to have to pay the price for his failure.

I stumble around the corner, almost running face first into a tau fire warrior emerging from a door to my left. I react quicker, smashing my autogun across his face, snapping his helmet backwards. His rifle tumbles from his grip and I snatch it up. Behind him are three more fire warriors, but startled, they fail to act, and I pull the trigger on the rifle. It has no kick to it at all, the heavy shell smashing straight through the closest tau and punching the next in line from his feet. The third brings up his rifle, but far too late. The next shot almost takes his head off completely, his body flopping messily to the ground. I step clumsily over the bodies and crash through the doorway.

Coldwind punches me across the chin, a weak blow that barely registers. I lash out with my good foot, kicking his legs from underneath him. He stares at me with no emotion. I place my boot on his chest and pin him down.

'You bit off more than you can chew this time, ambassador,' I say quietly, bringing the barrel of the rifle up to his face.

'I regret nothing,' he replies calmly, meeting my angry gaze with a passionless expression.

'That's good. Nobody should die with regrets on their mind,' I tell him. Sounds of sporadic gunfire outside attract my attention, but they soon quiet. 'Any other confessions to make, to clear your soul?'

'All that I have done, I have done for the tau'va,' he says evenly. 'I foresaw that I might die. I am not afraid. I have served the tau'va. We shall continue to grow.'

'But why the double-cross?' I ask, curious. 'Why risk this happening? Why sour the deal?'

'To teach you humans that your time is finished,' he says with a short nod of amusement. 'You are old and decrepit, like the crumbling mansions your rulers inhabit. Your time has passed, and yet you so jealously cling on to the remnants of what you once had. We are superior. The tau'va is far superior to your dead Emperor.'

'You might be superior, but we've had a lot more practice,' I grin at him, tossing the rifle to one side. 'I'm not going to shoot you.'

'You are not?' he replies, hope rising.

'No, I'm going to strangle you,' I tell him, my voice dropping to a cold whisper. I grab him by the throat and he tries to struggle, but his blows are feeble and undirected. I slam him against the wall, my fingers tightening around his neck. 'Your last sight is going to be of a human throttling the life from you. I hope you enjoy it!'

'You will all die. Victory will yet be mine,' he gasps, smiling, and I drop him to the floor.

'What do you mean?' I demand, dragging him back to his feet.

'It appears that your pilot took to the role of mercenary even better than you intended,' he says, hanging limply in my grip. 'You will never get off Es'tau alive.'

'Neither will you, alien,' I snarl, dashing his head against the wall, snapping his neck with a single blow. I drop him at the foot of the wall. I have to find the others, tell them about the change of plan. If they're heading to the pick-up point, chances are they'll be walking into a trap. Added to the fact that Quidlon got himself killed before shutting off the travel line power, this place could be swarming by now. Right about now I wonder if the Colonel's decision not to bring comm-links was a good idea. He'd been worried that any signals we made would be intercepted by the aliens.

But it's no use worrying about what you haven't got, I remind myself, just as I told the others back in training. I snatch up the tau rifle and head for the front of the building, passing by a charred staircase into a short entrance hall. Easing the door open, I peek outside, but there's no sign of the enemy. I haven't got a clue where I am; this wasn't part of the set-up in the training bay back aboard the *Laurels of Glory*. I decide to head back to the square and see if I can pick up some kind of trail from there. There's no way I'm getting off this planet alive if I try to go it alone.

I manage to get back to the square without running into any more trouble, and crouch in the devastated ruins of the building where I met the others, still smoking from the rocket bombardment. Flashes of light attract my attention, and I note the crackle of gunfire not far off. I work my way stealthily around the edge of the square, carefully checking each building and street. A main boulevard runs off opposite my position, and I can see flames burning in a building a couple of hundred metres down. Squinting against the light, I make out figures dashing across the wide road, their long, tapered helmets clearly marking them out as tau. Two of them are pitched off their feet by hits and I hear two reports of a rifle echo around the quiet town. Scanning the buildings, I try to make out Tanya's position, as I guess she's the one picking off the enemy with such precision, all scruples obviously gone.

I can't see her from here though, and decide to break across the square, pausing to take cover by the remnants of the two destroyed battle suits before running painfully to the far side. Moving slowly along the front wall of a building at the junction of the boulevard and square, I stop at the corner and look down the street. I can see a few tau, and the ominous shape of another battle suit stalking past the burning building.

In the firelight, I catch a movement in a doorway on the opposite side of the street, and watch as a long barrel extends out from the shadows.

There's a small flash and a bang, and one of the tau is spun to the ground by a clean hit to the chest. I see Tanya get up and move further down the street, hopping over an intervening wall and taking position on the wide steps leading up to the next building.

I sprint across the road, head down, and land in a heap on the far side, trying to push myself further into the wall. Gasping now, feeling my broken ribs rubbing against my lungs, I edge along the wall, closing in on Tanya. She fires again, and then moves back towards me, keeping low and out of sight. I hiss her name as she's about to duck into a side road about fifteen metres away, stopping her in her tracks.

'Last Chance?' she hisses back urgently. 'We thought you were dead.'

'Takes a lot to kill me,' I tell her, moving out of cover and joining her. 'Where are the others?'

'The entrance to this chamber is just a few hundred metres this way,' she says, pointing down the side street. 'The tau are blocking the way out though. I've been protecting their backs; more tau are coming through from the opposite side.'

'We have to get them to pull back,' I tell her. 'Strelli's sold out to the tau, there's no shuttle waiting for us.'

'Damn!' she curses, glancing over my shoulder towards the square. 'More battle suits!'

I look back and see it's true. Three more huge shapes stand over the ruins of their comrades' vehicles, weapons tracking the buildings around the square. A cluster of drones hover around them, glowing slightly.

'Let's get to the others,' she says, heading down the road. I can't believe the change in confidence in her. She seems calm, assured, almost enjoying herself.

'What made you finally take that shot?' I ask, struggling alongside her. She looks over me and hooks my right arm over her shoulders, pulling me more upright.

'I realised it was him or you,' she tells me, no hint of embarrassment.

'Never realised you cared,' I laugh back, which turns into a cough.

'I don't,' she replies harshly. 'But it made me realise that Brightsword would have killed hundreds, thousands more. Just like you said. So I shot him.'

'And?' I prompt her, feeling she has something more to say.

'I just thought of all those people. The rest was easy,' she admits. 'It gave me satisfaction, shooting that monster.'

'It always gets easier, Tanya,' I agree with her, limping alongside the sniper.

'My name's Sharpshooter,' she snaps back, turning us down a narrower street to the left. 'You taught me that. It's what I do.'

'I guess it is,' I say, nodding in agreement.

We run into Trost a couple of buildings further down the street. I tell him there's a change of plan and he leads us to the Colonel and Oriel.

Standing with them is the Space Marine. He's even more impressive this close, my head barely comes up to his chest. His armour is scratched, pitted and cracked in dozens of places, but he doesn't seem bothered in the least. He whips round as we enter, power sword raised, throwing a blue glow across the smooth, rounded panels of his black armour.

'Where the hell did he come from?' I ask Trost as I limp towards Schaeffer.

'I guess you weren't the only ones I was creating a diversion for,' he replies, glancing nervously at the massive figure.

'Colonel, it's worse than you think,' I gasp, my breath getting shorter and shorter. I think blood's getting into my lungs, my own life fluid slowly drowning me. I need medical attention and I need it quick. 'Strelli cut a deal with Coldwind, he's not waiting for us.'

'What?' Oriel snaps, stepping away from a window on the far side of the room.

'Coldwind admitted it before I killed him,' I explain. 'There'll be no shuttle waiting for us at the transport terminal.'

'The tau will already have a heavy presence in the terminal,' the Colonel says after a moment's thought. He turns to Oriel. 'What other ways out of the dome are there, inquisitor?'

'None that won't be heavily guarded by now,' he sighs, closing his eyes and rubbing the bridge of his nose as if he's got a headache.

'They're attacking: three squads, two battle suits!' I hear Moerck call from another part of the building.

'Trost, can you blast us a new exit?' Oriel asks the ex-Officio Sabatorum agent.

'Get me to the exterior wall, and Demolition Man can make you a door!' he snarls back, patting his bag of explosives.

'Right, everyone pull out,' the Colonel barks. 'The wall to this chamber is only a hundred metres away. We will blast our way out of here into the next arena. On the other side of that is the outer dome.'

'The tau are coming in from every direction,' Tanya points out. 'They'll be after us like hounds at the chase.'

'I will hold the breach,' the Space Marine says, his voice deep, given a metallic ring by the external vocalisers of his helmet.

'No, Brother Dionis, you are needed to ensure the inquisitor is safe,' Moerck argues. 'Give me the spare ammunition, I'll hold off the tau.'

'Still Hero, eh?' I say, pushing past Moerck. 'You're welcome to it.'

'Inquisitor?' Dionis asks for confirmation, his helmeted head turning towards Oriel, red eyes glowing in the gloom. 'What are your orders?'

'We all leave this damned city, head for the open ground in the next arena,' he confirms, striding towards the door, chainsword in hand. 'Moerck can act as rearguard. Give him your spare magazines and power cells. We move fast, don't wait for stragglers.'

We file out of the building, looking around cautiously. I see squads of tau running parallel to us, down the other streets, closing in on our position. A plume of jets heralds the arrival of more battle suits as they land on the roof of a high building maybe a hundred metres to our right.

'Move out,' whispers the Colonel, waving us on.

Like shadows, we ghost down the dark streets, Dionis on point, his power sword dimmed for the moment. He moves swiftly, despite his bulky power armour. Tanya helps me along, her sniper rifle slung over her shoulder, not the best weapon for a close range firefight anyway. I grasp the alien weapon in both hands, ready to fire in an instant.

From building to building we flit, pausing at every corner, glancing behind us regularly. It takes a few minutes to reach the wall of the huge chamber, which stretches up into the fake night sky above us.

'Okay, Demolition Man, get us an opening,' I say, patting him on the back.

Meanwhile, the others pass their spare clips to Moerck, who gathers them in his pack, which he slings over one shoulder.

'Melta-bombs, step back,' I hear Trost say, and we move away from the wall a few paces. There's a rapid succession of bright glows, and a section of the wall falls away, just lower than head height. Light pours through from the other side, blinding after the false night of the mock Sarcassa town.

'Sorry big fella,' Trost says with a shrug as Dionis crouches down to look through the small hole.

'It is of no concern, trooper,' the Space Marine replies, straightening up again. He raises a booted foot bigger than my head and kicks at the wall. Twice more his heavy boot crashes against it, dislodging a cracked chunk of rubble which nearly doubles the height of the hole. Without a word, the Space Marine ducks through, his power sword glowing again.

A scream in the air attracts our attention, and I see the trails of half a dozen rockets arcing over the buildings towards us. Oriel and the Colonel dive through the hole next, followed by Tanya, Trost and then me. Moerck backs through the hole, firing now at targets we can't see.

'Something special for you,' I say, dropping an object into his pack. He grunts without turning round, and I set off after the others, who are running over the dusty dunes of the next training area. I crest the nearest hillock, and realise that we're in some kind of ash wastes, the grey expanse stretching out in every direction. It'll be a killing field, no real cover, if the tau catch us in here.

'Run for all you are worth!' shouts Oriel, scrabbling up the next dune. I hear muffled explosions, and look up. The ceiling high above our heads seems to shake, motes of dust start drifting down. I pay it no heed, preferring to concentrate on pushing myself through the sliding dust and ash of the battle ground. Another explosion, at ground level and behind us, heralds the detonation of the charge I placed in Moerck's ammo bag.

'What the hell was that?' Tanya asks, stopping and glancing back over her shoulder to see what I can see: a large portion of the wall shattering and collapsing, crushing tau and battle suits underneath the artificial avalanche.

'Insurance,' I tell her, dragging her back into a run. 'Moerck was never gonna hold them off for more than a heartbeat. Still, he did make for a good booby trap.'

'You're a cold bastard,' she snarls, letting go of me and hauling herself ahead.

'Actually,' I call after her, dropping to my hands and knees and crawling up the dune, it's quicker than trying to walk, 'I'm not cold. I enjoyed that.'

'So how much explosive to get through?' Oriel asks Trost, as the demolitions expert examines the wall.

'Thought I'd use everything I've got,' he replies, stepping back after placing the last of his explosives against the base of the wall.

We exchange bemused glances and begin to back away across the dunes, breaking into a run as Trost picks up speed and accelerates past us. Looking back out into the artificial ash waste, I see tau battle suits soaring into the air, about half a kilometre away and to our left.

'Do it now!' the Colonel yells, and we all dive to the ground except Dionis, who simply goes down on one knee and turns so that his remaining shoulder pad shields his head.

The detonation seems to build in volume as the secondary bombs go up, rising to a deafening crescendo that's joined by the screech of tortured metal. A blast wave passes over me, scorching the hairs on the back of my neck and fluttering my clothes around me. There's a dull rumble and I look back, seeing a crack splitting up the dome wall.

'Oh frag,' I mutter to myself, painfully getting to my feet.

'Run!' screams Trost, breaking into a sprint, and we race after him as the crack widens, showering chunks of the dome down into the grit and dust.

My legs burn with pain as I force myself through the clogging dunes, pieces of debris dropping around us. Gritting my teeth I urge myself on even faster, dragging my feet one in front of the other. I slip and start to slide down the dune, but someone grabs the back of my shirt. Dionis hauls me up in one hand as he runs past, ploughing through the dust like a tank, his arms and legs pumping ceaselessly accompanied by the whine of servos within his armour, carrying me as easily as I might carry a new born babe.

A massive triangular section of the dome begins to fall inwards, crashing down and sending up a billowing cloud of dust and ash which sweeps over us, engulfing us in a rolling wave of air that buffets me in the Space Marine's grip.

'Okay, put me down,' I yell at Dionis, who slides to a halt and dumps me in a heap on the ash, making me cough and splutter and sending a stab of pain from my broken ribs. We turn back and head for the gouge blown out of the wall, stretching some thirty metres above our heads in a jagged wedge. The tau are closing in, shots begin to send up plumes of dust around us as we scramble over the shattered rubble, floundering through the newly created drifts of ash.

Just then something flashes inside, through the opening: a bolt of light that catches one of the battle suits in mid-jump, turning it into a fiery ball of slag.

'What the frag?' I exclaim, dragging myself over a jagged piece of debris and looking out through the massive rent in the dome wall.

Outside is a warzone, and no mistake. Small tau buildings stretch into the desert from this side of the dome, some of them reduced to rubble, others burning. Explosions light up the sky all over the townscape, as Imperial drop ships plummet groundwards, bombs and missiles heralding their approach, cratering the wide roads and smashing the buildings to pieces. Imperial Guardsmen are running everywhere, fighting with tau fire warriors and battle suits. A Hammerhead tau tank glides into view, its nose-mounted cannons chattering wildly, mowing down a squad of guardsmen advancing through the burning ruins of a tau building. I look over at Oriel as a platoon of guardsmen run past dressed in mismatched uniforms, carrying all sorts of weapons. One of them sets up a lascannon, steadying it on its tripod, before firing again at the tau, the bolt of energy going wide this time. The tau are returning fire, explosions ripping along the ground towards us. We break into a run again and I find myself next to the inquisitor.

'You know anything about this?' I ask him, knowing the answer already.

'More forces I had in orbit in case Coldwind got a sudden rush of intelligence,' he says with a smile, which changes to a wince as a rocket explodes close by, showering us with dust and pieces of rock. We're not safe yet, and the Colonel leads us through the breach.

We make it out into the open, but it's no safer here than inside, there are aliens everywhere – squadrons of battle suits advancing from the left, fire warriors piling out of the back of three hovering APCs to our right.

'Make for open ground, more drop ships will be landing,' the Colonel tells us, pointing to a gap between two shattered buildings just ahead. We dash from cover to cover through the crossfire between the two forces, in as much danger from friendly fire as from the tau. We run into a squad setting up a communications unit in the shell of a cracked tau dome, a small subsidiary building only seven or eight metres high. I recognise the officer in charge, he's the leader of the mercenaries we met in the bar, still wearing his white armband.

'Well, Emperor damn my soul,' he laughs, seeing us. 'I suggest you stick to starting bar room brawls in the future!'

'Captain Destrien, I presume,' Oriel says, nodding to the officer. 'I am Inquisitor Oriel of the Ordo Xenos. I believe you have been waiting for me.'

'When I got the signal to start the assault, I could hardly believe it,' he declares, serious now, folding his muscled arms across his chest. His jaw drops as Dionis strides in behind us. 'Well, if I ain't seen it all now.'

Out of a blasted doorway I can see the open desert surrounding the battle dome, now littered with drop ships as more troops land, dozens and dozens of men and women pouring down the gangways. Tank carriers land, their heavy ramps dropping quickly, Leman Russ rumble out of the holds, their battle cannons turning towards the tau force as soon as their tracks hit the sand.

There's a rush of air, and sand is billowed up from the ground only a dozen metres away as a drop ship lands close by, its jets kicking up a dust storm that swirls into the buildings. I turn my attention back to Oriel, who's just finished talking to the captain.

'We have had enough fighting for one day, and I need a rest,' he tells us all wearily, his shoulders sagging. 'We'll commandeer that drop ship and get back to orbit.'

'It'll be safer in orbit?' Tanya asks. 'I thought Brightsword had a fleet.'

'The fleet's already left, and we have forces boarding the two orbital stations as we speak,' Captain Destrien tells us, glancing at Oriel. 'Whoever came up with this plan certainly thought everything through.'

'I just want to know where that bastard Strelli is,' barks Trost, face screwed up in anger.

'Don't worry about that traitor,' Oriel assures us, his eyes hard. 'There's a tracker on his shuttle and we'll find him soon enough.'

The inquisitor smiles humourlessly at us for a second before striding towards the newly arrived shuttle. As we wait for the squad to disembark, another two drop ships land close by, and soon the air is filled with a choking, roiling dust cloud and the whine of engines powering down. I step on to the now empty ramp, following the others, and look around. The fight between the guard and the tau has mostly moved inside the battle dome. Turning away, I notice smoke rising from the main city in a dozen places, and look up to see the vapour trails of planes returning to orbit.

I get to the top of the ramp and look back, squinting through the light and swirling sand, my eyes tired, my head fuddled with fatigue and pain. I swear I see an illusion. Leading the squad out of the next drop ship along is a woman, with short-cropped, pure white hair, and pale skin, dressed in various shades of brown desert camo. She looks just like Lori – but Lori died in Coritanorum. She and her squad disappear from view behind another drop ship and I'm about to set off after her when the ramp begins to rise.

I turn and Oriel is stood there, watching the battle.

'Was that who I think it was?' I ask him as the door shuts
with a clang and the drop ship begins to rumble with the
build-up of power in the engines.

'I have no idea what you are talking about,' Oriel replies,
meeting my gaze steadily.

'I just saw Lori,' I confess. 'Or, I think I did.'

'But you were the only survivor from Coritanorum,' he points
out.

'That's true,' I agree, stumbling along the gangway to the
main compartment. I flop down into the seat and begin to
buckle myself in to the safety harness, stowing the tau rifle as a
souvenir under the bench.

Oriel walks past and is just about to go through the other
door when something occurs to me.

'I thought you died at Coritanorum as well,' I call out to him.
'You escaped on the second shuttle.'

'Yes, I did,' he answers curtly, before closing the door behind
him.

THE NEXT DAY, back aboard ship and all patched up with a good
night's sleep, I feel much better. Happy in fact. The bad guys
got killed and the Last Chancers did the job. So it's with a sense
of satisfaction that I make my way with the others to the officers' lounge for a debriefing by Oriel and the Colonel. We enter
the wide, oval room, gawking at the splendour of the wood
panelled walls, the thick red carpet underfoot and the low, vel-
vet-covered chairs. Oriel is waiting for us, standing in front of a
bookshelf, looking at the volumes. We settle into the seats as
the Colonel walks in from another door and nods for us to do
so. There's no sign of Dionis. He disappeared into the forward
chamber of the shuttle without a word when we left Es'tau, and
none of us have seen him since.

Oriel turns, a smile on his face.

'Well, Last Chancers,' he addresses us, looking at each of us in
turn. 'By my reckoning, a complete success.'

He paces away from the bookshelf and stands in the centre
of the room.

'As you have probably guessed, you have been caught up in a
game of sorts,' he tells us, becoming serious. 'It is a game that I
and other members of the Inquisition must play on a daily
basis. It is a deadly game, not just for us, but for others, like

yourselves, who are ultimately the pieces we play with. Yesterday, we won the game, and that is important. For some of you, that will be the only time you are involved. For others,' he looks at the Colonel, then at me, 'you shall be asked to play it again perhaps.'

'Excuse me, inquisitor,' Trost asks, raising a hand. 'I like the fancy speech, but could you just tell me what the frag this was all about? This was more than just offing some rogue commander, wasn't it?'

The inquisitor doesn't answer straight away, but instead looks at us, lips pursed. He strokes his beard a couple of times, and then looks at us again, weighing us up. He glances at the Colonel before speaking again.

'You will all be sworn to secrecy anyway,' he tells us. 'You have done well, and I cannot see that it will do any harm for you to know a little more now. You are right, this was more than simply a matter of preventing O'var from invading the Sarcassa system, although that did provide me with a reason for instigating a much wider scheme and killing two birds with one bullet, so to speak.'

I notice that Oriel's smooth talking has returned, a contrast from the tired and anxious inquisitor who fled the battle dome with us, the shells as likely to take him out as anyone else.

'The tau are a threat to our future in this part of the galaxy,' he explains, pacing up and down. 'It is a threat that we are unable to deal with fully at this moment in time. Other pressing matters, such as the advance of tyranid Hive Fleet Kraken, draw away the military resources we would need to wage war on the Tau Empire. That much is true, as you have been told before. That the tau are not keen to start a serious military engagement with the Imperium either, that much is also true. However, they had the upper hand. They thought that we could not combat the spread of their empire in this sector, and without this intervention we could not. However, by their own complicity in the assassination of Commander Brightsword, they provided me with a golden opportunity to give them an object lesson in the nature of the foe they face. They think they are clever, learning tricks of manipulation from the eldar, but they are young. The Imperium may not be perfect, but it does have one thing they do not have. Experience. For countless generations, inquisitors such as myself have been fighting against the menace of alien expansion, and the invasion of our worlds. Over those long centuries and millennia, we have learned a trick or two. To put it bluntly, we're sneakier than they could hope to be, given the right conditions.'

'So what have we actually done, except start a war with them, something you say we can't afford to do?' asks Tanya, voicing my own thoughts.

'Es'tau is just an outpost, little more than a fire caste staging area for O'var and his warriors,' Oriel answers, picking his words carefully. 'The loss of Es'tau, which by the way should be called Skal's Breach as it is marked on our star charts until they took it from us, is not a major blow to the Tau Empire. Except in one regard. No longer can they feel they can encroach upon our territory without reproach. No longer will they be certain that we won't respond to their aggressive advances into our space. We cannot hold back the expansion of their empire with might and guns. Not in the straightforward sense. But we can make them pause and think. Perhaps to turn their attention elsewhere, to easier areas to colonise which do not belong to us yet. We have sent them a message that will give them pause for consideration. That was my larger purpose in this enterprise. I wanted Brightsword dead, make no mistake about that, but not to stop him invading Sarcassa. I wanted him dead so that the chain of command was broken, so that the tau were disrupted, so that their attention was focussed on the battle dome and not on the half a dozen Imperial transports in orbit, packed with guard masquerading as renegades and mercenaries. Even now, three thousand more troopers are landing on the surface, eliminating the resistance that remains.'

His smile returns and he gestures to the Colonel, who picks up two scrolls from a desk to one side of the room. Pardons; I recognise them from before.

'Truly have you earnt redemption in the eyes of the Emperor,' Oriel tells us, his smile broadening into a genuine grin. 'Truly have you earnt the right to live again as free servants of the Emperor. You did not assassinate an alien yesterday. You conquered a world!'

I watch detached as the Colonel hands out the parchments, clearing Trost and Tanya of all crimes. Just the two of them remain, from the eight I picked half a year ago. Those are the two survivors then. I smile to myself, glad that I kept the promise to Tanya to keep her alive. I hope she enjoys the next sunrise.

Then my heart goes heavy. It's all over again. I'll be going back to prison. No pardon for poor old Kage, N; 14-3889, 13th Penal Legion. Not that I give a damn about that, I wasn't expecting one. No, my mind's on something else.

I walk over to Oriel, where he's stood by the bookshelf again.

'When I accused you of being a witch, why did you say that of all people I should not judge you?' I ask.

'You're intelligent, Kage, you'll work it out for yourself,' he says, not looking at me.

'What does that mean?' I demand, making him turn around and look at me.

'When you're back in your cell, you'll have time to think about it,' is all he says, tapping the side of his head before walking off.

EIGHT
EPILOGUE

THE AIR WAS filled with swirling grey dust, whipped up into a
storm by a wind that shrieked across the hard, black granite of
the tower. The bleak edifice soared into the turbulent skies,
windowless but studded with hundreds of blazing lights whose
yellow beams were swallowed quickly by the dust storm. For
three hundred metres the tower climbed into the raging skies
of Ghovul's third moon, an almost perfect cylinder of unbroken and unforgiving rock, hewn from the infertile mesa on
which the gulag stood. A narrow-beamed red laser sprang into
life from its summit, penetrating the gloom of the cloud-
shrouded night. A moment later it was answered by a triangle
of white glares as a shuttle descended towards the landing pad.
In the bathing glow of the landing lights, technicians scurried
back and forth across the pad, protected against the violent climate with bulky work suits made from fine metal mesh, their
hands covered with heavy gloves, thick-soled boots upon their
feet.

With a whine of engines cutting back, the shuttle's three feet
touched down with a loud clang on the metal decking of the
landing area. A moment later a portal in the side swung open
and a docking ramp jerkily extended itself on hissing

hydraulics to meet with the hatchway. A tall figure ducked
through the low opening and stepped out on to the walkway.
He stood there for a moment, his heavy dress coat whipping
around him, a gloved hand clamping his officer's cap to his
head. With his back as straight as a rod despite the horrendous
conditions, the new arrival strode across the docking gantry
with a purposeful gait, never once breaking his gaze from
straight ahead.

Behind him, another figure emerged from the shuttle,
swathed in a ragged uniform, his head and face bared to the
elements, seemingly oblivious to the searing dust storm. His
face was pitted and scarred with a dozen cuts and fleshy craters,
his scalp bearing a particularly horrendous weal just behind
the left ear. He walked with a slight limp as he followed the
officer more slowly, looking around him at his surroundings.

He caught up with the other man in the small elevator chamber, where a nervous guard stood. When the warden saw the
scarred man his eyes widened in surprise and fear. He glanced
at the officer in the heavy coat before fixing his gaze on the
newly arrived prisoner. The guard gulped heavily, and shuffled
nervously back a pace.

The prisoner turned and winked.

'Don't worry,' the man said, a savage grin wrinkling his many
scars. 'I won't be here forever.'

ABOUT THE AUTHOR

Gav Thorpe is currently working for Games Workshop, guiding the Warhammer creative team in his role as Loremaster. He has been writing short stories for several years now, and certainly hopes to continue adding more novels to his CV. For those who have been following his life saga, you may like to know that Dennis the mechanical hamster is still well and good, but his batteries are beginning to run a little low.

Coming soon from the Black Library

DEATHWING

A collection of stirring tales from the dark universe
of Warhammer 40,000

from
SUFFER NOT THE UNCLEAN TO LIVE
by Gav Thorpe

YAKOV'S AUDIENCE WITH the cardinal had lasted most of the afternoon and once again the sun was beginning to set as he made his way back to the shanty town. As on the previous night there were many of the mutants gathered around the shrine. Rumour of his visit to the cardinal had spread and he was met by a crowd of eager faces. One look at his own expression quelled their anticipation and an angry murmur sprang up. It was Menevon who stepped forward, a troublemaker by nature in Yakov's opinion. He looked down at Menevon's bestial features and not for the first time wondered if he had been sired by unholy union with a dog or bear. Tufts of coarse hair sprung in patches all across his body, and his jaw was elongated and studded with tusk-like teeth stained yellow. Menevon looked back at him with small, beady eyes.

'He does nothing,' the mutant stated. 'We die and they all do nothing!'

'The Emperor's Will be done,' replied Yakov sternly, automatically echoed by some of the gathered mutants.

'The Emperor I trust and adore,' Menevon declared hotly, 'but the governor I wouldn't spit on if he were burning.'

'That is seditious talk, Menevon, and you would do well to curb your tongue,' warned Yakov, stooping to talk quietly to the rabble-rouser.

'I say we make him help us!' shouted Menevon, ignoring Yakov and turning towards the crowd. 'It's time we made ourselves heard!'

There were discontented growls of agreement from the others, some shouted out their approval.

'Too long have they lorded over us, too long we've been ignored!' continued Menevon. 'Enough is enough! No more!'

'No more!' repeated the crowd with a guttural roar.

'Silence!' bellowed Yakov, holding his arms up to silence them. The crowd fell quiet instantly at his commanding tone. 'This discord will serve for nothing. If the governor will not listen to me, your preacher, he will not listen to you. Your masters will not tolerate this outburst lightly. Go back to your homes and pray! Look not to the governor, but to yourselves and the master of us all, the Holy Emperor. Go now!'

Menevon shot the preacher a murderous look as the crowd heeded his words, dispersing with backward glances and muttered curses.

'Go back to your family Menevon, you can do them no good dead on a scaffold,' Yakov told him quietly.

The defiance in the mutant's eyes disappeared and he nodded sadly. He cast a long, despairing glance at the preacher and then he too turned away.

THE TOUCH OF something cold woke Yakov and when he opened his eyes his gaze fell first upon the glittering knife blade held in front of his face. Tearing his eyes away from the sharpened steel, he followed the arm to the knife's wielder and his look was met by the whitened orbs of the mutant he knew to be called Byzanthus.

Like Lathesia, he was a renegade, and hunted by the Special Security Agents. His face was solemn, his eyes intent upon the preacher. The ridged and wrinkled grey skin that covered his body was dull in the silvery light which occasionally broke through the curtain swaying in the glassless window of the small chamber.

'I had your promise,' Yakov heard Lathesia speak from the shadows. A moment later she stepped forwards, her hair catching the moonlight as she passed in front of the window.

'I asked. They said no,' Yakov replied, pushing Byzanthus's arm away and sitting up, the thin blanket falling to his waist to reveal the taut muscles of his stomach and chest.

'You keep in good shape,' she commented, noticing his lean physique.

'The daily walk to the capital keeps me fit,' Yakov replied, feeling no discomfort as her penetrating gaze swept over his body. 'I must stay physically as well as spiritually fit to serve the Emperor well.'

A flickering yellow light drew the preacher's attention to the window and he rose from the thin mattress to pace over and look.

Lathesia smiled at his nakedness but he ignored her; fleshy matters such as his own nudity were beneath him. Pulling aside the ragged curtain, Yakov saw the light came from dozens of blazing torches and when he listened carefully he could hear voices raised in argument.

One of them sounded like Menevon's, and as his eyes adjusted he could see the hairy mutant in the torchlight, gesticulating towards the city.

'Emperor damn him,' cursed Yakov, pushing past Lathesia to grab his robes from a chair behind her. Pulling on his vestments, he rounded on the mutant girl.

'You put him up to this?' he demanded.

'Menevon has been an associate of mine for quite some time,' she admitted, not meeting his gaze.

'Why?' Yakov asked simply. 'The governor will not stand for this discontent.'

'Too long we have allowed this tyranny to continue,' she said with feeling. 'Just as in the revolution, the slaves have tired of the lash, it is time to strike back.'

'The revolutionary council was backed by two-thirds of the old king's army,' spat Yakov, fumbling in the darkness for his boots. 'You will all die.'

'Menevon's brother is dead,' Byzanthus growled from behind Yakov. 'Murdered.'

Yakov rounded on the grey-skinned man. 'You know this? For sure?'

'Unless he slit his own throat, yes!' replied Lathesia. 'The masters did this, and no one will investigate because it is just one of the slaves who has died. Justice must be served.'

'The Emperor judges us all in time,' Yakov replied instinctively. He pointed out of the window.

'And he'll be judging some of them this evening if you let this foolishness continue. Damn your souls to Chaos, don't you care that they'll die?'

'Better to die fighting,' Lathesia whispered back, 'than on our knees begging for scraps and offal.'

The preacher snarled wordlessly and hurried out through the chapel into the street. As he rounded the corner he was met by the mutant mob, their faces twisted in anger, their raucous, raging cries springing to life as they saw him. Menevon was at their head, holding a burning brand high in the air, the embodiment of the revolutionary ringleader. But he wasn't, Yakov thought bitterly, that honour belonged to the manipulative, headstrong teenage girl back in his room.

'What in the name of the Emperor do you think you are doing?' demanded Yakov, his deep voice rising to a deafening shout over the din of the mob. They ignored him and Menevon pushed him aside as the crowd swept along the street. The preacher recognised many faces in the torchlight as the mob passed by, some of them children. He felt someone step up beside him, and he turned and saw Lathesia watching the mutants marching past, her face triumphant.

'How did one so young become so bloodthirsty?' muttered Yakov, directing a venomous glare at her before setting off after the mutants. They were moving at some speed and Yakov had to force his way through the crowd with long strides, pulling and elbowing aside mutants to get to the front. As they neared the edge of the ghetto the crowd began to slow and he broke through to the front of the mob, where he saw what had stalled their advance. Across the main thoroughfare stood a small detachment of the SSA, their grey and black uniforms dark against the glare of a troop transport's searchlamp behind them. Each cradled a shotgun in their hands, their visored helms reflecting the flames of the torches. Yakov stopped and let the mutants swirl around him, his mouth dry with fear. Next to him the pretty young girl, Katinia, was staring at the SSA officers. She seemed to notice Yakov suddenly and looked up at the preacher with a small, uncertain smile. He didn't smile back, but focussed his attention on the law enforcers ahead.

'Turn back now, you are in violation of the Slave Encampment Laws,' screeched a voice over a loudhailer.

'No more!' shouted Menevon, hurling his torch at the security agents, his cry voiced by others. Stones and torches rattled off the cobbles and walls of the street and one of the officers went down to a thrown bottle which smashed across his darkened helmet.

'You were warned, mutant scum,' snarled the SSA officer's voice over the hailer. At some unheard command the agents raised their shotguns. Yakov hurled himself across Katinia just as gunfire exploded all around him. There were sudden screams and shouts, a wail of agony shrieked from his left as he and the girl rolled to the ground. He felt something pluck at his robes as another salvo roared out. The mutants were fleeing, disorder reigned as they scrabbled and tore at one another to fight their way clear. Bare and booted feet stamped on Yakov's fingers as he held himself over Katinia, who was mewling and sobbing beneath him. Biting back a yell of pain as a heel crushed his left thumb between two cobbles, Yakov forced himself upright. Within moments he and the girl were alone in the street.

The boulevard was littered with dead and wounded mutants. Limbs, bodies and pools of blood were scattered over the cobblestones, a few conscious mutants groaned or sobbed. To his right, a couple he had wed just after arriving were on their knees, hugging each other, wailing over the nearly unrecognisable corpse of their son. Wherever he looked, lifeless eyes stared back at him in the harsh glare of the searchlight. The SSA were picking their way through the mounds of bodies, kicking over corpses and peering at faces.

Yakov heard the girl give a ragged gasp and he looked down. Half her mother's face lay on the road almost within reach. He bent and gathered her up in his left arm, and she buried her face in his robes, weeping uncontrollably. It was then he noticed the silver helmet of a sergeant as he clambered down from the turret of the armoured car.

'You!' bellowed Yakov, pointing with his free hand at the SSA man, his anger welling up inside him. 'Come here now!'

The officer gave a start and hurried over. His face was hidden by the visor of his helmet, but he seemed to be trembling.

'Take off your helmet,' Yakov commanded, and he did so, letting it drop from quivering fingers. The man's eyes were wide with fear as he looked up at the tall preacher. Yakov felt himself getting even angrier and he grabbed the man by the throat, his long, strong fingers tightening on the sergeant's windpipe. The man gave a choked cough as Yakov used all of the leverage afforded by his height to push him down to his knees.

'You have fired on a member of the Ministorum, sergeant,' Yakov hissed. The man began to stammer something but a quick tightening of Yakov's grip silenced him. Releasing his hold, Yakov moved his hand to the top of the sergeant's head, forcing him to bow forward.

'Pray for forgiveness,' whispered Yakov, his voice as sharp as razor. The other agents had stopped the search and helmets bobbed left and right as they exchanged glances. He heard someone swearing from the crackling intercom inside the sergeant's helmet on the floor.

'Pray to the Emperor to forgive this most grievous of sins,' Yakov repeated. The sergeant started praying, his voice spilling almost incoherently from his lips, his tears splashing down his cheeks into the blood slicking the cobbles.

'Forgive me, almighty Emperor, forgive me!' pleaded the man, looking up at Yakov as he released his hold, his cheeks streaked with tears, his face a mask of terror.

'One hour's prayer every sunrise for the rest of your life,' Yakov pronounced his judgement. As he looked again at the bloodied remnants of the massacred mutants and felt the tears of Katinia soaking through his tattered priestly robes, he added, 'And one day's physical penance a week for the next five years.'

As he turned away from the horrific scene Yakov heard the sergeant retching and vomiting. Five years of self-flagellation would teach him not to fire on a preacher, Yakov thought grimly as he stepped numbly through the blood and gore.

YAKOV WAS TIRED and even more irritable than normal when the sun rose the next day. He had taken Katinia back to her home, where her brother was in a fitful, nightmare-laden sleep, and then returned to the site of the cold-blooded execution to identify the dead. Some of the mutants he did not recognise from his congregation, and he assumed they were more of Lathesia's misguided freedom fighters.

When he finally returned to the shanty town, the preacher saw several dozen SSA standing guard throughout the ghetto, each carrying a heavy pistol and a charged shock maul. As he dragged himself wearily up the steps to the chapel, a familiar face was waiting for him. Just outside the curtained portal stood Sparcek, the oldest mutant he knew and informal mayor-cum-judge of the ghetto.

Yakov delved into his last reserves of energy as the old mutant met him halfway, his twisted, crippled body making hard work of the shallow steps.

'A grim night, preacher,' said Sparcek in his broken, hoarse voice.

Yakov noticed the man's left arm was splinted and bound with bandages and he held it across his chest as much as his deformed shoulder and elbow allowed.

'You were up there?' Yakov asked, pointing limply at Sparcek's broken arm.

'This?' Sparcek glanced down and then shook his head sadly. 'No, the SSA broke into my home just after, accused me of being the leader. I said they couldn't prove that and they did this, saying they needed no proof.'

'Your people need you now, before they...' Yakov's voice trailed off as his befuddled mind tried to tell him something. 'What did you just say?'

'I said they couldn't prove anything...' he started.

'That's it!' snapped Yakov, startling the old mutant.

'What? Talk sense, you're tired,' Sparcek snapped back, obviously annoyed at the preacher's outburst.'

'Nothing for you to worry about,' Yakov tried to calm him with a waved hand. 'Now, I am about to ask you something, and whether you answer me or not, I need your promise that you will never tell another living soul what it is.'

'You can trust me. Did I not help you when you first arrived, did I not tell you about your congregation, their secrets and traits?' Sparcek assured him.

'I need to speak to Lathesia, and quickly,' Yakov said, bending close so that he could whisper.

'The rebel leader?' Sparcek whispered back, clearly amazed. He thought for a moment before continuing. 'I cannot promise anything but I may be able to send her word that you wish to see her.'

'Do it, and do it quickly!' insisted Yakov, laying a gentle hand on the mutant's good arm. 'With all of these trigger happy agents around, she's bound to do something reckless and get more of your people killed. If I can speak to her, I may be able to avoid more bloodshed.'

'I will do as you ask, preacher,' Sparcek nodded as he spoke, almost to himself.

THE DANK SEWERS resounded with running water and constant dripping, punctuated by the odd splash as Yakov placed a booted foot in a puddle or a rat scurried past through the rivulets seeping through the worn brick walls. Ahead, the glowlamp of Byzanthus bobbed and weaved in the mutant's raised hand as he led the way to Lathesia's hidden lair. Though one of the larger drainage systems, the tunnel was still cramped for the tall preacher and his neck was sore from half an hour's constant stooping. His nose had become more accustomed to the noxious smell which had assaulted his nostrils when the grey-skinned mutant had first opened the storm drain cover, and his eyes were now used to the dim, blue glow of the lantern.

He was thoroughly lost, he was sure of that, and he half-suspected this was the point of the drawn out journey. They must have been walking in circles, otherwise they would be beyond the boundaries of the mutant encampment in the city proper, or out in the fields.

After several more minutes of back-breaking walking, Byzanthus finally stopped beside an access door in the sewer wall. He banged four times, paused, then banged twice more. Rusted locks squealed and the door opened a moment later on shrieking hinges.

'You should loot some oil,' Yakov couldn't stop himself from saying, earning himself a cheerless smile from Byzanthus, who waved him inside with the lantern.

There was no sign of the doorkeeper, but as Yakov preceded Byzanthus up the wooden steps just inside the door he heard it noisily swinging shut again.

'Shy?' Yakov asked, looking at Byzanthus over his shoulder as he climbed the stairwell.

'Suspicious of you,' the mutant replied bluntly, giving him a hard stare.

The steps led them into a small hallway, decorated with flaking murals on the walls, they were obviously inside one of the abandoned buildings of the royal district.

'Second door on the left,' Byzanthus said curtly, indicating the room with a nod of his head as he extinguished the lamp.

Yakov strode down the corridor quickly, his hard-soled boots clacking on the cracked tiles. Just as he reached the door, it opened to reveal Lathesia, dressed in ill-fitting SSA combat fatigues.

'Come in, make yourself at home,' she said as she stepped back and took in the room with a wide sweep of her arm. The small chamber was bare except for a couple of straw pallets and a rickety table strewn with scatters of parchment and what looked like a schematic of the sewer system. The frescoes had been all but obliterated by crudely daubed black paint, which had puddled on the scuffed wooden floor. The remnants of a fire smouldered in one corner, the smoke drifting lazily out of a cracked window.

'We had to burn the carpet last winter,' Lathesia said apologetically, noting the direction of his gaze.

'And the walls?' Yakov asked, dropping his haversack onto the bare floor.

'Byzanthus in a fit of pique when he heard we'd been found guilty of treason,' she explained hurriedly, moving over to drop down on one of the mattresses.

'You share the same room?' Yakov asked, recoiling from her in disgust. 'Out of wedlock?'

'What of it?' she replied, genuinely perplexed.

'Is there no sin you are not guilty of?' he demanded hotly, regretting his decision to have anything to do with the wayward mutant. He fancied he could feel the fires of Chaos burning his soul as he stood there. It would take many weeks of repentance to atone for even coming here.

'Better that than freezing because we only have enough fuel to heat a few rooms,' she told him plainly before a smile broke over her pretty face.

'You think that Byzanthus and I... Oh, Yakov, please, allow me some standards.'

'I'm sure he doesn't see it that way,' Yakov pointed out to her with a meaningful look. 'I saw the way he looked at you in my bedchamber last night.'

'Enough of this!' Lathesia snapped back petulantly. 'I didn't ask you to come here to preach to me, you wanted to see me!'

'Yes, you are right, I did,' Yakov admitted, collecting his thoughts before continuing. 'Have you any other trouble planned for tonight?'

'What concern is it of yours, preacher?' she asked, her black eyes narrowing with suspicion.

'You must not do anything, the SSA will retaliate with even more brutal force than last time,' he warned her.

'Actually, we were thinking of killing some of them, strutting around with their bludgeons and pistols as if their laws apply here,' she replied venomously, her cracked hands balling into fists.

Yakov went over and sat down beside her slowly, meeting her gaze firmly.

'Do you trust me?' he asked gently.

'No, why should I?' she said, surprised.

'Why did you come to me before, to ask the cardinal for help?' he countered, leaning back on one hand but keeping his eyes on hers.

'Because… It was… I was desperate, it was foolish of me, I shouldn't have,' she mumbled back, turning her gaze away.

'You are nothing more than a child, let me help you,' Yakov persisted, feeling his soul starting to roast at the edges even as he said it.

'Stop it!' she wailed suddenly, springing to her feet and backing away. 'If I don't do this, no one will help us!'

'Have it your way,' sighed Yakov, sitting upright again. 'There is more to this than the casual murder of Menevon's brother. I do not yet know what, but I need your help to find out.'

'Why do you think so?' she asked, her defiance forgotten as curiosity took over.

'You say his throat was slit?' Yakov asked and she nodded. 'Why? Any court on Karis Cephalon will order a mutant hung on the word of a citizen, so why the murder? It must be because nobody could know who was involved, or why he died. I think he saw something or someone and was murdered so he couldn't talk.'

'But that means, if a master didn't do it…' Lathesia started before her eyes widened in realisation. 'One of us did this? No, I won't believe it!'

'You might not have to,' Yakov countered quickly, raising his hand to calm her. 'In fact it's unlikely. The only way we can find out is to go to where Menevon's brother died, and see what we can find.'

'He worked in one of the cemeteries not far from here, just outside the encampment boundary,' she told the preacher. 'We'll take you there.'

She half-ran, half-skipped to the open door and called through excitedly, 'Byzanthus! Byzanthus, fetch Odrik and Klain, we're going on an expedition tonight!'

THE FUNCTIONAL FERROCRETE tombstones had little grandeur about them, merely rectangular slabs plainly inscribed with the name of the family. The moon was riding high in the sky as Yakov, Lathesia and the other mutants searched the graveyard for any sign of what had happened. Yakov entered the small wooden shack that served as the gravedigger's shelter, finding various picks and shovels stacked neatly in one corner. There was an unmistakable red stain on the unfinished planks of the floor, which to Yakov's untrained eye seemed to have spread from near the doorway. He stood there for a moment, gazing out into the cemetery to see what was in view. It was Byzanthus who caught his attention with a waved arm, and they all gathered on him. He pointed to a grave, which was covered with a tarpaulin weighted with rocks. Lathesia gave Byzanthus a nod and he pulled back the sheeting.

The grave was deep and long, perhaps three metres from end to end and two metres down. Inside was a plain metal casket, wrapped in heavy chains from which hung numerous padlocks.

'Why would anyone want to lock up a coffin?' asked Lathesia, looking at Yakov.

Read the entirety of this story and many others in
DEATHWING, coming soon from the Black Library.

More Warhammer 40,000 from the Black Library

13th LEGION
A Last Chancers novel
by Gav Thorpe

Glancing over my shoulder I see that we're at the steps to the command tower now. You can follow the trail of our retreat, five dead Last Chancers lie among more than two dozen alien bodies and a swathe of shotgun cases and bolt pistol cartridges litters the floor. A few eldar manage to dart through our fusillade, almost naked except for a few pieces of bladed red armour strapped across vital body parts. Almost skipping with light steps, they duck left and right with unnatural speed. In their hands they hold vicious-looking whips and two-bladed daggers that drip with some kind of venom that smokes as it drops to the metal decking. Their fierce grins show exquisitely white teeth as they close for the kill, their bright oval eyes burning with unholy passion.

ACROSS A HUNDRED *blasted war-zones upon a dozen bloody worlds, the convict soldiers of the 13th Penal Legion fight a desperate battle for redemption in the eyes of the immortal Emperor. In this endless war against savage orks, merciless eldar and the insidious threat of Chaos, Lieutenant Kage and the Last Chancers must fight, not to win, but merely to survive!*

More Warhammer 40,000 from the Black Library

XENOS
Book 1 of the Eisenhorn trilogy
by Dan Abnett

The thundering sound rolled through the thawing vaults
of Processional Two-Twelve. Fists and palms, beating at
coffin hoods. The sleepers were waking, their frigid bodies trapped in their caskets. I could hear footsteps above
the screams. Eyclone was running. I ran after, passing
gallery after gallery of frenzied, flailing forms. The
screaming, the pounding... God-Emperor help me, I will
never forget that. Thousands of souls waking up to death,
frantic, agonised. Damn Eyclone. Damn him to hell and
back.

*THE INQUISITION MOVES amongst mankind like an avenging
shadow, striking down the enemies of humanity with uncompromising ruthlessness. Inquisitor Eisenhorn faces a vast
interstellar cabal and the dark power of daemons, all racing
to recover an arcane text of abominable power – an ancient
tome known as the Necroteuch.*

More Warhammer 40,000 from the Black Library

EXECUTION HOUR
A Warhammer 40,000 novel
by Gordon Rennie

An inhabited world. An Imperial world, far from the
nearest warzone. Once again, the guidance of the Powers
of the Warp has served him well. Already the name and
location of this new target are being relayed to the rest of
the fleet. The Planet Killer is making ready to strike
another blow for the Dark Gods. The doomed inhabi-
tants could not possibly realise or understand it yet, but
the hour of their appointed execution has just been set.

*THE VILE AND unholy shadow of Chaos falls across the Gothic
Sector at the onslaught of Warmaster Abaddon's infernal
Black Crusade. Fighting a desperate rearguard action, the
Imperial Battlefleet has no choice but to sacrifice dozens of
worlds and millions of lives to buy precious time for their
scattered fleets to regroup. But what possible chance do they
have when Abaddon's unholy forces have the power not just
to kill men, but also to murder worlds?*

More Warhammer 40,000 from the Black Library

PAWNS OF CHAOS
A Warhammer 40,000 novel
by Brian Craig

Gavalon had already begun thinking of the bulk of his forces as 'gunfodder', even though they had never faced guns before. The guns produced by the Imperium in their planetary-based factories were by no means as powerful as those they had brought from the star-worlds, but they were guns nevertheless and there was nothing in Gulzacandra that could compete with them – except, of course, magic. If the Imperium was to be stopped, magic would be the force that would do it.

IN THE GRIM *future of Warhammer 40,000,
mankind is engaged in an eternal conflict with the armies of
Chaos. On the medieval world of Sigmatus, the hated
Imperium is flexing its power with ruthless efficiency. The
rebels have a plan to fight back: summon a powerful daemon
from the warp and unleash it upon their enemies!*

More Warhammer 40,000 from the Black Library

FIRST & ONLY
A Gaunt's Ghosts novel
by Dan Abnett

'The Tanith are strong fighters, general, so I have heard.'
The scar tissue of his cheek pinched and twitched slightly,
as it often did when he was tense. 'Gaunt is said to be a
resourceful leader.'

'You know him?' The general looked up, questioningly.

'I know *of* him, sir. In the main by reputation.'

GAUNT GOT TO his feet, wet with blood and Chaos pus. His
Ghosts were moving up the ramp to secure the position.
Above them, at the top of the elevator shaft, were over a
million Shriven, secure in their bunker batteries. Gaunt's
expeditionary force was inside, right at the heart of the
enemy stronghold. Commissar Ibram Gaunt smiled.

*IT IS THE nightmare future of Warhammer 40,000, and
mankind teeters on the brink of extinction. The galaxy-
spanning Imperium is riven with dangers, and in the Chaos-
infested Sabbat system, Imperial Commissar Gaunt must lead
his men through as much in-fighting amongst rival regiments
as against the forces of Chaos. FIRST AND ONLY is an epic
saga of planetary conquest, grand ambition, treachery and
honour.*

More Warhammer 40,000 from the Black Library

GHOSTMAKER
A Gaunt's Ghosts novel
by Dan Abnett

They were a good two hours into the dark, black-trunked forests, tracks churning the filthy ooze and the roar of their engines resonating from the sickly canopy of leaves above, when Colonel Ortiz saw death.

It wore red, and stood in the trees to the right of the track, in plain sight, unmoving, watching his column of Basilisks as they passed along the trackway. It was the lack of movement that chilled Ortiz.

Almost twice a man's height, frighteningly broad, armour the colour of rusty blood, crested by recurve brass antlers. The face was a graven death's head. Daemon. Chaos Warrior. *World Eater!*

In the nightmare future of Warhammer 40,000, mankind teeters on the brink of extinction. The Imperial Guard are humanity's first line of defence against the remorseless assaults of the enemy. For the men of the Tanith First-and-Only and their fearless commander, Commissar Ibram Gaunt, it is a war in which they must be prepared to lay down, not just their bodies, but their very souls.

More Warhammer 40,000 from the Black Library

NECROPOLIS
A Gaunt's Ghosts novel
by Dan Abnett

Gaunt was shaking, and breathing hard. He'd lost his cap somewhere, his jacket was torn and he was splattered with blood. Something flickered behind him and he wheeled, his blade flashing as it made contact. A tall, black figure lurched backwards. It was thin but powerful, and much taller than him, dressed in glossy black armour and a hooded cape. The visage under the hood was feral and non-human, like the snarling skull of a great wolfhound with the skin scraped off. It clutched a sabre bladed power sword in its gloved hands. The cold blue energies of his own powersword clashed against the sparking, blood red fires of the Deathwatcher's weapon.

ON THE SHATTERED world of Verghast, Gaunt and his Ghosts find themselves embroiled within an ancient and deadly civil war as a mighty hive-city is besieged by an unrelenting foe. When treachery from within brings the city's defences crashing down, rivalry and corruption threaten to bring the Tanith Ghosts to the brink of defeat. Imperial Commissar Ibram Gaunt must find new allies and new Ghosts if he is to save Vervunhive from the deadliest threat of all – the dread legions of Chaos.

More Warhammer 40,000 from the Black Library

HONOUR GUARD
A Gaunt's Ghosts novel
by Dan Abnett

There was an impact, and a spray of dust and blood. Vamberfeld fell over clumsily, a corpse on top of him. Blinded for a moment, face down in the dirt, he slowly found his vision returning. He was suffused in blue light. Power sword smoking, Ibram Gaunt dragged him up by the hand.

'Good work, Vamberfeld. We've taken the breach,' he said. Vamberfeld was dumbstruck. And also covered in blood. 'Stay sane,' Gaunt told him. 'It gets better...'

The vox-link went mad. Gaunt could hear sustained bursts of las-fire and auto weapons. Herdsmen, suddenly several dozen in number, were surging out from the cover of their agitated animals. They had weapons. As their robes fell away, he saw body art and green silk. He grabbed his bolt pistol. The Infardi were all over them...

COMMISSAR GAUNT AND his Ghosts are back in action at the forefront of battle on a vital shrine-world of the deepest tactical and spiritual importance. But the vile forces of Chaos will never allow them to hold their prize for long and, as the counter-attack rages, Gaunt is sent after the most priceless relic of all: the remains of the ancient saint who first led humanity to these stars.

More Warhammer 40,000 from the Black Library

SPACE WOLF
A Warhammer 40,000 novel
by William King

Ragnar leapt up from his hiding place, bolt pistol spitting death. The nightgangers could not help but notice where he was, and with a mighty roar of frenzied rage they raced towards him. Ragnar answered their war cry with a wolfish howl of his own, and was reassured to hear it echoed back from the throats of the surrounding Blood Claws. He pulled the trigger again and again as the frenzied mass of mutants approached, sending bolter shell after bolter shell rocketing into his targets. Ragnar laughed aloud, feeling the full battle rage come upon him. The beast roared within his soul, demanding to be unleashed.

IN THE GRIM future of Warhammer 40,000, the Space Marines of the Adeptus Astartes are humanity's last hope. On the planet Fenris, young Ragnar is chosen to be inducted into the noble yet savage Space Wolves chapter. But with his ancient primal instincts unleashed by the implanting of the sacred Canis Helix, Ragnar must learn to control the beast within and fight for the greater good of the wolf pack.

More Warhammer 40,000 from the Black Library

RAGNAR'S CLAW
A Warhammer 40,000 novel
by William King

One of the enemy officers, wearing the peaked cap and greatcoat of a lieutenant, dared to stick his head above the parapet. Without breaking stride, Ragnar raised his bolt pistol and put a shell through the man's head. It exploded like a melon hit with a sledgehammer. Shouts of confusion echoed from behind the wall of sandbags, then a few heretics, braver and more experienced than the rest, stuck their heads up in order to take a shot at their attackers. Another mistake: a wave of withering fire from the Space Marines behind Ragnar scythed through them, sending their corpses tumbling back amongst their comrades.

FROM THE DEATH-WORLD of Fenris come the Space Wolves, the most savage of the Emperor's Space Marines. Ragnar's Claw explores the bloody beginnings of Space Wolf Ragnar's first mission as a young Blood Claw warrior. From the jungle hell of Galt to the polluted cities of Hive World Venam, Ragnar's mission takes him on an epic trek across the galaxy to face the very heart of Evil itself.